Praise for
Monica Burns

"Burns doesn't disappoint!"
— RTBOOKreviews

Monica Burns writes with sensitivity and panache.
— Sabrina Jeffries, NYT bestselling author

"powerfully done…the scenes between Tobias and Jane mesmerized me. I loved it."
— Joey W. Hill

"No one sets fire to the page like Monica Burns."
— eCataromance

"Definitely recommended reading."
— The Romance Studio

"Ms. Burns is masterful at escalating the sexual tension and suspense with her characters."
— Coffeetime Romance

Forever

My Lass

The Forevermore Series, Book 3

by

Monica Burns

Table of Contents

Prologue

1962
Long Island, New York

"Come, Amelia, sit with me for a moment. Although, I think it is quite likely you will think me a delusional old woman in short order."

Patting the cushion of the chair next to her, Anna smiled as she silently invited the young woman to join her. With a quiet laugh, Amelia Whitworth shook her head and sat down in the seat beside Anna.

"Forgive me, Lady Starling, but I am the least qualified person in determining someone's state of delusion," the American said as she leaned forward and spoke in a sotto voice. "I hold certain beliefs that most people would deem worthy of having me committed. I'm fortunate Michael loves me enough to overlook my eccentricities."

Amusement sparkled in the young woman's blue eyes before she turned to look at the young man speaking with Anna's son-in-law, Andrew, and another man whose name Anna didn't remember. Almost as if sensing his wife watching him, Michael Whitworth turned his head and smiled at her.

Anna's granddaughter, Emma, had introduced the newlyweds to her a week ago at a small dinner party. She'd taken an immediate liking to the couple, and it wasn't until last night that she'd realized who the young woman was.

Now, as Anna witnessed the silent exchange between the newlyweds, it touched the deep wound in her heart that had opened up the night her dark angel had died. Even in the hour before he closed his eyes for the last time, Sebastian had looked at Anna the same way. Amelia suddenly drew in a breath of remorse and jerked her gaze away from her husband's.

"I am sorry, Lady Starling, I'm being rude—"

"There is nothing to forgive, my dear." Anna snorted with amusement and smiled at the young woman. "I remember moments when the world fell away every time my dark angel and I looked at each other. That never changed over the years."

"How long were you and Lord Starling married?" Amelia asked quietly.

"Forty wonderful years."

Anna stared down at her wedding rings as happy memories and sorrowful ones filled her head. There had been passionate arguments, too. Disagreements that had been resolved with equal passion. Anna knew what she was about to do would definitely have instigated an argument if Sebastian were still alive. But then she'd always managed to make her dark angel understand it was the rare exception when she would share her visions with someone other than him or another family member.

From the moment Emma had introduced Amelia to her, Anna had felt a connection to the younger woman, who had seemed so familiar. It had taken her several days to realize why. Then last night, she remembered the first visit she and Sebastian had made to Muchalls Hall years ago.

Sebastian had been looking into purchasing some land near Aberdeen and had frequently done business with Lord Glenburnie. Her dark angel had liked the other man, and when Sebastian had sought the Scotsman's advice, the baron had invited them to stay at Muchalls Hall while they were in Scotland.

It was there she'd met Madeline Whitworth. The first time she'd shook Madeline's hand, Anna had known the other woman was from a different place and time. What had puzzled her was how the woman had come to be at Muchalls Hall.

That mystery had been cleared up when she'd learned about the shipwreck and met the baron's daughter, Grace. Now as she stared at the young woman seated next to her, Anna saw where Madeline's warm, mischievous smile came from.

"I'm sorry if my asking about your husband has upset you, Lady Starling." The quiet apology jerked Anna out of her thoughts.

"Now it is my turn to apologize," she said with a shake of her head. "You've not upset me, my dear. I was simply caught up in happy memories. One of which involves you."

"Me?" The young woman arched her eyebrows in puzzlement. "I don't understand."

"And it's quite possible you'll *still* be confused after I've finished speaking." Anna winced as she heard Sebastian's objections clearly in her head. But she knew not to question her instincts and forged ahead. "I'm going to share something that would make most people call me delusional. Although I confess it is easier to broach the subject with you after having overheard your conversation with Emma the other day."

"Our conversation?" Amelia Whitworth's eyes widened as uncertainty and dismay swept across her pretty face. Anna quickly reached out to touch the young woman's arm in a gesture of reassurance.

"Of all my grandchildren, Emma is the one most like me. Where do you think her beliefs came from?"

"Oh." The short reply vibrated with relief, and Anna laughed softly as Amelia's face reddened. "There's no need to feel embarrassed, my dear girl. There are more people in this world who believe in reincarnation than you might think."

"Michael doesn't like me to mention it in public as he is somewhat on the fence when it comes to the topic," Amelia said with a glance in her husband's direction.

"Sebastian was equally stubborn in his acceptance of the idea, but the night he died, he promised we'd be together again." Anna stared off into space for a moment before she returned her gaze to the young American. "But the fact that you *do* believe in past lives makes it much easier to tell you something that is not only extraordinary, but will require a leap of faith on your part."

"I actually do quite well with those kinds of leaps." Amelia smiled with confidence.

"Very well." Anna pinned her gaze on the young woman. "I met your granddaughter years ago when Sebastian and I visited Aberdeen, Scotland."

Amelia jerked backward slightly, puzzlement and confusion darkening her face.

"I don't understand. How could you possibly meet my granddaughter in the past? A granddaughter I don't have?"

"It's difficult to explain, but I know you will have a granddaughter named Madeline." Anna hesitated, trying to explain without revealing exactly how Madeline had landed in the distant past.

"This makes no sense at all. I think you are teasing me, Lady Starling." Amelia shook her head and smiled, clearly believing Anna was joking with her.

"I understand it makes no sense, but Madeline will cross the boundaries of time, where she will be the governess to Baron Glenburnie's twin daughters." Anna sighed at the dismissive look of disbelief on the younger woman's face. The American's eyes narrowed on Anna.

"Are you telling me you think I'm going to have a granddaughter who's going to be a time traveler?"

"As I said, it requires a leap of faith to believe what I'm telling you." She eyed Amelia steadily. "But even if you cannot take that leap, you are still important to Madeline's survival."

"Survival?" The young American's dubious expression strengthened, and Anna inhaled a breath of frustration before blowing it out harshly.

"I did warn you that you would think me a delusional old woman."

"Yes, you did, and while I don't think—"

"*Amelia, listen to me*," Anna said in a low, sharp voice as she caught the young woman's hands in hers. "You do not have to believe anything I'm saying. But you *do* need to *listen*, and listen carefully. Your granddaughter's life and happiness will depend a great deal on you."

Amelia eyed her with uneasiness and obvious misgiving. The moment the young American glanced across the room at her husband, Anna squeezed the woman's hands tightly. Immediately, Amelia winced and jerked her head back toward Anna. With a shake of her head, the young woman frowned in dismay.

"Let me find Emma for you, Lady Starling. I think—"

"You do that," Anna snapped, as she waved her hand in a sharp, dismissive gesture. "Go. Find my granddaughter. Emma knows I do not open myself up to ridicule unless it's absolutely necessary. *She* will tell you to listen to me."

Anna turned away from the woman, her gaze searching the room for her granddaughter. A hand lightly touched her arm, and Anna arched her eyebrows in her best imitation of Sebastian's most arrogant look as she eyed the young woman beside her.

"I'm sorry, Lady Starling. I will not lie when I say what you're telling me sounds farfetched." Amelia winced with regret at the soft snort of disgust Anna made. "But I *will* listen to you, *and* if I have a granddaughter, as you say I will, then I will remember what you tell me this evening."

Anna remained silent for a long moment. Then, with an abrupt nod, she eyed Amelia sternly.

"From the time she's a young girl, your granddaughter will have dreams of a man standing on a cliff overlooking the North Sea. There is a terrible storm, and a ship is fighting dangerous waters to reach a small inlet. Madeline will be on that ship."

"You've seen this?" Amelia stared at Anna in amazement and a touch of fear.

"No, Madeline shared her story when we met years ago. She was convinced your words saved her life." Anna narrowed her gaze at the young American woman, knowing she couldn't tell Amelia how well she'd come to know Madeline over the years. "Madeline said you warned her several times not to be afraid to let go. She said you'd reassured her several times he would be there to catch her, and she should just let go."

"I don't understand…" Amelia shook her head in confusion.

"Nor do I, Amelia. But Madeline is not the first woman I've met in the past that was out of place." Anna paused as she remembered her friend Victoria. "All I know is that Madeline said your words saved her life. Words that you must memorize and share with your granddaughter when the time is right."

Anna reached out to squeeze the woman's hand as Amelia stared at her in dismay and fear before the young woman nodded slowly. It pained Anna to know what the woman's future held, but she was certain Amelia would do whatever it took to save Madeline.

Chapter 1

Present Day

The icy rain bit into her skin like tiny needles stinging with each drop the wind flung at her. Overhead, the dark sky worked to snuff out the last remnants of daylight. With something close to desperation, her gaze swept across the rugged landscape until she saw his tall figure. He stood on the edge of the cliff staring out at the ocean, while the harsh wind made his long, black overcoat flap wildly around his legs.

Although she wasn't close enough to hear the sound his coat made as it slapped against his legs, she could hear the sharp cracks in her head. Something familiar swept through her as she studied the isolated figure against the backdrop of the storm. Slowly, she turned her gaze to look out at the vast stretch of water he was watching so intently.

The storm was in full force, and jagged flashes of quicksilver streaked through the black clouds hovering close to the turbulent ocean. Giant waves opened huge crevices in the water before crashing closed with a deadly savagery that made her heart crash into her chest as it continued to pound at a wild, frantic pace. Fear streaked through her, making it difficult to breathe, while panic made her stomach churn.

It was then she saw it. The ship pitched wildly upward, then downward with each raging wave that hammered at its hull. It was a large ship, and despite its size, she could tell it was struggling against the churning water. She drew in a sharp breath of fear as the ship disappeared, then a second later shot up and over the tall wave that had hidden it from view. A white sail at the top of one mast was the only thing to indicate a ship was fighting the raging sea as the ship vanished beneath another high wave.

Almost as if the ocean were spitting out an unpalatable morsel, the ship surged upward into view. This time, it was closer to the shore and seemed to be headed for the cliff where the man stood. She looked down to see a narrow inlet and its small stretch of sand. If the ship could find its way through the massive rock formations on either side of the natural harbor, it would be safe.

Once more, the ship dropped out of view before it shot back up to sit high on the water. It was now close enough to the shore to see men fighting against the raging storm to keep the ship on course toward the narrow path to safety. Another wave crashed over the top of the ship's deck, followed by a wave that surged up beneath the ship and tossed it toward the natural harbor.

In the next breath, like a cat toying with a mouse, the sea threw the ship almost directly into the inlet before a second wave sent the vessel crashing against one of the rock formations that bordered the natural harbor. Metal screamed as the ship scraped across the rocks, while the sound of wood cracking and splintering filled the air in a cacophony of sound. Suddenly, she was in the water. Salt water filled her nostrils and mouth as she fought to find air. As she sank deeper into the depths of the sea, her body jerked violently.

Madeline cried out softly as she sat upright in her chair, dragging in deep breaths of air as the nightmare receded and released its hold on her. Her heart still racing, tension eased from her body as she realized she was in the house she'd grown up in after her parents died. The soft glow of the nightlight illuminated the room well enough to see her grandmother watching her from her hospital bed.

"The same dream?"

At the quiet question, Madeline jerked her head in confirmation as she rose to her feet to check the monitor that beeped softly at the side of her grandmother's bed. Satisfied with the readings, she turned and straightened the sheet and blanket that covered her grandmother's frail form.

Less than six weeks ago, Amelia Whitworth had been a robust, cheerful bundle of energy. Now she was wasting away from cancer. Madeline's throat closed as she fought back tears. A fragile excuse for a hand caught hers and squeezed Madeline's fingers with a strength that belied her grandmother's weakened state.

"It's going to be all right, Maddie," her grandmother said softly, using the nickname she'd always used when comforting Madeline. "I know your grandfather is waiting for me. Your parents, too."

"I know I'm being selfish, but I don't want you to go. Who's going to text me out of the blue with nothing but heart emoticons because you somehow know I'm having a bad day?" Her tear-filled voice made her grandmother squeeze her hand again.

"We're all selfish when we lose someone we love, Maddie. But those bad days are about to end, sweetheart. Destiny has something special in mind for you." The words made Madeline force a smile to her lips.

"I'm sure you're right, Grandma." The reply earned her a gentle slap on the hand.

"Do not patronize me, Madeline Amelia Whitworth." Her grandmother eyed her with a familiar stern expression that was as fierce as when she'd been a rebellious teenager. "You've had the same dream since you were a child, but they're more frequent now, which tells me something's coming."

"They're just dreams," Madeline lied. In truth, they were nightmares. Terrible dreams where she was trapped and drowning in the sea.

"And you know what I've always said about your dreams. They're—"

"Memories of a past life." Madeline tried not to roll her eyes and failed.

"That sarcasm of yours is going to come back to bite you, Maddie."

A believer in past lives, her grandmother had always said Madeline's dreams were connected to a life she'd lived before. From the time she'd turned thirteen, she'd dreamed about the stranger on the cliff. Through the years, she'd always awoken feeling sad from the dream.

All of that had changed about a month after her grandmother had become sick. The dreams had become longer, more frequent, and for the past week, the dream had haunted her sleep every night. Even more disturbing was the vividness of the nightmares. In the past, they'd been nothing more than movies she watched from a distance. Now they were visceral, tangible sensations that left her shaken, confused, and exhausted when she woke up.

The dream always ended the same way, with her desperately struggling not to drown. Tonight had been the worst. She could still taste the sea water in her mouth. A shudder rippled through Madeline at the memory. The dream had left her with a feeling of helplessness. It had been as if she had no control over anything.

It didn't help that she was a strong swimmer and had never had a fear of drowning. Madeline swam on a regular basis at the gym's indoor pool, and until a few minutes ago, the idea of being trapped underwater had never occurred to her. The books from psych class in nursing school probably could explain her emotional reaction, but she hadn't bothered to research it. A quiet sigh pulled Madeline out of her thoughts.

"Are you in pain?" Guilt nipped at her as she focused her attention on her grandmother. "Do you want something to drink?"

"No, I was just thinking about our trip to Scotland."

"Our trip—that was just wishful thinking," Madeline said with a laugh. "It was fun to look up things and talk about what we'd do when we got there."

"And the accents," Amelia Whitworth said with a smile. "There's nothing sexier than a man with a Scottish accent."

"Has Harriet been reading one of those steamy medieval romance books to you again?" Smiling, Madeline rolled her eyes as she studied her grandmother's face.

"Maybe." A flash of mischief darted across her grandmother's weary and gaunt features before she closed her eyes. "But at the moment, not even a Scottish burr would be enough to make me feel energetic."

"Why don't you try to get some sleep? I'll give you a little more pain medicine," she said softly as she adjusted the IV drip.

"Thank you, sweetheart." Her grandmother's eyes fluttered open as she caught Madeline's hand again and squeezed it tight. "I love you, Maddie."

"I love you too, Grandma."

Madeline leaned over the bed and pressed a loving kiss to the older woman's brow. A small smile curved her grandmother's lips as her eyes closed and she drifted off to sleep. With one last check of the vitals monitor, Madeline turned away from the hospital bed. A second later, an almost inaudible whisper filled her ears.

"Don't be afraid, Maddie. Don't be afraid to let go. He'll be there to catch you."

With a jerk, she whirled around on her heel to stare at her grandmother. It was obvious the ill woman was already asleep, and Madeline put the whisper down to her imagination. She was tired and overwhelmed by the heartache that had been assaulting her for weeks. Madeline knew she should be grateful for the precious moments she'd been given to say goodbye, but it wasn't enough.

She wanted more time. She wanted to talk about the birds her grandmother loved to identify from her kitchen window. She wanted to hear her grandmother warbling at the piano and sit next to her as they sang a duet. She wanted more texts of red hearts. There were so many things she wanted, but with an overwhelming sense of loss, she knew she wouldn't ever have those things again.

Days had dwindled to hours, and Madeline knew it wouldn't be long now. Her harbor of safety, warmth, and love was about to vanish, and her deepening grief would batter her in the same way the rocks had the ship in her dreams.

Chapter 2

Muchalls, Scotland
August 1896

Iain Fraser, Baron of Glenburnie, growled in frustration as he rubbed his forehead in an attempt to stave off the migraine hovering on the edge of his senses. It didn't matter how many times he calculated the figures. Unless Destiny's Dream arrived safely in Aberdeen in a few days with his cargo, he would be forced to do the unthinkable.

He would have to either sell some of his lands to that smug bastard, Robert Lindsay, or ask Andrew for a loan. Neither prospect was a palpable one. A well-known philanthropist in America, his cousin Andrew would send money without hesitation the moment Iain asked for a loan.

It didn't help that his cousin would insist on making it a gift. Even if he convinced Andrew to extend a line of credit, his cousin would make the interest rate so low it would still be more of a gift than a debt to repay. Iain released another snarl of anger as he threw his pen down with suppressed violence.

The throbbing in his head grew stronger, and closing his eyes, he leaned back into his leather desk chair. The soft squeak of his study door made Iain peer through the slits of his eyes to see who had dared to enter his sanctuary without knocking. He saw Grace studying him in silence.

"What is it, Grace?"

"Faither, I…I…"

The hesitation in Grace's soft voice made him open his eyes to see a look of fear on his daughter's face. Concern immediately flooded through him.

"What is it, Grace? Is it Ainslie? What has she done now?"

Iain suppressed the groan of pain threatening to escape him as his oldest daughter by mere minutes rushed toward his desk with a vehement shake of her head.

"Oh, nae, *Faither.* Ainslie has nae done anything. But I…I am…"

The moment Grace's voice trailed off, Iain gestured for his daughter to come to his side. The throbbing in his head increased as he saw the fear on the girl's sweet face. Iain swallowed hard as he fought through the pain.

"It's all right, lass. Is it the *an dara sealladh*?"

"Aye. I cannae…"

Whatever his daughter had seen, it had troubled her deeply. It was unlike her to show fear at a vision she'd seen. Even more worrisome was how pale his daughter looked. He couldn't remember ever having seen her so upset, and her expression heightened his concern. If there was one thing he couldn't protect his daughter from, it was the *an dara sealladh*.

"There's nothing tae fear, *mo nighean dubh*. Just tell me what ye saw." Just as he had when she was a baby, he lapsed into the soft, lilting brogue he'd learned to control years ago at Glenalmond College.

"A ship. I saw a ship sinking. And there was a lady."

The moment Grace mentioned a ship, Iain's muscles tighten. If it had been Destiny's Dream his daughter had seen in her vision, then it meant he would be forced to do what he didn't want to do. He would have to sell land or ask Andrew for a loan. He tried not to think the worst. Instead, he reminded himself that the *an dara sealladh* came to Grace in images that were all mixed together and sometimes completely unrelated.

"She was verra pretty, *Faither*, but she was…she was drowning, and I could nae help her. I dinnae want her to die." Sadness and fear in his daughter's voice made him pull her toward him, then wrap his arm around her slender frame.

"Dinnae ye fash, lass. Ye know the *an dara sealladh* is nae always reliable. Ye know it never shows ye everything."

"I ken, but the lady was frightened, and…"

The pounding in Iain's head would soon become blinding, but the emotion he saw flash in Grace's violet eyes made him push through the pain to focus his full attention on his daughter. The child wasn't just upset by what she'd seen. She was terrified.

"It's all right, lass. Ye ken that sharing what ye have seen helps ye not be afraid."

"Nae…*Faither*. It is…I saw Ainslie…she was with the lady." Grace stammered her words in an almost inaudible whisper.

"In the water?" Iain choked out the words as fear scraped away at his insides, before an invisible sledgehammer hit first one temple and then another.

"Nae," Grace said with a sharp shake of her head. "But the lady was drowning, and Ainslie was crying. Ainslie never cries."

Iain's stomach churned as he struggled to think. Where was Ainslie now? He relaxed slightly as Iain remembered Angus saying Ainslie had gone over to Squire Tewel's house with a cake Bridget had made. A tear slid down Grace's cheek, and Iain pulled his daughter close.

"I'm sure there's nothing tae worry about, *mo nighean dubh*," he murmured as he wiped the tears welling up in her eyes. "We will simply keep a closer eye on Ainslie. As for the woman, I am sure someone will help her, whoever she is."

Grace didn't answer him. She simply nodded, then buried her face in his shoulder. As she cried against his shoulder, Iain closed his eyes and rested his head on the back of his chair. A few moments later, Grace lifted her head and gasped with dismay.

"Ye have a migraine, *Faither*. Why dinnae ye tell me? I could have waited tae tell ye about the *an dara sealladh*."

"It is nae that bad, lass."

"I dinnae believe ye. Ye are too pale. Ye should be in bed."

"I will feel better after a brief nap here," Iain said. He tightened his lips as the pain hammering away at him threatened to make him wretch until his lunch was no longer in his stomach.

"I will make ye a poultice," Grace whispered.

The child was gone in a rush of soft air, and the moment he heard the study door close behind her, he released a low groan of pain. Christ Jesus, he'd not had a headache this bad in months. Slowly, Iain rose from his desk to move toward the wing-backed chair in front of the fireplace. The movement cost him, and sinking down into the fireside chair, he released a groan of relief and pain. Eyes closed, he prayed for sleep. Pain never followed him when he was asleep. Occasionally it would wake him, but sleep usually helped ease the pounding in his head to a mere throb.

Iain heard the door squeak softly a short time later, but he didn't open his eyes. Although he couldn't see Grace's small, almost too thin frame, the soft scent of lavender and herbs drifted into his nostrils as she reached his side. He released a quiet grunt as his daughter placed a soft, lavender-filled cloth on his forehead.

"You should lie down, *Faither*."

"The poultice will suffice, lass." Despite the brusque response, it was obvious his daughter heard the note of affection buried beneath it as she brushed her lips across his cheeks.

"All right, but I will send Angus to check on you shortly. If anyone can convince you to lie down, he can."

"Leave me be, Grace." he growled with restrained ferocity. "I'll nap here for a bit, and then I will feel better."

His daughter's only response was another kiss to his cheek before she left the study as soundlessly as she'd entered. The child was far too quiet and wise beyond her ten years. Grace was her mother's daughter. Gentle, intuitive, and caring.

The girl's twin sister, Ainslie, was the exact opposite. Ainslie had inherited every undesirable trait he'd ever possessed in his youth, as well as his brother's disregard for risk. Complicating Ainslie's wild ways was her ability to charm the most surly of ill-tempered Scotsmen, including himself. Even Thane would have found himself outmatched by his niece's ability to twist people around her little finger.

They needed a governess, which he could ill afford at the moment. Another solution whispered its way through his head, but he rejected it outright. He had no intention of marrying again. A knifelike pang stabbed viciously at his temple, and he sucked in a sharp breath at the pain. With determination, Iain forced himself to clear his head and relax his tense muscles. The throbbing seemed to lessen, and he waited for the blessed peace of oblivion.

Iain wasn't sure how long he'd napped, but something jarred him out of his sleep. Eyes closed, he didn't move for a long moment. The lavender essence of the poultice filled his nostrils, and a sigh of relief blew past his lips. The throbbing persisted, but had been reduced to a minor irritation. Between Grace's medicine and his nap, the majority of his pain had subsided. Relief surged through him. The headache had been the worst he'd had in a long time, but at least he'd been spared a more debilitating migraine. As he opened his eyes, his gaze fell on the open ledger on his desk.

Instantly, his jaw locked with tension as his problems returned to taunt him. Iain leaned forward and closed the accounting book with a vicious flip of his wrist. The violent action penalized him with a sharp twinge in his temple. A grunt of discomfort broke out of him as he stood up and sluggishly made his way across the floor to stare out the study's tall window.

Beyond the cliffs that bordered his lands was the North Sea. Angry, bluish-gray storm clouds brushed up against the dark waters on the horizon. A storm was brewing and would most likely reach land in a few hours. Iain opened the window and drank in a deep breath of the sea air being pushed inland. It created the sudden urge to walk out along the cliffs. The fresh air would do him good, and it would be a while before the storm reached landfall.

His decision made, Iain walked out of his study and into the main hall. He was shrugging into his overcoat when the front door flew open, and Ainslie barreled into the manor covered in dirt with hair askew. Her look of excitement died the moment she saw him, and a more sober look replaced her exhilaration. Resignation made Iain suppress a sigh. Whatever Ainslie had been doing, he had no doubt it was inappropriate for a young girl. Iain clasped his hands behind his back and eyed her with disapproval.

"Well, lass? What mischief are you running from now?" His clipped question made Ainslie wince. He could almost see the wheels spinning in her head, and he cleared his throat in a silent command for an answer.

"I beat Ethan," she said as she straightened her shoulders and lifted her chin with a look of satisfaction.

"I see. Might I ask what you beat him at?" he murmured.

Something undefinable crossed Ainslie's pretty countenance, and a twinge of pain lashed out at his forehead. Whatever she'd done to beat Squire Tewel's boy, he doubted her story would please him. As he pinned his gaze on her, his daughter winced and bowed her head. Now, he was certain he would not like the explanation she was about to give him.

"We raced from the cairn to the cliffs and back."

For a moment, Iain simply stared at her in stunned amazement. As the full impact of her actions penetrated his head, fear and horror snaked through him. The child could have been hurt far worse than the broken arm she'd suffered last year when she'd tried to take Macklin over a tall hedge. He could have lost her.

The thought made his stomach twist violently. The ground she'd raced her horse over was riddled with holes that could easily cause an animal to stumble. Without thinking, he reached out to catch her by her arms and shook her hard as his voice took on a rough burr.

"*Damnation, Ainslie.* Do ye nae have any idea what could have happened tae ye or Macklin?"

"I didn't ride Macklin. I rode Taren," she replied blithely.

"Taren!"

The color drained from Ainslie's cheeks at his angry roar. Fear held her frozen stiffly in his grasp, and regret whipped through him. Ainslie's dread was visible only for a moment before it disappeared and was replaced with a calm stoicism. But he saw the fear, hurt, and defiance in blue eyes so like his own. They were emotions he understood better than she knew, because as a child, he'd experienced the same ones on a daily basis with his father.

When he'd become a father, he'd taken a solemn oath with himself that he would never give his children cause to fear him. Although he was stern with his daughters, he was always patient and would explain his reasons for being upset with them. But of late, Ainslie's recklessness had sorely tested his patience, and he had found himself sliding closer and closer toward a line he'd vowed he would never cross.

Now he'd done the unthinkable. He'd frightened his daughter. Not once had he ever shouted at either of his daughters, let alone do anything physical to emphasize his anger at their transgressions. With a jerk, he released Ainslie as guilt slammed through him. A second later, a sharp bolt of fire crashed against his temple, and he flinched. Iain closed his eyes and fought to quiet the anger and fear threatening to ignite his headache again.

As he suppressed his outrage, his headache retreated slowly, and he looked at his daughter again. Other than her rigid posture and the pain in her gaze, her trepidation was undetectable. Clearing his throat, Iain kept his voice quiet, yet fiercely stern.

"Ye raced my horse across ground that has enough holes to bring a horse to its knees."

"But he didn't, *Faither*—"

"Did last summer nae teach ye what can happen when thrown from a horse, child? Taren is difficult to manage on a good day. Ye could have been killed," he bit out as a terrifying image filled his head of Ainslie and when she'd broken her arm. "What if Taren had stumbled and broken his leg? I would have had tae put him down. I can barely put food on the table now, let alone replace Taren."

Horror swept over Ainslie's face before her expression crumpled into a look of deep remorse. Blue eyes darkened with regret before they shimmered with unshed tears.

"I'm sorry, *Faither*. I didn't think—"

"Ye never do," he snapped before he could stop himself. With a sigh, he pinched the bridge of his nose with his fingers. "Go tae your room, Ainslie. Ye are nae to come out until I send for ye. Is that clear?"

"Yes, *Faither*," Ainslie whispered as she walked around him, then stopped. "I truly am sorry, *Faither*."

Ainslie tentatively touched his arm. Iain looked down at her hand on his sleeve and covered it with his. He acknowledged her apology with a slight nod.

"I've nae doubt of that, lass. But I dinnae want something terrible to happen to you." Wide-eyed, she stared up at him for a moment and he bent to brush his lips across her forehead. "Ye and your sister mean a great deal tae me, Ainslie. I dinnae ken what I would do if I lost either of ye."

His somber words made her eyes grow round as saucers. Clearly, his fear had struck a chord in her as she nodded with understanding.

"I promise to try harder, *Faither*," she said in a quiet voice. She didn't wait for his reply. Instead, she hurried across the stone floor and up the main staircase.

As Iain watched her disappear, he muttered an oath, then retrieved his Macintosh and threw it over his arm before walking out the manor's front door. The child was growing more reckless each day. He exhaled a breath of disgust. Not all of it was her fault. He was to blame, too. She needed a woman's touch. But the idea of losing a second wife to childbirth simply to produce an heir was something he couldn't stomach. He'd married Flora out of duty and to honor his father's demand for an heir to the Glenburnie title.

In the beginning, he'd found his bride a pleasant companion, and over the course of their first year of marriage, he'd become quite fond of her. It would have been difficult not to. Flora had been kind, gentle, and sweet. But she'd always been fragile. Childbirth had been an ordeal for her, and she'd not had any strength left after giving birth to their twin daughters.

Iain wondered how his wife would have managed Ainslie's wild ways. He was certain she would have been less quick to anger, but he knew Flora would have been horrified to have learned Ainslie had ridden Taren. The child could have been killed, and as much as his daughter tried his patience, he loved her dearly. The thought of something happening to either of his daughters was enough to send an icy chill barreling through him.

The scent of salt in his nostrils pulled him out of the past. The smell of the sea was stronger than usual as he breathed in the faint mist that had blown inland. The North Sea would be treacherous waters to sail tonight. Iain made his way around the house and along the path leading to the cliffs overlooking the sea. The color of the sky where it met the waterline had changed little from when he'd viewed it from the study window. If anything, it appeared darker.

Jagged streaks of lightning danced through the sky as if the gods were doing battle inside the dark clouds, and Iain counted slowly until a low, distant rumble echoed out into the air. The storm was closer than he thought. When he reached the cliffs, he shrugged his coat on, then stared out at the churning sea, wondering what to do with Ainslie. If his pockets weren't so badly to let, he would send her away to school.

Even hiring a governess was an expense he could ill afford at the moment. His coat stirred against his legs, then flew outward with a snap. Startled out of his thoughts, he realized the wind driving the storm inland had reached the shoreline. The suddenness of its arrival surprised him.

The wind's strength whipped around him and the power of it made his black, seal-skin coat flap wildly about his legs. It emphasized how dangerous it must be out on the water. Below him, the sea pounded the inlet with a loud roar, that on a calm day, was just a soft murmur. The ferocity of the waves sent its spray upward where the wind carried it even higher to where he stood on the cliffs, where it became a soft mist brushing across his face.

Iain looked over his shoulder toward the manor as a light rain began to fall. If he didn't return to the house, he'd be thoroughly soaked from a deluge of rain. Out of the corner of his eye, something moved at the edge of the cliffs, and he jerked his head in its direction. Braced against the wind that continued to increase in strength was a tall figure. The distance between the two of them was about the length of Aberdeen University's football field. Startled that someone else was willing to weather the wind and rain to watch the approaching storm, he frowned.

At first he thought he was looking at a man until the force of the wind pressed a white shirt and dark trousers against a body soft with womanly curves. What in God's name was a woman doing out on the cliffs in this kind of weather? She stood stiff and frozen as she stared out at the turbulent water. Despite the distance between them, he could sense her desperation and panic. In the next instant, her hands covered her mouth as if she'd stifled a scream. Iain followed the direction of his gaze, and his eyes widened. Christ Jesus. An old steamer.

The three mast, single-funnel ship was battling her way toward Muchalls Inlet below. There was no smoke coming from the stack, which meant the propeller wasn't in operation. Whether the captain had deliberately turned off the coal furnaces or not, the ship had her main sails reefed, and she was battling the sea with her smaller sails. The ship disappeared in a churning wave of water before surging back into view.

The captain was clearly heading for the inlet. Vicious waves tossed the ship about, and Iain was amazed the sea hadn't already claimed the vessel as a prize. Only a master sailor could keep a ship afloat in waters such as these. A captain like Dougal McLeod.

It was impossible to tell from this distance whether it was Destiny's Dream, but McLeod's ship was as old as this one. If it was the old sailor at the helm, then Iain's future hung in the balance because the ship was taking a battering that could easily tear her apart.

His gut twisting at the thought, Iain watched the vessel as it battled its way toward the inlet before turning his attention back to the woman. The rain was falling harder and blurred his vision slightly, but she was still there. It was as if she was waiting for someone or something.

Was her man on the ship? No sooner had the question pierced his thoughts than he saw the woman's figure shimmer. In the blink of an eye, she'd become a faint, transparent image. Iain blinked water out of his eyes as he shook his head hard in an effort to improve his vision. In the next instant, she disappeared.

Stunned, he stared at the spot where she'd been standing. She'd simply vanished. It was as if she'd evaporated in a wisp of smoke. Iain shook his head as he rejected the fanciful thought. The daft woman had to have gone down the path leading to the inlet.

With a growl of frustration, he knew he would have to go after her, just to ensure her safety. It was a treacherous path down to the beach, unless she knew where the rope handrail was. One slip of the foot, and she'd fall to her death. The fact he'd not recognized her said he could win a hefty sum by wagering she didn't know the path at all.

Iain broke out into a run to save the woman from her foolhardy act. He'd only gone a few paces when he heard a shout behind him. He didn't stop running, but looked over his shoulder to see a small group of men and one or two women hurrying in his direction. Leading the way was his man, Angus McFayden, who was quickly gaining on him. As the Scotsman drew up alongside him, Angus pointed to the ship that was still making its way toward the inlet.

"Squire Tewel saw the ship sailing inland and brought some of his tenants tae help survivors…and whatever cargo can be saved."

The quiet resignation in the man's voice brought Iain's fears to the surface once more. McFayden was clearly thinking the same thing as Iain. If the ship was Destiny's Dream, Angus knew how crucial it was for McLeod's ship to reach safe harbor. Deep inside, he'd been hoping it wasn't Captain McLeod at the helm. But the tall Scotsman's fatalism made him realize that in all likelihood he was watching his future battling its way toward shore. As he slid to a halt where the path met the top of the cliff, Iain nodded his head toward the inlet.

"We need to move quickly," he raised his voice to be heard over the storm as he started down the path leading to the beach.

On a good day, it was not without its dangers. Iain's heart slammed into his chest at the memory of Ainslie asking permission to go to the inlet last summer. He'd quickly forbidden it with the promise of dire punishment if she disobeyed. His gaze focused on the path once more. Along the narrow, rocky trail, grommet-headed spikes had been driven into the rock. Threaded through the iron loops was a heavily braided hemp that served as a railing along the rock face. Twilight had only just set in a short time ago, and there was still enough light at the top of the cliff to see well.

The rocky path downward was a different matter altogether. Dark storm clouds overhead had combined with the shadows of the cliff to reduce visibility to near darkness.

Bolts of lightning split the sky every few moments to offset the low light. Every jagged flash of light gave him a clear view of the rocks below, but there was no sign of the woman anywhere.

"You've bloody well lost your mind, Fraser. You imagined her," he muttered.

A grunt escaped him as his feet tried to slip out from under him. When he'd regained his balance, he looked back the way he'd come. Another flash of light revealed the rest of the rescue party close behind him, with his manservant in the lead.

"The rock's wet along here, Angus," he shouted over the storm. "Tell the others to maintain a firm grip on the rope."

"Aye."

Iain barely heard the man's reply over the noise of the storm as he continued to make his way downward. A few moments later, he was standing on wet sand mixed with small pebbles. In front of him, he saw the steamer set on a straight line for the middle of the cove. In stunned admiration, Iain watched as the ship reached the entrance of the inlet and was dead center between the rocks that lined the natural harbor. Damnation, the man was actually going to succeed in grounding his vessel safely.

Iain had never seen anything like it in his life. Whoever the steamer's captain was, his skill in navigating his ship so precisely into the inlet in this storm was exceptional. The moment the thought entered his head, a large wave formed and headed toward the ship. It gained momentum before it crested at the height of the ship's deck and crashed into the vessel with a strength that threw her off course. The master sailor had just realigned the ship's heading when another wall of water lifted the ship's bow up out of the water and tossed the vessel toward the rocks.

In seconds, a screeching cry of iron and wood splintering against the rocks rose up above the noise of the storm. It was the sound of death. Chaos erupted as the ship's terrible shriek mixed with shouts of panic from the vessel's sailors. Fear echoed in the cries that almost drowned out the noise of the storm. Not content with having sent the ship onto the rocks, the angry sea sent another wave cresting up into the air. With an almost vicious precision, a wall of water crashed down onto the ship's deck. Any shouts of fear were instantly drowned out as the wave retreated and pulled three sailors into the water and below the surface.

Without thinking, Iain quickly discarded his overcoat then ran toward the section of beach where the rocks met the curve of the inlet and jutted out to where the ship lay precariously against the sea-carved formation. The stretch of sand he was accustomed to crossing to reach the rocks was now a pool of angry water. He waited for the waves to retreat, then ran forward.

He was only halfway to the rocks when the sea tried to reclaim the small area of the beach between him and the only path to the shipwreck. A powerful wave slammed into him and soaked his trousers, while the undertow tried to knock him off balance and pull him into deeper waters.

In a split-second, the past wrapped an invisible band of steel around Iain's chest and squeezed the air out of his lungs. He was in the sea cave again, and the waves were strong and dangerous. Panic and fear surged through him as the incoming tide filled his mouth with sea water and he sank below the surface.

Fear, unlike anything he'd ever known, drove him to thrash about in a desperate effort to find a pocket of air. A moment later, Thane's hand latched tightly onto Iain's arm and pulled him up out of the water into the dark cavern. Coughing up water, he dragged in deep breaths of precious air. Iain lifted his head, and the look on his brother's face made his heart slam into his chest with renewed fear. Thane was about to tell him the worst was yet to come.

A hard wave slammed into Iain's legs and jolted him out of the past. *Christ Jesus*, what the hell was he thinking to lose his concentration like that? His heart slammed into his chest before it began to beat like pistons pounding fiercely inside a steam engine. Iain stared down at the water almost up to his thighs, and his fear rapidly changed into full-blown panic. The undercurrent tugged at his legs, and he fought the urge to plunge forward toward the safety of the rocks.

"Don't feed the bloody monster, Fraser. Wait until the water recedes, then ye run."

His mouth dry, he waited for the water to retreat before he moved forward. Water-filled sand sucked at his boots as he splashed his way forward to the rocks. Out of the corner of his eye, Iain saw water rushing toward him. It sent adrenalin pumping through his body, and he scrambled up the rocky formation until he stood on a flat surface of stone. Bent over at the waist, he drank in harsh breaths of relief and jumped as a strong hand clamped down on his shoulder.

"Are ye all right, my lord?" Angus asked in a gruff tone. The Scotsman had been with his family since Iain had been a young boy. Angus knew why Iain feared the water.

"Yes," he bit out between clenched teeth and bobbed his head toward the shipwreck. "We need to move fast before the sea tears her off the rocks."

"Aye."

His equilibrium restored, Iain moved quickly toward the vessel that clung perilously to the rocks. As he reached the ship, he extended a hand to a sailor struggling to find a firm grip on the wet stone. Iain pulled the man up to safety, who turned to help a shipmate. Not lingering, Iain moved further out along the rock formation to where he saw other sailors trying to climb up to the top of the rocks.

Waves smashed against the rocks, their spray sending salt water in his face. One arm wiping the water out of his eyes, he helped one man after another off the ship. An older man with weathered features was about to climb onto the rocks when someone cried out. The man turned and caught sight of someone Iain couldn't see. The ship creaked loudly as she shifted her position on the rocks.

Without hesitating, the white-bearded sailor ran across the deck to help an injured shipmate to his feet. The man's arm wrapped around his shoulders, the old sailor half-carried, half-dragged the man toward Iain. A moment later, the two men were standing beside him on the rock formation. As the captain confirmed all hands were off the ship, Iain directed the sailor toward the place where the rocks met the beach.

About to follow the captain, something just outside his line of vision made Iain turn his head. As he studied the turbulent sea, he saw a flash of white bob up from under the bow of the ship. At first he dismissed it as a whitecap, but something deep inside urged him to look harder. The white vanished beneath the waves, but seconds later he saw a boy trying to swim toward the rocks. God help the lad.

"Angus, I need a rope. *now*," he bellowed over his shoulder. He heard the Scotsman shout something, but the man's words were drowned out by the roar of the waves as Iain descended the rock face toward the water. Slick with water and kelp, the sea-carved rocks made it difficult to keep his footing. It wasn't until he reached the waterline that he realized how close he was to the pounding surf.

Fear twisted his gut as the instinct for survival demanded he climb back to safety. His earlier panic hardened every muscle in his body as he pressed himself deep into the kelp lining the rock. In the back of his head, his father's voice taunted him for being a coward. It was enough to make him ignore the sickening twist of his gut as his hand found a small indentation in the rock to serve as a natural anchor.

Despite his fear, he forced himself to shift his position until his hip pressed into the kelp. Water from a wave sprayed up over him, and he shook his head to clear his vision. It took him several seconds to find the boy in the roiling sea, but he finally caught sight of him trying to swim to the rocks.

"Come on, lad," he shouted. "Swim toward me."

The moment the boy turned his head in Iain's direction, shock pounded its way through him. A woman. He watched her fall beneath the surface, then bob up again and abruptly alter her course to where Iain clung precariously to the rock formation.

Her progress was hampered by waves trying to drive her backward, but she continued to swim in his direction. It was obvious the woman was a strong swimmer, but he could tell she was tiring. Fingers digging into the stone anchor, he crouched and stretched out his hand.

"Take my hand, lass. I'll not let go."

At his shout, he saw her push herself through the water with another powerful breaststroke until she was almost within his grasp. Iain stretched his body out over the water as far as he could. In the back of his head, he heard a shout of warning, but he buried it deep in the recesses of his mind.

Icy fingers skimmed across his, but she slipped out of reach a second later as the water pulled her away from him. Bleak resignation swept over her pale features the moment he failed to catch her hand. The defeat in her brown eyes sent a powerful rush of adrenaline through him.

Determined not to surrender her to the depths of the North Sea, Iain stretched himself outward even further until he was holding his entire weight on the tips of his fingers. Another wave pushed her closer to him, and he caught hold of the sodden material of her shirtsleeve. With a hard tug, he used her shirt to pull her closer to him.

Reluctant to lose its prize, the sea fought back with a wave that hit her from the side. Her sleeve tore away from the shoulder of the shirt, and his heart sank. Suddenly, the woman's feet broke the water's surface as she kicked herself forward. It was just enough for Iain to wrap his hand around her wrist, then tug her into his side. Without prompting, her arms wrapped around his waist as he pulled her into his chest and her head came to rest on his shoulder. Tremors shook their way from her body into his, and he bent his head to press his mouth against her ear.

"Ye did it, my brave lass," he said with admiration.

The only answer he received was a muffled sob. She was entitled to the cry. Few people could have done what she had, including him. Iain knew his fear would have made it almost impossible to do anything but flounder in the water until the sea dragged him under. In the back of his head, Iain heard his father's voice shouting at him for surviving and not Thane.

A loud cry from above made him look up to see Angus holding a rope that he cast down to him. Satisfied the woman had a secure grip on his waist, Iain released his hold on her and caught the rope. It was looped off with a hitch knot so it could be placed over their heads and tightened under their arms, enabling the Scotsman to pull them up to safety. Gently, he dropped the sturdy hemp over her head.

"I need you to put your arms through the rope." At his instruction, her arms tightened around him as she silently rejected his instructions. "Just one at a time. My man, Angus, will pull you up to safety."

After several seconds, she hesitantly lifted one hand up and through the loop. With his fingers still digging deep into the indentation to hold them steady, he made her grasp the section of rope stretched taut over their heads.

"Now the other one." When she hesitated, he pressed his mouth to her ear again. "Come on, my brave bonnie lass. You'll be safe in less than a minute. Just put your other arm through the rope."

As she pulled her arm away from him, he heard a chorus of shouts from above. Iain glanced over his shoulder and saw a large wave cresting as it headed straight for them. Although she'd not put her other arm through the loop, Iain tugged hard on the rope so it closed snug around her. She jerked her head toward him in surprise, then looked over her shoulder. A wordless cry parted her mouth as her gaze swung back to him.

"Pull her up now, Angus," he shouted and released his hold on her the instant he felt the Scotsman tug on the rope. As the woman was pulled upward to safety, Iain tightened his grip on the indentation and grabbed a stalk of kelp just as the wave slammed into his back and pounded his body into the rock.

The brutal force of the wave knocked the air out of him before it sent the sea crashing down over him. Water filled his nose and mouth, stealing the last bit of breath he had. For a second time in his life, he experienced what it was like to drown. The sea retreated and left him coughing up water, threatening to choke the life out of him. His forehead pressed into a patch of slimy kelp, Iain clung to the rocky formation, pulling in deep breaths of life-sustaining air.

Wet, rough hemp slapped lightly against his cheek, but he didn't move. The rope hit him again with greater force, and Iain opened his eyes. A cold knot twisted his stomach as he glanced over his shoulder and saw an even larger wave rising upward to lash out at him.

"Christ Jesus," he groaned.

His fingers were numb from biting into the indentation of the rock, and he was certain not even his death-like grip would save him from the strength of the wave heading toward him. Releasing his hold on the stalk of kelp, he shoved his head and arm through the lifeline. Deep inside, a voice ordered him to let go of the rock, but he couldn't move.

"Let go, you bloody bastard," he snarled with fear, but his mind refused to obey. A hard tug of the rope made the noose under his arm dig painfully into his side, and he looked up to see Angus glaring down at him.

"*Now, mon*, before ye drown."

With a low growl of fear, Iain let go of the rock and wrapped both of his hands around the thick, braided rope. He muttered a harshly worded prayer and allowed Angus to pull him to safety.

Chapter 3

May, Present Day

Madeline's stomach lurched as a wave crashed over the bow of the sailboat. When they'd sailed out of the Aberdeen harbor two hours ago, the weather had been wonderful. The owner of the bed-and-breakfast had said she'd picked the perfect day for sailing. He'd told her it was warmer than usual for the end of May, and that she'd be fine on the water with a lightweight jacket.

As the sailboat had traveled south, she'd chatted with the other four passengers on the boat, as well as the captain. Captain Mury and his crew had entertained them with stories about Scottish clans and famous shipwrecks. Everything had been perfect until the clouds appeared over the beautiful Scottish coastline. Over the next few minutes, the clouds darken, and the captain quickly turned the boat around. His demeanor confident and calm, the captain told them not to worry about the change in direction. He'd indicated Aberdeen was the closest harbor, and he simply preferred to err on the side of caution for everyone's safety.

It hadn't taken long for the man at the helm to appear uneasy. Madeline was beginning to wonder if the captain had made a mistake by turning around. She glanced over her shoulder at the black storm clouds hanging over the water. Thirty minutes ago, they'd not been so dark, and she was certain they were even closer now. Worse, the water had become increasingly choppy and violent. Each wave the boat bounced over gave her a bit of air time up off her bench seat.

The sailboat suddenly dropped downward in the water as a wave crashed into the hull. A second later, it rose up to land hard on the crest of another wave. The captain shouted something at one of his crew members and pointed toward the shoreline. Madeline's gaze followed the direction of the man's gesture and saw what looked like a small inlet. Was the man going to try to dock there?

No sooner had the thought flitted through her head when the sailor turned the boat's spoked wheel. Relief streaked through her as the vessel changed direction for a second time. Almost as if the sea were angry at the captain's attempt to evade the storm, an enormous wave of water flew up over the side of the boat onto the deck to soak her tennis shoes. Madeline grimaced at how cold the water was.

Overhead, the sails flapped, then bulged against the gusts of wind as the boat shifted its heading. Her gaze flitted back to study the captain's weather-worn face. As a hospice nurse, she'd learned to read facial expressions and body language to know when her patients were in pain. Although the man behind the ship's wheel smiled at her when he met her gaze, she knew he was a lot more worried than he was willing to let anyone see.

The captain barked an order at one of his crew as a wave slammed into the side of the sailboat. Madeline watched the sailor nod sharply, then scurry along the deck toward the bow. The shoreline was close now, and Madeline frowned as she studied the inlet they were heading toward. It looked familiar, but she couldn't figure out why. She didn't have time to think about it as a tall wall of water rose over her head, then crashed down on her and the other passengers.

Madeline gasped as the icy sea water drenched every inch of her. The vessel bounced up and over another wave, then downward, only to shoot upward again. Fear streaked through her as she double-checked to ensure the clasps on her life vest were properly secured. She was a strong swimmer, but no one, not even an Olympic medal holder, stood a chance of making it to shore from this far out. If the worst happened, at least she'd have enough buoyancy to stay afloat while trying to kick her way toward shore. If she could even do that, a voice of panic cried out inside her head.

Madeline raised her head and focused her gaze on the small cove they were headed toward. They were close now, and she could see the small beach in the center of a horseshoe of menacing rock formations. The majority of it looked like small pebbles and jagged rocks. If there was sand, she didn't see any, and she didn't care. It was solid ground. It offered safety and a guarantee she wouldn't drown off the coast of Scotland.

Her breath caught in her throat as the water beneath the sailboat tossed them to one side. She whispered a small prayer that the captain could avoid the rocks. Madeline suddenly stiffened as she recognized the inlet and the rocks forming a gateway into the cove. It was the one she'd seen in her dreams over the years. Almost afraid to look, her gaze flew upward to the top of the cliffs to see the lone male figure standing on the precipice high above the inlet.

She drew in a sharp breath of surprise. Was it him? It was the first time she'd ever seen him from this angle. In her dreams, he was always on her left and too far away to see his features clearly. Unable to take her eyes off of him, she saw his long, dark coat fly outward and flap violently around his legs. Her heart skipped a beat. It was just like in her dreams. Only she wasn't on the cliff now. She was on a boat heading toward the inlet.

A volley of harsh instructions roared out of the captain. Madeline jerked her gaze away from the man on the cliffs and looked back toward the helm. In quick succession, the helmsman rattled off orders as the ship bounced hard against the water and made its way past the outer edges of the rocks lining the cove. Staring at something over Madeline's shoulder, the captain's tanned skin became gray as the color drained from his face. Before she could turn her head to follow his gaze, a violent wave hit the side of the sailboat. The strength of it lifted the boat up on its side.

Screams filled the air as she tried to grab hold of the steel bar behind her, but her fingers slipped right off the wet metal. Arms flailing, she tried to find something to hold on to as she slid across the deck and into the water. An instant later, the ship rolled over. Pain slammed through her as her head hit something hard. A grunt escaped her and sea water flooded her mouth as she drifted downward into an ocean of black water.

Dank air filled Madeline's nostrils as her eyes fluttered open. It was pitch black, and her teeth were chattering from the icy water she was immersed in up to her neck. God, where was she? She fought to remember, and the soft tendril of a memory drifted through her head. The instant it reached the forefront of her brain, she gasped.

The sailboat. It had capsized. A pocket of air must have formed as the boat had hit the water, but she couldn't remember how she'd found it. The last thing she remembered was something hitting her head, then trying to remain conscious as sea water flooded her mouth and choked the air from her lungs.

Oh God, was she dead?

Panic fanned its way through her, and she frantically dog paddled as she blindly searched the blackness for something to hold on to until her fingers brushed across a strip of wood. Desperately, she wrapped her stiff fingers around the edges and clung to it as she tried to control her fear. Fighting to remain calm, she focused on how unusual the wood felt beneath her fingers. It was roughhewn and slimy. The wood certainly didn't feel like something on the sailboat. It reminded her of a wet piece of wood one might find on the beach after a storm.

For the first time, Madeline realized she was no longer wearing a life vest, she continued to cling to the wood with one hand, while wildly slapping the surface of the water in search of the floatation device. An explosive screech of wood and metal filled the air, and her heart slammed into her chest. She didn't have a clue what had made the sound. *Liar, you know exactly what it is, Madeline. The boat is on the rocks.*

Fear slithered through her, and her heart pounded in her chest. A voice in the back of her head ordered her to relax. Panic wouldn't help her escape, and she could easily die of shock before hypothermia set in completely. She tried to slow her breathing and succeeded a small fraction before she tried to form a plan of action.

"Think…Madeline. Think," she said fiercely as her teeth chattered a loud noise in her ears. "Okay, the ship is…upside down, that means…the surface…air…is above me. Brilliant, Madeline. How…do…we get up there?"

Christ, if she had some light, she could figure out which way to go. What if she followed the hull of the ship upward? No, she might not have enough air for that, and if the boat was on the rocks then she—if? *Don't be an idiot, Madeline. That sound had to have been the hull scraping against the rocks.* If she were to swim up along the bottom of the boat, she could easily be crushed between the rocks and the ship. Worst-case scenario, she swam in the wrong direction, and she might not find this pocket of air again.

"So what are you going to do, Madeline?"

The only answer that came back to her was the last thing she wanted to do. She needed to take a deep breath and go underwater to see if there was a source of light to show her the water's surface. The question was whether she'd be able to see something, and if she did, could she reach it? One thing was certain. She sure as hell couldn't stay here.

If she didn't drown, at best she had an hour before she succumbed to hypothermia, and she was damn sure the air would run out long before that happened. The ship shifted slightly, accompanied by more sounds of metal and wood screeching against the rocks. It was a terrifying sound, and she gasped with fear.

"Oh God, please. I don't want to die," she whispered as she closed her eyes.

"Don't be afraid, Maddie. Let go. He'll be there." The quiet reassurance in her grandmother's voice made Madeline draw in a sharp breath.

"Grandma?" she whispered.

"Let go now, Maddie. Let go now, before it's too late."

Without questioning the voice, Madeline drew in a deep breath, then pushed herself down and outward, away from the ship. Above her head, a flash of light revealed a path upward to the surface. With a vicious kick of her legs, she swam as hard as she could. Seconds later, her head was above water. She took a breath only to have sea water rush into her mouth as a wave tossed her beneath the water before she kicked her way up again. Coughing, she twisted around in the water, trying to find the inlet's beach. There was still light out, and she could see the dark hull of the ship outlined in the gray darkness.

For a moment, she stared at it in confusion. The vessel was tilted to one side, with her bottom impaled on top of the rocks. Lightning flashed, and her mouth filled with sea water again as she gasped at the sight of a large smokestack funnel with three masts sharply outlined in the near darkness.

"What the—"

She didn't get to finish her sentence as a wave rolled over her head and pushed her downward. When she bobbed to the surface again, she saw lights a short distance away. Another flash of light overhead revealed people standing on the rocks near the shipwreck. Every muscle in her body was contracting, which made it difficult to stay afloat as her legs were beginning to stop doing what her brain was telling them to do. It was now or never. With as hard a kick as she could, she floundered her way toward the rocks. She'd gone only two strokes when another wave rolled over her and pushed her beneath the water.

With a cry, Madeline shot upright in bed. Her arms outstretched in a disoriented fashion, she coughed violently, trying to breathe something other than sea water. Gasping for air, she pressed her hands into her chest and waited for her terror to recede as it always did. She wasn't in the water. She was in her own bed.

Relief made Madeline curl into a ball, pulling her legs up into her chest as she wrapped her arms around them. The soft sheet covering the lower half of her body was soft against her skin as she rested her forehead on her knees. Inside her chest, her heart continued to pound wildly out of control.

"Christ," she mumbled, and blew out a harsh breath of relief.

That had to be the worst nightmare she'd ever had about the stranger. It had been terrifyingly real and tangible. The thought made Madeline's stomach lurch violently, and she forced herself to take deep breaths. The fresh scent of the sheets filled her nose, and it had a soothing effect on her.

They smelled of sunshine and clean air, just like when her grandmother had allowed sheets to dry in the open air and sunshine. As she drank in the scent, the nightmare slowly faded. Her heartbeat returning to normal, she lifted her head. In front of her, a stream of sunlight fell through the window onto the foot of the bed where a dark green coverlet lay twisted in a wild heap.

The memory of thrashing about in the water as she tried to keep her head above the waves made her close her eyes for a brief moment. The thought vanished as she looked around the room with a frown. This wasn't her room. Panic streaked through her for a moment before she groaned and her head flopped back into the mattress.

"Oh, for God's sake, Madeline. Of course it's not your room, you idiot. You're in Scotland. Remember?"

How could she have forgotten that? One arm flung over her eyes, she fought back tears as the image of her grandmother's attorney pushing an envelope across the desk at her filled her head. Inside had been a note from her grandmother. It had been short, and she remembered every word.

Dear Maddie,

Bill is going to give you instructions I know you won't like. But I want you to remember you promised me you would follow my last wishes to the letter. You're not to protest or argue. All you're allowed to do is remember your promise to obey my instructions.

All my love,
Grandma
P.S. Don't be afraid to let go, Maddie, he'll be there.

With a wry twist of her lips, Madeline stared up at the ceiling. Her grandmother had been right. She'd not been happy with the instructions Bill Simmons had given her. In fact, she had objected by bursting into tears in the attorney's office. Mr. Simmons had quietly pushed a box of tissues within reach, then patiently waited for her to collect herself.

Scotland.

Her grandmother had been planning and saving for the trip for a long time, Bill Simmons had said. It was supposed to have been a birthday surprise for Madeline, but her grandmother had become sick. She'd seen to it that her attorney made all the arrangements so Madeline wouldn't be able to find an excuse not to make the trip. He'd even done the preliminary work of acquiring a passport for her.

Madeline closed her eyes again. At least her grandmother had missed the sailboat cruise from hell. Immediately, every muscle in her body stiffened. With a jerk, she sat upright in bed. The sailboat had to have reached Aberdeen if she was in her hotel room. Madeline frowned.

Why didn't she remember the sailboat returning to the harbor?

She drew in a deep breath of amazement as she remembered the captain heading toward the inlet…toward him. The man. She'd seen him on the cliff just before the last wave had hit. Had he rescued her? But how? Is that what her grandmother had meant in her dream? Deep down, a voice tried to tell her something unpleasant, but she ignored it—refused to listen to it.

"Think, Maddie. How in the hell did you get back to the hotel?" she muttered. She glanced down at the linen nightgown she was wearing with annoyance. "And why in God's name would you think wearing this thing to bed would be comfortable?"

Fingers pressing into her temples, she closed her eyes and tried to remember. Had she actually taken the sailboat cruise, or had it been a nightmare? Had it been nothing more than a terrible dream like all the others, where she'd stood on the edge of a cliff watching the man standing alone on the cliffs with her?

A quiet knock on her door made her jump, and before she could say anything, a young woman entered the room. Stunned that someone had simply entered her room without permission, Madeline stared in silent amazement at the girl. The young woman, carrying a tray of food and what looked like a dress over her arm, walked quickly past the bed toward a table near a large chifforobe.

With dark auburn hair and dressed in a period costume, the girl was the stereotype of a Scottish woman from another century. The hotel's advertised promise of an authentic historical ambiance was one it had delivered on from the time she'd checked-in the day before yesterday. All the staff wore period costumes, something her grandmother would have loved as there were men in kilts with brogues everywhere. As the young woman turned toward Madeline, the girl smiled politely.

"Good morning, miss. How are you feeling?"

"I'm sorry?" Madeline shook her head, confused by the question.

"You were pale as death last night when his lordship carried you into the house." The girl set her tray down, then laid a dress on the foot of the bed. "They say he risked his life to save you."

"Saved me?" What had someone saved her from? A chill swept through her.

"Aye, that he did, miss. Dinnae ye remember?"

When Madeline didn't answer, the girl frowned then hurried to the side of the bed. Without warning, she leaned forward and pressed the back of her hand to Madeline's forehead. Relief replaced the maid's look of concern.

"Goodness, ye gave me a fright. I thought ye might have taken a fever."

"I'm sorry, but who are you?"

"I'm Eileen McFayden, miss." The girl smiled broadly and gestured toward the tray. "Me *màthair* thought ye might like some tea with a few scones."

"Your mother?"

"Aye. My parents work for Lord Glenburnie. He's the one who saved you. My *màthair* is his cook, and me *faither* looks after the stables and the manor."

"I'm sorry, I'm a bit confused." Madeline eyed the maid with a growing sense of disorientation.

"Och, tis no wonder either. Ye would have drowned if not for his lordship," the girl said with a dreamy expression. "His lordship is terrified of the water. But this morning me *faither* said his lordship wasn't afraid last night. *Faither* said the mon snatched you straight out of the sea with the strength of The Bruce himself."

Madeline closed her eyes for a moment as her stomach lurched violently. It hadn't been a dream, after all. The sailboat cruise had ended in disaster, but she'd survived. The others.

"What about the others?" she whispered in horror. "Did they get off the boat? The captain?"

"Aye, only five sailors were lost. May the good Lord keep them."

Madeline sucked in a sharp breath of horror at the girl's reply. There had only been eight people on the sailboat, which meant only she and two others had survived. She'd almost died. A voice deep inside whispered something else had happened, but she couldn't hear what it was trying to tell her.

"Miss? Miss? Ye've gone as pale as a ghost. Are ye all right?"

"Yes," she choked out as her fingers latched onto the sheet and curled up into tight fists.

Eileen's voice sounded in her ears as if from a distance while an overwhelming wave of relief rolled over her. She was alive. All of it had been real, and she'd survive the unthinkable. She could have easily been one of those who'd lost their lives. Relief warmed her for a brief moment at the thought before guilt sent an icy chill spreading across her skin.

How could she be so heartless as to be glad she wasn't one of those who'd died? How was she any more deserving to live than someone else? The question sent a shudder rocking through her as she closed her eyes and bit back tears. A gentle arm wrapped around her shoulders as Eileen sat down on the bed beside her.

"It's all right to cry, miss. There was nothing ye could do. The good Lord wanted ye to live. Ye need not be sorry for that."

Slowly Madeline lifted her head to stare out the window at the wide expanse of land racing to meet the sea. The water was as calm today as it was yesterday when the sailboat had left Aberdeen's harbor. It had all happened so quickly. The storm, the sailboat capsizing, getting hit on the head, finding herself in the pocket of air, and her grandmother's voice.

That last one she could only put down to her mind using whatever it could to make her overcome her fear and swim up to the surface. But the voice had been right. He had been there, calling out to her. She couldn't remember what he looked like, only the encouragement in his voice as he'd urged her to swim toward him.

"Are ye feeling all right, miss?"

"No—yes. I need to get dressed so I can say thank you to the man you said saved me."

"That would be Lord Glenburnie ye need tae speak with."

"I also want to speak with the others who…survived."

"The ship's captain and his crew left for Aberdeen at first light."

"Left?" Madeline shook her head slightly in bemusement. "I don't understand. Isn't this the Chester Hotel in Aberdeen?"

"Oh no, miss, this is Muchalls Hall," Eileen said with a shake of her head.

As Eileen left Madeline's side to stand next to the bed, Madeline stared blankly at the maid. Where the hell was Muchalls Hall, and why wasn't—the inlet. Captain Mury had been headed for the small beach between the rock. Muchalls Hall must be the home of the man who'd pulled her out of the water. So why didn't she remember him, and for that matter, anything else except her dream?

And she didn't appreciate Captain Mury leaving her behind. Wherever behind really was, because she was clueless as to where Muchalls Hall was in relation to Aberdeen. She would not be happy if the captain hadn't made arrangements for her return to the city. First order of business was getting dressed and then finding a way back to her hotel in Aberdeen. Her gaze focused on the girl.

"I need to get dressed. Do you know where my shirt and pants are?" At her question, the maid's eyes widened in horror.

"Oh, miss. Ye cannae wear those. It's nae proper."

"Why? Everyone in Aberdeen is wearing them." Madeline slipped out of bed, eyeing the other woman with puzzlement. Eileen's eyes narrowed slightly as she studied

Madeline intently. With a firm shake of her head, the maid rejected Madeline's comment.

"'Tis nae proper, miss. Even if ye could, the clothes ye were wearing when his lordship pulled ye out of the water need repairing. Me màthair thought this dress would do until your other clothes dry out." Eileen pointed to the dress lying on the foot of the bed. "The stays from your trunk are still drying, but me màthair found some undergarments and an old corset her ladyship wore before she died."

"Stays?"

Madeline found herself floundering in confusion again as Eileen gestured toward a chifforobe that stood next to the window. What trunk was the woman talking about? Everything she had brought with her on her trip was at the Chester Hotel, except for her purse, which she'd taken with her on the sailboat. It had her wallet, her passport, and her phone with the pictures she'd taken since arriving in Scotland. The phone, wallet, and credit cards she could replace. But her passport? Getting that replaced was bound to be a major headache. She could only hope there was an US Embassy in Aberdeen.

When Madeline didn't move, the maid scurried toward the tall mahogany chest. Two seconds later, Eileen held up an undergarment that looked like the bustiers that had been in fashion off and on over the last few years. Madeline had always loved the look on others, but on her not so much. With large breasts, she always looked like she was going to pop out of the damn things.

"Me màthair said Lord Glenburnie's wife ordered it from Paris when she was alive. God rest her soul. It's a wee scandalous, but me màthair thinks it will fit ye."

Madeline eyed the garment the maid was holding up in the air with misgivings. What the hell did she need a corset for, let alone a gown? Didn't these people have an extra pair of jeans or t-shirt she could use until she got back to Aberdeen and her luggage? Madeline slowly stepped forward to take the corset from the maid. As she eyed the garment warily, Eileen tipped her head slightly with a look that said she found Madeline's reaction extremely peculiar.

"Do ye need help to dress, miss?"

"No. No, thank you," Madeline said as she stared down at the corset. "It hooks up the front, so I'll figure it out."

"If ye are sure, miss."

"I'll be fine." Madeline forced a smile to her lips as she met Eileen's uncertain gaze. After a second, the maid nodded slowly.

"All right, the bath is just down the hall, and I laid out towels for ye. The water will be hot, and a good soak will do ye good. And, ye need tae eat something." Eileen's voice was quiet but stern. As if realizing she'd spoken too sharply, the girl smiled. "Me màthair makes the best scones in the Mearns, miss. I know ye will enjoy them."

The maid smiled and patted Madeline's hand reassuringly, then left the room. Alone once more, Madeline looked down at the odd underwear and dress on the bed, before her gaze shifted back to the corset in her hand. Lord, she'd heard of people living the part, but these people seemed to take it to the extreme by expecting their guests to do the same. She snorted with amusement as she dropped the corset on the bed and made her way to the bathroom.

Madeline wasn't sure what she'd been expecting, but the bathtub and sink were antiques. A short time later, reclined against the back of the tub, she reveled in the hot water. Eileen had been right about soaking in the tub. The hot water had loosened her muscles considerably, and she wasn't feeling quite as stiff as when she'd woken up. As the water grew tepid, Madeline knew she would have to brave the cooler temperature of the bathroom. Better now than never.

Quickly scrambling out of the tub, she rubbed off as much water as she could with one of the thin towels Eileen had laid out for her. Shivering, she quickly threw the nightgown over her shoulders, grumbling as she shoved her arms through the sleeves. The linen material clung to her still wet skin, making it difficult to straighten. She uttered a noise of frustration. What she wouldn't give right now for a t-shirt and a pair of pajama bottoms.

The warmth of the bathroom disappeared as she opened the door leading into the hall. Immediately, the cold air of the corridor skimmed over her skin despite the nightgown's long sleeves. The change in temperature made her draw in a sharp breath before she hurried toward her room.

Still towel drying her hair as she moved down the hallway, she suddenly slammed into an immovable object. A small cry escaped her as Madeline stumbled over her feet, and two large hands caught her by the arms to hold her upright. Tugging the towel off her head, she found herself staring at a wide chest and broad shoulders in a dark brown jacket.

Her brain registered a brown pouch and dark green kilt with muted stripes as her gaze dropped downward. She'd always enjoyed muscular arms and legs on a man, and while his jacket hid his arms, this guy's legs were sexy as hell. A soft sound rumbled in his chest, and Madeline jerked her head up to meet a piercing blue-eyed gaze that sent her heart pounding hard in her chest.

Good Lord, the man was tall. She wasn't short by any means, but this man was at least six-five if not taller. He seemed to tower over her. It made her feel small and, oddly enough, quite feminine. The man wasn't what she would call handsome, but his features were masculine and rugged in a way that would make it impossible for anyone to ignore him whenever he entered a room.

His hair was as dark as coal, with a slight sheen that made her want to run her fingers through it to see if it was as soft as it looked. But it was his dark blue eyes that sent a rush of heat skimming across her skin. As the heat dissipated, a tingling sensation took its place until every nerve ending in her body hummed with awareness. It took a lot to intimidate her, but this guy unsettled her in a way that made her stomach tighten and skin tingle. He had sexy bad boy written all over him. Just the kind of guy she avoided at all costs. Men like this were trouble.

Martin had been almost as hot as this guy, and she'd fallen hard for her ex-fiancé. Mocking laughter flitted through her head. Martin had never made every nerve ending in her body tingle with awareness like this man did. This guy oozed sex appeal. If his voice was anywhere near as hot as his body, she was certain he could make any woman dance to whatever tune he wanted to play.

She swallowed hard at the thought. Heat suffused her skin again as she saw his gaze slide down over her body with an expression of sinful appreciation. It was just the right amount of smoldering assessment that would make a woman melt in his arms. Who was she kidding? She was already melting, and he'd not even opened his mouth.

Afraid she'd failed to put the nightgown on correctly, she followed the path of his gaze downward. Embarrassment rolled through her as she realized the gown had absorbed a great deal more water than she'd thought. The linen clung to her chest, highlighting her stiff nipples as they pressed outward against the material. In the back of her mind, a voice debated whether they were hard from the chilly air or her reaction to the man.

Sucking in a sharp breath, Madeline jerked her towel upward and pressed it to her chest as she met his gaze again. Blue eyes narrowing, his firm mouth twisted slightly in what might have been either amusement or disapproval. She wasn't sure which, and his eyes were unreadable. Without saying a word, he simply stepped aside and swept his hand out in front of him in a silent command for her to continue along her way.

Madeline hesitated for a moment, then like a scared rabbit, hurried past him. Behind her, a quiet sound escaped him that might have been laughter. She was too embarrassed to glance over her shoulder and find out. When she reached the safety of her room, Madeline stood with her back pressed against the door with her eyes closed.

Other than her father, Eileen hadn't mentioned any other men being in the house. That left one of two possibilities. Either the man she'd just run into was Eileen's father or Lord Glenburnie. Eileen had to be at least twenty, and the man she'd just ran into was too young to be the maid's father. So that left Lord Glenburnie.

Now she understood Eileen's reaction as she'd explained how the master of the house had rescued Madeline. The maid had sighed with good reason. The man was unbelievably hot. A vague memory pushed its way forward as she recalled an outstretched arm and a deep voice commanding her to take his hand. If she was right in thinking the man she'd just met was the same one who'd saved her from drowning, she didn't believe for a minute he was afraid of anything, let alone water.

Embarrassment slid through her again, and her cheeks grew hot as she recalled the way his gaze had swept over her. It had been a leisurely appraisal, and he'd taken his time to study her from top to bottom. Thank God the man hadn't said a word. If his voice was even half as devastating as the rest of him, it wasn't too much of a leap to think he was one of those men who could seduce a woman with a smile and a few words whispered in her ear, especially in a Scottish brogue.

"Enough, Madeline," she muttered with disgust. "You didn't come to Scotland for any one-night stands, and you are definitely not interested in a guy who doesn't look like commitment material. Not by a long shot. Not to mention he's Scottish and you're a Yank."

With a shake of her head, she pushed herself away from the door and crossed the floor to the bed. She dubiously studied the underwear Eileen had left her. Still rattled by everything that had happened in the past twenty-four hours, it took Madeline almost an hour to dress. If she'd had her own clothes, she would have been ready in minutes.

The frilly laced legs of the drawers had been easy to figure out, but she didn't know whether the camisole went under or over the corset. She opted for under. The corset had been a bit cumbersome, but the fact that it hooked up in the front made it easy to put on. The dress had been the most difficult, with all its buttons running down the back.

By the time she was ready to put on the shoes Eileen had set out on the floor, Madeline was in a stage of revolt. She held the shoes up in the air to study them with antipathy. They buttoned up the side and looked extremely uncomfortable. Madeline shook her head. No. Just no. She'd just have to go barefoot until she returned to Aberdeen. When she finished dressing, she appraised herself in the mirror. Other than for her short hair and her bare feet hidden under the floor-length dress, she looked as if she'd stepped out of the past.

Satisfied with her appearance, she was about to leave her room when the mirror reflected something fluttering in the air outside her window. Crossing the floor, she peered out the windowpane searching for whatever she'd seen in the mirror. Today, the sea looked nothing like it had yesterday. Although it was windy, there wasn't a dark cloud in the sky. The wind danced across the North Sea's surface, creating small whitecaps that rolled toward the shore. The flutter of movement caught her attention once more.

Madeline turned her head to the right and saw a piece of white sail billow outward in the breeze before falling lifeless against its mast. They were the rocks she'd seen in her dream, but the shipwreck wasn't the sailboat. The boat in front of her was much larger and older than the sailboat. It had a funnel and three masts awkwardly jutting up into the sky. Madeline blinked, then stared at the shipwreck again, but the view didn't change. Where was Destiny's Dream? A wave of uncertainty swept through her as she stared at the rocks. Something was wrong, and she didn't like the queasy sensation stirring in her stomach. Where the hell was she?

Chapter 4

Iain tried to maintain his focus on the news article in the daily Scotsman. It was proving to be a losing battle as his thoughts kept drifting back to the woman he'd rescued from the Phoenix Rising last night. The memory of how close they'd both come to drowning sent a chill surging through his blood until his body could feel the icy water soaking him.

With a grunt, he shoved the memory into a dark compartment in his head. He'd saved the woman, and now he had a mystery on his hands. Captain Napier had been adamant that the woman hadn't been on board the vessel. The man had insisted the woman had to have been a stowaway.

From the clothes she'd been wearing, Iain was inclined to think the same thing. The pants and shirt she'd had on when he'd carried her back to the house had been of excellent quality, but had clearly been made for a man. The problem was her trunk.

Fingers drumming lightly against the newspaper on his desk, Iain shook his head in bafflement. The steamer trunk that had washed up on shore was a mystery. Stowaways didn't travel with baggage. If she'd been a stowaway, how had her trunk gotten on board? It was a question that perplexed him, especially considering Napier's insistence the woman had not been a passenger.

The gowns hanging in the dress compartment of the trunk had been of a material and design only found in a shop that catered to noblewomen or women of means. Then there was the brass plate just above the sturdy lock with the raised initials MW bolted down on the sheet of metal. The baggage was hardly that of a member of the working class. It made him wonder if Captain Napier had been lying. Perhaps the man had taken her on as a passenger and pocketed the money without telling his employer. If the woman were running from something or someone, she might have paid a large sum for Napier to take her on as a passenger.

Iain leaned back in his desk chair and closed his eyes. The image of the woman was still fresh in his mind from their encounter in the upstairs hall. Last night her shirt and trousers had clung to her, outlining a full, lushly curved body. But it had been a fleeting observation, as his thoughts had been grappling with their near brush with death.

Their meeting in the hallway almost an hour ago had been a much different encounter. She'd obviously just emerged from her bath, as her nightgown had hugged her body almost as well as her wet clothes last night, with one exception. The stiff nipples pressing against the white linen of her nightgown had been an erotic sight. The fierce urge to pull one of those rosy peaks into his mouth while his hand cradled the other full breast in his hand had stirred his cock beneath his work kilt.

The woman wasn't a beauty, but there was something alluring about her. It was as if she'd come from a different world with her large, brown eyes that could hold a man prisoner with just a look. Even in the dim light of the upper hallway, they'd been luminous and beguiling. Perhaps the most enticing of all were her lips.

Full and plump, her mouth had made him long to see if she tasted as sweet as she looked. The only thing that seemed out of place was the short length of her hair. It was cut almost as short as his, but unlike his black hair, hers was dark brown.

The brown color held faint touches of light that enhanced the wavy soft curls.

The memory of how she'd looked in the upstairs hallway made his body tighten. There had been an ethereal quality about her that had set his imagination on fire. An image of her lying in a soft bed of heather, as if she were one of the fae calling him to join her, sent a strong surge of desire barreling through his veins.

Irritated by his fanciful thinking, he released a low growl of self-disgust. It had been a while since he'd bedded a woman, and his reaction to his unexpected guest was confirmation of the fact. His hand slapped the top of his desk and created a loud crack in the study as he launched himself out of his chair in a rapid movement.

Iain strode to the window to stare out at the sea that had tossed the woman up on his doorstep. The last thing he needed was an extra mouth to feed. He was also willing to wager money he didn't have, the woman would disrupt his household almost as much as Ainslie's daily antics. Household? He snorted with self-disgust. The only disruption would be to his sleep, given his less than restful slumber last night. At the sound of a quiet knock on the door, he glanced over his shoulder.

"Enter."

The harsh command echoed sharply in the room as he waited for whomever was on the opposite side of the door. The door didn't open immediately, which indicated the person on the other side had hesitated before venturing into his domain. As the door slowly swung open, he turned around and watched his unexpected guest walk into the study. Hands clasped behind his back, he studied her in silence for a moment, remembering the last time they had met.

"Good morning…again."

Iain's quiet greeting sent a pink color cresting up over her cheeks, forcing him to bite back a smile. He shouldn't tease her, but something provoked him to do so. She met his gaze for an instant, then averted her eyes as the flush in her cheeks darkened.

"Hello…I am…are you, Lord Glenburnie?"

"Aye." His cryptic reply made her look uncomfortable, and he cleared his throat as he met her gaze. "And you are?"

"Madeline Whitworth."

"Well, Miss Whitworth, I am assuming it's Miss." At his speculative observation, she verified her unmarried state with a bob of her head. He paused for a brief moment as he remembered the initials on the steamer trunk. That was one mystery solved. Iain ignored how much her unattached status pleased him. "You, Miss Whitworth, are a very lucky woman."

"I don't remember much, but I understand you pulled me out of the water. Thank you," she replied quietly. "I would have died if not for you."

"You should give yourself a great more credit, lass." Iain shook his head as he remembered how valiantly she'd swam toward him last night. "I simply gave you something to hold on to. You were the one who battled the sea to reach the rocks."

Silence stretched between them, and Iain experienced a unique feeling of awkwardness. He'd not been this tongue-tied since he'd asked Maggie MacLean to dance at the county fair when he was still a boy. He cleared his throat, then walked toward his desk. It provided something solid between the two of them. As to why he thought he needed a barrier between them, he wasn't sure.

"The captain—"

"I wanted—" Her full lips twisted in a wry grin as she met his gaze. Determined not to allow himself to get lost in her soft, brown-eyed gaze or think about the sweet curve of her mouth, Iain waved his hand in the air.

"Please, proceed." His taciturn command made her wince slightly before she nodded.

"I don't wish to impose on you any longer than necessary, but did the captain make arrangements for me to return to my hotel in Aberdeen?"

"Hotel?" Iain eyed her in puzzlement.

"Yes, and if you have a telephone I could use, that would be wonderful. I need to contact the US embassy in Aberdeen." The woman's lovely mouth twisted up in a small moue as she seemed to think out loud. "At least I hope there's an embassy there. My passport is at the bottom of the ocean., and I need a replacement."

"A telephone?"

Iain frowned for a moment. In the past ten years, the telephone had become fairly common in the homes of those with unlimited means. But even if he could afford the luxury, the technology had yet to reach the countryside. He shook his head.

"Unfortunately, we don't have one. I can send my stable boy to the village to send a telegram to the hotel."

He pulled a sheet of paper out of his desk, removed the cap from his fountain pen, and bent his head over his stationery, waiting for her to speak. When she remained silent, Iain lifted his head to see her staring at him as if he had two heads.

"You don't have a telephone? Not even a cell phone?"

"I believe I just confirmed that." He arched an eyebrow in annoyance at being questioned. He didn't know what a cell phone was, but it must have been similar to a telephone. Madeline's gaze narrowed at him, and she cautiously retreated towards the study door.

"Do you have a car that could take me to Aberdeen?"

"A car?" Iain frowned.

"Yes, a car. It has an engine and takes you places."

Brown eyes wide with alarm, Madeline Whitworth paled as she took another step toward the exit. Fear flashed crossed her face as she stared at him in obvious alarm. Puzzled by her behavior, Iain dropped his pen onto the desktop and narrowed his gaze at her.

"I'm well-acquainted with automobiles, but I don't own one of those either. But, if you would kindly sit down, I can make arrangements to send you wherever you wish to go."

With a sweep of his hand, Iain gestured toward the chair facing his desk as he slowly walked around the dark mahogany furniture. The moment he moved, she took several quick steps backward until her hand was wrapped around the doorknob.

For all her womanly charms, Madeline Whitworth was proving to be quite difficult. He should have expected this. A woman dressed in men's clothing, who was most likely a stowaway, should have been warning enough.

"Miss Whitworth, come sit down before you collapse to the floor," he bit out between clenched teeth. When she didn't move, Iain released a soft growl of irritation. "I can assure you, Miss Whitworth, I mean you no harm. Now, stop acting like an addlebrained female about to have the vapors and sit down."

She immediately straightened to her full height and glared at him. The woman obviously didn't like someone dictating to her. In the back of his head, he admired the way she'd pushed aside her fear in her refusal to be intimidated. The thought increased his annoyance. He needed to find out where this woman belonged and send her on her way. The sooner she was gone, the better. Iain was beginning to think she wouldn't listen to him when she suddenly walked toward the chair.

The only plausible explanation for her odd behavior was that she was still disoriented from her brush with death. That wouldn't surprise Iain, given his own reaction a little while ago. Iain's stomach knotted tightly in his gut as the old fear made his mouth go dry. As Madeline perched on the edge of the chair's seat, he moved to sit down behind the desk.

Before he could say anything, she reached out to pick up the newspaper he'd casually dropped on the desktop. She turned the paper right-side up so she could read it, and a second later she made a gurgling sound in the back of her throat. If possible, she'd grown even paler than just a few seconds ago.

"Is this some sort of game?" she rasped as she looked at him. Fear darkened her eyes, and Iain shook his head in puzzlement. The woman was trying his patience much in the way Ainslie did.

"A game?"

"This newspaper, it says 1896."

"It's the fifth of August 1896, to be exact." Iain pinned his gaze on her with irritation.

"That's not possible," she whispered in horror. The panic and fear in her made him frown with concern. She shook her head as her palm pressed into her stomach as if she was in some form of distress. "I was just in Aberdeen with cars and telephones and computers…the sailboat."

In a flash of movement, the woman was out of her seat and running to the door. Iain muttered an oath as he lunged to his feet to follow her. As he reached the entrance hall, Madeline had already thrown open the front door and charged out of the house. He winced at the bright light streaming into the entryway.

"*Fuck*," he snarled as he ran after her. So help him, if the woman caused him to have another headache, he would wring her neck.

Iain looked down the drive, expecting to see Madeline running toward the main road. There was no sign of her, and he uttered another oath beneath his breath and ran toward the side of the house. As he rounded the corner of the manor, he saw her racing toward the cliffs.

The memory of the phantom he'd seen on the precipice last night made Iain run faster. If she threw herself off the cliffs, there would be an inquest, something that would be even more disruptive than Madeline Whitworth was at the moment. He saw her stop at the edge of the cliff to stare down at the inlet. What the devil was wrong with the woman? In the next breath, she bolted toward the path that led down to the beach. A string of curses rolled past Iain's lips as he reached the path leading down to the sandy shore and followed her.

"*Madeline, stop,*" he shouted angrily.

Either she ignored his command or didn't hear him as she continued scurrying down the stony path. Iain frowned as he watched her darting downward. There was something about her gait that made it look as though she thought there were hot coals under her feet. Iain's gaze fell on the stony path, and he sucked in a sharp breath at the small trail of blood sprinkled over the ground. She was bleeding. Grunting with anger and growing concern, he increased his pace, half skidding, half running downward along the narrow path.

When he reached the foot of the cliffs, he saw Madeline standing at the edge of the sea. The waves were rolling onto the shore, and the hem of her gown was dark from the water swirling around her legs. As he closed the distance between them, Iain watched her pacing back and forth while shaking her head. Every second or so, she would stop and stare out at what was left of the Phoenix Rising, lying battered against the rocks. It wasn't until he was a couple of feet away that he could hear her.

"It's not possible. It's just not possible." The panic in her words as she paced the sandy shore line startled him. Madeline didn't even glance in his direction as he stopped a few feet away from her. She simply walked back and forth, muttering to herself. "It can't be 1896. This is just one of your nightmares, Madeline. You'll wake up soon and be back home."

"Madeline."

When she didn't respond, Iain thought she might not have heard him. A few seconds later, she abruptly halted her pacing to stand stiff and motionless as she stared out at the shipwreck. Iain said her name again, and she whirled around in a sharp movement. Her cheeks were wet with tears, and his heart slammed into his chest at her confused look of horror.

"I'm not supposed to be here. I don't belong here," she said as she stretched out her hand to him. "I don't even know where here is."

Something twisted in Iain's gut as he took her hand in his and gently pulled her into his arms. Her face buried in his shoulder, she sagged against him. Instantly, Iain swept her up into his arms, and she cried in a heartbroken manner against his chest.

Glancing down at her feet, he sucked in a sharp breath of shock. She was barefoot. With a shift of his arm, Iain swung her legs up high enough so he could crane his neck and look at the bottom of her feet.

"*Màthair of God,*" he exclaimed in horror at the cuts across her soles. "*Where* are your shoes, lass?"

The only reply Madeline gave was a tearful sob. A grim resignation swept over him as she continued to cry in his arms. Whatever was wrong with her, it was bad enough for her to ignore the cuts on her feet. The salt from the sea water had to have exacerbated the pain, but she seemed oblivious to the fact. In silence, he carried her toward the path leading to the top of the cliffs. As they reached the narrow trail upward, Iain came to a halt.

"Madeline, I need tae put ye over my shoulder, I cannae carry ye up the path like this. We'll fall tae our deaths." She stirred in his arms and raised her head. Eyes red from crying, she met his gaze and shook her head.

"I can walk," she whispered. The hopelessness he saw in her brown eyes aroused a protective instinct inside him.

"Dinnae be a fool, woman. Your feet are too badly cut tae walk up the path."

"I can walk on my own."

Madeline's voice was stronger now, and there was an obstinate air about her that made Iain groan with frustration. He already had one stubborn female in his life, and this one was proving to be as bull-headed as Ainslie. Setting her down on a nearby rock, he pulled his *sgian dubh* from his hose and squatted in front of her. In quick succession, he cut the hem of her dress off into several strips. Iain tucked the small knife back in his stocking and lifted his head.

"This is apt tae hurt, lass."

Madeline met his gaze and gave him a sharp nod of understanding. As gently as he could, Iain began to wrap her feet in the wet cloth. The only sound she made was a sharp hiss of air, but he knew she had to be in pain as she held herself rigid. When her feet were bound, he straightened and offered his hand to her.

"Are ye certain ye want tae do this?"

"Yes." Her voice was little more than a whisper as she placed her hand in his.

As she stood up, Madeline's mouth twisted in a grimace of pain, but she didn't utter a sound. Instead, she limped her way to the path and started upward. Iain followed behind her and marveled at her perseverance as she slowly made her way up the rocky trail. Her stubborn determination to make her way to the top of the cliffs on her own only strengthened his impression of how much she reminded him of his daughter.

It took them twice as long to climb the path as normal with Madeline limping her way upward. By the time they reached the top of the cliffs, her limp had become an uneven stagger. Iain could only imagine how badly her feet hurt as he came up behind her and lifted her up into his arms. While he was tempted to send for the doctor, he knew Grace could tend to Madeline's feet easily enough. It was her emotional state that concerned him more.

A hard shudder rocked its way out of her and into his chest the moment she was cradled against him. One arm wrapped around his neck, she pressed her face into his jacket. There was a sense of defeat about her that troubled Iain. It created a deep-seated urge to protect her, no matter the cost. The power of the emotion caught him by surprise as his arms tightened around her. With a grimace of confusion at the feelings assaulting him, Iain carried Madeline back to the manor at a fast pace.

Chapter 5

Pain was the first thing that pierced Madeline's consciousness. Her feet hurt like hell. Slowly opening her eyes, she breathed in the soft aroma of the outdoors. The smell drifted down from a soft linen pouch resting on her forehead. She recognized soft traces of lavender mixed with pine, but there was something else mixed in with the aroma she couldn't place. She reached up to touch the sack, but a small, warm hand prevented her from touching it.

"Stop," a quiet voice commanded. A second later, a young girl she'd not seen before leaned over her and removed the pouch off Madeline's forehead. "I dinnae want ye to spill the herbs all over ye."

For a moment, Madeline stared up at the girl, whose hair was the bluish black color of midnight. It was pulled away from the sides of her face and tied at the back of her head in a half-ponytail. Long and silky looking, her hair fell down over her back and shoulders in a gentle wave.

Slender and frail looking, her eyes had a slight tilt to them with long, black lashes that emphasized their violet color. As the girl smiled down at her, Madeline's gaze swept around the room. It was the same room she'd woken up in this morning. The only difference was it had been bright and sunny then. It was nighttime now.

Two oil lamps cast a soft glow on the walls of the room. Each one had a brass base that supported a clear glass container filled with oil. Although she couldn't see the flame inside the pale white, opaque ball on top of the burner, she could see its shadow dancing behind the glass. Smoke from the burning oil drifted up out of the globe's slender chimney in a thin white stream before it dissipated in the air.

Her gaze shifted around the room, and her heart sank as she closed her eyes again. She was still in Lord Glenburnie's house. She was still in 1896. The memory of the inlet she'd dreamed about all her life pushed its way into Madeline's head followed by the image of the shipwreck on the rocks. She knew the difference between a sailboat and a ship. The vessel down in the inlet resembled an old sailing ship with one of the Titanic's black funnel smokestacks plunked in between its masts.

But where was Destiny's Dream? The sudden memory of her head hitting the deck and her mouth filling with sea water as she slid into a dark void, made her tremble. Fear cascaded over her like the hard waves that had pushed her deep into the sea, and she shuddered.

She was dead. She had to be. There could be no other explanation, because time travel wasn't possible. None of this could be real, and yet everything was a tangible stroke against her senses. The scent of flowers, the freshly laundered sheets against her skin, the warmth of the girl's touch and the child's soothing voice. Even the thin, cloudy white, streams of smoke drifting out of the glass chimney of each oil lamp looked real. Madeline closed her eyes.

"It's not real. I'm dreaming," she whispered to herself. "I can't be dead."

"Nae, miss," the girl exclaimed softly. "Ye dinnae die here. Ye came here. Ye are safe here."

The girl's words sent another tremor through Madeline. What did the girl mean that she'd not died here? An ominous thought swirled up out of the dark recesses of her brain. Madeline immediately snuffed out the question as if it were a flame flickering in the oil lamp. Eyes squeezed tightly shut,

Madeline fought back against the fear and confusion threatening to send tears streaming down her cheeks.

"Do nae cry, miss. Please do nae cry. Ye are safe now. "

Small fingers brushed away the tears that found their way out from under Madeline's eyelids. Blinking her eyes to bring everything into focus, she looked up at the girl and forced a smile to her lips.

The girl eyed her with worry, and Madeline knew her effort to act as if nothing was wrong was a weak one at best. Determined to regain control of her senses, she ordered her brain not to make assumptions. Facts. That's what she needed. Just facts. Information that would tell her what was happening and where she was.

"I'm all right. I'm just a bit overwhelmed at the moment," Madeline choked out.

"I dinnae ever cry." Another voice echoed in the room that was much stronger than the girl at her bedside. Startled, Madeline jerked her head in the direction of the voice. Just inside the door of her room stood another girl, who looked identical to the one at her bedside. The fear returned.

"Oh, God. Please tell me you have a twin," Madeline whispered as she looked back at the girl who had removed the poultice from her head.

"Aye," the child said as she directed a sisterly glare of disgust at the other girl. "I'm Grace Fraser, and this is my sister, Ainslie. Lord Glenburnie is our *faither*."

Relief spiraled through her that she wasn't seeing things as well. The soft creak of the door's hinges made Madeline turn her head back to where Ainslie stood, and the door swung open wider. In the next breath, Lord Glenburnie stepped into the room, followed by Eileen carrying a tray. The room had been comfortable in size a second ago, but this man made the room suddenly feel much smaller. Firm lips thin with irritation, he pinned his gaze on the girl next to the door.

"You were told not to bother our guest, Ainslie."

His quiet words echoed with steel inflexibility and disapproval. Trepidation flashed across the girl's features, but she straightened to her full height before she tilted her chin upward and met her father's gaze with confidence.

"I thought Grace might have need of my help."

"Did you now."

Skepticism twisted Lord Glenburnie's mouth as he studied his daughter for a long moment. Something about the silent battle the two were engaged in made Madeline believe Ainslie Fraser tested her father's patience on a regular basis. But she empathized with the child. She'd been equally rebellious after her parents had died. Fortunately, her grandmother had loved her despite Madeline's mutinous behavior. The question was, did Lord Glenburnie love his daughter?

"Ainslie's not bothered me at all. I'm sure she only meant to help," she said with a sympathetic look at the girl.

As she came to Ainslie's defense, the girl stared at Madeline in surprise before looking back at her father. The child remained silent, and Lord Glenburnie narrowed his gaze at Madeline before returning his attention to his daughter. With an affectionate squeeze of the girl's shoulder, a small smile tipped the corners of his mouth.

"Go along now, lass. Bridget almost has dinner ready."

Ainslie didn't argue, she simply bobbed her head with understanding and darted out of the room. The man's gaze settled on Grace, and he jerked his head in the door's direction.

"Go with your sister, Grace. I'll be along shortly."

"Yes, *Faither*," Grace nodded obediently, then bent over Madeline and touched her arm. "I'll come back later to change the bandages on your feet."

The girl's remark brought into focus the way the soles of her feet stung. Running down a rocky path barefoot hadn't been the brightest thing she'd ever done. But at least she had a good excuse. It wasn't everyday she found herself in a situation like the one she was in currently. The pain was also a fact she could use. It was a tangible sensation, just like Grace's consoling pat on Madeline's arm. As the girl headed toward the door and started past her father, he touched her shoulder to halt her progress.

"You did well, lass. I'm proud of you."

"Ainslie really did come tae help, *Faither*. But I had already finished bandaging Miss Whitworth's feet."

The girl's words made Lord Glenburnie nod his head, but his skepticism returned as he arched an eyebrow at his daughter.

"I suspect curiosity made your sister so eager to be of assistance." The man's mouth twisted in a wry smile, and his daughter grinned up at him.

"Aye, but it was good I dinnae need her help. She does nae like it when I am in charge."

"Off with you, imp," Lord Glenburnie said with a quiet chuckle.

Grace hesitated at her father's command, and she looked over her shoulder at Madeline. A strange expression darkened the child's pretty features, and Madeline frowned in bewilderment. It was as if the girl wanted to say something, but she didn't. Instead, she turned back to her father and murmured something Madeline couldn't hear.

A puzzled frown drew the tall Scotsman's eyebrows upward as he stared down at his daughter for a brief moment, before he jerked his head up to look at Madeline. It was as if he'd had a sudden revelation, although Madeline didn't have a clue as to what that might be. The man turned his attention back to his daughter and quietly ordered her to leave. With one last glance over her shoulder, Grace hurried from the room. As the child disappeared, the tall Scotsman turned to face Madeline. Surprise no longer visible on his face, he nodded toward the maid.

"Eileen has brought you dinner."

An encouraging smile tipped the girl's mouth, but the moment Madeline pushed herself upright in bed, the maid gasped in obvious horror. Startled, she looked at the younger woman, whose cheeks were bright red, and Madeline shook her head in confusion.

"I'm certain Miss Whitworth has a bed jacket in her trunk, Eileen."

Lord Glenburnie's statement was a veiled command, and the maid hastily darted toward a tall chifforobe. Seconds later, the young woman retrieved a feminine jacket with lace edging on the sleeves and neckline. Eileen scurried back to the bedside, her face still bright with color. Muttering something beneath her breath, she urged Madeline to put the jacket on.

Madeline gave the maid a dubious look as she pushed her arms through the sleeves. Her gaze flitted toward Lord Glenburnie. He was observing the incident with an unreadable expression, but she could have sworn she saw amusement flickering in his blue eyes, as well as something else that made her breath hitch.

When Eileen was satisfied Madeline was suitably covered, the maid sighed with obvious relief. Pink color still flaring in her cheeks, the maid bobbed her head in an approving manner.

"There now, Miss. That's much better."

"Thank you," Madeline said as she bit back a smile. If Eileen thought this high-necked, long-sleeved nightgown was too revealing, the woman would faint at Madeline's normal nightwear. The young woman smiled with satisfaction as she set a bed tray in front of Madeline, then adjusted the legs to ensure it was stable.

"That will be all, Eileen. You may return for the tray later." As her host met his servant's gaze, the maid frowned as if she meant to argue. When her employer narrowed his eyes at her, Eileen flushed again.

"Aye, me lord. I will leave the door open so I can hear Miss Whitworth call out if she needs anything else."

"An excellent idea," he said as his mouth thinned with irritation. "However, as my guest, Miss Whitworth's reputation is quite safe."

Cheeks bright red once more, the maid fled the room, and Madeline barely managed to not laugh out loud. She knew it wasn't right to laugh at the young woman's embarrassment, but it was difficult not to when her nightgown was far from revealing. Madeline's gaze shifted back to Lord Glenburnie to find him eyeing her with an arched eyebrow. Now it was her turn for her cheeks to grow hot beneath his penetrating gaze.

"I'm sorry. I'm not used to… I mean, I don't think about what I'm wearing when I'm at home."

"Given this morning's events and your subsequent injuries, it would surprise me to discover otherwise."

The irony in his voice made her cheeks burn hotter, and she wasn't sure if he was simply making an observation or censuring her. He crossed the floor to a chair pressed against the wall and easily lifted it with one hand to carry it to the side of her bed. In the back of her mind, she wondered if he went commando under his kilt.

Madeline swallowed hard at the thought. That kind of curiosity was almost as insane as believing she was in the past. But her decision to view things from a factual, scientific viewpoint, forced her to consider every possibility that she was in the past. Especially when, as illogical and fantastical as the idea was, everything pointed in that direction. The realization immediately threw questions at her like darts flying toward a dart board. How in God's name had she been thrown back to 1896? How had she been on the Destiny's Dream one minute only to wind up in the water and under a different ship altogether? A shipwreck she was surprised she'd survived.

Maybe she hadn't. Her stomach lurched at the thought. But if she hadn't survived the capsizing of the Destiny's Dream, how had she landed in the past? Then again, what if she was in a deep sleep? She'd heard patients' stories of near-death experiences, where they'd visited another dimension. Now, she really was going off the deep end. She might not know how she'd arrived here, but she was certain she wasn't asleep. All of it was too real and tangible to be a dream.

As Lord Glenburnie sat down in the chair, Madeline breathed in the masculine scent of pine, musk, and the outdoors. No, she was definitely not asleep. The man confirmed that in spades. Dark-blue eyes studied Madeline intently for a long moment.

The intensity and assessment of his gaze sent a frisson skimming across the surface of her skin. Heart pounding, her mouth went dry as an image of the man kissing her flitted through her mind. The mental picture tightened every one of her muscles and constricted her lungs until it was almost difficult to breathe, while her brain gleefully fired off several more arousing images.

Desperate to ease the growing tension in her body, she fought to form a coherent sentence and break the silence between them. Lord, not even when she'd first met Martin had she experienced such an awkward, tongue-tied emotion.

"I've been…been a lot of trouble, and I'm…I'm sorry." Madeline stumbled over her words as she succeeded in pushing her fantasies aside by staring down at her dinner.

"I'll nae deny things have been…interesting, since I pulled you out of the water." The wry comment made Madeline glance at him to see a small smile of amusement on his sensual mouth.

Earlier today in his study, before her mad dash down to the sea, his accent had been softer and more refined. Now, although his voice still had a polished edge to it, there was more than just a hint of the Scottish accent in the dark, silky sound. With just a few seductive words, all this man had to do was crook his finger and whatever woman he wanted would come running.

Without any doubt, she fell into that category of women. Everything about this man made her want to break every rule in the book and then some. Another arousing image flitted through her head, and she batted it away in her struggle to regain control of her senses. Refusing to give in to all the delicious fantasies tumbling over one another in her head, Madeline focused on the fact that he'd probably found her a troublesome guest. One corner of her mouth twisted in a wry grimace.

"I'm happy to help."

At the soft note of sarcasm in her voice, he laughed. It was a pleasant sound. Her brain instantly threw out an image of him laughing as he hovered over her just before kissing her. Madeline scowled at him, uncertain whether it was because he might be laughing at her or to destroy the fantasies filling her head. He folded his arms across his chest, a smile still curving his sensual lips. Another fantasy flitted through her head, and she batted it into oblivion.

"I'm beginning to think you might have Scottish blood in you, Madeline. That glare is worthy of the best Highland lass." The teasing observation earned him another glare, and he laughed again.

"Has anyone ever told you how annoying you are, Lord Glenburnie?" She glowered at him, not enjoying the sensation of being forced to be so formal while he wasn't. "And this title thing isn't working for me. What's your real name?"

"My real name?" He didn't answer her for a moment, and she saw a glint of devilment in his eyes. She didn't know why, but something about his expression said he was thinking it might be amusing not to answer her question. He smiled again. "Iain Fraser, Baron of Glenburnie."

It was a good, strong name. It suited him. He arched an eyebrow at her, and his mouth twitched as if he wanted to laugh again. Determined not to give him any other ammunition to tease her with, Madeline focused her gaze on the plate of food in front of her. Silence fell between them for a few seconds before he cleared his throat.

"Is something wrong with your meal, Madeline?" The quiet words made her jerk her gaze up to meet his.

"I'm not really hungry."

Madeline frowned as she stared down at her plate again. It wasn't quite the truth. She just wasn't sure if she was balking because his watching her made her nervous, or if she feared insulting him by not eating some of the food on her plate. The roasted chicken leg and mashed potatoes were favorites of hers, but the words 'I do not like green eggs and ham' rang out clearly in her head when it came to the beets.

"You must eat." The adamant statement made her roll her eyes at him. A low sound rumbled in his chest that sounded like amused frustration. "Eat, Madeline. I have no wish to see you collapse from hunger."

"Oh, I don't think that will happen anytime soon," she mumbled with self-deprecation as she stared at the mashed potatoes filled with carbs. "I have more than my fair share of pounds to ensure I survive the apocalypse."

When he didn't order her to eat again, she lifted her head to meet his gaze. The expression on his features made her heart slam into her chest. Just like this morning, his gaze slid down along the length of her body in a leisurely manner. The slow appraisal made her feel as though he could see every inch of her through the covers. She swallowed hard as his gaze met hers.

"You do yourself a grave disservice, *mo bhòidhchead fuilt dorcha*."

The quiet words were a soft caress against her senses and sent a shiver of excitement down Madeline's spine. Amusement and something else flared in the depths of his dark-blue eyes. She didn't have a clue what *mo bhòidhchead fuilt dorcha* meant, but she was certain it had to be one of those casual endearments people used like sweetheart or babe.

Coming from any other guy, she would have interpreted the comment as sexual innuendo. While this man's words and tone of voice held a definite hint of desire, there was an appreciation in his voice, too. The type of appreciation he might have for a painting or sculpture. It made her feel beautiful. Whatever he'd said, he'd made it sound like a sincere compliment, and she was ready to melt.

Madeline swallowed hard as she tried to remember what they'd been discussing. Right, eating. Quickly jerking her gaze away, she decided to eat the food she recognized. She reached for her fork and took a bite of the mashed potatoes. The roasted leg of chicken was next. It had no spices, just a little salt and pepper. A quiet chuckle echoed out of him, and she glanced his way to see a satisfied smile on his face.

"It appears you were hungry, after all."

"There's no need to gloat," she grumbled. She rolled her eyes in aggravation at his self-satisfied expression.

"I'm simply satisfied you did as I asked."

"Asked? Umm, you didn't ask," she said with another eye roll. "You gave me an order, which makes me think you're someone who likes to get their way all the time."

"I usually do," he said off-handedly with a slight shrug. Madeline refrained from making a sarcastic retort, certain it would backfire on her. Instead, she cut a piece of chicken off the bone.

"Tell me where your home is, Madeline." The sound of her name rolled off his tongue and wrapped itself around her senses in a seductively breathtaking manner. Determined not to fall victim to more vivid fantasies, Madeline took another bite of mashed potatoes. When she'd swallowed the bite, she put her fork down and met his gaze.

"I'm from the States—St. Paul, Minnesota to be exact."

"States?"

"America. I came to Scotland… on vacation." A wave of sorrow pounded at her heart as she remembered how her grandmother had arranged for this trip.

"Vacation?" he mused in puzzlement before his expression suddenly changed to one of comprehension. "You're on holiday."

"Yes, I spent some time in Edinburgh, then traveled to Aberdeen. I don't know why, it just seemed to call to me."

Madeline frowned as a voice in her head whispered she knew exactly why she'd gone to Aberdeen, and why she'd decided to take a cruise along the shoreline. She'd been hoping to see the man from her dreams. The sudden memory of the figure she'd seen on the cliffs from the sailboat during the storm made her muscles tense. What if the man she'd seen was Iain? Was it possible there was some sort of time portal near the baron's home? With an inward sigh, she dismissed the absurd thought.

"Called to you?" His head tipped slightly to one side as his gaze narrowed with assessment. "Do you have the *an dara sealladh*?"

"The what?"

"The gift of sight."

"If I had the gift of sight, I wouldn't have gotten on that damn sailboat," she huffed with a healthy dose of sarcastic amusement.

Surprise darkened his features as Iain studied her with an odd expression. She winced. Lovely. She'd forgotten women of this time period didn't talk like sailors. From his expression, he probably wasn't even used to hearing one of the tamer words in her salty vocabulary coming out of a woman's mouth. He arched an eyebrow in obvious disapproval, and she cringed. Okay, that sealed it. She'd have to watch her mouth.

"But you *did* board the ship." His piercing blue gaze was riveted on her face.

"Yes, but not…it's complicated."

"Complicated," he murmured as he continued to study her. "You just said you boarded the Phoenix Rising. Did you, or didn't you?"

"I wasn't on that ship. At least not the one out there on the rocks. I was on a sailboat called Destiny's Dream. It was supposed to—"

"Where did you board Destiny's Dream?" Iain's abrupt question startled her, but it was the abrasive sound of his voice that made her jump. Rigid in his seat, Iain's features were no longer open and pleasant. His face now looked as if someone had chiseled it out of stone.

"In Aberdeen."

"Aberdeen?" Although his features were still grim, there was a bewilderment in his voice as he continued to mutter to himself. "Why would McLeod sail down the coast instead of making port in Aberdeen?"

"Who's McLeod?" Madeline frowned in confusion.

"The captain of Destiny's Dream."

Clearly distracted, he continued to talk to himself in a quiet rumble of sound. She had no idea why he was so upset, but she knew good and well the captain's name of the boat she'd been on hadn't been McLeod.

"The captain of the sailboat I was on was Captain Mury."

"That's not possible." He dismissed her statement with a sharp gesture of his hand, his eyes narrowing in anger at her. "Captain McLeod has been the master of Destiny's Dream for the past five years."

"Well, the captain of the ship I was on was Captain Mury."

Iain sprang to his feet at her fierce rebuttal. He shook his head as his mouth thinned into a tight line. Startled by his reaction, Madeline stiffened as he leaned over her until there were mere inches between them. She didn't like that he intimidated her, but there was a ferocity about his anger that said he wasn't a man to be crossed. Madeline quickly pressed herself back into the bed's headboard in an attempt to put some distance between them. It only gained her an inch

"Either your memory is failing or ye are lying, and I dinnae tolerate liars, woman."

The abrasive accusation astonished Madeline, and she stared at him in stunned silence for a moment as she came to grips with the fact that he'd just called her a liar. Somewhere in the back of her mind, she noticed his brogue had thickened a great deal more than when he had been calm and quiet. It was a mere blip on her radar as she clenched her jaw in anger and leaned forward slightly to put her face closer to his. It was a pitiful attempt at intimidation, but it demonstrated she intended to stand her ground.

"I am *not* a liar," she bit out fiercely. "And my memory is *not* failing. I distinctly remember Captain Mury spelling out his last name M-U-R-Y."

The sudden, vivid image of the captain's gray features and slack-jawed look of horror as he'd stared over her shoulder filled Madeline's head. He must have seen the huge wave headed straight for them and realized the boat would not be able to remain upright on the water.

Instantly, all the memories of her terrifying ordeal came rushing back at her, and an icy chill coated her skin. Madeline closed her eyes and shuddered as those last moments on the Destiny's Dream replayed in her head in graphic detail.

It was as if some cruel part of her brain was taunting her by showing her the events in slow motion. The giant wave crashing down on her before it rolled the boat over, as if it were a toy. The way her arms had flailed, trying to find something to hold on to as she'd gone sliding across the deck toward the sea.

The fleeting sensation of cold metal brushing across her fingertips before she was tossed into the freezing water mocked her. As the churning water engulfed her, the icy temperature made her gasp in shock. Looking upward, she saw the wood planks of the deck heading toward her as the sailboat flipped over.

The moment her head slammed into the deck. She cried out in pain, only to have the sea rush in and steal her breath away. Plunged back into that horrifying moment, Madeline found herself choking and gasping for air, while her body became as cold as the water she'd been pulled from. Still caught up in the horror of those traumatic moments, she barely heard Iain's sharp oath pierce the air.

A shiver streaked through her as the terror of the accident sent her heart racing out of control. Her tremor was quickly followed by another and another until she was shuddering violently. In seconds, Iain removed the dinner tray from her bed and seated himself beside her.

"It's all right, lass. It's over now. You're safe."

The gentle reassurance in his voice was accompanied by a sinewy arm wrapped around her. A second later, the hard warmth of his body engulfed her. Despite the soothing note in his voice, she continued to tremble against him. The heat of Iain's body penetrated her clothing and sank into her pores until her tremors slowly eased.

But his warmth wasn't enough to push aside the memory of how desperately she'd prayed to live, as she had breathed in the dank air in that pitch-black pocket beneath the ship. Then there had been the battle with the waves as she'd struggled to reach the rocks, only to be pushed back down below the water, one wave after another.

If not for him pulling her out of the water, she would have drowned. Quickly following on the heels of that thought was a tendril of something darker that whispered in the back of her head. Madeline quickly buried it. The possibility was too horrible to even consider. Unable to hold back the tears pushing against her eyelids, she sobbed into a broad shoulder. Immediately, Iain's strong arm tightened around her.

"It will be all right, Madeline. I promise you that, lass." The soft reassurance in his voice was a quiet, sturdy sound. "Everything will be all right."

She'd known the man for less than a day, but his comfort and silent understanding made her cling to him as she pressed her face into his jacket. Madeline had never had a man console her like this before, not even Martin, who'd said he loved her. The entire time they'd been together, she'd learned to comfort herself because she couldn't rely on Martin for moral support of any kind.

Madeline started to sob harder as she remembered her grandmother was the reason she was in Scotland in the first place. After several moments, her tears subsided, and Madeline pushed herself away from Iain's chest to sit up straight. A moment later, a handkerchief was pressed into her hand. Madeline wiped her tears away as she met Iain's dark blue eyes.

"Lord, I'm not usually such a crybaby," she sniffled.

"A what?" The puzzlement on his face tugged a small smile to Madeline's mouth as she sniffed again.

"Someone who cries all the time, wanting attention." Her explanation made him nod with understanding as he slowly moved from the mattress to the chair he'd been sitting in earlier.

"You survived a traumatic experience, it's to be expected."

The moment he retreated, Madeline wanted to pull him back. She didn't understand why, but she wanted to cling to him. This man's bravery in pulling her from the sea and his silent consolation just now made all the men in her past seem small and insignificant.

"I'm beginning to sound like a parrot." Madeline winced. "But I need to say I'm sorry again."

"There is no need to apologize for being frightened. I know what it is to face death and survive." Dark emotions crossed his face in quick succession before his features became unreadable. "Unfortunately, you will most likely experience more moments like this in the future, but as time passes, they will become less frightening."

"I know that from my training, I've just never experienced something like this before," Madeline mused softly with a nod.

A frown of puzzlement on his rugged features, he'd just parted his lips to say something when an older woman rapped her knuckles on the open door of Madeline's room. There was a look of disapproval on her face as she met the baron's gaze.

"Eileen's busy in the kitchen, and I've come for Miss Whitworth's tray, my lord."

"Thank you, Bridget."

Iain stepped back to let the woman retrieve the tray he'd placed on the floor before consoling Madeline. The woman's expression was dark with condemnation as she moved forward and picked up the tray of half-eaten food. Eyeing

Madeline with more than a hint of censure, the older woman turned to face her employer.

"Ye supper will nae doubt grow colder if ye dinnae go down now, my lord," she said sternly as she looked at her employer and bobbed her head toward the door.

Iain arched his eyebrow with an arrogance that said he tolerated the woman's abrupt statement only because he chose to. When Mrs. McFadyen's expression didn't change, he turned and caught Madeline's hand in his. She inhaled a sharp breath of surprise as he bowed over her hand to brush his mouth across the tips of her fingers.

"If you require anything, simply pull the cord to ring for Eileen or her mother, Mrs. McFayden, here. They'll come check on you." Iain nodded toward the narrow panel of material with its fringed tassel that hung next to her bed. "Tomorrow, we shall discuss how to send you home."

The words sent a small shudder through her. It was highly doubtful Iain would be able to send her back to present day. As much as she wanted to return home, she had a feeling she wouldn't be leaving the past any time soon—if ever. The thought made her grimace slightly, and he eyed her with curiosity. Madeline forced a small smile to her lips as she nodded her head.

"Thank you," she replied quietly, unwilling to say anything more as she glanced in Bridget McFayden's direction.

The woman was hovering nearby with a scowl of disapproval on her features. Almost like a mother hen protecting a chick, Mrs. McFayden looked pointedly at the door as Iain nodded at the woman with a slight twist of his lips. The man was clearly amused by the woman's fierce manner.

Without commenting, he gestured toward the door and allowed Mrs. McFayden to precede him. As he pulled the door shut behind him, Iain looked over his shoulder to meet Madeline's gaze. His expression revealed nothing, but something in his eyes sent her heart skidding out of control.

The soft thud of the door closing behind the baron made Madeline release the breath she hadn't realized she was holding. What the hell was going on? It would be easy to tell herself that she was experiencing some kind of wild and crazy hallucination. But she knew better. Wherever she was, it wasn't a reality television show, and it definitely wasn't one of those historical immersion vacation deals. As difficult as it was to believe, there was only one conclusion she could come to. Somehow, she'd landed in the lap of Baron Glenburnie in the year 1896.

So, exactly how was she supposed to explain how she got here? Telling the truth would land her in a psych ward faster than confessing to murder. Lying was a dangerous path to follow. It would be too easy to forget something, not to mention Iain's reaction when she'd argued with him about the Destiny's Dream. While she hadn't appreciated being called a liar, she understood why he would challenge her.

As Madeline remembered his reaction, she recalled the note of panic and worry underlying the fury in his voice. Iain was more than just a little familiar with the Destiny's Dream in this era. Was he the owner of the vessel? Maybe he knew someone who was a passenger on board the ship? It could be carrying cargo he owned.

Whatever his connection to the Destiny's Dream in this time period, she'd definitely thrown him for a loop by not backing down about Captain Mury. And she was certain Iain Fraser, Baron of Glenburnie, was not a man who ever let much of anything phase him. He was far too confident.

Well, maybe not *that* confident. It was unlikely the man would just brush aside her assertion she was from the future. That would definitely throw him off kilter. No, he'd just look at her like she was a crazy person, and call someone to take her away. She winced at the thought and pinched the bridge of her nose. What was she going to do? A faint voice echoed in the back of her mind. Nothing. There wasn't anything she could do. Not exactly a comforting thought.

Another whisper echoed in her head, only this one was insidious and garbled. An icy sensation of fear skated down her spine, but it was quickly silenced by a scoffing laugh. Madeline shivered as she remembered how strong her recollection of the shipwreck had been moments ago. It had actually felt as if she were reliving the wave overturning Destiny's Dream and tossing her into the icy water of the North Sea.

Close on the heels of that frightening memory had been the sense of security that had enveloped her as Iain had wrapped his arm around her in an obvious attempt to comfort and reassure her. The memory of mesmerizing blue eyes and a voice as smooth, yet fiery, as cognac caused her mouth to go dry.

When it came to men like Iain Fraser, she'd always given them a wide berth. They were always the ones who could take you to the heights of heaven, and the moment they left, you were dropped into the depths of hell. She'd learned that with Martin, even though she'd been the one to break off their engagement.

When she'd given Martin his ring back, he'd been upset. What she hadn't realized, was his reaction hadn't been because he loved her. It was because she'd struck a blow to his ego. A fact that had been driven home when he'd started dating less than a month after their breakup.

Madeline had no idea why she'd been so surprised and hurt at Martin's quick recovery. She should have expected it. At the time, she'd thought it was because she was still in love with him. For some inexplicable reason, she'd wondered if there was something wrong with her to expect more out of a relationship. Madeline had even had the stupidity to think she wasn't good enough for him.

That misconception had been nothing more than her buying into Martin's constant reminder of how lucky she was to have him. When you were in a relationship with a guy whose focus was solely on himself, it meant you weren't a priority. Madeline couldn't count the number of times he'd told her how many other women wanted him, but that he'd chosen her. Not once had he ever said he was lucky to have her in his life.

Hell, not once had he ever said she was beautiful, even though he didn't have a problem pointing out other women he thought were beautiful. The sudden memory of Iain leisurely running his gaze along her body less than an hour ago pushed its way into her thoughts.

Martin had always acted like a fifth grader whenever he'd seen her naked or dressed up for a night out. He'd snicker like a little boy seeing candy and tried to squeeze a boob or grab at her crotch. It had always made her feel as though the only thing she was good for was sex.

When Iain had taken his time running his gaze over her from head to toe, it had been incredibly arousing, but not in a cringing way. It was as if he'd been studying a work of art and taking pleasure in what he saw. For the first time in her life, she'd felt beautiful, even alluring. Then there was the man's quiet strength.

When she'd broken down into a massive puddle of tears as she'd relived her terrifying moments in the water, Iain had been kind and understanding. If he'd been Martin, she would have received a few pats on the back until she stopped crying. The moment her tears dried up, the focus would return to him. It was how she'd learned to console herself without anyone else's support.

It wasn't until Iain had pulled her close that Madeline realized how much she'd needed to lean on someone else for comfort. The past couple of months of grief and loneliness had been difficult, with no one to turn to for support or comfort. Even if she and Martin had still been engaged, he would have balked at spending emotional capital trying to ease her grief.

And Martin sure as hell would never have reacted like Iain by offering her his shoulder to cry on while he held her in silence. Heaven forbid she mess up one of his pristine jackets with her tears. It was ironic a stranger in the distant past had offered her more solace than the man she had been prepared to marry. Even more astounding was how Iain's fierce anger had changed to gentle kindness in the space of seconds. His ability to override his anger and offer solace instead of dismissing her fear made him an unusual man, no matter what the time period.

There had been pain in his voice when he'd reassured her that her reaction was a normal one. It made Madeline believe he'd experienced something equally traumatic in his life. An event that gave him a better understanding than most people, of the shock and fear she'd relived moments ago. Whatever had happened to him, it had given him the ability to understand her terror.

Madeline could only hope he was wrong about a repeat performance. She didn't like the idea of reliving those terrifying moments again. Although she didn't have a clue how she would get home, at least she was alive. It was an important fact to remember the next time she relived those terrifying moments in the water. From deep in the recesses of her mind, a dark whisper tried to tell her something she didn't want to hear. Madeline quickly shoved it into the back of her mind. She wasn't ready to go there yet.

$\mathfrak{C}$hapter 6

$\mathfrak{G}$ain tugged hard on the drapes to close off the last bit of sunlight pouring into his study. With the last window covered by the dark curtains, the room was lit by nothing more than a thin border of sunlight that forced its way past the outer edges of the drapes. With most of the bright light blocked out of the room, he released a harsh sigh of relief. Shutting out the light was the first thing he'd done the moment he'd entered his study a few moments ago.

The brilliant sunshine pouring into the room would only worsen the minor headache he'd been nursing. Fingers massaging his forehead, he tried to ease the faint, but persistent throbbing that had started in the early morning hours. He blamed it on his sleepless night. A night of tossing and turning brought on by the mystery surrounding his far too tempting guest.

Yesterday, while Madeline was recovering from her frantic race down to the sea, he'd sent his stable hand to Aberdeen to inquire as to the arrival of the Destiny's Dream. His fear that McLeod's ship had suffered a similar fate as the Phoenix Rising had been alleviated less than an hour ago when Cecil had returned with good news.

Captain McLeod had asked the Rotterdam harbor master to telegraph Aberdeen that the Destiny's Dream had set sail with the morning tide. It meant that with fair weather, the screw propeller steamship would most likely reach Aberdeen by tomorrow night, along with his cargo.

If he could secure a good price for the silk, lace, and the small load of steel he'd been able to add to his investment, he would have little debt hanging over his head by this time next week. There would even be enough left over to cover back wages for Cecil and the McFaydens. There might even be enough for a few new dresses for the girls. While there wouldn't be enough money to send them away to school, he was hopeful he could hire a governess for their schooling.

If his next trip proved to be an equally profitable investment, he could send them to school then. He would also be able to repair things in the house that had been left to languish in the past year of financial losses. The first thing would be to finish the piping for the bathrooms. He liked the convenience of having hot running water and plumbing in his suite. But he wanted to add plumbing to the servant quarters as well as the guest rooms. Not that he had many visitors.

The sudden memory of Madeline standing in front of him in the hallway after her bath filled his head. If the guest rooms had been plumbed, his sleep last night would have been far less eventful. Instead, his dreams had been filled with images of him caressing Madeline's lush breasts while tasting her sweetly curved mouth. Iain groaned softly at the erotic thought. If he didn't send the woman on her way quickly, he was apt to find himself in a *sair fecht* as Angus was fond of saying when he was struggling with a particularly troublesome problem.

The difficulty was, where was he supposed to send her? Cecil had checked with the MacDonald Norwood Hall and Douglas hotels, but neither of them had a guest registered by the name of Miss Whitworth. Nor had the hotels had her on their list of expected arrivals. The lad had also checked several other reputable lodgings in the city. No one had heard of the woman.

That left him with a mystery he wasn't sure how to solve. Captain Napier had been adamant Madeline hadn't been aboard the Phoenix Rising. Madeline had been equally adamant that she'd been on the Destiny's Dream. Now, as he pondered Madeline's mysterious arrival, he remembered Grace and the *an dara sealladh*.

Last night, when his oldest daughter had whispered that Madeline was the woman she'd seen drowning in her vision, Iain had been more relieved than startled. Grace's gift rarely revealed a complete picture of events, but when his daughter had seen her twin sister in the same vision with Madeline two days ago, it had alarmed him.

But last night, he'd known Ainslie was safe and sound, eating her meal in the dining room. So that still left the question as to how Madeline had come to be in the water? The memory of the woman he'd seen on the cliffs filled his head.

The cliffs weren't frequented by many people. In fact, he rarely met anyone whenever he took a stroll along the edge of the precipice. There was also no conceivable way anyone could have landed in the water if they'd jumped from the cliffs that towered over the inlet. Even at high tide, the inlet was a sizable expanse of beach with rocks abutting the face of the cliffs.

Ghost stories were prevalent among the villagers, but he'd never heard any stories of a woman haunting the cliffs above the inlet. What made it particularly difficult to believe he'd seen a ghost, was the woman's close resemblance to Madeline.

Both women had the same short, light-brown hair, although he'd not been close enough to tell if the woman's hair had possessed the golden highlights Madeline's did. But the woman on the cliffs had been just as tall as Madeline, and both women had the same lush, womanly curves. On the cliffs, the wind and rain had made the woman's clothing outline her curves in the same way Madeline's bath water had made her nightgown cling to her in such a delectable manner.

Then there was the fact that the two women had been dressed exactly the same. It was one of half a dozen things he'd noted about Madeline as he'd carried her back to the house the night of the storm.

Iain had scoffed at himself the first time he'd even considered the ludicrous possibility that the two women were the same person. Logically, he knew if the woman he'd seen on the cliffs had actually jumped, they would have found her body on the rocks at the bottom of the cliff. Iain had no explanation for anything other than he was mad and had imagined the woman disappearing before his eyes or the fae had been at work.

Then there was Madeline's reaction yesterday morning. It had only added to the mystery surrounding his guest. It wasn't just her disbelief and astonishment over the fact he owned neither a telephone nor a car he found puzzling. The moment he'd told her the date, she'd become paler than anyone he'd ever seen.

He'd fully expected her to faint. Instead, she'd raced frantically out of the house and down to the inlet. Everything about her behavior had been that of someone in a deep state of panic and shock. When he'd reached her on the beach yesterday, he'd been so preoccupied with his concern for her welfare that he'd forgotten her questioning the date until now.

Iain frowned as he recalled her agitation and strange mutterings about not believing the year was 1896. He could understand why she might be surprised by having lost track of a few days, but she'd clearly been questioning the year. It made him wonder if she'd been a patient in a convalescent home for a long period and had just learned what year it was. A strange whisper of a thought told him it was something altogether different.

His lips twisted slightly in a small grimace as he remembered carrying Madeline back to the house after her mad dash down to the sea. It had been much more than simple concern for her that had pushed her strange words out of his head. The unexpected strength of his desire to comfort and protect her had startled him. Even last night, as she'd relived her harrowing brush with death, he'd been stunned by his intense need to console her.

As he remembered the look of terror on her face, another memory from deep in the recesses of his mind pushed its way forward. Iain understood her fear. He understood the way it could cripple you, but even worse was the guilt. It was something he'd lived with ever since that terrible day in the sea cave. The moment the memories tried to push their way firmly into his conscious mind, the throbbing against his temples strengthened. With a grunt, he crushed the past and thrust it back into the darkness where it always hid.

Determined to fight off another migraine, he sank down in one of the wing-back chairs facing the fireplace. Stretching his legs out in front of him, he rested his head against the cushions and closed his eyes. Forcing himself to relax, he focused on slowing his breathing and pushed all of his problems out of his mind. As he calmed his thoughts, he slipped into the quiet darkness of sleep.

A loud noise pierced Iain's light slumber, and he jerked upright in his chair. The sight of a glowing piece of charred wood pressed against the andirons in the fireplace made him grab the poker to push it back into place. When he'd finished stoking the fire, Iain leaned back into his chair again to stare into the flames. His brief nap had removed all traces of his headache, but it hadn't cleared his thoughts of Madeline.

From her clothing, to her mannerisms, to her language, she was unlike anyone he'd ever met. While he knew Americans were an unusual lot, Madeline appeared to be even more eccentric than what he'd heard from others right down to her unconventional short hair. It suited her, but other than the woman on the cliff, he'd never seen a woman with her hair cut so short.

Last night, when she'd brazenly sat upright in bed without a bed jacket, she'd obviously been puzzled, then amused, by his maid's reaction. It was as if she found a bed jacket an unnecessary garment. Her curse had been even more startling. Even yesterday morning, when she'd stood in front of him in nothing but a nightgown, she'd shown no embarrassment about her appearance.

No, that wasn't quite true. The instant she saw his fascination with her stiff nipples pressing into the damp bodice of her nightgown, her cheeks had filled with color. A rosy pink that had only emphasized the idea that one of the fae had landed in his home.

While her colorful speech last night had taken him aback, it was the clothing she'd been wearing when he'd pulled her from the water that intrigued him. It hadn't simply been that she was dressed in men's trousers. It was the type of fabric they were made of.

The pants were made of a denim unlike any he'd ever seen before. The American fabric had been created for miners almost forty years ago, but the denim used for miner clothing was a coarse, sturdy material. Madeline's pants had been soft despite the water-logged garment's weight.

Then there had been the strange corset she'd worn beneath her clothing. The sea had made her long-sleeved shirt cling to her skin, outlining the shape of the unusual undergarment supporting her breasts. Bridget McFayden hadn't shown him the article of clothing after undressing Madeline, but the housekeeper had commented on the scandalous nature of her undergarments.

Everything she'd been wearing when he'd pulled her out of the water was the complete opposite of the clothing he'd found in the trunk that had washed up on shore. It had been reasonable to assume it belonged to her. But it wasn't until she'd said her name was Madeline Whitworth that he'd been certain. The initials MW on the baggage's plated latch convinced him the trunk was hers. The memory of finding two lace-edged corsets and other feminine undergarments in the baggage he'd briefly examined sent an image of Madeline dressed in nothing but a corset flashing through his head.

Iain closed his eyes as the vivid picture took hold of not only his mind, but his senses as well. It took only a second for him to imagine all the different ways to explore her body.

The idea of sliding his mouth up along her leg to delve into the secrets at the apex of her thighs made his cock stir beneath his kilt. The imagery faded slightly as a knock on his study door echoed through the air. In a detached manner, he commanded the person outside the study to enter while he struggled to clear his head of his erotic imaginings about his mysterious guest.

"Am I disturbing you?"

The quiet question from across the room tightened his muscles. He'd already accepted that Madeline's voice was one he'd recognize in the dark. The image that had faded from his head returned. The idea of how much he would enjoy hearing her voice in his bed at night was far too appealing.

Iain turned his head to see Madeline standing in the middle of his study. In the darkened room, the fire burning in the fireplace cast its light on her profile. The warm glow of firelight softened her features, and without thinking, his gaze focused on her mouth. Christ Jesus, if he'd thought her a fae yesterday in the hallway, today she resembled a siren. Was she *disturbing* him? It wasn't a question he intended to answer. He rose from his chair to face her.

"You are feeling better?"

"Yes, although if I wasn't, it wouldn't be anyone's fault but my own. I was an idiot to run around outside barefoot." The wry twist of her lips drew his attention back to her mouth before he met her gaze again.

"Then I take it you are wearing shoes today," he said wryly.

It wasn't a question, but she immediately lifted one side of her gown to her knee. The moment she revealed a sleek, stocking-encased leg, his throat closed until it was difficult to breathe. Head bent as she twisted her foot back and forth to examine the shoe, she shook her head slightly.

"Yes, and surprisingly, they're much more comfortable than they look."

He barely heard her reply as he imagined his hand caressing her sleek calf as he slowly rolled the stocking off her long leg. The erotic images he'd banished from his thoughts only a moment ago returned in full-force. Last night, when she'd stated she could easily survive Armageddon, he'd been startled. Did the woman not know what a tantalizing creature she was?

She had the full hips, lush thighs, and legs that were made to wrap around a man. As his gaze had slowly run the length of her body and its full curves last night, he'd been sorely tempted to show her just how enticing her body was. He knew without a doubt this woman would make bed sport exciting and immensely pleasurable. The direction of his thoughts made his body harden everywhere.

As if suddenly aware of his intense assessment, she lifted her head to meet his gaze. Her eyes widening with surprise, a flush of pink rose in her cheeks, and she quickly straightened upright. In a split-second, the silk of her gown hid temptation from his view. His gaze locked with hers, and the flash of awareness in her brown eyes made him believe she wouldn't object to his advances.

Iain suppressed a groan at the thought. God help him. He was definitely in trouble where this woman was concerned. With a gesture toward one of the chairs facing his desk, he silently encouraged her to take a seat. Arms folded across his chest, he watched her attempt to sit down in the chair closest to him. Frustration tugged her mouth into a thin line as she struggled with the bustle of her gown. It was as if she'd never worn one before, and he frowned with puzzlement.

She'd not had trouble yesterday morning, but then she'd been perched on the edge of her seat. It was unlikely the bustle, which was more like a small padded pillow, would have caused her any problem then. Madeline muttered something, and he was certain it was a much harsher oath than the one she'd used last night. He stepped forward and forced her to stand in front of the chair.

"Raise the back of your gown slightly beneath the bustle, here, then lift the back up as you sit down to avoid sitting on the feminine contraption."

His hands pressed into her hips as he showed her how to manage the gown. With a sharp nod of irritation, Madeline's fingers brushed across his as she gathered the material in her hands to follow his instructions. The instant she touched him, a bolt of electricity streaked up his arm. He flinched at the shock.

Fortunately, she was too distracted by her gown to notice his reaction. Relieved by her preoccupation, Iain took a quick step back, but not before the light scent of lavender filled his nostrils. It made him want to pull her against him so he could continue to breathe in the sweet smell. He quickly increased the distance between them even more and heard Madeline release a quiet sound of satisfaction as she sank down into the depth of the chair's seat. She looked up at him and winced.

"This isn't what I usually—" Her expression revealed she'd said she'd been about to reveal something she'd not meant to. The momentary hesitation made Iain lean forward slightly.

"It's not something you usually wear." The moment he finished her sentence in a sardonic voice, she winced.

"Something like that."

"As I recall, you referenced the same fact last night after Eileen insisted you wear a bed jacket."

When she didn't answer, Iain arched his eyebrows as he waited for her to provide an explanation for her words. Instead, she averted her gaze and nibbled at her bottom lip. The action made him want to run his thumb across the bruised spot. Exasperated with the direction of his thoughts, he allowed her evasiveness to go unchallenged for the moment.

"I have news."

"News?" She eyed him warily.

"I sent my stable hand to Aberdeen yesterday to see if any of the hotels had you registered as a guest. No one had heard of you."

"Well, that's not a…good."

As she stumbled over her words, Iain narrowed his gaze at her, and color filled her cheeks once more. This time, the flush was accompanied by an expression of guilt. Madeline shrugged slightly and bit down on her lip once more. Again, he was forced to suppress his physical reaction. What in God's name was wrong with him? Narrowing his gaze at her, he leaned back against the edge of his desk, folding his arms across his chest.

"Why do I have the impression you really meant to say you aren't surprised?" The observation made her jump slightly before she nodded.

"I'm not actually. Surprised that is."

"Why?" At his clipped, single word question, the color vanished from her cheeks as she bowed her head.

"I can't explain it."

"What, can't you explain?"

"How I got here."

The resignation in her voice was accompanied by a helpless look that flitted across her face as she met his gaze for a split second, then looked away. Frustrated by her vague answers, he shook his head, and a twinge of pain tugged at his temples.

"Ye are nae making any sense."

"Do you honestly think I don't know that," she snapped as her eyes flashed with frustration and a hint of fear. "It's not like I asked to come here."

"Ye said ye were on holiday." Iain scowled with irritation at the way she changed her story from one minute to the next.

"I am. I was," she said emphatically as she glared at him. A second later, her anger vanished and the helpless look returned to darken her features. "It's complicated."

"So ye said last night."

"If you're going to call me a liar again, I suggest you think twice about it." Madeline's mouth thinned with defiance as she glared at him. Frustrated, he scowled back.

"It is difficult nae tae think such a thing with the Destiny's Dream on her way from Rotterdam to Aberdeen as we speak," he bit out between clenched teeth.

The burr in his voice had thickened, which meant his anger was close to besting his self-restraint. Worst of all, his head was beginning to ache again. A slight pain, but an unpleasant one. Why did the woman insist she'd been on the Destiny's Dream when the damned ship had just set sail from Rotterdam this morning?

It was not his imagination that he'd faced an old terror to pull her out of the angry sea. Deep in the back of his brain, a voice tried to convince him to accept her evasive explanations. He swatted the foolish notion aside and winced at the twinge of discomfort it caused. When she didn't respond to his comment, he glared at her.

"*Damn it*, woman. Tell me the truth. How did ye come tae be in the water if ye weren't on the Phoenix Rising?" He immediately regretted raising his voice as his head protested. The throbbing had escalated quickly and was now a full-on assault inside his head.

"I don't know," she said in a voice that pleaded with him to accept her at her word. "I wish I had an explanation. I really do. But I don't."

"And yet your lack of explanation leads me tae believe you're lying or hiding something."

"I am *not lying*." Madeline spat out the words in bitter objection as she sprang to her feet with suppressed outrage. She took a step forward, then quickly retreated as her anger evaporated, and a silent plea for understanding darkened her expressive eyes. "I don't expect you to believe me. I'm having a hard time believing what's happening myself."

Her last comment was barely above a whisper as she met his gaze. It was rare for him to forgive a lie, but damn if he wasn't close to doing so with this woman. The fear, confusion, and bleak despair on her lovely face said her protests were sincere.

Iain turn away from her and moved to stand in front of the fireplace. Perhaps if she wasn't facing him, it would be easier for her to answer his next question. As he studied the flames licking their way across the logs, he considered his words carefully. Iain cleared his throat, but kept his back to her.

"Do ye remember what ye were saying when I reached ye on the beach yesterday morning?"

The question was met with an uneasy silence, but he remained still. The stillness was suddenly broken by the chime of the mantle clock. It echoed in his head as if he were standing next to a church bell. Iain stretched out his hand to touch the timepiece's smooth wood casing, silently commanding the normally quiet ring to stop. When the clock finished sounding the hour of three, Iain drew in a deep breath of relief. A moment later, her soft voice filled the air between them.

"Yes, I remember."

Startled that she'd actually answered him, Iain almost spun around on his heel to face her. He managed to prevent himself at the last moment.

"Tell me why ye questioned the year."

"If I told you that, you'd think I'm crazy, which I'm not. And I'm definitely not about to say something that will get me locked up." Despite the mutinous tone in her voice, fear was layered beneath it.

"Lock ye up?"

This time he turned around and saw her pacing the floor behind her chair as if she were trying to reach a decision. His jaw tightened. Had he been correct about her having escaped a hospital?

"Were ye a patient in a hospital?"

"As in a mental hospital? Do I act like someone who's crazy?" Madeline uttered a small sound of laughter, which was clearly not one of amusement, then waved her hand as she began pacing the floor again. "Don't answer that. But to answer your question, no. I've never been in a psych ward before."

The word she used was unfamiliar, but it seemed reasonable to assume she was referring to an institution for the mentally insane. Iain said nothing. He simply studied her as she continued to move restlessly back and forth until she abruptly stopped and turned to face him.

"You don't believe me, do you?" Madeline closed her eyes when he didn't reply, and her expression was that of someone debating a weighty matter. When she looked at him again, she met his gaze steadily, while straightening her back to stand stiff and defiant in front of him.

"If you want me to, I'll swear to it on a bible, but I am telling you the truth. I have never been a patient in a mental hospital, and I have never been in trouble with the law."

The emphatic denial rang out in the study with a quiet strength of truth that was accentuated by the proud, upward tilt of her chin. She'd even preempted him from asking about any criminal activities. When she didn't flinch beneath his gaze, Iain nodded his head. His silent acknowledgement that he believed her made Madeline sag slightly in obvious relief.

Iain clenched his jaw as another sharp jab of pain slashed at his temple. Despite believing she'd never been committed or broken any laws, it still didn't solve the question of how she'd come to be in the water. Did it really matter? When she left Muchalls Hall, she would no longer be his problem. Clasping his hands behind his back, he cleared his throat.

"We should contact your family in America. I'm certain they'll be relieved tae hear you're safe and well."

Madeline paled as anguish flitted across her face. With an abrupt jerk of her head, she rejected his suggestion. Her gaze met his for a brief moment, before she bent her head to stare at her hands clasped tightly together. Her knuckles were white from the strength of her fingers intertwined in a fierce grasp.

"There's no one there."

"Another lie?" The throbbing in his temple made his question sharp and critical. Madeline's head jerked up as if he'd slapped her.

"My grandmother was the only family I had left, and she died less than three months ago." The grief in her voice echoed with unshed tears and remorse crashed through him. Iain closed his eyes. He was a heartless bastard.

"Forgive me. Ye have my condolences." His apology was met with a small roll of her shoulders as she looked down at her hands again.

"You didn't know."

"And there's no one ye can call upon for help? A father? Uncle? Cousin?"

The only answer she gave was a shake of her head. What the devil was he supposed to do with the woman? Fire and ice streaked its way from the back of his head to the front. It was an agonizing bolt of pain, and Iain bit back a groan as he massaged the side of his head with his fingertips. It failed to ease the throbbing that was continuing to grow and intensify.

"I don't suppose you found any money in the trunk?" Her question broke the silence, and he shook his head. It was a monumental mistake, and Iain barely managed not to release a shout of pain.

"No. Did you expect there to be?"

He hadn't meant to make his reply so harsh, and the sharp, caustic words made her draw in a quick breath. Iain's hand dropped to his side as massaging his temple failed to produce any relief, and he lifted his head. Madeline's full mouth was a thin line of anger, and she eyed him with icy contempt.

"Look, all I did was pay for a day trip sailing down the Scottish coast, and I got a hell of a lot more than I bargained for." Her anger was almost tangible, but so was her fear. "I didn't ask to be here, and if I'd known I was going to be interrogated by an irritating, half-witted jackass of a Scotsman, I would have booked a different trip."

Iain stiffened at her insult and took an angry step forward. The thunderbolt slamming into the back of his eye told him he'd made a serious mistake. The intense pain made his stomach churn, as nausea threatened to compete with the pain in his head. A soft gasp filtered its way through his haze of pain, and a second later, she was at his side. Gently, she touched his arm.

"You're not well."

Somewhere in the part of his head that wasn't hurting, he realized he didn't like appearing weak in front of her. His actions rough and jerky, Iain tugged his arm out of her grasp. The action cost him dearly. With a low groan, he staggered to one side. He heard her mutter something before her hand gripped his arm firmly and pulled him toward the fireside chair. Iain stumbled forward and fell into the leather cushioned seat.

Chapter 7

"I should have added pig-headed to that insult," she said with a touch of sarcasm in her voice. Madeline frowned as she studied the pallor of his rugged features. His eyes were closed, and his lips were a thin, hard line that emphasized the amount of pain he was in.

"It's simply a headache. I'm accustomed tae them. It will go away," he said hoarsely.

"I'd say it's more than a minor headache. It's so dark in here, I'm guessing the light hurts your eyes," she said softly to avoid exacerbating his pain. "What do you take for it?"

"Nothing."

"God, spare me the male ego, and the asinine refusal to accept help," she muttered and blew out a harsh puff of air at his stubbornness. "Will you let me try something to ease the pain?"

"I have nae need for drugs. If I remain still, it will go away on its own."

"From the look of pain on your face, I'm betting you're going to be down for the count for some time if you don't have something."

"Grace will be here shortly with a poultice." The quiet reply made Madeline eye him in puzzlement for a moment, before she realized he must have asked his daughter to make something for him. Still, he looked as if he were in so much pain, she refused not to try to alleviate his discomfort.

"I know a technique that might help ease your pain. Would you let me try?"

At her question, Iain opened one eye and squinted as he looked up at Madeline. She didn't give him a chance to reject her offer. With a nod of encouragement, she circled his chair to lean over the back and gently pressed her forefinger against the spot in between his eyebrows.

Iain murmured something, but she failed to make it out. Instead, she slowly counted to sixty, then changed the position of her fingers until they pressed into the side of his temples close to his eyebrows. Madeline repeated her counting then moved around the chair to sit down on a small ottoman in front of him and took his hand in hers.

Instantly, a small shock pulsed from his strong hand into hers and set off a tingling in her fingers. The electrical charge streaked up her arm and spread its way throughout the rest of her body. It was a startling sensation that caused her to drag in a sharp breath of surprise. Iain's eyes fluttered, and she quickly dropped her head rather than being forced to stare into that piercing blue gaze of his.

If there was one thing she'd already learned about Iain Fraser, Baron of Glenburnie, it was how the man had a way of knocking her for a loop. Not in a bad way, but the man definitely left her breathless. Madeline forced herself to focus on the powerful hand turned palm up in hers. Remembering what she was supposed to be doing, she examined the inside of his wrist, then applied pressure to the appropriate place. When she'd finished, she looked up to see him watching her with bewildered astonishment. She smiled.

"I take it you're feeling better?"

"Aye. I dinnae ken what you did, lass, but thank you."

"You're welcome."

At her reply, their gazes locked, and it was as if she'd suddenly been swept out to sea. The dark blue of his eyes resembled the stormy hue of thunderclouds, and her heart slammed into her chest. Suddenly aware that she was still holding his hand, Madeline jerked away from him as if she'd been burned. It wasn't far from the truth. Drawing in a breath to replenish the air that had left her lungs, Madeline forced herself to look away from his hypnotic gaze.

"We have still nae resolved the matter of what tae do with you."

The quiet words held no hint of innuendo, but the first thought that flashed through her mind had little to do with her current situation. Rather she imagined more than one thing she would enjoy him doing to her. Tension flooded her senses, and she quickly averted her gaze praying she'd not revealed her thoughts.

Madeline struggled to breathe evenly and forced herself to focus on her current predicament. She had no idea if there was a way back to her time, but for the moment she was stuck here. Homeless and without money, she was dead in the water. The irony of the cliché might have struck her as funny at any other time, but right now, she was in real trouble.

"I suppose I'll have to find a job."

Although she knew her nursing skills and knowledge were exceptional, she had a feeling she'd find it hard to find employment. Just the fact that Iain had asked if she had a male family member to look after her emphasized she was in an era where women had few, if any rights. He frowned in concentration as he studied her for a moment.

"What work have ye done in the past, or have ye even had tae work?"

The suggestion that she'd been reliant on a man to provide for her made Madeline shake her head with a snort of sarcasm.

"If you're suggesting I'm a helpless female who needs someone to look after her, think again. I have—had a job."

"Had?"

Suspicion threaded its way through his single word question. His reaction made Madeline uneasy at his sudden distrust. It probably wasn't a good idea to speak of her life in the future in the past tense, unless she told him the truth. Instinctively, she knew telling him she was from the future was a bad idea. No, it was a *really bad* idea. She had no doubt he'd deem her a candidate for long-term commitment to a psych ward and would more than likely send for someone to come take her away. It wasn't a pleasant thought.

People still had trouble talking about mental health in her own time. It was a certainty conditions would be much worse here in 1896. Then there was the possibility of changing something in the future. Madeline frowned as she debated just how much she could tell him.

Although she'd never been a big fan of science fiction, she had a vague recollection of a theory that said the future could be easily altered if someone revealed too much. Unwilling to test the idea, she decided she would keep her explanations simple and honest without being too specific.

"At home, I'm a hospice nurse."

"Hospice?"

"Yes, I care for people who are dying."

"An admirable occupation." Approval glittered in his dark eyes, but his distrust remained, albeit significantly diminished. "However, I'm unaware of any positions that call for a skill such as that. Perhaps ye might serve as a companion to an elderly lady?"

"Maybe," Madeline murmured as she considered the possibility.

She enjoyed being around older people, especially when they shared their life stories. Several of her patients had lived through tragedies and great joy. Listening to their reminiscing had always been an enjoyable experience. In most cases, the patient appreciated the simple fact that someone was willing to listen to their stories.

Madeline was about to ask how to go about finding such a job, when a quiet knock echoed off the door, then it opened with a squeak. Grace entered quietly carrying a small bag of what Madeline assumed was a poultice for her father. The girl's eyes widen with surprise as she saw Iain sitting upright in his chair with no pain visible on his face.

"*Faither*, I thought…" Grace's voice trailed off as she stared at the two of them in confusion.

"Madeline performed some form of magic to make the pain disappear." His description made Madeline shake her head.

"It wasn't magic. I'm a nurse in my—in America. It's an ancient technique I learned. If you like, I can teach it to you." The moment she made the offer, Grace nodded her acceptance of Madeline's offer then hurried forward.

"Yes, I should like that very much," the girl said in an excited, yet hushed voice. The child was clearly used to speaking softly when her father was unwell.

Madeline's mouth tilted upward in a small smile at her enthusiasm as she rose to her feet then guided the girl to stand behind Iain. With Grace standing in front of her, Madeline guided the girl's hand and quietly instructed her how to apply pressure to first the pressure point on her father's forehead and then temples.

When she took Iain's hand to show Grace the pressure point on his wrist, his hand muscles flexed slightly the moment she touched him. Worried she might have caused him pain, she glanced up at him ready to apologize. The words about to pass her lips died a quick death as she met a penetrating gaze that was dark with an emotion she recognized as desire.

Heat pulsed through her in a split-second, sending her heartbeat skittering until it was pounding wildly in her chest. Madeline's mouth went dry, and she hastily looked away and placed his hand in his daughter's smaller one in a quick move. When she was no longer touching him, she showed Grace where to apply pressure to her father's wrist.

Unwilling to touch him again, Madeline guided the girl's fingers to the pressure point on his wrist to avoid her own fingers coming into contact with Iain. The girl was a quick study, and Madeline smiled her approval when the lesson was complete.

"Well done, Grace. You're an excellent student. It's a simple technique, but it usually eases the patient's suffering fairly quickly. Probably faster than a poultice, although using the two together isn't a bad idea at all. The pressure points don't always alleviate all the pain someone is suffering, but in almost every case it lessens it."

"Thank ye, Miss Whitworth. I shall try this the next time *Faither* has a migraine."

"You're welcome."

The lesson complete, the girl grinned broadly at Iain, and Madeline watched him return his daughter's smile with love and fatherly pride. Suddenly, Iain's smile died, and he frowned.

"Where is your sister?"

"She said she was going for a walk," Grace murmured.

"Did she say where?"

Tension radiated off of Iain, and Madeline immediately wondered if stress was the culprit responsible for his headaches. It was obvious Ainslie was headstrong, impulsive, and perhaps even rebellious. She couldn't be an easy child to manage if one was struggling with debilitating migraines. At her father's question, Grace winced, but remained silent. The child clearly didn't want to get her twin into trouble, but when her father narrowed his gaze at her, Grace lowered her head.

"I think she might have gone down to the inlet to see if anything else had washed up on the shore."

"*Christ Almighty.*" The color drained from Iain's cheeks as he stared at his daughter in horror. "Are ye certain? Of course, ye are."

Iain quickly rose to his feet and swayed slightly. It was enough to convince Madeline that he'd not fully recovered. She stepped forward to block his way out of the study.

"*Sit down,*" she ordered in her best and sternest nurse's voice. He stared at her in surprise before outrage darkened his face. The minute his mouth parted to object, Madeline narrowed her eyes at him. "I *said*, sit down. *Now.*"

The moment he hesitated, she pressed her hands into his hard shoulders and forced him to sit down in his chair. Although he balked, Iain sank down into the wing-backed chair the moment she pushed him downward.

"I will go look for Ainslie. It's obvious to me that you're still not feeling good, and I know my way down to the inlet. You are *not* to move from that chair or this room, is that understood." At her severe tone, Iain looked ready to protest, but she pinned him with a hard look. "Do *not* say a word. Grace, stay with your father. If he moves, remind him he'll have me to deal with when I return with your sister, and I'm not a nice person when I'm angry."

Madeline shifted her gaze from Grace to the girl's father. Beneath her fierce glare, Iain's mouth thinned with anger. It was obvious he didn't appreciate taking orders, and she leaned forward to bend over him.

"I won't think twice about ripping you a new ass, if you don't do as I say."

Shock registered on his face at her fiercely worded command, and Madeline heard Grace gasp behind her. Aware that in the heat of her anger, she'd failed to control her tongue, she debated whether to apologize. She chose not to, and instead, she glared down at him.

"Grace, make sure he doesn't move. I'll be back in a few minutes."

With that final parting shot, Madeline hurried out of the study and then the house. Quickly following the path she'd taken to the inlet yesterday, she ran as fast as she could to the cliffs. Ainslie was nowhere to be seen, and Madeline understood Iain's fear for the child.

If the girl had gone down the path lining the cliff wall to the inlet, it would take only one misstep for her to slip and fall to her death or suffer a serious injury. As she reached the edge of the cliff overlooking the inlet, she breathed a sigh of relief when she saw Ainslie throwing rocks out into the water. Now to convince the child to return to the house. Madeline carefully made her way down to the inlet and walked across the sand toward the girl.

"Hello, Ainslie."

The moment Madeline greeted her, the girl whirled around to face her with first shock and a bit of fear, both of which vanished quickly to become rebellious defiance. Madeline smiled at her then turned to look out over the water.

"It's quite beautiful, isn't it?"

"I suppose." There was a hint of bewilderment in the girl's response. Madeline turned her head and offered her a brief smile before she looked away to stare out at the Phoenix Rising.

"Has anything else from the shipwreck washed up on shore?"

"Nae. At least nothing interesting."

Madeline simply nodded at the child's response, keeping her attention focused on the flat surface of the water. It was a tranquil picture compared to the night Iain had pulled her from the water. The waves gently brushed against the shore, and she noted it was even calmer than yesterday when she'd raced down the steep path along the cliff to the water. There was a peaceful serenity about the inlet today that made it hard to imagine she'd been fighting for her life in the same water two days ago.

"Do you ever have picnics on the beach?" Madeline asked, turning her head to study the girl. Surprise crossed Ainslie's pretty features as she nodded. "Aye, Eileen brings us sometimes. Nae with *Faither*, though. He dinnae like the inlet."

"He doesn't like the water?" Madeline eyed the girl with curiosity.

"Nae. Something bad happened here a long time ago. He will nae talk about it, but I think tis about my Uncle Thane." Ainslie shrugged slightly her expression one of pensive curiosity. "My uncle died in the sea cave when *Faither* was a boy."

"The sea cave?"

"Aye, ye cannae see them now because the tide has come in, and they are full of water, but at low tide ye can go inside. They are on the other side of the outcrop." A frown of discontentment furrowed Ainslie's brow. "But *Faither* made me swear never tae go into the sea cave. I dinnae want tae swear, but I did, and I cannae break my oath."

"I think that's very honorable of you, Ainslie. Integrity is something very special. It says no one has the ability to make you do something you know is wrong. It also shows how trustworthy you are when you give your word to someone else and don't break your promise."

The child didn't answer her for a long moment, she simply studied Madeline with a frown of concentration. Suddenly, she nodded and smiled.

"I dinnae think about it like that before." The small note of satisfaction in her voice made Madeline bite back a smile.

"Well, I think I'll go back to the house now. I'm hungry, and I'm hoping Mrs. McFayden will have lunch soon."

Without waiting for Ainslie to reply, Madeline turned and headed toward the path leading to the top of the cliff. She prayed she'd earned enough of the girl's trust that Ainslie would follow her. A second later, her prayer was answered as the girl appeared at her side. At the foot of the path, Ainslie touched Madeline's arm.

"Let me go first. I can show ye the slippery spots, and dinnae let go of the rope." At the girl's authoritative tone, Madeline nodded and bit back another smile. Ainslie was clearly her father's daughter.

When they reached the top of the cliff, the two of them walked back to the house with Ainslie pointing out different landmarks and what she liked about them. As they walked through the front door of the hall, Iain emerged from the study with a fierce expression on his face. Not about to have him send the child back into her shell, Madeline deliberately stumbled, making it appear as if she'd tripped over her dress. In a split-second, Ainslie was at her side to steady her.

"Thank you, Ainslie." She smiled at the girl as she glanced up to see Iain staring at them slack jawed. "Would you do me a favor, please? Would you find out when Mrs. McFayden will have lunch ready. I'm starving."

With a bob of her head, the girl darted away, and when she was out of earshot, Iain shook his head in amazement.

"Are you sure that is my daughter, or did you switch her with one of the fae?"

"The fae?" Madeline frowned at the word.

"Fairy folk."

"It's not magic to simply listen," she stated quietly before she narrowed her gaze at him. "And I have a feeling you weren't in any mood to listen when Ainslie and I entered the house."

"My daughter is impulsive and takes far too many risks. It is a family trait that often has unpleasant, tragic consequences." His posture was rigid as he eyed Madeline with cold anger at having been admonished by her. "As her father, it is my duty tae keep her safe."

"I'm sorry. I wasn't trying to tell you how to be a parent." The words sounded hollow because she knew that was exactly what she'd been telling him. She sighed, and this time her apology was filled with sincerity. "I truly am sorry. It's just that Ainslie reminds me of myself when I was much younger. I was rebellious, impulsive, and unthinking of potential danger."

Iain glanced over his shoulder in the direction Ainslie had headed before he turned back to Madeline and gestured for her to move into his study. When she hesitated, he narrowed his eyes at her in a clear message that said she wasn't to argue. Irritated by his arrogant manner, Madeline glared back before she walked into the study. To her surprise, the drapes were partially open now, which indicated Iain's migraine was almost non-existent or completely gone.

The sound of the door closing behind her made Madeline spin around. His chilly anger had vanished, but she could tell he still wasn't happy with her. Iain stalked past

Madeline, heading toward his desk. As he circled the large, mahogany piece of furniture, he sank down in his chair. When he gestured for her to take a seat in front of his desk, Madeline experienced the urge not to blindly heed the man's silent command. Instead, she tilted her chin upward in a small gesture of defiance.

"Our earlier conversation was interrupted. As I recall, we were discussing what positions would best suit your skills." When she remained silent, he glanced at a photograph frame on his desk before he met her gaze. "It's evident your options are not extensive, and I have a proposal for you."

"What kind of proposal?" Madeline tipped her head slightly as she studied him warily.

"It's obvious someone needs tae provide for ye, and I'm willing tae offer my protection in exchange for ye becoming governess tae my daughters." The suggestion that she needed protection made her narrow her gaze at the man.

"*First off,* I *do not* need someone to provide for me. *Secondly,* I don't have the *slightest* idea how to be a governess."

"Ye dinnae have difficulty challenging my abilities as a parent, which leads me tae believe ye are not unfamiliar with how tae deal with children." For not the first time, she realized she'd always be able to tell when he was irritated, annoyed, or upset, because he always slipped into a deep brogue. Apparently, his cultured accent was something he'd learned, while his Scottish accent flowed off his tongue as sensually as silk drifting over her skin, even when he was angry.

"I've already apologized for criticizing you, and all I did was listen to Ainslie. I understand you were worried, but berating her would not have helped the situation," she huffed with a breath of exasperation. "And it's most definitely *not* a good example of my suitability for a job as a governess."

"Then how do ye propose tae pay for your room and board? I am a generous host, but there are limits tae my generosity."

The quiet question made her flinch, and her cheeks grew cold, a sign that the color had drained from her face. He was right. She couldn't rely on him to keep supporting her. On the heels of that thought was the realization she had nowhere else to go. She had no idea how long it would take for her to find a job or if she even could. In the back of her head, she heard the sharp, grating sound of a jail cell door clanging shut. It left her feeling trapped, and she tried to quell the panic rising inside of her.

"Well, Madeline?" The ultimatum in his voice said he knew she only had one option.

"Fine," she snapped.

"Good."

The single word echoed with the sound of satisfaction, and she eyed him with antipathy. Her reaction caused his mouth to quirk in a small smile. Clearly he was amused by her irritation.

"There is a room next to the children's' bedroom. I believe it will provide ample space for a schoolroom. I will inform Ainslie and Grace at lunch. Ye will take your meals with us tae ensure my children are instructed as tae proper etiquette at the table."

"That should be interesting," she muttered. She hadn't the foggiest notion as to what would be deemed proper behavior at a table in 1896. As with everything else in this new reality, she would have to wing it.

"I am leaving for Aberdeen tomorrow morning, so Ainslie and Grace will be your complete responsibility while I'm gone."

"Yes, my lord," she murmured with sarcasm. Her reply caused him to eye her with irritation, before his mouth suddenly twitched with amusement. Not about to let him say something that would drive her blood pressure up even higher, she raised her chin haughtily. "If you'll excuse me, I apparently now have a job to do."

Spinning about on the heel of her foot, she stalked to the door of the study. Her hand on the crystal doorknob, she froze then slowly turned to face him.

"By the way, what is the salary of a governess these days?" The question made him frown at her.

"I dinnae mention a salary."

"Well, I'm pretty sure, room and board is *in addition* to the annual salary."

"I will pay ye twenty-three pounds a year."

"*Twenty-three pounds.* That's all?" she gasped.

That wouldn't even buy her a new pair of shoes at home. Although she knew things were much cheaper in this time period, than at home, she still had nothing to compare the amount to.

"Twenty-five and nae a shilling more," he growled.

Something told her the amount was a generous one, but it still sounded like poverty-level wages. With an abrupt nod, she jerked the door open and stalked out of the room, slamming the door behind her. The man was as arrogant as they came, but in the back of her mind, a voice said it made him sexy as hell.

Annoyed that she'd even admitted the fact, she ran up the stairs to the only sanctuary she had in the house. She slammed that door behind her too, then sank down on her bed to stare at the wall. How in the hell had she landed in 1896, and how was she going to get home?

Chapter 8

Madeline looked over her shoulder and considered the proportions of Muchalls Hall from her vantage point. An educated guess said she'd walked at least a mile and a half, possibly even two. Sunday afternoons were apparently the only time off the household staff received each week, and she'd chosen to go for a walk.

Although she wasn't sure she could say she was working all that hard. Iain had left several days ago, leaving her to flounder about in her new role of governess. Madeline didn't have a clue what she was doing and was winging it when it came to coming up with an education plan for Ainslie and Grace.

For sanity's sake, she'd decided to focus on the natural talents the girls possessed. Ainslie was exceptional at math and had a talent for working with animals. It didn't surprise her that Grace excelled at botany, but the child was quite skilled at drawing too. Madeline had encouraged the girl to write down her poultice recipes, while drawing and identifying the ingredients.

The one thing working with Iain's daughters had done was to occupy her time, so she didn't have to dwell on her predicament. Actually, that wasn't quite true, it was always there in the back of her mind. It was worse when she was trying to fall asleep. All she had were questions, and there were no answers forthcoming from anywhere. Not even her nightmares gave her any hints as to how she'd arrived at Muchalls Hall.

Although she had vague memories of Iain's hand gripping her wrist and pulling her toward him, she had only the vague memory of him saying something to her before she'd been roughly pulled upward and out of his embrace. It was the last thing she remembered of her rescue.

Madeline's memories of the Destiny's Dream were altogether different. Those were far too vivid and terrifying. Her nightmares were filled with images of the storm, the man on the cliff, and the captain's gray features just before the wave tossed the sailboat upside down as if it had been a toy.

Equally vivid was the memory of hitting her head on something hard, and everything going dark a split-second later. Then, in the next instant, she was suddenly breathing air permeated with the dank odor of wood that had been in the water for a long time.

Perhaps most vivid and discernible had been the crisp sound of her grandmother's voice. If anyone were to suggest Madeline had heard it in her head, she would vehemently argue they were wrong. Sharp and clear, her grandmother's distinctive mid-west accent had filled that small space as if she'd been right next to Madeline. It had been an actual voice echoing clearly in that pocket of life-sustaining air. A confident voice Madeline hadn't hesitated to question as she'd obeyed the command.

But of all the memories that filled her nightmares, it was the darkness that horrified her the most. It punctured her dreams with such a terrifying strength, she always awoke as her body jerked upright in bed with her heart pounding wildly in her chest. There had been such a finality to the darkness. The sensation was one she couldn't shake, and in the back of her mind, a whisper of something she didn't want to consider tried hard to push its way into her consciousness.

With a disgusted sigh, Madeline climbed the steep hill in front of her. As she reached the top of the knoll, she stared down at a rather large pond. The water shimmered in the sunlight and made her draw in her breath at the lovely sight. A thin rivulet of sweat rolled down her back, reminding her how hot she was from her exercise. She didn't have a swimsuit, but she could at least go wading to cool herself off. Walking quickly down the incline, she reached the edge of the water within minutes.

Madeline took off her shoes and stockings, then lifted the skirt of her gown high on her thighs and strode into the water. The water was colder than she expected, but as her feet adjusted to the temperature, Madeline wished she could simply take off her clothes and go for a swim. She waded deeper into the pond, then closed her eyes and stood still enjoying the coolness of water swirling gently around her legs.

After a few moments, she realized she was still hot, and she frowned with irritation. At home she would actually be swimming. The thought made Madeline huff out a sharp breath of air as she made a decision. She quickly surveyed the surrounding landscape to ensure she was completely alone before she waded out of the water to remove everything, but her combination garment.

For a brief moment, she debated going nude, then opted not to. Her luck of late hadn't exactly been worthy of investing in a lot of lottery tickets. She'd only draw more attention to herself if someone stumbled upon her naked in the pond. A moment later, she ran back into the water, then threw herself forward into a low dive and sank beneath the cold water.

Coming back up for air, she propelled herself back and forth across the length of the pond with smooth kicks and arm strokes. As she swam, her pace increased as she released all the pent-up emotions and energy she'd been internalizing. She'd not known until that moment, how badly she'd needed an outlet for everything that had been locked inside of her for almost a week.

Madeline didn't know how long she'd been in the water, before her body began to tire. Slowly, she swam toward the edge of the pond where she'd left her clothes. When she reached shallow water, Madeline waded out of the pond and tried wringing the water out of her undergarments. It was an impossible task and hands braced against her hips, she rolled her eyes with a shake of her head.

"Well, Madeline, you should have gone naked after all," she muttered sarcastically to herself.

Glaring down at the soggy underwear that clung to her body like a second skin, she uttered a small sound of disgust. Faced with the choice of putting her dress on over her soaked undergarments or going commando to stay dry, Madeline hesitated before her shoulders rolled up in a careless shrug. Commando it was then. Moving quickly, she undid the front of the wet garment and pushed it off her body.

The moment she'd stepped out of the dripping undergarment, she heard a sound behind her that made her heart sink. Frantically, she reached for her gown as the soft thunder of hoofbeats echoed through the air behind her. Clutching her dress to the front of her body, she whirled around to face the approaching rider.

The sight of Iain racing at breakneck speed in her direction made her eyes widen in surprise. With a hard tug on the reins, he brought the animal to a sliding halt and dismounted. As she watched him approach her with a long, quick stride, the grim expression on his rugged features made her stare at him with trepidation. She should have kept her underwear on, soaking wet or not.

"Are ye hurt, lass?"

The question was the last thing she expected to hear pass his lips. She'd been steeling herself for him to unleash the wrath of hell down onto her head for her lack of clothing, not him asking if she was hurt. Bewildered, she shook her head.

"Hurt? No… I'm fine. What makes you think I'm hurt?"

"Because ye fell into the pond," he snarled as his fingers dug into her bare arms and something that resembled horror flashed in his dark blue gaze. Confused, Madeline tipped her head slightly to one side.

"I didn't fall into the pond. I—"

"Sweet màthair of God, is Ainslie in—"

"No, the girls are at the house." She rushed to reassure him and flinched at the look of horror on his face. "They're fine. I just went for a swim. I was hot, and—"

"Ye did what?" Anger darkened Iain's face, and he shook her roughly. Stunned by his reaction, Madeline stared at him in disbelief. "What in the name of God would make ye do such a thing. Dinnae ye ken ye could have drowned."

"I swim all the time at home, and—"

"Ye are *nae* at home, ye wee Sassenach eejit." Iain's breathing had become ragged as a shudder rocked through his body. The tremor pulsed its way into her through the firm hands that tightened their grip on her arms. She winced as his fingers dug painfully into her arms, and he shook her again. "I dinnae pull ye out of that fucking sea tae see ye drown in a pond."

There was something in his voice that made Madeline realize he was afraid. No, not afraid. Panicked terror vibrated off of him with a physical force that stunned her. From the fury in his voice to the gray, ashen color of his face, he possessed the air of a man caught up in a full-blown panic attack. His harsh breaths emphasized the tension holding him rigid, and she was certain she would have bruises tomorrow where his fingers pressed fiercely into her arms. She winced as he gave her another vicious shake.

"Dinnae ye ken how dangerous the water is?"

"Iain, I'm sorry. I didn't mean to upset you," she whispered as she pressed her hand into his chest.

The intensity of his emotions rolled over her in a tangible vibration, and his grip on her didn't slacken. Eyes as dark and stormy as the North Sea he'd pulled her from, he showed no sign of having heard her. Beneath her palm, his heart pounded violently in his chest, and the way it was racing at such an alarming speed frightened her. Worried he might suffer another migraine or worse, faint from hyperventilating, she took a step into him, while keeping her hand against his chest.

"It's all right, Iain. Everything is all right. I'm safe, now." Madeline kept her voice soft and soothing as she pressed her palm deeper into his chest. "I want you to breathe slowly. Can you do that for me?"

A dazed expression swept across his rugged features as his breathing remained fast and heavy, but she saw him making a concerted effort to do as she asked. Over the next minute or two, Madeline gently and quietly encouraged him to take deep breaths and slow his breathing. As he followed her instructions, his breathing began to slow and even out, while the frantic beat of his heart against her palm lessened to a more reasonable rate.

Iain's head dropped until his forehead rested against hers in a sign of exhaustion. A savage shudder shook his tall, hard frame, and he dragged in a deep breath then blew it out forcefully. It was a harsh sound. It signaled his desperate attempt to free himself of the terror that had held him in its fierce grip seconds ago. Still concerned for him, Madeline lifted her hand from his chest to his cheek.

"Better?"

"Aye." The hoarse whisper sent relief streaking through Madeline.

Although Iain appeared to be past the worst of his attack, she knew he would need several moments to recover. What on earth had made him so terrified for her safety? The memory of Iain's face a few days ago when Ainslie had gone down to the inlet triggered the memory of Eileen's comment the first morning she'd awoken at Muchalls Hall. The maid had said Iain was afraid of the water.

Then there was Ainslie's mention of the sea cave and something about her uncle dying there. Had Iain's brother drowned? Fear could make people react in a lot of different ways. She remembered her own reaction to being on the Destiny's Dream and almost dying. The sudden sound of Iain drawing in a deep breath then exhaling it, jerked her out of her thoughts.

For the first time, the warmth of his face against her hand penetrated her consciousness. Quickly pulling her hand away from him, she pressed it into the gown she clutched tightly against her breasts. It was the only thing separating them, and she didn't know how she was going to extricate herself from the situation. She wasn't sure how long they'd stood standing in silence, when Iain drew in a deep breath then slowly released it.

"Thank ye, lass. It's been a long time since that's happened tae me."

"You're welcome, I'm just sorry I was the reason for your attack."

"Ye are nae tae go swimming again without someone close by." Iain lifted his head slightly to stare down into her eyes. His features were stern and implacable.

"But I—"

"Dinnae argue with me, Madeline. If ye truly are sorry for making me fear the worst, then ye will give me your word that ye will do as I ask."

"You *aren't* asking," she muttered.

"Nae, I'm not. But I'll have your word all the same."

"*Fine.* You have my word."

Satisfied with her answer, he straightened then stiffened as his gaze drifted downward. Frozen where she stood, she prepared herself for the reckoning to come. Heat spread its way through her cheeks the moment his gaze returned to hers. Immediately, her pulse skidded out of control at the desire darkening his eyes. Oh God, she was in trouble. *Big* trouble.

"Do ye swim without clothes at home, *mo bhòidhchead fuilt dorcha?*" There was that sexy-sounding Gaelic phrase again.

"No. And I didn't just now either. I wore my underwear," she said breathlessly. She jerked her head toward the sodden white linen lying behind her, while she tried to control her reaction to the sudden change in him. Madeline's body hummed with a wild sensation as his thumbs rubbed small circles against the flesh of her arms. "But I didn't…I didn't want my dress to get soaked, too. So I thought…I was…*oh why* am I explaining myself *to you.*"

Scowling at him, Madeline pushed him away, then took two quick steps backward. One eyebrow shot upward as a small smile tugged at Iain's mouth.

"Turn around," she snapped. When he didn't seem inclined to obey her command, she narrowed her gaze at him. "I *said,* turn around, Lord Glenburnie."

"Does this mean ye have no need of a maidservant, lass?"

"It means exactly what I said. Turn around, before someone else comes along to embarrass me further." At her sharp words, his small smile broadened, but he did as she ordered. "And close your eyes."

"It's a bit late for that, Madeline. I have an excellent memory of a bonnie lass with a thin nightgown clinging to a sweetly curved body."

The soft words sent a hot frisson dancing across her skin. Madeline sucked in a sharp breath before she silently chided herself for her reaction. Quickly scrunching up the back of the gown, she ducked her head under the skirt, while trying to keep the rest of the gown covering her as best as she could.

Awkwardly, she pushed her arms through the sleeves as the skirt of the dress fell down to her ankles. Reaching behind her, Madeline tried to button the back of the gown. It had been a hell of a lot easier to undo the damn thing.

"Oh, for Christ's sake," she muttered with frustration.

"Are ye having trouble with the buttons, *mo bhòidhchead fuilt dorcha?*"

The laughter in his voice made her glare at his back. There was no sign of the man who, just a short time ago, had been shuddering in her arms in a state of sheer panic. Instead, that man had been replaced by a devastating Scotsman, whose voice could easily coax a woman to do just about anything.

"I don't know what you're calling me, but stop it."

"I can assure you, it's a compliment, Madeline." The surprise in his voice made her grimace. One part of her brain wanted to know what he was saying, while the other half refused to go there. Iain uttered a noise of impatience. "Will ye allow me tae turn around and help ye, or are ye going tae wait until nightfall before you sneak back into the manor with your gown agape?"

"Fine."

"Ye are as stubborn as Ainslie," he grumbled with irritation as his hands landed on her shoulders to turn her around.

"Oh, that's rich, considering the apple doesn't fall far from the tree."

She smiled smugly to herself at the low sound of displeasure that echoed out of him. Her self-complacency evaporated the instant his fingers brushed against her back as he began to button up her gown. Madeline went rigid as fire streaked across her skin like a wildfire consuming everything in its path. Heat engulfed her body, and she tried to keep breathing as she trembled slightly.

"Are ye cold?"

"A little," she lied.

The last thing she intended to do was let him know how a mere touch of his fingers brushing across her skin had ignited an incendiary reaction in her. As he finished doing up the back of her gown, his hands glided across her shoulders. The light caress made Madeline dart away from him to pick up her underwear. Without looking at him, she focused her attention on wringing out the garment.

"Come, I'll take you home."

"I can walk just fine."

"I *said*, I'll take ye home, Madeline."

There was a warning in his words that made her glance over her shoulder. Lips tight with determination, Iain narrowed his gaze at her. His expression dared her to thwart him, and something in his stormy gaze indicated he wouldn't hesitate to throw her over his horse's back like a sack of feed if she refused to do as he commanded.

Unwilling to test his resolve, she nodded. Madeline turned her back to him and sank to the ground to pull on her hose and shoes. When she was ready, she scrambled to her feet and with one last twist of her wet underwear, she followed him to his horse. As he swung himself up into the saddle, his dark green and blue plaid kilt with its muted reddish stripes fluttered against well-toned, muscular thighs. The boots he wore rose above his ankles about three inches, while his dark hose covered firm calves and stopped just short of his knees.

The sudden memory of a conversation she'd had with her grandmother several months ago made her bite back a smile. If her grandmother were here, she wouldn't have hesitated to ask if Scotsmen went commando under their kilts. The horse suddenly shifted its position and sidled toward her in two steps. Startled, Madeline jumped back. A low chuckle whispered through the air, and she jerked her gaze up to Iain.

"There's nothing tae be afraid of, lass. Taren is simply eager for the oats he knows are waiting for him at home."

"I'm not afraid, I'm just not sure how I'm supposed to jump up behind you in this dress."

Madeline glanced down at her gown before she lifted her gaze to eye his horse warily. With a sharp flick of his fingers, Iain gestured for her to step forward. The moment she stepped forward, he leaned down and wrapped his hands around her waist. Startled by his action, she gasped in surprise as he lifted her up and set her on the horse in front of him.

"I dinnae say anything about riding behind me."

The moment her body was pressed against the man's chest, Madeline found it difficult to breathe. Forcing herself to draw air into her lungs, she immediately regretted doing so. Horse, leather, pine, and a spicy scent she didn't recognize flooded her senses. Iain smelled heavenly.

Tension slid through her as Iain made a soft sound and urged the animal into a slow canter. Deliberately keeping her eyes trained on the manor in front of her, Madeline straightened her back and tried to keep from leaning against the man. It was a futile effort. Instead, she sat rigid in front of him, desperately trying to ignore the way her body hummed with awareness. A low chuckle drifted past her ear.

"Taren will nae bolt, lass."

"What?" She glanced up at him over her shoulder.

"Ye are stiff as a piece of hardwood. Relax, the horse will sense your fear."

"I am *not* afraid of the horse."

"Then what *are* ye afraid of, Madeline?"

The wicked glint in his eye made her immediately avert her gaze. When she remained silent, he laughed softly, but didn't press her for an answer. The only sound filling the air for the next several minutes was the jingling of Taren's tack, the horse's soft snorts, and the faint sound of the animal's shoes hitting the ground. After a long moment, Iain cleared his throat.

"Where did ye learn tae swim, Madeline? It is an unusual talent for a woman." His question made her dart a look at him out of the corner of her eye before focusing again on the house in front of her.

"My father taught me."

"Father?" The word held a strong note of suspicion, and Madeline nodded.

"Yes, he and my mother died in an accident a month after I turned twelve, and I went to live with my grandmother." A bittersweet smile curved her mouth. "She's why I came to Scotland."

"I dinnae understand, lass."

"She always wanted to visit Scotland," Madeline said with a shake of her head. "For the past couple of years, we would look up places and then make a note of the castles and battlefields we wanted to visit."

"Battlefields," he murmured softly. It wasn't a question, but the amusement in his voice made her glance up at him. When Iain's lips curled in a complacent smile, she narrowed her gaze at him.

"What?" she demanded.

"I dinnae say anything."

"But you're dying to make some kind of wisecrack, aren't you? So, out with it," she snapped irritably.

"I was simply thinking the Frasers at Falkirk and Culloden would have welcomed ye with open arms to fight with them against the enemy."

"Are you making fun of me?" Madeline huffed. He laughed.

"Nae, *mo bhòidhchead fuilt dorcha*. Ye have a fire in ye, lass, that only a Scotsman can appreciate."

Iain's voice had softened, and the sound of it brushed across her senses as if he'd caressed her with his hand. It sent a jolt of electricity skimming along her nerve endings until her skin hummed with awareness. Something dangerous flared in his piercing blue gaze as she looked at him, and Madeline experienced a lethargic fluttering in her stomach.

Madeline quickly jerked her body around to face forward again. Her gaze focused on the manor house that was so close, and yet it was still far enough away that she might not be able to resist melting back into his chest.

"Has nae mon ever told ye how brilliantly your eyes sparkle when your feathers are ruffled, Madeline?" When she didn't answer, a quiet laugh stirred the short curls on the top of her head. "Perhaps I should compliment ye more often, Madeline, if my doing so renders you speechless."

"I am not speechless," she bit out through clenched teeth, unwilling to give him any encouragement. "If my eyes are sparkling, it's because I'm angry."

"Indeed."

A provocative challenge whispered its way through the word, and Madeline clenched her fists to stop herself from responding. It was a struggle not to turn around and read him the riot act, but she succeeded in maintaining her tranquil appearance. At least, she *tried* to make herself believe she appeared serene and unaffected by his teasing.

The manor was close, and she mouthed a silent prayer of thanks as Taren carried her and Iain over the last bit of grass and onto the drive made of small pebbles. When the animal trotted to a halt, Iain leapt down from the animal to forestall her from dismounting without his assistance.

Strong hands gripped her waist, and he lifted her out of the saddle. Her body slid down over his chest, and the instant his mouth came near hers, Madeline drew in a sharp breath. Iain instantly froze at the sound, and as their gazes locked, heat pulsed between them. For a moment, she wondered what he would do if she lightly brushed her lips over his.

Horrified at the direction of her thoughts, Madeline grew rigid with dismay. The instant he set her on the ground, she tugged free of his grasp to put several feet between them. With a breathless word of thanks, Madeline didn't bother to worry what it might look like as she bolted for the front door of the manor.

At the moment, all she cared about was escaping this man who had her body ready to spontaneously combust. If the hounds of hell had been on her heels, they couldn't have made her run any faster, and she didn't stop running until she reached her room. Her heart racing, Madeline closed her eyes as the back of her head rested against her bedroom door. God, she was in trouble with a capital T, and she was at a complete loss as to what she was going to do.

Chapter 9

Iain entered the dining room where his daughters and Madeline were eating breakfast. He'd not seen Madeline since he'd brought her home from the pond yesterday evening, and the sound of her laughter edged its way through him like a warm summer breeze.

"Good morning, *Faither*." Grace and Ainslie spoke simultaneously, their expressions bright with excitement.

"Good morning, lassies," he said with a grin before he looked at Madeline. "Good morning, Madeline."

"Good morning," she replied quietly, quickly averting her gaze to look down at her plate.

The faint flush of color dusting her cheeks made Iain bite back a smile of amusement. For a woman who was unabashedly straightforward and confident, she blushed with the innocence of a schoolgirl. Ainslie fidgeting in her chair pulled his attention away from Madeline as he moved to the buffet server to fix a plate of eggs, sausage, and tattie scones.

It was obvious both girls were on pins and needles. They knew he always brought home a small gift or two for them whenever he traveled to Aberdeen, and he knew Ainslie would be the first to broach the topic.

"Did ye have a good trip, *Faither?*"

"Aye, I did," he said as he smiled over his shoulder at his daughter. His youngest by several minutes was showing restraint for a change.

Frustration furrowed Ainslie's forehead at his noncommittal reply, and Iain suppressed a grin as he carried his plate, along with a bowl of porridge, to the table. Sitting down at the opposite end of the table from Madeline, he focused his attention on Ainslie.

"What did you learn while I was gone?"

"Madeline gave me math problems tae do. They were harder than I thought they would be, but I answered all of them correctly. I also did an inventory of the larder for Bridget, and I helped Angus with the new calf that has been doing poorly all summer."

"Inventory? Calf?" Startled, Iain looked down the length of the table at Madeline and frowned.

"Ainslie has a gift for working with animals. I had her write what she did while helping Angus in the barn," Madeline said as she smiled at his daughter. "Since she's good with numbers, I thought doing some form of inventory would help her learn the basics of accounting."

The reply wasn't exactly what Iain had been expecting. In truth, he wasn't really sure *what* he'd thought Madeline would teach his children. But if he had made a list of expectations, hearing that his daughter had been working in the larder and stables would not have been on it.

"So Ainslie has spent the last several days working in the stables," he said with a sense of growing frustration. "Exactly *what* has *Grace* been doing?"

"I've been writing out my poultice recipes then drawing and labeling the plants I use, *Faither*," Grace said in a cheerful voice. "I dinnae think tae do that before. Madeline says I am excellent at drawing."

"Botany is obviously one of Grace's greatest strengths, so I thought she could focus on her poultices while using math and drawing skills at the same time."

"Do you plan on teaching them needlework as well?" Iain scowled as he stared down the length of the table at Madeline. Surely the woman understood his daughters needed to know how to use a needle and thread.

"Needlework?" Confusion flashed across Madeline's face before understanding lightened her oval features. "Oh, sewing. I don't know how to sew."

"And the piano? Will you be teaching them music?"

"Unfortunately, I was never very good at playing musical instruments." Madeline winced as he arched his eyebrows at her in amazement. She narrowed her gaze at him. "I seem to recall telling you I didn't know how to be a governess."

"Aye, that you did," he muttered with an ironic twist of his lips.

Clearly, he'd not thought things through when it came to the education of his daughters. His gaze met Madeline's, and there was regret, as well as hopelessness, on her face that made him draw in a quiet breath before he released it with resignation. Sending the girls off to school would need to happen sooner than later. But if his next investment paid off as well as the one he'd just benefitted from, he would be more than able to send his daughters to a suitable school.

"*Faither?*" Ainslie shifted in her chair again with suppressed excitement as she waited for his full attention. He turned his head to meet a pair of violet eyes wide with anticipation.

"Yes, Ainslie?"

"Did you bring us something, *Faither?*"

"Bring you something?" he asked as he feigned a frown of surprise and arched his eyebrows at her.

"Dinnae tease us, *Faither.* Ye always bring us something when you come home from a trip." Grace's voice was filled with almost as much excitement as Ainslie's.

"Hmm, perhaps there was something that found its way onto the wagon."

"What is it, *Faither?* What did ye get for us?" The chorus of excited questions layered over each other, and he leaned back in his chair.

"Cecil should be here with the wagon soon. You'll have to wait until then."

"But Cecil is old, and he drives so slow. Cannae ye just tell us now?" Ainslie pleaded.

"If you knew what it was, it wouldn't be a surprise anymore," Madeline laughed as she teased the twins. "Anticipation is part of the fun."

His daughters eyed her with a mixture of disgruntlement and begrudging acceptance. Something about Madeline sitting at the opposite end of his table filled him with an unusual sense of contentment. It was a feeling that said all was right within his world. Iain knew the emotions should alarm him, but for the time being, he was willing to allow himself the pleasure the sight of her gave him.

Even more striking was the relationship she'd developed so quickly with his daughters. Despite her unusual teaching style, Grace and Ainslie displayed an animation and excitement about their lessons that said there was great merit in Madeline's method of instruction. She was an enigma with her strange ways and mysterious arrival. But there was always something she held back as if she was frightened.

Although, the only time Iain had ever seen Madeline exhibit any real fear had been the morning after he'd pulled her from the sea. She was spirited, intelligent, and she had a pleasing laugh. Madeline also possessed a unique mix of compassion and understanding when it came to someone in distress.

It was an ability she'd demonstrated twice now. First with his headache, then yesterday at the pond when she'd helped him fight off his demons. Although her commands had been stern and resolute, the soothing sound of her voice had been the lifeline he'd clung to while battling his way back to sanity. Then moments later, all rational thought had vanished from his head.

A new battle had erupted inside him as he'd reacted to her state of undress. The feel of her soft skin against his fingertips had only strengthened the way his body ached for her. It had been a reaction he'd barely managed to control when the only barrier between her skin and his mouth was the gown she'd clutched to her breasts. The intensity of his arousal hadn't surprised him. He'd already had more than one erotic image of Madeline since her arrival at Muchalls Hall.

What had startled him as he'd struggled with his reaction to her, had been the desire he'd seen in her doe-eyed gaze. The warm brown eyes that had locked with his had held a slumberous expression of arousal. The sultry blaze he'd seen glowing in her lovely brown eyes had caused his cock to stiffen beneath his kilt. Equally tantalizing had been her lush pink mouth. Her breathing had been rapid and her rosy-hued lips had been parted as if begging to be kissed.

Everything about her reaction had convinced him a similar fire had been burning in her as well. The tension between them had seemed to grow in strength as her soft curves had pressed into him on the ride back to the manor. When he'd helped her dismount Taren in the stable yard, the heat of her sliding down over his chest had only heightened the desire assaulting his body.

As her mouth had come close to his, Madeline had released a small sound of awareness that had sent Iain's heart slamming into his chest. Seconds later, she'd twisted free of his grasp then darted away from him and disappeared into the house.

He'd not seen her again until he walked into the dining room for breakfast. Iain heard Ainslie muttering a protest, and he shook his head, while studying the woman at the opposite end of the table.

"Madeline is right." The moment her startled gaze met his, a small smile tugged at his lips. "Anticipation is part of the pleasure. It heightens the excitement and intensity of one's reaction the moment *all* is revealed."

The instant a blush darkened her cheeks, Iain knew she understood his subtle reference to yesterday afternoon. Under his work kilt, his cock stirred, and he quickly suppressed the desire threatening to rage its way through his blood. Cheeks bright with pink color, Madeline quickly shifted her gaze to first Ainslie and then Grace.

"The one thing that's for certain is that the two of you have lessons that need to be completed before you find out what the surprise is."

With an alacrity that amazed him, both girls requested to be excused from the table, and Iain nodded. The twins hastily pushed back their chairs and raced from the room. Madeline moved almost as quickly, but Iain rose to his feet and called out to her before she could flee the dining room.

"My surprise for Ainslie and Grace is not the only thing I brought home with me. I brought something for you as well, Madeline, but it's packed in the crates along with what I bought for the girls." Her startled trepidation made him smile. "I promise its nothing as intimate as the wet linen garment you discarded yesterday, *mo bhòidhchead fuilt dorcha.*"

"Well, *that's* a relief."

Her sarcasm was accompanied by a scowl in his direction, but it didn't stop another blush from cresting over her cheeks. Despite her obvious exasperation at his teasing, the breathless note in her reply betrayed her flustered state. It convinced Iain he'd not imagined her attraction to him yesterday.

Still smiling, he walked the length of the table until he was little more than an arm's length away from her. Iain saw the way her throat bobbed as she swallowed hard, and he could tell she was fighting not to retreat. That she stood her ground only emphasized the strength he'd seen in her from the moment she'd defied the sea and fought her way toward him the night he'd pulled her from the water.

It said she wouldn't flee any perceived or real sense of danger, and yet, he knew she was afraid of something. The problem was he didn't know what that something was. She'd said she wasn't running from anyone, but she was running. He was certain of that.

"My daughters appear to be enjoying their lessons, despite your unique teaching style." The moment she bristled at his observation, he raised his hand in a gesture of appeasement. "It is not a criticism, Madeline. It's a compliment. I knew Grace would not be a challenge. Ainslie, on the other hand, can be difficult, but the child didn't argue or hesitate when you told the girls they had lessons to do."

"So, you're all right with the way I've been doing things?" Madeline eyed him warily.

"Aye. While your methods are most irregular, they're clearly effective, and I have no objection to you continuing as you have been."

"Thank you." She met his gaze for a brief moment then looked away. "If you'll excuse me, I'll—"

"Before you go, I thought you would like to know that I made additional inquiries while I was in town," he said quietly.

"Inquiries?"

"I was concerned Cecil might have overlooked something when I sent him tae Aberdeen after the shipwreck. As Ainslie said, he's old, and the man is sometimes forgetful. So, I decided tae do some investigating myself."

His quiet revelation made her grow rigid, and he narrowed his gaze at her. From the moment Madeline had entered Muchalls Hall, she'd been a mystery he'd wanted to solve. But every single inquiry he'd made over the past five days had proven futile. It had only deepened the mystery surrounding her.

The day after Madeline had raced down to the sea in a state of panic, Iain had wired Andrew with a request for him to try to uncover any information about her. But not even his cousin, with all his wealth and resources in America, had found anything. It was as if Madeline had materialized out of thin air only a moment or two before he'd pulled her from the water.

Then there was her reaction the morning after the shipwreck. The instant he'd confirmed the date, she'd fled his office in a state of sheer panic. When he'd found her on the beach, she'd been muttering gibberish about nightmares and the date.

Now, with each passing day and all his unanswered questions, the memory of the woman he'd seen on the cliff the day of the shipwreck had become a persistent thought in his mind. Despite watching her suddenly fade from view, he'd convinced himself the woman had taken the path down the side of the cliff. The fact that he'd even considered the possibility that the woman on the cliff and Madeline were connected had him questioning his sanity.

But he also knew there were things and events that logic could never explain. Grace's gift of the *an dara sealladh* had taught him that, and he was beginning to think Madeline Whitworth's presence here was unexplainable. As he met Madeline's gaze, her reaction to the fact he'd conducted his own investigation clearly alarmed her.

"I don't understand." Fear flashed in her eyes before she looked away from him.

"I sent a telegram tae my cousin in America. I asked him tae check passenger manifests on ships crossing the Atlantic for the past three months. There's nae been anyone with the last name of Whitworth crossing the Atlantic in all that time."

Iain studied her in silence waiting for her to offer some form of explanation as to how she'd come to be on the Phoenix Rising, not the Destiny's Dream as she'd so emphatically insisted. He frowned when she didn't answer him.

"Who is the man you're running from, lass?"

"Man?" Her eyes widened as she met his gaze with bewildered surprise.

"Your manner is far too worldly tae suggest you're a young woman unacquainted with men. So, whoever you're running from—"

"*Unacquainted with*…are you calling me a slut?" Her posture became rigid with outrage as she eyed him with contempt. Iain winced. He'd plainly worded his explanation wrong.

"Forgive me, Madeline. I am nae suggesting such a thing. I am simply stating ye are nae an innocent afraid of her own shadow when she's in the same room as a man."

"Every time you open your mouth, my lord, the hole you're digging gets deeper. So I suggest you stop before you're in so deep you can't get out." The sarcasm in her voice was sharply edged with anger. Iain released a small noise of frustration.

"I am simply pointing out that I think you're running from someone, and I want tae know if it's a husband or a lover."

"I am *not* running from anything *or anyone*." The terse, angry reply made him shake his head in disbelief. Irritated by her persistent denial that she wasn't running from some kind of threat, Iain glared at her.

"Then explain why I can't find anything that says ye even exist."

"You wouldn't believe me even if I *could* explain it," she bit out sharply.

"*Damn it*, Madeline. I cannae help ye if ye dinnae trust me."

"Did I *ask* for your help?" The fiery glare she directed at him made Iain grit his teeth.

"Nae, but there's something ye are nae telling me. Something that terrifies ye."

The panic and fear he sensed in her earlier had become an almost tangible sensation. Studying her intently, the unshed tears shimmering in her soft, brown eyes aroused the urge to pull her into his arms and offer his shoulder for her to cry on. It was so strong it made him take another step toward her. The moment she turned her head away from him, Iain reached out to catch her chin in his fingers and forced her to look at him. His thumb rubbed across the plump lower lip of her pink mouth.

"Trust me, *mo bhòidhchead fuilt dorcha*," he murmured as if soothing a frightened animal. "Let me help ye. Tell me what frightens ye so badly. It will make it easier if ye share your burden with someone else."

"No. It won't. If I thought you could help me, I would have asked you already. But you can't."

"I dinnae believe that."

"Can you send me into the future?" The fierce, bitter question made him stare at her in confusion.

"I dinnae understand, lass."

"I *said*, can you send me to the *future? Back* to my time? I wasn't born in this century. I won't be born for more than another hundred years."

Iain stared at her as if she had two heads, and Madeline flinched. Her stomach lurched as she realized what she'd done. She'd allowed that sexy brogue of his to lull her into a false sense of security. A silent belief that he would understand if she told him the truth. Fear expanded inside Madeline, and bile rose in her throat.

She pulled free of his light grasp and turned to flee, but his strong hand caught her arm again to prevent her from escaping. Without a word, Iain ushered her out of the dining room and pulled her toward his study.

"Let me go," she snapped in a hushed voice as she tried to free herself.

The last thing she wanted was for someone to come help the man hold her prisoner as he sent for someone to take her to the asylum. Iain ignored her demand, and pulled her into the study, then closed the door behind him. With a sharp tug, Madeline jerked free of his grasp and took several quick steps backward. He stood with his back to the door, obviously not about to let her escape that way. She ran toward the window, but his voice rang out with a harsh command to stop.

"I will catch ye before ye can unlock the windows, Madeline," he declared quietly. "Now, come sit down."

"Why? So you can tie me down, while you send for someone to take me away and lock me up?"

"I am nae going tae send ye away, lass. Now, *sit down*."

Arms folded across his chest, Iain bobbed his head toward the chair in front of his desk and waited for her to comply with the command. Without looking away from him, Madeline slowly walked toward the chair. As she sank down into the cushioned seat, Iain strode forward. Tension made her sit rigidly, preparing herself to flee the moment he let his guard down. She had no idea where she'd go, but she couldn't stay here.

"I said tae trust me, *mo bhòidhchead fuilt dorcha*," he said softly as he stood in front of her and leaned back against his desk.

The position gave him the appearance of being completely relaxed, but Madeline knew how fast he could move. That, she'd witnessed yesterday when he'd easily lifted her off the ground and set her on his horse in front of him. Beneath that layer of nonchalance was a power she wouldn't want unleashed on her head if he were angry.

It wasn't difficult to imagine him as a Highland warrior with his tall, sinewy body. Everything about him said he was strong enough to easily break a man in half. But it was the intangible force inside him she found enthralling and alarming at the same time. Iain Fraser was dangerous. Yesterday had emphasized just how much when he'd helped her off his horse.

His strong arms had held her tight against him as he'd slowly allowed her to slide down over his body. The tantalizing scent of the outdoors had mixed with the warm smells of leather, pine, and something spicey. Engulfed by the heat of him, she'd desperately fought off the urge to bury her face in his neck and breathe him into her senses.

The strength of him had been underscored by his hard, muscular body pressing into hers. Before her feet touched the ground, she was already wondering what it would be like to make love with the man. The memory sent her heartbeat skidding out of control, and Madeline immediately pushed her chair backward in a meager attempt to put space between them, hoping her thoughts would follow suit.

"I want tae ask ye a question, Madeline, and I want ye tae answer me honestly."

Wary of a possible trap, she studied Iain in silence. There was something in his voice that eased some of her tension, and she flinched. God, she was doing it again. She was allowing that quiet, gentle brogue of his to lull her into a false sense of security. Madeline's gaze darted toward the door, and Iain released a harsh sound of frustration.

"*Look at me*, Madeline. You're safe here. I will nae let anyone take ye away. Now then, I want ye tae answer my question truthfully." Iain narrowed his gaze at her as he waited for her to agree. Madeline nodded her head sharply. Satisfied, he studied her carefully for a moment then cleared his throat. "Before ye arrived at Muchalls Hall, had ye ever seen the cliffs or the inlet before?"

Startled by his question, Madeline wasn't sure whether to tell him about the dreams she'd had all her life or to simply deny everything. She could just tell him she'd lied about being from the future because she'd been trying to keep him from asking more questions. No, that wouldn't work. Iain wasn't just an intelligent man, he was incredibly intuitive.

She was pretty sure he'd be able to tell she was lying if she tried to backtrack her irrational declaration. Did it matter if she sounded crazy? If he already thought she was out of touch with reality, what harm would it do to take one more step in that direction?

"Yes. In my dreams." Madeline flinched as she remembered how in recent weeks, the dreams had become stronger, more vivid. "I've had the same dream, over and over, since I was a girl."

"Exactly what do ye see in this dream, lass?"

The quiet question made a knot rise in her throat. How *exactly*, was she supposed to answer that? He eyed her sternly with a silent warning to tell him the truth. Madeline wasn't sure what made her decide to answer him, but she found herself speaking without stammering.

"I'm standing on the cliffs, looking out at the North Sea. It's raining, and there's a man on the cliff with me, and he's staring out at the sea."

The instant he jerked in surprise, Madeline studied him in puzzlement and noted a strange expression of bewildered amazement on his face. The emotion vanished the moment he realized she was watching him.

"Do you know this man?"

"No. At least, I don't think I do. The rain makes it difficult to see clearly, and he's too far away for me to see his face."

She shook her head. The sudden memory of being on the Destiny's Dream and seeing the man standing on the cliff above the inlet flitted through her head. She'd barely had time to wonder who he was before all hell had broken loose and the sailboat had capsized. Had he been the same man she'd always dreamed about? Madeline brushed the silent question aside. She was already beginning to feel borderline psychotic. She didn't need to exacerbate the situation.

"What else do you see in these dreams?"

"There's a ship heading for the inlet." Madeline drew in a sharp breath as she remembered what the ship looked like. Even though she'd couldn't see the name on the side of the vessel, she recognized it. Madeline's heart began pounding like a horse racing toward the finish line. "It's the Phoenix Rising. She's headed toward the inlet, but a huge wave throws her onto the rocks. Then I'm suddenly in the water, and it feels like I'm drowning, and that's when I wake up."

Trembling, Madeline clenched her jaw and deliberately forced herself to shut out the horrifying memory of being trapped underwater the night of the storm. For the first time, she realized how her dreams about drowning were identical to what had happened to her when the Destiny's Dream had capsized. She drew in a deep breath, and slowly released it to calm her racing heart.

Madeline raised her head to see Iain staring down at the floor with a frown of contemplation. Although she could still see the latent power in his stance, there was a quiet strength about him that made her feel safe. This was a man she could turn to if she was in trouble. Was that why she'd told him about her dreams? She remained silent as he looked up to study her for a long moment. Iain drew in a shallow breath then released it. With a nod that indicated he'd reached some sort of decision, he cleared his throat.

"For both our sakes, Madeline, I think it best we dinnae mention any of this tae anyone else."

"Ya think?" Her sarcasm sent his eyebrows shooting upward. Madeline rolled her eyes at him. "I'm not an idiot. I'm sure you think I'm crazy, but I'm also pretty sure that you don't want anyone else to know you hired an insane person as a governess for your daughters."

"Insane?" The chuckle that filled the air made Madeline stare at Iain with varying levels of anger and bewilderment. "Nae, lass. If anyone is insane, it's me."

"I don't understand."

"The Scots respect, and sometimes revere, those with the *an dara sealladh*. They would nae question what Grace saw. As for me—"

"Grace has the ability to see things and talk to the dead?" she exclaimed softly as something insidious tried to wind its way through her mind.

"Nae, she cannae speak to the dead, but the lass often sees things, knows things before they happen," Iain said quietly.

"And she saw *me*?" The moment she asked the question, she felt more than saw Iain's body tense, and she immediately demanded an answer. "*Tell me*."

"Several hours before the Phoenix Rising crashed on the rocks, Grace saw ye in the water." The way he seemed to choose his words carefully made Madeline stiffen.

"What else?" Her curt question made Iain frown before he drew in a breath and expelled it.

"The lass said ye was drowning. She was deeply troubled because she could nae help ye."

"Oh, God." Her whispered words made Iain lean toward her.

"But ye did nae drown, Madeline. Ye are here." He suddenly reached out and caught her hand in his. The electric current that streaked up her arm made her jump. Iain squeezed her hand and smiled reassuringly. "See, I'm real. You're real. Ye dinnae drown, Madeline."

"But what if Grace…" her voice trailed off as she took in Iain's words. He shook his head at her unfinished question.

"Even Grace knows that what she sees is nae always the way things happen."

A small tremor rippled through Madeline as she struggled with the thought of Grace seeing her drown. How was that possible? Madeline almost snorted out loud at the idiotic thought. She was stuck in the past and questioning Grace's ability to see things? But what if she really was insane?

If she was, then her psychosis was unlike anything she'd read about in her textbooks. Everything was so real and tangible. The sensation of Iain's hand holding hers was as real as any touch she'd experienced in her own time. Even if she was delusional and living in a reality only she could see and feel, it meant she hadn't drowned. She was still alive, just like Iain had pointed out seconds ago. Another shiver rippled through her as she suddenly remembered Iain had mentioned himself. Had he seen her drowning too?

"Do you have this dara, or whatever you called it, too?"

"Nae," he shook his head. Madeline narrowed her eyes at him.

"But you *saw* something that night, didn't you?" He slowly released her hand, and clearing his throat, he straightened upright once more.

"Aye…I saw a woman on the cliffs who looked like you."

"Like me?" she barely breathed the words.

"Aye. When she disappeared, I thought she'd gone down the path tae the inlet. I went after her, but she wasn't anywhere tae be found."

"Is that why you asked me if I'd seen the inlet before?" At her question, he nodded.

"After I pulled ye from the water and carried ye back tae the house, I realized ye were dressed exactly like the woman I saw."

"You think I'm the woman you saw on the cliffs?" Madeline stared at Iain in amazement.

"Aye, the only other explanation is that I'm mad, but I know I'm not. It's why I believe ye." At his soft statement, Madeline stared at him dumbfounded. Wry amusement tilted his lips. "Ye cannae be any more astonished than me, *mo bhòidhchead fuilt dorcha*. But I *do* believe ye are telling me the truth."

"You do?" Madeline shook her head as she tried to take in his words.

"Aye, but as I said, it's best we dinnae mention this tae anyone else, or we shall both be carted off tae the asylum."

Still thunderstruck, she stared at him in silence. He believed her. It didn't matter how or why. It was simply enough that he believed her. Tension released its grip on her muscles, and she sagged slightly in her chair.

"Thank you," she said in a hoarse voice.

Slowly, she pushed herself up out of her seat to sway slightly in front of him. Strong hands gripped her arms to steady her. Instantly, the heat of his touch sank through her clothes, down into the pores of her skin until it reached her blood. In seconds, his warmth cascaded through her until her entire body was feverish. It sent a tremor through her, and Iain frowned with worry.

"Are ye unwell, Madeline?" The rough concern in that silky soft brogue of his made her shake her head sharply, while fighting to maintain her equilibrium.

"No. I'm fine."

"Ye dinnae look fine."

"Well, I should know whether or not I'm fine," she snapped as she scowled up at him. Exasperation echoed in the low rumble of sound that escaped him.

"Aside from Ainslie, I dinnae think I've ever met a more mulish lass," he growled with exasperation. Despite knowing she could be bull-headed and stubborn, the less than flattering observation made Madeline stiffen, and her irritation helped her find her balance again.

"I am *not* hardheaded." The lie tumbled off her lips before she could stop herself.

"And if I said the sky was blue, no doubt ye would say it was purple." Iain snorted with a healthy dose of sardonic amusement. Madeline glanced at the window to see the overcast skies then looked up at him and smiled mockingly.

"Go ahead. Say it. Say the sky's blue, because at the moment, it's gray outside." At her smug reply, Iain jerked his head to look out the window, and she grinned with satisfaction. "Next time make sure you're right before you try to prove your point."

Iain slowly turned back to her, and a small smile of something wicked touched his firm, incredibly delicious-looking mouth. Fire flared in his dark-blue eyes as he arched an eyebrow at her. Madeline swallowed hard, failing to stop the tremor shaking its way through her. The instant his hand cupped her chin, she sucked in a quick, sharp breath of air. She'd barely breathed in a second breath, when his thumb rubbed its way across her bottom lip. The sensual caress caused her heart to crash to a halt then resume its pounding as her entire body tightened with anticipation.

"There is one thing ye need tae ken about me, Madeline Whitworth. Dinnae ever dare me tae do something." The moment he leaned into her, his tantalizing scent filled her senses. For a moment, his mouth hovered close to hers, before his head tipped to one side, and he nibbled at her earlobe. "Ye will nae win, especially if there is only a mere piece of fabric between my mouth and your sweet curves."

The words immediately made it almost impossible to breathe as she tried to pull badly needed air into her lungs. Of their own volition, the muscles at the apex of her thighs tightened in response to his seductive brogue and the image his voice had created in her head. Heaven help her, in less than five seconds, the man had her on the brink of throwing herself at him. She gulped at the realization. Struggling to breathe, Madeline shivered as his mouth feathered light, almost intangible, kisses along her jawline.

"As much as I wanted tae, I dinnae give way to temptation yesterday, lass." The whisper was a soft caress over her senses, and her eyes fluttered shut despite her best efforts to resist the hypnotic sound of his voice. "But ye did say tae make sure I am right before I prove a point, *mo bhòidhchead fuilt dorcha*, and I need tae ken if ye lips are as sweet-tasting as they look, if only tae prove tae myself that I'm right."

God, the man could make a dictionary sound sexy as hell, but whatever he was calling her in that Gaelic language of his was enough to make her willing to do just about anything he asked of her. Ready to melt from the heat rushing through her, Madeline dragged in a sharp breath just before his mouth covered hers in a light kiss.

Frozen where she stood, a tremor rocked its way into every inch of her body as his mouth hardened against hers. Strong muscular arms wrapped around her waist and pulled her into his sinewy frame. Hands splayed against the steely hardness of his chest, her lips eagerly parted beneath his.

A low sound rumbled in his chest, and it vibrated through his muscles to dance against her fingertips as his tongue mated with hers. The spicy, orange flavor of the jam they'd had at breakfast flooded her mouth. It held the faintest hint of honey and whiskey. God, the man was a veritable feast of everything hot and male.

Desire spiraled through her limbs, while her nipples hardened. The corset she wore was low enough that the hard edge of it brushed against the stiff peaks causing them to tighten and ache with an almost painful pleasure.

The moment a large hand slid up from her waist to brush across the top of her breasts, a soft moan whispered out of her. Beneath the gown's bodice, the tip of her breasts tightened even more until she whimpered with need. In the back of her mind, she knew this kiss was madness, but she was beyond all sense of reason. The only thing her body wanted—needed—right now was his touch. Everything else was lost in a mind-numbing bliss.

Chapter 10

The sweetness of Madeline's lips against his made Iain's heart slam into his chest like a sledgehammer. Every erotic thought he'd ever had about her clouded his head as he savored the hot taste of her. The soft scent of lavender filled his nostrils, and he pulled her soft curves even tighter into his body. Beneath his kilt, his cock was hard as iron.

It had been a long time since he'd had a woman, but he couldn't remember ever having a woman in his arms as intoxicating as Madeline. The soft sigh of delight he heard pass her lips stirred a need in him to carry her upstairs to his room and revel in her warm, fragrant skin.

He wanted to explore every inch of her with his mouth and hands. Most of all, he wanted to sink into her hot, silky folds. He wanted to feel her body clutching his as she cried out his name, just before her body shuddered beneath his with wild abandon as she came fast and hard.

Like a sleek kitten aching to be stroked, her body moved against his in a silent plea for him to satisfy them both. His hands cupped her buttocks to tug her hips forward until his cock was nestled between her voluptuous thighs with only her gown and his kilt preventing him from taking her this second.

Raw, carnal need surged through his veins as he struggled not to sit her on his desk, lift her skirts, and slide into her. Knowing he was on the precipice of doing just that, he pushed her back until she was an arm's length away from him. Passion softened her features as she stared up at him with surprise and disappointment.

Self-disgust sailed through him. Christ, the woman was a guest in his home, and he'd been on the verge of taking his pleasure with her. Iain shook his head as if doing so would clear the fog that still blinded him to almost everything in the room except her.

"Forgive me, Madeline." He swallowed hard. "I should nae have—"

"There's no need for an apology. We're both adults."

Shoulders rolling in a nonchalant shrug, she turned away and took a step toward the door. There was something about her stiff posture that made Iain reach out to catch her arm. She looked over her shoulder at him, and he saw something unfamiliar flicker in her gaze. Unable to decipher the emotion, he studied her intently.

"Ye misunderstand, *mo leannan*. I dinnae regret the kiss. I found it immensely pleasurable, but I took advantage of the situation."

"I don't regret it either," she breathed softly. "And it was… I enjoyed it very much."

Color flooded her cheeks, and with a gentle tug, she freed her arm from his grasp then fled the room. As the study door closed behind her with a solid thud, Iain shoved his hand through his hair. Madeline Whitworth was beginning to be a problem for him.

A delectable one, but a problem nonetheless. Iain dragged in a harsh breath. He'd nearly lost control a few minutes ago. No woman had ever affected him like Madeline had. His chest tightened as he remembered the tantalizing heat of her mouth against his.

She'd been every bit as tempting and exquisite as he had imagined she'd be. But the last thing he wanted was for her to think there could be anything permanent between them. He had Thane's and Flora's deaths on his hands, Iain refused to be responsible for a third.

With a sharp turn on his heel, Iain turned and walked to the window to stare out at the sea as he remembered the conversation that had led up to their kiss. Her claim that she was from the future had made her sound like a madwoman. If not for the woman he'd seen on the cliffs the night the Phoenix Rising sank, he would have thought Madeline demented.

Perhaps they both were. Madeline for saying she was from the future. Him for believing she was the woman who'd vanished mere minutes before the sea had smashed the Phoenix Rising on the rocks. But every detail of Madeline's dream matched up precisely with what had happened the night he'd stood on the cliff watching the Phoenix Rising fighting to reach safe harbor.

The only thing missing from her description was how she'd disappeared like a phantom right in front of him. What had happened to her at that precise moment? She'd said her dreams always ended the same way before she awoke. She was drowning.

Iain released a harsh breath as he remembered Grace's vision. The *an dara sealladh* had shown Grace images of Madeline drowning. Thinking back to the day of the storm, Iain remembered how badly shaken Grace had been by what she'd seen. The night his daughter had tended to Madeline's injuries, she'd reminded him of her vision before he'd sent her down to supper.

Later that evening, when he asked his daughter if she was certain Madeline was the woman in her vision, Grace had been unshakeable in her conviction about what she'd seen. Grace had been emphatic that the *an dara sealladh* had shown Madeline drowning. Iain drew in a small breath as he remembered how his daughter had said Madeline had drowned somewhere else, but not here.

Was such a thing possible? Could Madeline really be from the future? Could she have—no, Grace had to be misinterpreting her vision. Madeline hadn't drowned. She'd bravely swum through the rough sea to him, and he'd pulled her from the water himself. He shook his head at the memory of her clinging to him as the waves pounded the two of them against the rocks. Iain didn't have an explanation for anything where Madeline was concerned. At the moment, the only thing he understood was that both of them might be mad as hatters.

Iain smiled as his daughters charged out of the front door of the manor. Yesterday afternoon, the prospect of rain had forced him to change his plans for surprising the twins. They'd not been happy when they'd been told they would have to wait until today for their surprise, and he was grateful the sun was out so they weren't disappointed again.

Following behind the girls at a more sedate pace was Madeline. As she stepped out into the sunshine, he allowed himself to enjoy the sight of her. The sun gave her skin a warm glow and made her brown hair shimmer in the light. She looked delectable, and the moment his gaze swept over her, pink color crested over her cheeks.

Ainslie was the first to utter a shout of delight as she pointed toward the stakes and wire wickets Angus had helped him set up a short time ago. Grace released a loud cry of pleasure that was completely out of character for her, and Iain eyed her in astonishment.

Color invaded the child's cheeks as she glanced over her shoulder at Madeline who smiled with approval. Immediately, his oldest turned back to him and shrugged slightly. A wide grin on her sweet face, Grace ran after Ainslie, who had reached the tall box of croquet mallets. While the two girls talked excitedly with each other, Iain arched his eyebrows at Madeline in a silent demand as to his daughter's unusual reaction.

"I've told Grace it's perfectly fine to be enthusiastic in certain situations. She needs to enjoy being a child."

At the explanation, Iain nodded as he turned back to his daughters. Madeline had succeeded where he had failed. In a relatively short time, she'd helped Ainslie control her impulsive, unrestrained behavior, while encouraging Grace not to be quite so reserved. The change in his daughters was remarkable, which pleased him greatly. The twins whirled away from the box of mallets and threw themselves at him with renewed cries of excitement and happiness.

"Oh, *Faither*, it's wonderful," Grace exclaimed with a wide smile, while Ainslie hugged him tightly.

"It's magnificent, *Faither*. Thank you."

The girls thanked him several more times before they returned to the croquet set to select their mallets. With a teasing grin, Iain gestured toward the tall wooden box.

"Would you care to join us, Madeline?"

"I've never been good at sports, so I think I'll just cheer everyone on from the sidelines." Her reply was accompanied by a wry twist of her lovely mouth.

"But ye must play, Madeline. It will nae be as much fun without ye." Ainslie darted forward to tug on Madeline's arm and tried to pull her toward the wooden box of mallets.

"Aye, Ainslie is right. Please say ye will play, Madeline." Grace echoed her twin's plea as the girl flanked her governess to aid in her sister's efforts to drag Madeline to the box. Iain eyed her with amusement.

"Perhaps Madeline is afraid to do battle with us, lassies." His mouth twitched with amusement as she resisted his daughters' efforts to convince her to play.

"Oh, I'm not afraid," Madeline said with a laugh as she wrapped an arm around the shoulders of her two charges. "I just know the minute I pick up a mallet, I've already lost the battle."

"Which battle?" Iain chuckled and nodded toward his daughters as another round of pleading filled the air. "The game or their determination to have you join us?"

"*All right*, all right, I'll play." Madeline capitulated with laughter as the twins pulled her to the croquet set.

"The lassies already have their choice of battle weapons, so I'll allow you to choose your mallet before me."

Iain smiled at the impish way Madeline scowled and wrinkled her nose at him in mock irritation. Heaving a sigh of resigned amusement, she stared down at the remaining four mallets, then pulled one out of the box. The girls cried out with glee and led Madeline toward the starting point.

More than an hour and a half later, Iain murmured an oath as Madeline's ball sent his rolling off the playing field. The cheerful smile she sent in his direction made him glare at her with exasperation.

"I thought ye dinnae play this game verra well."

"I don't," she said, and her smile broadened to a grin at his frustration. "I've just been lucky."

"Lucky?" he muttered in annoyance. "Lucky is when I win a wager on a beast that is a longshot."

"Stop grumbling, and go get your ball," she laughed.

Still muttering to himself, Iain stalked away from her to where his ball had landed outside the boundaries. As he picked up the ball and carried it to the edge of the course, then watched Ainslie knocking her ball through the final arch and hitting the stake. His partner ran to his side with an encouraging smile.

"Ye only have the last arch to go through, *Faither*. Madeline cannae reach it before ye do."

Iain nodded at his daughter's confidence, as he watched Grace send her ball through the last arch and hit the stake. His palm wrapped around the head of the mallet, Iain pressed the top of the stick against the ground to lean on it slightly. For a long moment, he studied the course, debating where to send his ball with his next whack.

Suddenly, his gaze fell on Madeline's ball, which was lined up perfectly to go through the next to last-arch. Iain studied its placement for a long moment, debating whether he could knock it out-of-place while still lining his own ball up for the last arch. The sound of Madeline's laughter floated toward him.

"I think you're about to lose, my lord."

At her light-hearted gloating, Iain lifted his head to meet her gaze. With a mocking smile, he pointed his mallet toward her ball in a silent promise that he intended to knock her out of place. Beside him, Ainslie gasped, but remained silent as Madeline's eyes widened in disbelief.

"*Don't you dare,*" she protested with a note of pique in her voice.

Without replying, Iain lined himself up for the shot, and a moment later, a loud crack split the air as his mallet hit his ball. Straightening, he watched it roll speedily toward Madeline's ball and land with a gentle bump against hers. Ainslie released a shout of disbelief and admiration at the successful strike and enthusiastically hugged him.

Iain grinned down at his daughter, before he headed toward Madeline. Not saying a word, he adjusted his ball next to hers, placed his foot on it, then whacked it hard. A second later, Madeline's ball raced backward over the length of the course to land a few feet away from the starting point. Straightening, he grinned at her scowl, then took two steps forward to lean over her until his mouth brushed against her ear.

"Dinnae I tell ye yesterday never tae dare me, *mo bhòidhchead fuilt dorcha.*" Iain allowed himself to enjoy her sweet, soft scent for a second, before he straightened to grin down at her, chuckling as a rosy hue darkened her cheeks.

With a huff of air parting her full lips, she remained silent as she directed one last baleful glance in his direction before heading toward her ball. Iain laughed as she walked away from him. Whether or not she was lucky, the game was about to go to him and Ainslie.

A minute later, Iain sent his ball through the final arch where it hit the stake to win the game. Ainslie shouted in glee as she ran forward to hug him with jubilation. From where she stood at the next to the last arch on the course, Madeline shook her head and turned to Grace who was running toward her.

"I'm sorry sweetie, my luck ran out."

"We can beat them the next game."

"Oh, *that* won't be happening," she said with a laugh just as Iain and Ainslie reached where she was standing with Grace. With a rueful smile curving her lips, she looked at him, then Ainslie. "Congratulations, you two. You played a good game."

"Ye would nae have lost if *Faither* had nae been able tae *roquêt* your ball," his youngest daughter said in a sympathetic tone of voice.

"You're right," Madeline said as she directed an amused scowl in Iain's direction.

"Let's play again," Ainslie said with a grin, and Grace bobbed her head in enthusiastic agreement.

"Not me. I've had my fill for the day. I'm going to sit on the sidelines and watch." Madeline nodded toward the wrought-iron bench in front of one of the lawn's hedges that Iain had added to the grounds several years ago.

"I believe I will do the same," Iain said as he urged his daughters to play against each other.

Dejection clouded their features as the girls turned away from him, but in seconds they were taunting each other good-naturedly as to which one of them would win their game. Madeline was already seated on the bench, and she smiled at him as he sank down into the space beside her. Instantly, his muscles tightened at the effect her scent had on him. The soft fragrance of lavender and roses made her smell like a sunny spring day.

"You seem to have performed a miracle with my daughters."

"A miracle?" Madeline released a quiet sound of skeptical amusement, eyeing him as if he'd lost his mind. "*Right.*"

"Then explain the sudden change in Ainslie's behavior. She is much more subdued than she's ever been, and yet it's easy to see she's happy. As for Grace…" Iain shook his head. "She's a wise soul in a child's body, and yet you've taught her she doesn't have to act like an adult all the time."

"They simply needed a mother figure." Madeline turned her head to study him with curiosity. "Did you love your wife so much that you couldn't bear the thought of marrying again?"

The question made him jerk slightly as he glanced at her before returning his attention to his daughters. When he didn't reply immediately, he heard her draw in a soft breath of regret.

"I'm sorry. That's none of my business." Out of the corner of his eye, Iain saw the embarrassment on her face. Without looking away from his children, he cleared his throat.

"I'll never marry again," he said in a voice devoid of emotion. "I'll not put another woman's life in danger."

"I don't understand." Madeline turned toward him slightly. Iain turned his head in her direction.

"Flora died because I made her with child. She was nae capable of surviving the birth of our daughters." Iain dragged in a breath of pain as Thane's face flashed in front of him. "I already had one death on my hands when I lost my wife. I cannae put another life in danger."

"Another?" She barely paused before continuing. "You're not to blame for any of the things that went wrong with Flora or your first wife. Many women die in childbirth. It's sad, but true.

"I have only been married once." Iain shook his head as he remembered his father viciously blaming him for causing Thane's death.

"But you said—"

"I am responsible for my brother's death. Thane, died saving my life."

"Oh, Iain, I'm so sorry." Madeline's hand covered his in a gesture of sympathy. "He must have loved you very much to have given his life to save yours."

He didn't answer the silent question in her voice. The last thing he wanted was to remember all the times his father had said Thane was the one who should have lived, not Iain. Dragging in a deep breath into lungs empty of air, he watched Ainslie who was so much like Thane, despite bearing no physical resemblance to his brother.

Would his father have forgiven him if he'd lived long enough to see his granddaughter display the same qualities his brother had possessed? Bitterness swept through him. No, his father had never been a forgiving man.

The sudden warmth of Madeline's hand against his vanished as she drew away from him. Iain stared down at the hand she'd touched. It was no longer clutching his knee so tightly. Startled, he realized her soothing touch of comfort had eased some of his tension. The knowledge surprised him. Feeling her gaze still studying him, Iain turned toward her.

Madeline's curiosity was evident, but she'd obviously chosen not to question him about what had happened. With an eagerness that astonished him, he experienced the need to share what had happened that terrible day. It was a story he'd never told anyone, not even his father, because it would have sounded as if he was blaming his brother.

"My brother died helping me escape the sea cave." When she didn't appear surprised, he narrowed his gaze at her. With a small shrug, she nodded toward the girls working their way through the croquet course.

"Ainslie said she'd promised never to go near them. She'd told me it had something to do with her uncle, but she didn't tell me what." The reply made him jerk his head in acknowledgement.

"I've nae told her or Grace what happened, only that my brother died there. It's why the thought of Ainslie alone on the beach that day alarmed me so much. She is too much like Thane."

"I think any child being alone on the beach would be enough to scare anyone. I know how dangerous the water can be."

Fear flashed in her gaze as if she were remembering her own battle to survive the North Sea. He nodded and turned back to where he saw Ainslie laughing at her sister. Iain remembered similar moments where he'd feared for his brother, almost as much as he did for his youngest daughter.

"My brother was three years older than me, and there was nae anything he could nae do well. But swimming was his true gift. Even when Thane did something incredibly reckless, my father never hid how proud he was of my brother."

Iain paused for a moment as he remembered the day Thane swam out past the rocks at the opening of the inlet. He remembered standing on the edge of the rocks jutting out into the sea, shouting at Thane to come back. When his brother had finally turned around, he'd made it back to the beach safely, but had collapse onto the sand afterward.

It had taken a great deal of restraint for Iain not to pummel his brother for being so reckless. If there was one thing he did better than Thane, it was boxing. But he'd known his father would punish him, and not Thane, for fighting.

Worst of all, he'd idolized and admired his brother's boldness just as much as their father had. It was why he'd dismissed his brother's warning not to enter the sea cave that tragic afternoon. He closed his eyes for a moment before his gaze settled on Ainslie's tall figure. How much she reminded him of his brother. Iain glanced at Madeline who was patiently waiting for him to continue. He drew in another breath.

"But the day he died was different. Thane had told me the cave was dangerous. He said nae even he would go into the cave." Iain's throat closed as he remembered how he'd deliberately waited until the water was deep enough for him to swim into the cave rather than walk inside. "I dinnae believe him. I knew Thane was nae afraid of anything, and I thought he was simply trying to stop me from doing something he'd done."

"Did your brother see you swim into the cave?"

"Aye, Thane was on top of the outcrop of rocks, and shouted at me nae tae go in. I dinnae listen tae him. By the time I reached the deepest part of the cavern, I knew I'd made a mistake and had misjudged the timing of the tide." The knot swelling in his throat threatened his source of air just as the sea had done that dark day.

"You must have been terrified," Madeline whispered. Iain jerked his head in silent confirmation.

"The deepest part of the cave has a wide ledge ye can stand on. I had tae jump across a riptide pool tae reach it. I thought I could jump back, but I was wrong."

The memory of how he'd slipped on the wet stone as he'd leapt across the pool to reach the ledge sent a chill sliding through Iain. Almost falling into the riptide pool had been a horrifying experience. It was the primary reason he was to blame for Thane's death. He'd been too scared to jump back across the dangerous section of water. Unable to move, he'd simply stood frozen on the ledge. It was a visceral image that made a layer of ice form over his skin, and Iain clenched his jaw at the cold sensation holding him in its grip.

"By the time Thane reached me, I was in a state of panic. It took my brother several minutes tae convince me tae climb along the cavern wall tae reach the other side. By the time I reached my brother, the water was rising quickly. Thane told me there was enough air for us tae make it almost tae the entrance of the cave without having tae swim underwater, but he was wrong."

Iain dragged in a deep breath of air as he remembered trying to swim those last few feet out of the cave. A warm, feminine hand covered his again, and he shuddered at Madeline's touch. His father had been right to blame him for Thane's death. If he'd not gone into the cave, his brother would still be alive.

Madeline sat silently with her hand covering his as he remembered those terrifying moments swimming down the cavern's dark passageway. Not even the airholes the sea had carved out of the cave's ceiling, some almost as large as his fists, had offered any hope of air.

The sea didn't just rise inside the cave when the tide came it. It sent waves crashing over the top of the cavern itself to fill the holes with hard streams of water. Dragging in another deep breath, Iain stared straight in front of him, only seeing the darkness and the water.

"Thane made me go first because he could hold his breath longer than I could. He was right behind me, encouraging me nae tae stop until the moment the cave was completely filled with water. I only had tae swim a short distance tae reach the surface, and I was jubilant when I saw the top of Thane's head. But when I saw him floating face down in the water, I realized the worst had happened."

Iain bowed his head as guilt and sorrow became an invisible vise tightening around his chest until it felt as if a heavy stone was resting on his chest. Madeline didn't speak, she simply squeezed his hand again in a comforting manner. After several long moments, her soft voice drifted through the air.

"You were a child, Iain. We all make stupid mistakes and choices when we're children." The gentle note in the words made him shudder.

"A child who knew the cave was dangerous, but all I wanted tae do was show my brother that I was nae afraid tae be as daring as him."

Madeline didn't reply, she simply sat with her hand covering his in mute understanding. The sudden, sharp pain splitting through his head made him grimace. A moment later, the sound of the girls running toward him, made Madeline jerk away from him, and in seconds, the twins were standing breathlessly in front of them.

"*Faither*, are ye all right?" Ainslie's voice was filled with concern as she lowered her head to peer at his features.

"Do ye have another migraine, *Faither*?" Grace touched his shoulder, her voice echoing her sister's worry. Iain tried to shake his head. The action made him clench his jaw tight.

"It's only a slight headache, lass," he murmured. The response caused another jolt of pain to lash its way through his head. Beside him, Madeline must have seen his grimace of discomfort. She uttered a noise of annoyance and sprang to her feet.

"Grace, go prepare one of your poultices and send Angus if you see him. Ainslie and I will help your father back to the house after I try to ease some of his pain."

The soft sound of Madeline's voice filled his ears as she dispensed her commands and circled the bench to stand behind him. Without hesitating, Grace dropped her mallet to run toward the manor. Behind him, Madeline's fingers applied pressure to the spot above the bridge of his nose. There was a modicum of relief, and after a minute, her fingers pressed into the side of his temples.

A small hand gently turned his over as Madeline quietly directed Ainslie where to press her thumb into Iain's wrist. After a moment, his hand reached up to wrap his fingers around Madeline's wrist.

"I feel better," Iain croaked, the throbbing in his head having eased significantly. At his hoarse words, Madeline circled the bench to cup his elbow and urged him to stand. He waved her away with irritation. "I dinnae need any help walking back to the house."

"Did you win first prize for being the most stubborn damn Scotsman in the country, Lord Glenburnie? *Stop* being an ass, and let us help you back to the house." Madeline's quiet words didn't mask her fiery anger. Ainslie gasped and stared wide-eyed at her governess. The sound made Madeline jerk her head in his daughter's direction. "And don't think I'll tolerate you talking like that young lady."

At her stern warning, Ainslie bobbed her head in understanding. Madeline's fingers gently, but firmly, pressed into his arm as she cupped his elbow and encouraged him to stand. Giving way to her resolute manner, Iain's mouth twisted in a smile that was really little more than a grimace.

"I was nae wrong tae say ye must have Scottish blood in ye, Madeline Whitworth."

"Oh shut up," she muttered, her reply pulling another sound of amazement from his youngest. Madeline shot his daughter a warning look as she bobbed her head. "Ainslie, help me get your father back to the house."

Madeline wrapped her arm about his waist, and his daughter did the same as the two of them walked him toward the manor. His headache continued to abate, and his awareness of the woman at his side sent a rush of pleasure through him. It was the first time his headaches had ever offered him a benefit.

For a third time today, he breathed in Madeline's soft, feminine scent. If he'd not been feeling so uncomfortable, and they'd been alone, he would have pulled her into his arms and tasted her and most likely much more. The muscles in his jaw clenched. Clearly, the woman was even more of a problem for him than he'd thought yesterday.

Chapter 11

The morning sunshine warmed Madeline's shoulders as she sat on one of the benches behind the manor watching Ainslie working with Angus as they trained one of the two young colts Iain had bought while in Aberdeen more than two weeks ago. Madeline's gaze dropped to the thin book of nursing Iain had bought for her while in Aberdeen. He had presented the small volume to her at breakfast the morning after their croquet game. Heat immediately filled her cheeks as she remembered the events of that morning.

Without thinking, Madeline had accepted the gift with excitement, while impulsively kissing Iain's cheek and thanking him profusely. Eager to peruse the book, she'd immediately sunk down into her chair and opened it. Several seconds later, Madeline realized the girls, with the exception of their soft giggling, were more quiet than normal.

Puzzled by their unusual silence, she raised her head, and barely suppressed an audible groan of embarrassment. Fire burned her cheeks as she saw the sly speculation in the eyes of her students as they continued to giggle, while their gazes darted between her and Iain.

If possible, her cheeks became hotter, as her gaze darted to Iain. The sinful smile curving his beautiful mouth made Madeline's heart suddenly pound wildly in her chest. Something wicked flashed in his gaze and sent a frisson skimming over her skin. In that instant, she'd known that if they'd been alone, she would have been in his arms with that sexy voice of his arousing a host of emotions inside her.

Quickly jerking her gaze away from him, Madeline returned her attention to Iain's daughters, her cheeks still burning with humiliation. Unwilling for the girls to get the wrong idea, she'd swallowed hard as she struggled to come up with a reasonable explanation for her reaction to Iain's gift.

"Where I…I come from…it's…we…we often thank someone with a kiss on the cheek."

"Then I will remember to buy another book for you when I go to Aberdeen in a few weeks," Iain said with a grin as he winked at his daughters before ordering the girls to continue eating. Mortified, Madeline managed to finish her meal quickly without shoveling food into her mouth. In minutes, she was on her feet.

"If you'll excuse me, I have a few things to do in the classroom. Girls, I'll see you when you're done with breakfast." She wasn't about to add to her humiliation by saying anything to Iain, so she simply nodded her head in his direction and turned to flee.

"Before you go, Madeline," his voice was a quiet command for her to stop where she was, and she obeyed without even thinking twice.

Slowly, she turned to face him. Eyebrows arched as if silently asking her what the hurry was, Madeline clutched the book he'd given her tight against her chest. The girls lifted their heads to watch the small exchange.

"Yes?" Madeline breathed a small sigh of relief at how steady her voice sounded.

"I forgot to mention yesterday that I have a friend and his wife coming to Muchalls Hall next week for several days." Iain laid his napkin beside his plate. "I was hoping you would be kind enough to keep Lady Starling company while Sebastian and I visit several different properties in the area."

Startled, Madeline stared at him for a long moment. First, he'd wrangled her into being a governess. Now he wanted her to play hostess. What was he going to ask her to do next? The sudden image of his mouth kissing every inch of her filled her head. It was enough to ignite invisible flames that engulfed her in a fiery heat. She swallowed hard.

"That might be a little…awkward," she choked out. The moment she tried to say no without actually refusing his request, Iain reclined back in his chair, the fingers of one hand drumming softly on the arm of the table chair.

"Girls, you may be excused. Madeline will join you in the schoolroom shortly."

"But—" Ainslie immediately stopped speaking as her father eyed her sternly.

Without another word, the two girls rose from the table and headed toward the doorway leading into the hall. Grace smiled cheerfully at Madeline, while Ainslie frowned with disappointment at being sent out of the room. Madeline winced at the girl's expression, and she patted Ainslie on the shoulder as the girl paused next to her.

"I'll be there in a few minutes."

"Do nae let him bully ye, Madeline."

Ainslie's words were so soft, Madeline almost didn't hear the warning. Although she had no need of the child's cautionary words, she nodded her understanding. Iain cleared his throat, and the child glanced over her shoulder at her father. With a gentle squeeze of Madeline's hand, Ainslie hurried from the room. Iain rose from his seat and walked toward her.

"In my study, if you please."

The words were polite, even pleasant sounding, but Madeline heard the inflexible steel running underneath. Before she could protest, Iain had ushered her out of the dining room, down the hall, and into his office. As the door closed behind him, she jerked her arm out of his grasp, then put several feet between them before turning to glare at him.

"Okay, I went along with the governess bit because I knew I needed to pay my way, and I was grateful for a roof over my head. But I don't think entertaining your guests falls under the work you're paying me for, does it?" Madeline scowled at him for arrogantly assuming she would just fall into line with his dictates. "I'm not your—"

Madeline stopped herself just before she landed herself in a bed of hot coals. The last thing she wanted was to make the man think she was interested in climbing into his bed. Loud laughter resounded in the back of her head as she lied to herself. Iain's eyebrows rose, and he studied her intently for a long moment.

When he suddenly moved forward, Madeline stiffened with a wild mix of trepidation, anticipation, and excitement. She wanted to groan at the way her body reacted as each step he took brought him closer and closer. Damn it, her mouth had landed her in trouble again. The voice in her head whispered it was a good kind of trouble. She immediately pushed the suggestion deep into the back of her mind.

Madeline tried to look away from Iain, but she was all too aware that at home it would be labeled a big hashtag fail. A knot formed in her throat, and her mouth went dry at the wicked glint in his eye. Oh God, she was definitely in trouble if he even hinted at demanding a kiss.

"What were you about to say, Madeline?"

Iain reached out to brush a lock of hair off her forehead then slid his hand through her short wavy locks. The sensation of his fingers slowly moving across her scalp made it feel more like a caress. It made her stomach flutter, and she swallowed hard, trying to breathe normally. She didn't succeed as he arched his eyebrow at her, silently demanding she answer him.

"I was going to say I'm not your… I'm not responsible for acting as your hostess." She stumbled over her words, as she tried to come up with anything that didn't come close to the word wife.

"Hostess?" Iain's mouth twitched with amusement as he bent his head. Laughter echoed in his soft voice as his lips brushed across her ear. "I dinnae think that was what ye were about to say, *mo bhòidhchead fuilt dorcha.*"

"If you're suggesting that I act as mistress of the house, forget it." She jerked her head backward to glare up at him.

"Mistress of the house?" Warm fingers stroked her cheek until they cupped her chin. "An intriguing idea, *mo leannan.* Perhaps that's a role we should consider."

"That's not what I meant." Christ, she was the biggest liar in the world. She might not have meant to use the word, but that didn't mean she'd not been thinking it deep in the back of her mind. The laughter in Iain's dark blue gaze said he would have agreed with her.

"Are ye saying ye dinnae like the idea of warming my bed?"

"I…you…it isn't…"

God, how did one dodge a question like that? Silence. That's how. With a sharp shake of her head, she kept her mouth shut knowing it was the safest option. Anything else she said was bound to lead to places her body wanted to go, but it was a path riddled with pitfalls. The instant his mouth brushed against the corner of hers, she gulped back a small squeak of protest.

"I'm waiting Madeline. Will ye nae answer my question?" The soft rumble of his voice whispered across her skin like a hot, desert breeze.

Iain's lips seared the opposite corner of her mouth, and she barely suppressed a moan. Heat streaked through her blood at the burr in his voice and from the fire his light, tantalizing kisses ignited inside her. Unable to speak coherently, Madeline remained silent, certain that the moment she opened her mouth she'd stammer and trip over every word she tried to say.

Even worse was the possibility she'd say something that would dig a deeper hole than the one she was already in. He lifted his head slightly to stare down at her. In seconds, she was lost in the stormy dark blue eyes that danced with laughter and something that declared she was treading in dangerous waters.

"I would nae object if ye said yes, *mo leannan*. I cannae deny that the thought has nae crossed my mind more than once since the morning we first met in the upstairs hall."

The softly spoken words were a seductive, invisible caress across her skin, and it unleashed a heady exhilaration inside her. Madeline bit down on her bottom lip, struggling not to press her body into his and kiss him. Iain's eyes darkened as if he could read her thoughts. Was that what he wanted? Did he want her to take the initiative?

Suddenly throwing caution to the wind, her hand wrapped around the nape of his neck, and she pulled his head down to kiss him. The instant her lips met his, he stiffened. Regret immediately spiraled through her. Embarrassed by her impulsive act, she started to pull away from him, but was forestalled in the next instant when Iain's arms gathered her close and tight against him.

In a split second, the warm scent of him engulfed her senses, and the hard arms embracing her would have been impossible to escape, even if she'd wanted to. Her heartbeat thundered in her ears, and as his tongue slipped into her mouth, his fingers trailed from the base of her throat down to where the valley of her breasts was covered by her bodice. A growl of something dark and dangerous echoed out of him as he plundered her mouth. The hot caress blinded her to everything but him, and a small tremor pulsed through her. With a suddenness that startled her, Iain lifted his head then pressed his forehead against hers. Madeline murmured a quiet protest.

"I'll nae take ye here like this, *mo leannan*. I want tae take my time caressing every inch of ye with my hands and mouth."

The words sent a frisson racing down her back, and Madeline drew in a sharp breath at the thought of his mouth searing her skin. The hoarse note in his voice emphasized the desire she saw in his eyes as he pulled away from her slightly but didn't release her. Fire blazed in his dark eyes, and she reached up to touch his cheek. Immediately his hand caught hers, and he pressed his mouth against her wrist. She wanted to melt back into his arms.

"As much as... I'm not sure it's a good idea," she choked out and shook her head in a silent rejection of what she knew they both wanted.

"Aye, it is probably nae a good idea, but I cannae deny it's proving difficult for me tae keep my distance from ye, Madeline."

A tremor shook its way through her at the way her name rolled off his tongue in that rich, tantalizing voice of his. Another shiver streaked through her as his fingers brushed across her mouth. God, the way he was looking at her had her ready to ask him what time tonight and where.

Never in her life had she ever ached for a man's touch as much as she did Iain's. Just the thought of his hands and mouth gliding across her skin was enough to send her heart racing out of control. Desperately she tried to shove the image out of her mind. It was dangerous to involve herself any deeper than she already was. A voice snorted in the back of her head. Deeper than she already was? She was in over her head where Iain Fraser, Baron Glenburnie was concerned.

The tendril of a revelation drifted up into her conscious mind before she frantically pushed it back in fear. Admitting the truth and uncertainty of her current situation was difficult enough. If she allowed herself to believe what her heart was telling her, there would be no going back. Worse, it would mean certain heartbreak if she were suddenly thrown back to her own time.

Madeline's heart twisted viciously in her chest. It was already breaking. Iain had made it clear he would never marry again, but she was certain it wasn't marriage he feared. He was afraid of loving someone and losing them. The realization made her heart clench even more painfully.

Iain slowly released her and took a step back. The instant the warmth of him disappeared, her body cried out a loud protest. He cleared his throat and clasped his hands behind his back.

"This all began with you thinking I expected ye tae entertain my friends. It was nae my expectation that ye play hostess, Madeline. I simply thought ye might enjoy Lady Starling's company, while ensuring she isn't bored during her stay."

"Fine. I'll do what I can to make the woman feel welcome." At her belligerent response, Iain eyed her with amusement.

"I think you will like her. Anna has as strong a will as another lass I know." Madeline ignored the teasing laughter in his voice, desperate to escape before she did or said something stupid.

"Will there be anything else?" At her quiet question, Iain frowned in puzzlement.

"If you truly dinnae wish—"

"I agreed to entertain the woman," she snapped. "So, unless you have other duties you feel compelled to throw at me, the girls are waiting for me in the schoolroom."

Iain remained silent as he stared at her in bewilderment. The moment his confusion abated, his gaze suddenly narrowed at her. The astute assessment growing in his eyes made her realize she needed to run before he acted on his suspicions. With a quick bob of her head, Madeline spun around on her heel and hurried out of the room without a backward glance.

The memory of that day in Iain's study more than a week ago was interrupted by the sound of Lady Starling's voice behind Madeline. Closing her book, she rose to her feet and turned toward the viscountess. Iain had introduced her to the woman and her husband, late yesterday evening. Unlike last night, Lady Starling wasn't holding her infant daughter as she closed the last couple of yards between them.

"Good morning, Miss Whitworth," the viscountess said cheerfully as she came to a halt next to Madeline while studying the paddock and surrounding area for a moment. When she turned back to Madeline, Lady Starling smiled. "Today is the first day I've seen the sun since we arrived in Scotland two weeks ago. How on earth do the Scots survive the gray skies, I wonder."

"I don't really know. This is only the fifth or sixth day of sunshine I've seen since I arrived at Muchalls Hall." Madeline laughed.

Yesterday evening when the couple had arrived, she'd been relieved to find the woman had a pleasant, down-to-earth manner. It made Madeline believe the couple's stay would not be filled with awkward conversations. Lady Starling gestured toward the bench where Madeline had been sitting.

"May I join you?"

"Of course," Madeline nodded then sank back down onto the wrought-iron bench as the other woman sat next to her.

"What are you reading?" The viscountess tipped her head to one side to read the title of the book.

"A book on nursing. Lord Glenburnie found it while he was in Aberdeen last week."

"How interesting." Lady Starling eyed Madeline with an inquisitive gleam in her dark brown eyes. "Are you hoping to become a nurse?"

"I already am." Madeline glanced down at the book, which to her, read more like a first aid manual than an academic book.

"You are? Now I truly *am* intrigued." The viscountess laughed. "Sebastian told me you're from America. Is that where you learned how to be a nurse?"

"Yes. I went to school in St. Paul, Minnesota."

"I would love to travel to America, but it's not possible right now. Jane is still too young. In fact, Sebastian wanted to leave the two of us behind in London, but I wouldn't have it.

I don't like being apart from my husband for any great length of time."

"Have you been married long?"

"Our first anniversary is next week, and I never thought I could be this happy. Not even living on the Falcon did I ever feel this way."

"The Falcon?"

"My uncle's merchant ship. I had a rather unusual upbringing. I lived with my Uncle Charles on the Falcon after my mother died. I fell in love with the sea, and it wasn't until I met Sebastian that I could even bear the thought of living anywhere else." Lady Starling smiled.

"I can't imagine living on a ship. Actually, I don't think I'll ever be able to get on another boat again. *Ever*," Madeline said with a vigorous shake of her head. Her reply made Lady Starling's expression grow somber.

"Sebastian said you were in a shipwreck, and that Iain saved you from drowning."

Curiosity gleamed in the woman's gaze as she studied Madeline. The viscountess was clearly hoping to hear details of the event. Madeline nibbled at her lip slightly and looked away from the woman.

"He did. I don't remember much about what happened that night, but I've been told he placed himself in harm's way to rescue me."

"I've no doubt of that. Iain is a good man. I also know first-hand how dangerous the North Sea can be. Although I've never had to swim for my life as you apparently did." The woman studied her with a look of admiration. "Iain told Sebastian that if you'd not been a strong swimmer, you most likely would not have survived."

"Yes, I probably wouldn't be—" Madeline came to an abrupt halt as the memories pushed hard to escape the dark recesses of her mind where she'd buried them. Lady Starling made a small sound of regret.

"Forgive me. I'm certain it must have been a traumatic experience."

"You'll get no argument from me with that statement." Madeline nodded.

In an empathic gesture, Lady Starling reached out and gently squeezed Madeline's hand. Almost immediately, the woman stiffened. At the viscountess's reaction, her heart skipped a beat at the glazed expression on the other woman's face.

"Lady Starling, are you all right?"

Madeline's concern grew when the woman didn't respond. Hoping she would see Iain standing outside with Lord Starling, Madeline glanced over her shoulder toward the manor. Not spying either man, she jerked her head toward the paddock. Angus and Ainslie had disappeared, and Madeline debated whether she should run for help, but she didn't want to leave the other woman alone. Suddenly, Lady Starling drew in a sharp breath of air and she stared at Madeline in wide-eyed amazement and horror.

"Dear Lord," the woman whispered. "You're from a different place and time."

The woman's revelation made Madeline go rigid. How could the woman possibly know that? She shook her head and tried to act puzzled by the viscountess's observation. The dismay on Lady Starling's face made Madeline's stomach lurch. God, how could the woman know she was from the future? When she remained silent, the viscountess sighed and shook her head with regret.

"Madeline. May I call you Madeline?"

The woman waited for her response with a hesitant, yet hopeful expression. After a brief moment, Madeline responded with a slow nod. Relief lightened Lady Starling's sweet features as she released a sigh of what sounded like genuine relief. It also possessed a note of fear and regret.

"Then you must call me Anna. It's what my friends and family call me, and I'd like very much for us to be friends. Having a friend can make life easier to face at times." There was an earnestness about the woman's manner, which made Madeline relax slightly.

"All right." Her voice was little more than a whisper, and it caused a small smile to tip the corners of the other woman's mouth upward.

"No, that's not the correct answer." Lady Starling shook her head, her reply a gentle chastisement. "You're supposed to say, yes, *Anna.*"

"*Yes*, Anna." Her voice more energetic this time, Madeline found it impossible not to smile at the satisfaction that settled on the viscountess's face.

"That's a start, but we definitely need to work on your enthusiasm." Anna's disgruntled tone and expression of disappointment made Madeline laugh.

"Yes, Anna," Madeline said firmly and with quiet amusement. "Is that more to your liking?"

"Oh, that's much better." Anna's satisfied expression faded and became somber. "Now then, I need to explain my reaction a moment ago."

The viscountess nibbled on her bottom lip as she looked back toward the manor. Hesitation reflected in her eyes as she turned back to Madeline, then the other woman shrugged slightly.

"Sebastian will *not* be happy with me when he learns what I've done." Anna leaned forward the moment Madeline jerked in dismay and squeezed her hand reassuringly again. "You have nothing to fear. Even if Sebastian didn't love me as much as he does, he would still not betray my secret. The idea of scandal is abhorrent to my dark angel, and my ability would most *definitely* cause a scandal."

Madeline's level of fear dropped significantly at the viscountess's reassurance. For some unknown reason, she trusted the woman. There was something about the viscountess's manner that said she was someone who would never betray a friend. When she remained silent, Anna drew in a deep breath as if steeling herself for something unpleasant.

"As mad as it might sound, I have the ability to see things others can't." The soft words made Madeline jerk slightly as she met the other woman's gaze.

"You can see the future?" Madeline's quiet question made Anna eye her with surprise. With a shrug, a slight smile tugged at Madeline's mouth. "Where I'm from, there are some psychics who are quite popular."

"I'm not actually a psychic, though," Anna said with a small shake of her head. "I don't communicate with the dead. I simply have visions or a sense of knowing. Like I just did with you."

"Something that made you believe I was from the future?" The question made Anna nod then look away from Madeline. As she studied the viscountess's profile, she saw a look of dismay on the woman's face.

"Normally, Sebastian is nearby and all I have to do is look at him, and he knows to come lend me his support..." Anna swallowed hard then looked back at Madeline. "I was so startled, I spoke without thinking."

With a nod of understanding, Madeline turned her head toward the empty paddock. Uncertain what to say in response to Anna's revelation, she stared sightlessly at the fence that enclosed the large area of grass. Beside her, Anna remained silent for a long moment before she touched Madeline's hand.

"You know you cannot go back, don't you?" Anna's quiet words made Madeline turn toward the viscountess in stunned astonishment. At her reaction, the viscountess swallowed hard. "I thought you...I thought you understood."

"Understood what?" Madeline fought to suppress the tide of fear threatening to overtake her senses. "How do you know...*why* can't I go back to my own time?"

"Because..." An uneasy emotion darkened Anna's face, and the viscountess was clearly struggling with her words as she caught Madeline's hands in hers. "There's only one of you, Madeline, and you're here...at Muchalls Hall."

"But that doesn't tell me why you think I can't go home."

"Because you're…you're no longer present in the future, Madeline."

The look of deep dismay on Anna's face sent a jolt of panic driving its way into the very heart of Madeline as she met the viscountess's steady gaze. Something in the woman's eyes caused a layer of ice to coat her skin. Madeline shivered at the freezing cold pushing its way through her skin down into her bones until her body was stiff and frozen.

"Madeline, I wish—"

"Are you saying I drowned in my time?" she whispered in horror as the truth closed in on her.

Panic wrapped a powerful vise around her chest making it difficult to breathe properly. The night Grace had tended to the cuts on her feet after Madeline's mad dash down to the inlet without shoes, the young girl had told her the same thing. Denial had made her ignore the child's words.

It had been easy to dismiss Grace's reassurances that Madeline hadn't drowned, but had come to Muchalls Hall instead. But in the back of her head, she'd always understood what Grace had meant. Somehow, the girl knew Madeline had drowned in her own time, while landing in the past.

The horror of those moments after the Destiny's Dream capsized, rushed toward her like a wall of water. Something hard hit the back of her head, and she gasped in pain at the tangible sensation. It was the last breath she took as sea water filled her nose and mouth. Desperately, she fought for air, but there was none to be found.

Fear spun its way through her limbs as she struggled to find her way up to the surface, but there was no air left in her lungs as she slipped into a black void. A split-second later, she was in the small pocket of air beneath what she'd thought had been the sailboat.

As the terrible truth continued to press in on her, she heard her grandmother's voice again urging her to swim upward and that *he* would be there. With each breath she took, a new memory rose to confront her with the reality of what had happened. She remembered leaving the pocket of air under the boat to swim desperately upward.

The sea had fought hard to keep her from reaching the surface, and the icy water had only intensified the pain in her badly cramping legs and arms. Every muscle in her body had been in painful revolt against the commands her brain was issuing as she'd struggled to remain above the water. She'd been little more than a plaything for the sea to toss about, uncaring whether she lived or died.

It was then she'd seen Iain clinging to the rocks calling out to her. She'd been exhausted as she'd struggled to reach him. Part of her had simply wanted to give up and allow the water to take her. But something about Iain's shouts of encouragement had forced her to fight the relentless, icy waves tugging at her cold, pain-wracked limbs.

A tremor rippled through her at the memory of being tugged into Iain's hard, muscular chest. His strong arm wrapped tightly around her waist, his voice had soothed and reassured her. For the first time, she remembered the rough burr in his voice as his words 'ye did it, me brave lass' resounded in her ear while she had shuddered against him. Even as terrified as she'd been, his voice had calmed her as she'd clung to him, while the water had tried to smash them against the rock face.

All this time, Madeline had convinced herself the wreckage, sea, and a strange twist of fate had pushed her up into the dark oasis of air beneath the Destiny's Dream. She'd silently told herself that her involuntary reflexes had sent air rushing into her lungs the moment there was air for her to breathe. But she'd been wrong. She hadn't survived the sinking of the Destiny's Dream.

"*Madeline.*" The panic in Anna's voice sounded as if she were far away. "Madeline. Talk to me."

Sluggishly, Madeline's gaze focused on the viscountess as the memories receded, and she realized Anna was shaking her gently. Madeline raised a hand to her temple, and Anna exhaled a deep breath of relief.

"*Thank God.*" The woman exclaimed as she studied Madeline with an expression of deep concern on her pale features. "Are you all right?"

"Yes." Madeline's hand shook as she brushed her hair off her brow. "I…it just all came rushing back. I wasn't prepared for it."

"Prepared for me, you mean." Anna's voice was soft and contrite as she touched Madeline's arm. "I'm so terribly sorry for upsetting you. I shouldn't have said anything after my first *faux pas.*"

"Please don't blame yourself," she said quietly as she offered Anna a wan smile. "I think I've known the truth since the night Grace said something about what had happened. I just wasn't willing to consider the possibility."

"Iain's daughter said something to you?"

"Yes. Naturally, I didn't believe Iain when he said it was 1896. So, I ran barefoot down to the inlet to see the ship on the rocks up close. Running over sharp rocks without shoes wasn't one of my brightest moments."

Madeline's mouth twisted in a wry grimace as she swung her gaze away from the other woman to look out at the landscape beyond the paddock. When the line that split the land from the sky came into focus, Madeline shivered as her mind showed her an image of the inlet and the shipwreck on the rocks. Still staring out at the expanse of sea and sky, Madeline swallowed the panic that hovered in the back of her throat.

"Grace took care of me after Iain brought me back to the house. She said I hadn't died, that I'd come to Muchalls Hall instead. Iain told me a few days ago that Grace has the gift of sight. After what you've told me, her words make sense now. But even that night, I knew deep down what she meant. I just dismissed her words, because I wasn't willing to admit the truth."

"And now?" The quiet question made Madeline turn back to Anna.

"Now? If I was at home, I'd be asking for drugs to stop the hallucinations." Madeline inhaled a deep breath then released it slowly to calm the churning in her stomach. "If my grandmother was here, she'd simply be saying I told you so."

"I told you so?" The puzzlement in Anna's quizzical expression made Madeline smile ruefully.

"Ever since I was a child, I had dreams about a man standing on a cliff, and a ship trying to survive a terrible storm. My grandmother was a firm believer in past lives, and she was convinced my dreams were about another existence."

"And the man?" Anna tipped her head to one side to study Madeline with curiosity. "Was it Iain?"

"I never saw his face clearly, but just before the sailboat I was on capsized in my time, I saw someone on the cliffs overlooking the same inlet I'd dreamed about my entire life."

"Was it the man from your dreams?"

"I don't know. I know it sounds crazy, but before she died, my grandmother told me not to be afraid to let go. He'll be there, she said. I always thought it was simply her believing in past lives and such."

Madeline closed her eyes as she remembered hearing her grandmother's voice in the dark pocket of air when she'd been in the icy sea. She dragged in a deep breath.

"But when I found myself in that pocket of air after the boat flipped over, I heard my grandmother telling me to let go, that he'd be there to catch me."

"Heard her?" Curiosity lit up Anna's expression.

"Yes. It was as if she were right next to me in the water. She just kept saying, don't be afraid, Maddie. Let go. He'll be there." Madeline shrugged slightly as a small smile touched her lips. "So I listened to her."

"And here you are," Anna said with a gentle smile. "I'm terribly glad you listened to your grandmother."

"I'm still not sure I actually heard her or if it was—"

"*Never* doubt what you heard, Madeline." The viscountess reached out to squeeze Madeline's hand. "There are things in this universe that no one completely understands—things that cannot be explained. Your grandmother reached out to you because you were meant to live."

"Well, it would have been a lot less terrifying if she'd just told me not to get on the Destiny's Dream." She smiled ironically at Lady Starling. "But I'm still alive, and that's a positive outcome, even if I'm more than a hundred years in the past."

"Of course, it is," Anna exclaimed before an odd expression of assessment crossed her face. "Personally, I think you're *exactly* where you're meant to be."

"I'm not sure I'd go that far," Madeline snorted her disagreement. "I'm a nurse, working as a governess. Correction, I'm *pretending* to be a governess, and if this book is anything to go by, the forecast is pretty bleak when it comes to my nursing career."

Madeline held up the book Iain had given her before she dropped it back into her lap. Anna uttered a soft exclamation of dissension.

"Don't be a chowderhead. Things could always be worse." Anna pressed her hand against her chest. "What if you'd not come out of that catatonic state you were in a moment ago? *Poseidon's balls*, I would have needed to call for help, and Sebastian would have been *much* more than just unhappy with me. It would have been a *fucking* mess."

Madeline's eyes widened, while her brain replayed the woman's words. She shook her head slightly thinking she must have heard wrong. She was willing to bet money she didn't have, that women in 1896 didn't use the kind of foul language Anna just had. A grimace flitted across the other woman's face as her cheeks flamed bright red.

"*Christ*, Sebastian is right I don't know how to control my bloody tongue." The self-recrimination in Anna's words made Madeline snort with laughter.

"I'm the last one you need to apologize to. Fuck happens to be one of my favorite words. People who find it offensive, use words I find offensive."

Anna blinked in astonishment, and Madeline laughed again. Wide-eyed and mouth parted in mute shock, the viscountess shook her head in amazement. Another laugh passed Madeline's lips. Immediately, Anna's dazed look of surprise vanished as laughter sparkled in her brown eyes. In the next breath, the viscountess burst out laughing as well.

Every time their laughter subsided, the two only had to look at each other and start laughing again. They must have been laughing for five minutes straight when the sound of male voices echoed behind them. Their laughter slowly dying, Madeline and Anna looked over their shoulders to see Iain and Lord Starling headed in their direction. Madeline leaned toward her new friend.

"*Poseidon's balls*, what are we supposed to tell them we're laughing about?" The moment she whispered the question, Anna burst out into laughter.

"I don't…think we…can."

Holding her side as if in pain from laughing so hard, Anna shook her head. They were still laughing as Iain and the viscount came to a halt in front of them. As their laughter subsided, Madeline and Anna drew in deep breaths of air as Iain cleared his throat.

"Might Sebastian and I ask what the two of you find so amusing?"

The curiosity and amusement in Iain's voice matched the other man's expression as the viscount studied his wife. Anna and Madeline stared up at the men for a moment, before turning back to each other, which set off another round of laughter.

"It's obvious we will not be privy to whatever has thrown them into such a state of hysteria." At Lord Starling's dry reply, Anna narrowed her gaze at her husband.

"Are you suggesting your wife is hysterical, my lord?" His wife's pique caused the viscount to solemnly offer her an almost imperceptible bow.

"Forgive me, my lady. I believe I should have used the word passionate as I'm well-acquainted with how much you relish a healthy dose of laughter, among other things."

There was barely the hint of a pause before his last three words, but Madeline saw the man's mouth twitch slightly as if struggling not to laugh. Anna narrowed her gaze at her husband before she smiled lovingly at him.

"You are forgiven, my lord. Although, how I manage to put up with a fuh—" Anna stumbled slightly at the disapproval wrinkling her husband's forehead, before she smiled mischievously. "See, that frown of yours is exactly why I was about to call you a fuddy-duddy. You know good and well I possess all the patience and devotion every proper wife should have for her husband. A fact, I've proven repeatedly, *and* without complaint I might add."

The instant the viscount stiffened, Madeline knew Anna's circumspect reply referenced something only the two of them understood. The viscountess's arched eyebrow emphasized her amused satisfaction, and Madeline was certain her newfound friend had turned the tables on her husband.

Despite his obvious annoyance, something in his gaze said he adored his wife, and the sudden softening in Anna's eyes said the man's love was reciprocated. Envy sped through Madeline as she watched the silent exchange between the couple. How could she ever expect to find a love such as theirs in a time that wasn't her own?

What man would love her enough for her to trust him with her story. She would always have to guard her tongue. The memory of Iain saying he believed her drifted through her head. Without thinking, Madeline's gaze shifted to him and saw he was watching her intently. The emotion in his gaze was impossible to define, but it made her heart flutter in her breast.

In the next breath, the second truth she'd been denying since the day Iain had kissed her slammed into her with a force that would have driven her to her knees if she'd been standing. Oh God, she was in love with Iain Fraser. She flinched, and the moment her cheeks grew cold, Madeline knew the color had drained from her face. Iain's eyes immediately narrowed as his probing gaze met hers. It was obvious he was attempting to determine what was troubling her, and she quickly looked away.

Once more, the reality of her situation crashed down over her like one of the waves that had tried to push her into a watery grave. In the next breath, she remembered the sea had done just that in her own time. It took only that thought to make her queasiness return, and she quickly rose to her feet.

"If you'll excuse me, I'm satisfied Ainslie is completely absorbed with today's lessons. I should check in on Grace to ensure she's not having any problems." She forced a smile in the direction of the two men, then turned toward the other woman. "Thank you for…for an enlightening *and* irreverent conversation…Anna."

"A conversation I enjoyed as well." The viscountess's brown eyes were filled with a sudden concern as she caught Madeline's hands and gave them a small squeeze of understanding. "We shall see you at dinner?"

With a nod, Madeline turned and headed back toward the manor. As she walked away, she realized those few moments of laughter with Anna had only been a temporary reprieve from the emotions storming through her. The sudden urge to run away and hide spiraled through her, but she had nowhere and no one to run to.

The churning in her stomach hadn't eased by the time she entered the back door of the manor. For a moment, she debated going straight to her room. No, the minute Iain learned she hadn't spoken to Grace there would be questions. Uncertainty and dismay increased her nausea, but Madeline continued to make her way to the kitchen.

Madeline made a cursory review of what the girl had done, praised her efforts, then turned to leave the kitchen. Before she could flee upstairs, Grace blocked her way and eyed her carefully.

"Ye are nae well, Madeline."

"I'm just a little tired. I didn't sleep well last night," she lied as she tried to smile reassuringly at the child.

"I dinnae believe ye. Something is wrong." The fierce note of concern in the girl's voice made Madeline shake her head.

"I'm fine, Grace. I'm just a little tired." The lie was an understatement. She was completely drained. "In fact, I think I'll go take a short nap."

Madeline bent down and kissed the girl's forehead, then walked out of the kitchen and headed toward the stairs. Behind her, she heard Grace utter a sound of frustration, but she didn't acknowledge it. The turbulent emotions roiling inside her made her stumble slightly as she climbed the stairs. God help her. What was she going to do? She couldn't go back to her own time, and she'd fallen in love with a man who wouldn't allow himself to love again. It was a hopeless situation.

If she stayed, her heart would become even more entangled with Iain and his daughters than it already was. Simply as a protection for her own emotional well-being, she needed to find a way to make a life for herself away from Muchalls Hall.

Even if she hadn't fallen in love with the master of the house, there would come a time when the girls would no longer need a governess. Despite Iain's willingness to let her teach his daughters as she saw fit, she had a better chance of winning the lottery than finding another employer who wouldn't drop kick her the moment they realized she wasn't a real governess. The thought shot a bolt of fear through her.

Was it possible she could find employment working as a nurse? Surely there were doctors in London who could use a qualified nurse. Maybe it would be possible to open up a small practice of her own. Hopelessness cascaded over her. What the hell was she going to do to survive?

As she walked down the second-floor hallway, Madeline saw Bridget McFayden emerging from one of the guest rooms with a load of laundry in her arms. The woman smiled cheerfully at her and nodded as they passed each other. She'd gone only a few steps past the woman, when Madeline stopped and turned around.

"Mrs. McFayden, could I ask a favor of you, please?"

"Aye, what would ye be needing, Miss Whitworth." The Scotswoman faced her and eyed her with curiosity.

"I'd like to find a job as a nurse. It's what I was trained to do, and I think it's time for me to…to move on."

"I see," Mrs. McFayden nodded sagely as she narrowed her gaze at Madeline. "Are ye sure ye wish tae do so?"

"We both know I'm not what most people would call a governess, and the longer I stay, the more…I just need to do what I'm good at, which is nursing."

"Aye, ye are definitely nae what anyone would call a true governess, but I ken the wee bairns will nae be happy tae see ye go. They have come tae be quite fond of ye."

"Which is exactly why I need to go," Madeline said with renewed determination. "It's not healthy for them to become too attached to me."

"And his lordship? Does he ken how ye feel?" The question made Madeline stiffen. Dear God, were her feelings for Iain so transparent? Her mouth went dry as she met the woman's steady gaze.

"I've been trouble for Iain…Lord Glenburnie since he pulled me from the sea. I'm pretty sure he'll be happy to see the back of me. Relieved, in fact," she said with a forced laugh.

"Will he now?" the older woman asked softly.

The skepticism in the woman's voice was just enough to make Madeline wonder if the housekeeper thought Iain had feelings for her. She quickly dismissed the thought. It was wishful thinking to read something more into the woman's reply when it came to Iain. Madeline swallowed the knot that had formed in her throat and shook her head in silent rejection of Mrs. McFayden's words.

"Will you help me?"

"If ye are sure."

"I am," Madeline said with a nod. The housekeeper studied her for a moment in silence then bobbed her head.

"Verra well, I'll send Eileen up with paper and pen in a wee bit."

"Paper and pen?" Madeline shook her head in bewilderment.

"Aye, ye will need to write an advertisement telling others ye are seeking a position," Mrs. McFayden studied Madeline suspiciously.

"Oh, at home, the employer advertises in the paper and then I apply for the position." Her explanation made the Scotswoman raise her eyes to the heavens and release a disgusted sigh in obvious disapproval of foreigners.

"I'll send up the Scotsman and the Aberdeen Herald with Eileen so ye can see how others advertise their services."

"Thank you." Madeline nodded her understanding, and if possible, her heart seemed to sink even lower in her chest. It had become a physical ache, and she was fighting hard not to cry. As she turned away to continue to her room, the Scottish housekeeper made a quiet sound of concern.

"Ye dinnae look well, Miss Whitworth. Is there anything I can do for ye?"

As she'd done with first Iain and his friends, then Grace, and now Mrs. McFayden, Madeline forced a smile to her lips then glanced over her shoulder.

"No, thank you, Mrs. McFayden. I'm just tired. I didn't sleep well last night, and I thought I'd take a nap. Thank you again, for your help."

As she walked away from the woman, Madeline could sense the Scotswoman watching her, but she didn't look back. The moment she reached her room, she stood with her back pressed into the door's wood paneling and closed her eyes. She wasn't sure how, but she needed to find a way to hide her misery from the girls, and from Iain too.

Worse, she needed to prepare herself for the day when she left Muchalls Hall. She knew that day would come far too quickly, and it would be devastating for her. A tear pushed its way past a closed eyelid.

If she'd known before she boarded the Destiny's Dream her voyage would end in heartache, she would have walked the other way. But she hadn't, and here she was trapped in the past with no way to return. Exhausted physically and emotionally drained by the fear, uncertainty, and heartache weighing down on her, Madeline walked toward her bed. Within minutes of stretching out on the mattress, she was sound asleep.

Chapter 12

Iain laid down his fork then took a drink of wine from his goblet. Mrs. McFayden had outdone herself for the evening's meal in honor of his guests, including the roasted pheasant for dinner. There was only one thing missing. Madeline.

The moment her name whispered through his head, Iain's gaze immediately flew to the empty chair at the opposite end of the table. Before dinner had been announced, Eileen had informed him that Madeline wasn't feeling well and would not be joining them for dinner.

The news had immediately aroused his concern as he recalled Madeline's wan pallor earlier. Even despite her laughter, there had been a haunted air about her that had worried him. Sensing his concern, Grace had quietly told him that Madeline had looked ill when she'd returned to the house this afternoon. Like Iain, his oldest child had observed her teacher's distraught, lethargic manner. Madeline had reassured his daughter that she was simply tired, but Grace was certain her teacher had not been well at all.

Now, as Iain studied the empty chair opposite him, he realized how accustomed he was to seeing Madeline seated across from him at every meal. It was as if the light in the room always shone brighter when she was present. Iain knew the practice of one's governess taking meals with the family would be considered inappropriate in other households. Mrs.

McFayden had eyed him with distinct disapproval the first time he mentioned Madeline was to eat with the family.

In fact, even Angus had arched an eyebrow when he'd learned Madeline was taking her meals with him and his daughters. He'd waved off the couple's unasked questions by explaining Madeline was dining with the family to monitor his daughters' table etiquette. A loud snort of derisive laughter echoed in his mind, while another voice called him a liar.

"*Faither*, do ye have another headache?" Grace whispered as she leaned toward him. The question made him jerk his head to where his oldest sat next to him at his left.

"No, lass. What makes you ask me that?" The question caused the woman on his right to release a small laugh.

"Because you're scowling like the grumpiest of Scotsmen." The viscountess's comment reminded him of Madeline's observation the day after his return from Aberdeen.

"He's worried about Madeline," Ainslie said cheerfully as she eyed Iain with a sly grin. Not about to give his youngest any ammunition to use against him, he shook his head.

"Actually, I was thinking about the property Sebastian and I visited yesterday." He looked toward his friend who was studying him with a quiet assessment.

"So, you agree that the textile mill would be an excellent investment?"

"It will require a substantial amount of investment to make it safe for the workers, but I feel relatively confident the output will be doubled afterward. Workers who know their employer cares for their safety and well-being work harder than dissatisfied employees."

"I concur." Sebastian said with a nod of satisfaction. "The days of living off the rents of tenants is long gone. Our financial survival going forward means it's important we find ways to make Birchwood a working estate. The mill will expand the family holdings, while our livestock can supplement the wool we buy from farmers near the mill."

"I think it's a wise investment and business decision." Iain smiled at his friend.

"Just as it would be a wise move on your part to accept my offer." Sebastian grinned the moment Iain frowned.

"It's a fair offer, but I dinnae think I'm the right one for the job."

"Stop being such a stubborn, proud Scotsman. It's not an offer of charity. I proposed the idea because I want a man I trust overseeing the mill's foreperson."

"It seems a waste of finances," Iain said quietly.

"Not when I've seen what can happen when there *isn't* someone I trust overseeing one of my investments." Sebastian took a drink of wine before eyeing Iain over the rim of the glass with a determined look. "I've no intention of letting you say no, Iain."

"I said I would think about it." Iain bobbed his head slightly as he laid his napkin beside his plate.

"It sounds as if we are about to become regular visitors to Muchalls Hall, Iain. Are you sure you want that?" The laughter in Anna's voice made him smile.

"I think Madeline would enjoy that very much."

The moment he spoke, Anna raised her eyebrows slightly before looking at her husband. Iain wanted to groan at his response. What the devil had prompted him to mention Madeline, let alone suggest she was a permanent resident? All too aware of his daughters' wide-eyed gazes pinned on him, he bit down on the inside of his cheek at their looks of elation. What the devil had he been thinking? He hadn't. His cock had been doing that for him since the day Madeline had arrived. Iain met Anna's amused gaze.

"What I mean is that Madeline will be here for quite some time as Ainslie and Grace have benefited greatly from her rather unorthodox teaching style," Iain said as he took another drink of wine to wet his dry mouth. "I like that she is teaching my daughters how to think for themselves."

"I confess I enjoyed myself immensely in Madeline's company this afternoon." Anna smiled at him. "She sounds like a remarkable governess. I think I shall need to steal her away from you in a couple of years, when Jane is older."

"Nae, Grace and I will nae let *Faither* send her away."

"You must like her very much," Anna said with a soft smile at Ainslie.

"Aye. I wish she could—"

The moment Ainslie saw Iain's frown, she stopped speaking and quickly returned to eating again. Anna turned to look at him with amusement, and he gritted his teeth at the calculated gleam in the viscountess's brown eyes. Damnation, he could almost see the matchmaking wheels spinning in the woman's head. He had no intention of marrying again.

"Obviously, Madeline has made a very strong impression on your daughters."

"Aye, we like her verra much," Grace said in a voice that bordered on defiance as she glanced from Anna to her father. "We will nae let *Faither* send her away."

The sly smile on Lady Starling's lips as she darted another glance in Iain's direction made him look at Sebastian. At his silent plea for help, the viscount shook his head.

"I would rather face Gentleman Jim in the ring."

Sebastian ate the last bit of beef on his plate and eyed Iain with sympathy. The sound of rattling dishes echoed into the dining room, and Iain released a soundless breath of relief as Mrs. McFayden entered the room carrying dessert. Iain immediately relaxed as Ainslie and Grace exclaimed with delight at the cranachan and slices of Dundee cake on the tray. The last thing he needed was his children playing matchmaker.

His gaze met Anna's, and she lifted her goblet to her lips and eyed him with amusement over the rim of her glass. The sound of Sebastian clearing his throat made the viscountess turn her attention to the other man, and she smiled mischievously, but remained silent as Mrs. McFayden offered Anna a choice of dessert.

"What the devil possessed you to tell the woman anything at all," Sebastian snarled as he tugged off his jacket.

Anna flinched at the anger in her dark angel's voice, then frowned. They never kept secrets from each other, but she had begun to regret revealing what had happened in the garden with Madeline this afternoon. Anna pulled her night robe over her shoulders as she watched her husband's sharp movements as he undressed. She'd seen Sebastian angry before, but never like this since they were married.

Not since the argument they'd had the night she'd given herself to him for the first time, had Anna seen him so furious. She narrowed her eyes as she watched him fling his jacket over a nearby chair before he undid the thin tie at his neck and pushed his suspenders off his shoulders.

"*Answer me*, Anna," he commanded as he turned to face her.

"What do you want me to say, Sebastian?"

"I want to know why you decided it was perfectly fine to tell the woman she'd drowned in the future before miraculously appearing here—in the past."

"I *didn't* decide it was fine to tell her anything at all," she answered quietly. "I saw Madeline in the future, and I blurted it out before I even realized what I was saying."

"One day you're going to regret your inability to control that tongue of yours," he snapped.

Anna eyed Sebastian with assessment. Her husband's anger was out of proportion, even for her dark angel. Just last month, the man had praised her for biting her tongue and not insulting Lady Margaret at the opera. This argument wasn't just about her slip of the tongue this afternoon with Madeline.

Something else was bothering him. Anna bit down on her lip as she remembered he'd been grumpy ever since they'd left London. If she didn't know Sebastian so well, she might have been excused for thinking he'd been planning a liaison during his trip to Scotland. She knew better.

Her dark angel demonstrated his love for her on a regular basis. Whether it was rubbing her feet while she'd been pregnant with Jane, reaching for her hand in the dark at the theater, meeting her gaze from across the room, or in bed when he made love to her so tenderly and passionately, Sebastian's heart was hers.

"This argument isn't really about my telling Madeline what I know, is it, Sebastian?"

"What the devil is that supposed to mean?"

Guilt flashed so quickly across his face that if she'd not been looking for it, she wouldn't have seen it. Annoyed by his stubbornness in hiding what was troubling him, Anna planted her hands on her hips and eyed her husband with irritation.

"It means, you're still angry with me for insisting I come to Scotland with you. I would have thought you'd be happy that Jane and I are with you, but you certainly don't act like it." The fierce accusation made Sebastian stiffen as his gaze met hers before he quickly returned his attention to undressing.

"I am *not* angry with you for accompanying me." His voice had the same stilted note it always did when he was hiding his emotions behind the wall he would occasionally throw up between them.

"Aren't you? Ever since we left London, you've acted as if our daughter and I are a burden to you." Her accusation made Sebastian stare at her in stunned amazement. She sniffed her disgust at his reaction. "Don't you dare deny it, Lord Starling. However, I'll make it easy for you. I'll take Jane to Aberdeen tomorrow, and the two of us will take the first available train back to London."

"You'll do nothing of the sort," Sebastian snarled. "I'm not about to let my wife take any more risks with her health than absolutely necessary."

"*What?*" Anna's mouth fell open in astonishment for several seconds, before annoyed disgust made her hands fly up in a gesture of angry confusion. "What the hell are you talking about."

A groan escaped Sebastian as he shoved one hand through his hair and bowed his head. When he didn't answer her, Anna closed the distance between them and poked his chest with one finger.

"I asked you a question, Lord Starling. What risks am I taking?"

She'd barely finished asking her question, when Sebastian roughly pulled her into his arms and buried his face in the side of her neck. The shudder that rippled out of him and into her made Anna draw in a soft gasp of fear.

"Sebastian, please. Tell me what's wrong." When he didn't speak, Anna stroked the nape of his neck with her fingers in a soothing gesture. "Please, my dark angel. What makes you think I'm in some sort of danger?"

"Pennington said giving birth to Jane was very difficult for you." Sebastian dragged in a ragged breath as he lifted his head. "He said you needed to rest for several months, and traveling across Scotland is *not* what I call rest."

"Oh, for heaven's sake," Anna exclaimed angrily. "Resting doesn't mean I have to stay in bed for six months. That man knows as much about women and babies as Hamish or Smitty."

"He came highly recommended, Anna." Her dark angel's expression held a small bit of umbrage at her questioning his choice of doctor.

"A recommendation you received from other men, *not* their wives." Anna eyed him with exasperation. "For the record, Lord Starling, Dr. Pennington will never come near me or any of our children ever again."

"Whether or not the man attends you in the future is not the issue. I'm worried you're not getting enough rest. You fall asleep against my shoulder when we travel, and you have demonstrated an increasing tendency to sleep late."

"You seem to forget we have a daughter who needs attention, night and day. You sleep through the night. I don't."

"Then why haven't you asked for help?" The bewilderment in his voice made her heave a sigh of exasperation.

"I don't need help. I'm doing what every woman has done since the beginning of time, and I love doing it. So, would you please, stop acting like a mother hen." Anna scowled up at him before she gently cupped his cheeks. "I love you, my dark angel, but I'm made of much sterner stuff than that old goat of a doctor says."

Anna pulled his head down to kiss him gently, and Sebastian's arms wrapped tightly around her as he returned the caress. When he lifted his head, he smiled at her before another frown suddenly furrowed his brow.

"What now?" Exasperated, she rolled her eyes.

"No matchmaking." It wasn't a request. It was an order, and Anna shook her head.

"Matchmaking? What the devil are you talking about, now?" She feigned innocence, and Sebastian released a quiet sound of irritation.

"You know damn well, what I'm talking about, Lady Starling."

"Such language, my lord." Her pretense at being scandalized made Sebastian grunt with exasperation.

"Don't change the subject, Anna. You're not to meddle in Iain's personal affairs. I like him, and I need him to accept my offer to manage my investments in Aberdeen. I trust him to look out for our best interests. So *no* matchmaking schemes. Is that understood?"

"I'm not the one you and Iain need to be worried about." Eying him with restrained amusement, she snorted with laughter. "Grace and Ainslie are as stubborn as their father. I think the two of them will do whatever it takes to have Madeline become a permanent member of the household. The man is going to have his hands full with those two girls if he lets Madeline leave.”

“Then let Iain deal with them. I don’t want my wife trying to throw my friend and his governess together.”

“Exactly when have I ever played matchmaker?” she snorted with disgust. “You know I’m too direct for that.”

“That’s what I’m afraid of,” Sebastian said with a groan as he pressed his forehead against hers. “Isn’t taming one beast enough of a challenge for you, light of my life?”

“Now that you’ve broached the topic, I won’t deny you would often try the patience of Job himself.”

“And I remember telling you more than a year ago that you would need that kind of patience,” he sighed with resignation. “I do try, sweetheart.”

“I know you do,” she whispered, pressing her cheek against the warmth of his skin where his shirt splayed open. She suddenly pulled away from him to eye him with a mock glare.

“Oh, and for your edification, my lord. When we’re in polite company, my tongue is quite controlled.”

“Is it?” he murmured with an arched eyebrow. “As I recall, you almost called me a fuckwit this afternoon.”

“An excellent example of how well I’ve learned to control my tongue. Be grateful I called you something *other* than a fuckwit.”

“And fuddy-duddy was an improvement?” His eyebrows shot up again, but she saw the way his mouth twitched and the gleam of laughter in his dark gaze.

“There’s no pleasing you, is there?” Anna rolled her eyes as she laughed.

“Actually, I can think of several ways we can please each other, my love,” he whispered softly as his lips brushed against hers. “Ways that will make both of us quite happy.”

“Good Lord. Did you just propose we do something wicked, Lord Starling?” Anna caught his hand in hers and raised it to press a kiss to the back of his hand. With her eyes meeting his, she smiled slowly as she slid his forefinger into her mouth to gently suck on it. At his soft groan, she released him. "If you intend to prove you're not a fuck-wit, then I suggest you do it now, while I can still keep my eyes open."

"Oh, I can promise you'll not fall asleep, Lady Starling," he said with a grin. "I intend to make you sob my name as you admit I'm not a pompous ass." The world shifted as he lifted her up into his arms. Her arm wrapped around his neck, she sighed happily. A moment later his mouth brushed against her ear.

"I love you, Anna." The emotion in his voice made her heart soar, and she tipped her head back to meet his gaze.

"And I love you, my dark angel," she whispered back as he carried her to bed.

Chapter 13

Iain closed his book of accounts with a grunt of disgust. Everyone had gone to bed more than an hour ago, but he'd been feeling too restless to retire. Unwilling to lie awake staring up at the ceiling, he'd gone to his study to work. It had been a pointless effort. He couldn't concentrate, and he was still wide awake.

Rising to his feet, he blew out the oil lamp on his desk and headed upstairs. There were several books in his room. Perhaps reading one of them would help him fall asleep. Iain was halfway to his room when he heard a soft click drift through the quiet hallway. It took him a second to recognize the sound of a door opening, and before he could react, Madeline stepped out of the bathroom.

The two of them collided, and as she staggered backward, he pulled her into his chest to save her from falling. She gasped in surprise and clung to him for a brief moment to steady herself.

"I'm sorry. I wasn't expecting anyone to be up at this hour," she murmured quietly, pushing herself free of his embrace. Iain frowned as she avoided his gaze.

"You're feeling better?" His fingers tipped her head up, and she blinked in confusion then nodded.

"Yes, thank you."

"You were missed at dinner this evening. *I* missed you." Startled by his admission, a warning bell rang loudly in the back of his head. Madeline swallowed hard then looked away from him.

"Iain, I…I've decided to look for employment in the medical profession. I don't know how long it will take to find—"

"Ye are leaving?" Stunned, he stared down at her as shouts of protest drowned out the warning bell resounding in the back of his mind.

"Yes, I think it's time." Madeline nodded, and he caught her chin with his fingers, forcing her to look at him. The hopelessness shimmering in her eyes made his gut clench.

"I dinnae understand why ye wish to leave. Are ye unhappy here?"

"I think it's best for the girls. If I stay much longer…I don't want them to grow too attached to me. It's not healthy for them."

The fact that she'd not answered his question irritated him. She'd displayed no sign of being unhappy at Muchalls Hall over the past couple of weeks. Remembering the echo of laughter in the hall this morning as she'd refused to give way to Ainslie's protests in some unknown matter, Iain had heard the happiness in the sound.

Something had changed between that moment of laughter and the late afternoon. The memory of her wan appearance when he and Sebastian had found Madeline and Anna in the garden made him study her intently.

"Ye dinnae appear tae have any reservations about staying at Muchalls Hall this morning. What happened between breakfast and this afternoon while ye were with Anna in the garden."

"Nothing happened." She shook her head vehemently, but the moment she turned her head away from him, he knew she was lying. Anger tightened his limbs.

"Dinnae lie to me Madeline. Ye know I dinnae like liars."

The ferocity of his quiet words echoed much more loudly in the hall than he liked. Unwilling to let their argument rouse someone from their sleep, Iain caught her arm and pulled her the last few feet to his room. He ignored her gasp of surprised protest as he thrust open his bedroom door to drag her through the doorway, then shut them off from curious ears.

"What the hell do you think you're doing?" Madeline snapped as she glared up at him.

"I intend tae have the truth from ye."

"Truth? What truth?" Anger flared in her eyes, but it didn't mask her panic.

"I want to know what happened while ye were with Lady Starling this afternoon."

"What part of the word *nothing* don't you understand."

"The part where ye were happy this morning at breakfast, then a few hours later ye announce ye intend tae leave Muchalls Hall."

"It's the middle of the night, not just a few hours after breakfast."

"Dinnae ye try tae avoid answering my question, Madeline. I'll nae let ye leave until I hear the truth."

"You're an arrogant ass, Lord Glenburnie. I don't answer to you except when it comes to your daughters."

She shoved her way past him in an attempt to reach the door only a few steps away. Iain stopped her when she was only a foot from the barrier that shut out the rest of the world. Angered by her refusal to tell him what was wrong, Iain forced her to face him. The action sent the soft scent of roses mixed with lavender flooding his nostrils. Instantly, his body reacted, but he stifled the emotion stirring inside him.

"I meant what I said, Madeline. I'll have the truth from ye, and I'll nae let ye leave until I have an answer."

"I've already *answered* your question, *despite* the fact I don't owe you an explanation."

"Ye are as stubborn as Ainslie." Irritation tightened his muscles as he fought not to shake her for being so obstinate.

"Oh, that's rich coming from you when Ainslie comes by the trait naturally. The only thing that comes close to outweighing your arrogance is your bullheaded, autocratic behavior."

Iain glared down at her for a moment. The woman didn't just frustrate him, he found her maddening. And enticing. So enticing that every time she was near, he wanted to pull her into his arms and kiss her until she begged him not to stop. Iain took a small step forward, and she immediately retreated until her back was pressed into the door.

A small breath of surprise escaped her, and he saw an emotion flit across her face that caused an invisible vise to wrap itself around his chest. God in heaven, he'd never wanted a woman as much as he wanted Madeline right now. He wanted to tease her until he heard her soft laughter or saw her eyes flare with that fiery look usually reserved for a true Scotswoman.

He wanted to whisper sweet nothings into her ear just to see the color rise in her lovely face. But most of all, he wanted to hold her in his arms and caress every inch of her with his mouth until she pleaded with him to make her his. Slowly, he bent his head to brush his mouth against hers, and he heard the almost inaudible sound of her gasp that was almost a moan.

"Your stubbornness is enough tae drive the devil mad, *mo bhòidhchead fuilt dorcha*, while tempting the most pious of men tae give way tae temptation just to taste every inch of you."

One hand braced against the door, Iain traced his finger down the side of her neck then along the edge of her nightgown to where the garment parted just above her breasts. She quivered beneath his touch, while her lovely mouth parted to draw in a quick breath of air. Unable to stop himself, Iain tasted the sweetness of her lips in another light kiss. This time he allowed his lips to linger a little longer than before. She dragged in another breath.

"Iain, I… we've already said… this… it's not a good idea."

"Aye, that we did, *mo leannan*, but I also said I'm finding it difficult to stay away from ye, and I think ye feel the same way." He tipped his head to nibble at her earlobe, and her shudder reverberated against his lips. "Tell me ye dinnae want me tae explore every inch of ye with my mouth."

"It will…it will only complicate things." She pulled her head away from his mouth, unwittingly encouraging him to savor the silky warmth of her neck. A small moan whispered out of her.

"Aye, but ye dinnae say ye want me tae stop. Do ye want me tae stop, *mo leannan?* I will if ye ask me tae do so."

"I don't…oh God." His teeth lightly grazed her earlobe, and another quiet sound broke past her beautiful mouth. It aroused him in a way he'd never experienced before. The woman wasn't just maddening, she was intoxicating.

"I dinnae think I've ever tasted any woman so sweet. Ye go tae my head, Madeline. I cannae sleep without ye haunting my dreams. I want tae see ye writhing beneath me as I pleasure ye. I want tae hear ye cry out my name and beg me tae take ye again and again. But if ye want to leave, I'll nae stop ye, *mo leannan.*"

Despite his body's punishing protests, he quickly pulled back from her and put several feet between them to give her the freedom to go or stay. Every part of him ached for her not to leave. Eyes closed, she remained pressed against the door. A second later, he saw a hard tremor whip through her body as her eyelids fluttered open, and she stared into his eyes.

The fiery passion he saw flare in her gaze made his heart leap only to plummet downward as he watched her turn toward the door and wrap her fingers around the doorknob. It dealt his insides a hard blow of disappointment, followed by another emotion he refused to acknowledge. An overwhelming need to plead with her to stay became an almost tangible blow to his gut.

It stunned him. He'd never begged for anything in his life. A knot formed in his throat at the realization. Alarm rose to the top levels of his brain when Madeline suddenly spun around to face him. Desire darkened her brown eyes, and his heart raced as she hesitated, then ran toward him. Desire exploded inside him to obliterate every rational thought he possessed as her lips touched his.

The moment Madeline threw herself into Iain's arms, she knew there was no going back. Her brain was no longer in control of her emotions as she became locked in an embrace that signaled he wouldn't let her go until she surrendered to him completely. The man had no comprehension of how impossible it had been to resist him. He'd won her heart, and for this one singular moment in time, she didn't want to refuse him.

Just for tonight she wanted to silently express her love for him. Tomorrow she would find a way to manage the devastating heartache her decision would bring her. All she wanted tonight was to create a precious memory of his touch to sustain her in the months and years to come when she was no longer in his arms.

A large hand brushed over her breast, and she trembled at the light caress. Her lips parted against his, and a second later, he gave way to her as she explored the inner heat of his mouth. The flavor of whiskey swept across her tongue, and she relished the smooth taste of it. It reflected his hard, unyielding strength, just as the steely muscles of his arms did.

Eager to explore that strength with her fingertips, she pushed his jacket off his shoulders. Without breaking the wild, unrestrained passion of their kiss, he slipped one arm out of his coat, then tugged at his tie, as she pulled the jacket off him completely. As she fumbled with the buttons of his vest, he undid the ones at the top of his shirt. The back of his hand brushed against hers, and his quick movements indicated his own need for nothing to be between them, but hot skin on skin.

In seconds, his vest and then his shirt fell off him, giving her access to the scorching heat of his chest. She broke away from his fiery kiss to skim her lips downward over his skin to the top edge of his kilt. Without any urging, he removed his sporran, then pulled the plaid hugging his waist off of him. As much as she wanted to pleasure him with her mouth, she wanted him on top of her, thrusting into her over and over again.

Quickly removing her robe, she tossed it aside then pulled her nightgown upward. He helped tug the garment over her head, then suddenly stepped back to study her. The passion blazing in his gaze made her shudder with the need to have his arms wrapped around her again.

"Ye truly would tempt a pious man, *mo bhòidhchead fuilt dorcha.*"

The rough burr in his voice had strengthened to an even darker, throaty sound unlike all the other times he'd slipped from a cultured accent to his native one. Passion, desire, and raw need echoed in his words as his gaze roamed over every inch of her. It was as if his mouth was tasting her with invisible caresses, and she'd never experienced a sensation like it.

The moment he stepped forward and brushed his fingers across her hard nipples, she moaned softly. Her eyes fluttered closed in anticipation of his mouth suckling her sensitive flesh. Instead, his mouth kissed the skin below her breasts as his lips showered her skin with slow, fiery caresses. As his mouth teased her skin, her need for him strengthened.

Hard hands slid up along her legs as he knelt in front of her, and the moment his mouth reached her stomach, he roughly forced her to shift her stance until her legs were further apart. Startled, she looked down then gasped loudly as strong fingers parted her wet folds and his mouth found her sex. With her next breath, his teeth grazed the plump nub of flesh then nipped at it.

"Oh, my God."

Everything around her faded from view as his tongue dove into her, flicking and swirling against muscles taut with pleasure. The rush of her orgasm rose inside her fast and hard. As if sensing her impending release, his mouth returned to the swollen flesh at the edge of her sex. Heat consumed her the instant his teeth gently bit at her flesh, while her legs wobbled beneath her.

A strong hand cupped her buttocks and pulled her forward until her legs were braced against powerful, muscular shoulders. Over and over again, his tongue teased and pleasured her until another orgasm swirled upward to force a cry of ecstasy past her lips. Trembling violently against him, she pressed her hands into his solid shoulders, while her senses erupted in one fiery sensation after another.

With one last nip of her with his teeth, he rose to tower over her. Hard, masculine fingers dug into the soft curves of her bottom, as he tugged her into his hard frame. The tip of his erection brushed against her sex, and she dragged in a deep breath. She stared up at him, her gaze taking in the raw male passion hardening his sharply angled features. God how she loved this man.

His head bent to nuzzle her shoulder, his mouth caressed her skin as if preparing to forge a path downward. Unwilling to let him tease her anymore, she pushed him away slightly until he lifted his head with a growl of protest. Facial muscles taut with desire, his eyes blazed with a fiery hunger that matched the flames rising up to consume her. Using what little strength she had left in her legs, she hopped up and wrapped her legs around his waist.

Strong, muscular arms immediately cradled her buttocks, and a small smile touched his firm mouth. Hunger assaulted her senses as she stared up at him. She needed him desperately. Almost as desperately as she loved him. Tonight was all they would have, and she didn't want to waste a single moment of it. One hand spiked through silky black hair as she pulled his head downward to kiss him.

Against the heat of his tongue, she tasted her essence as well as the whiskey flavor of him. The two mixed together in a powerful blend of passion, and she tightened her legs around him. The instant his cock jumped against her bare bottom, she retreated from their kiss to stare up into a gaze that was a firestorm of desire.

"If you don't make love to me this minute, I'm going to walk out of here," she whispered hoarsely.

It was a lie and they both knew it, but her words tugged a low, harsh growl out of him. He didn't wait for her to repeat her demand. Instead, he quickly carried her to his bed. One knee pressed into the mattress, he laid her down, then followed her as she sank into the bed.

The dark passion on his rugged features made her heart skip a beat, and she shifted her body against his. This time the tip of him brushed against her sex, and her hands clutched at hard buttocks to pull him closer, while pushing herself forward.

"Iain, for the love of—"

Her plea was interrupted by intense pleasure as his body filled hers completely in one swift, unexpected thrust. Hard and thick inside her, her body rejoiced as one sensation after another rolled through her. In a silent plea, she pushed her hips up into his. He answered the unspoken demand with slow, deep strokes as his body claimed hers.

With each thrust of his powerful body into hers, he unknowingly tied her to him until she knew she could never let another man touch her. The life she would lead after tonight would be a lonely one, but it was a price she was willing to pay for this one night of exquisite pleasure.

Chapter 14

ain groaned with pleasure as he buried himself in Madeline's slick folds. She was every bit as hot and sweet as he'd imagined. When she'd removed her nightgown several moments ago, an invisible bolt of lightning had slashed through him.

Never in his life had he seen a woman so exquisite or tantalizing. His wife had possessed a lovely body, but he'd not lied when he'd said Madeline would be a pious man's undoing. He wanted to mark every inch of her with his mouth. The thought of doing so excited him, but it was the hunger to taste the heat of her that had made him kneel at her feet.

Twice her body had yielded to his intimate kisses, and the tart bite of her against his tongue had made his cock ache for the heat his mouth had explored. When she'd jumped up and wrapped her legs around his waist, her threat of leaving had compelled him to carry her to his bed.

He was certain her threat was a bluff, but he'd not been willing to take the chance. He needed her too much to deny himself the delights of her beautiful body. A low moan whispered out of her, and he responded to the cry by increasing the pace of his strokes. Her muscles tightened around him with an intensity that caused him to draw in a sharp hiss of air.

Christ almighty, the woman already had him on the edge of spilling his seed. Almost as if she could read his mind, her body contracted around him again. A hot, velvety vise could not have felt more punishing or intensely pleasurable. Soft fingers dug into his buttocks as she urged him to move faster.

Unable to refuse her, a foggy cloud of red-hot desire swept over him, and his body drove into hers at a blistering pace. Nothing existed outside of the soft musk of her desire, the taste of her sweet mouth against his, and the small mewls of rapture pouring out of her. The quiet moans grew in strength, and she bucked upward and cried out his name.

Shuddering beneath him, her hot core gripped him tightly before it eased only to flex around him a second later with greater strength. With each contraction around his cock, she pulled him closer and closer to his own release. Fast and hard, he pounded his body into hers. His ballocks drew up and tightened against the base of his cock until he uttered a restrained cry of release and throbbed inside her.

For a long moment, he hovered over her, his hands braced on either side of her. She was still shuddering around him, and he jerked as a hard spasm clenched at him pleasantly. Forehead pressed into hers, he breathed in the sweet, fragrant heat of her and enjoyed the ragged sound of her breathing. It was a sign that he'd satisfied her as much as she had him. Her beautiful breasts rose and fell rapidly as the aftereffects of their lovemaking slowly subsided.

Iain kissed her deeply then rolled away from her and fell backward into the mattress beside her. The silence stretched out between them with only their breathing breaking the quiet. Iain turned his head toward Madeline to see her staring up at the ceiling. Stretching out his hand, his fingers brushed across her cheek. She inhaled, then exhaled a deep breath before she looked at him. For a brief second, he saw an emotion flicker in her gaze that puzzled him.

"Do ye regret giving yourself tae me, *mo bhòidhchead fuilt dorcha?*" The question tugged a small smile to her beautiful lips.

"No, I have no regrets." She paused for a second as a frown furrowed her brow. "And I think it's time you tell me *exactly* what *mo bhòidhchead fuilt dorcha* means."

Iain chuckled at her mangled pronunciation. The glare she sent him made him laugh harder. He reached out to slide his fingers through her short, silky hair.

"It means my dark-haired beauty."

"*Oh.*"

He smiled at her soft gasp of surprise as her eyes widen, and pink color flooded her cheeks. A second later, she turned her head away from him. Iain went up on one elbow to lean down and kiss a cheek still aflame with color. Something resembling tenderness barreled through him.

"Ye disapprove, *mo leannan?*"

"What does *that* one mean?" She didn't look at him. The pink in her cheeks flared again, and he chuckled.

"Sweetheart." When he defined the Gaelic word, he waited for her to smile at him, but Madeline continued to stare up at the ceiling. Puzzled by her silence and stoic reaction, Iain eyed her with curiosity. "Do ye find that objectionable?"

"Objectionable?" Madeline jerked her head toward him as if he'd pulled her out of her thoughts. What he thought might be sadness flickered in her gaze. It vanished the moment she laughed.

"Not at all. What woman doesn't like to be called beautiful."

She looked back up at the ceiling again. There had been just the slightest bit of skepticism in her voice, and he frowned. Annoyed by her reply, Iain narrowed his gaze at her. Did she really believe his compliments were frivolous or insincere? They weren't.

"I would nae say something I dinnae believe, Madeline." At the quiet indignation in his voice, she turned her head to meet his gaze.

"Then I'll simply say thank you for the compliment."

Her remorse mollified his irritation, as he stared into her lovely eyes. Once more he thought he saw sadness flicker in their brown depths before she looked away. It made it impossible for him to shake off the idea she was hiding something from him. From the first moment he'd met her, Madeline had been an open book. Her facial expressions, her posture, and her eyes had always given him enough information for him to determine what she was thinking.

But tonight was different. There was a distance between them that hadn't been there prior to today or even this morning. She'd locked off a part of herself that he couldn't see, let alone touch. Even when she'd responded to his caresses a few moments ago with such wild abandon, he was certain she'd been holding something back from him.

"Madeline, will ye nae tell me what troubles you?" The soft question was answered with a harsh breath of exasperation blowing past her lovely lips. The look she sent him was almost one of antipathy.

"*Christ Almighty*, Iain, I've already told you there is *nothing* wrong." The barely restrained sharpness in her voice would have made others think she was simply irritated at his pressuring her. But the emotions that flashed and vanished in her gaze only strengthened his belief she wasn't telling him the truth. Something was wrong, he was certain of it. Frustration sailed through him as he gritted his teeth at her obstinate refusal to tell him what he wanted to know.

"Your eyes betray you, *mo bhòidhchead fuilt dorcha*."

His response made her stiffen, and Madeline's gaze locked with his for a long moment. In a swift, unexpected movement, she rolled over on top of him to straddle his waist. Pushing him deeper into the mattress a mischievous smile with just a hint of exasperation touched her mouth.

"Has anyone ever told you that you talk too much?"

Not even a fey princess could have smiled at him so enticingly. He'd seen this particular smile before when she was teasing Grace or Ainslie. The only time she'd ever directed the power and brilliance of it in his direction had been the day after his return from Aberdeen.

The smile on her rosy lips as she'd taunted him during their game of croquet held the same force now as it had that day. He'd been willing to swear a sledgehammer had hit his chest, but tonight something about her teasing was different. The mischief tilting her lips wasn't reflected in her brown eyes as she stared down at him.

The thought had barely filtered through his brain when she lowered her head and kissed him lightly. Before he could respond or deepen the sweet touch of her lips against his, her mouth glided over his cheek until it brushed against his ear.

"I don't want to talk anymore. I'd rather be doing something different, wouldn't you?" she whispered as she reached behind her to stroke his cock. Instantly, his body hardened everywhere. She lifted her head, and the sultry curve of her mouth made his chest ache as if someone had sent a caber into his chest. God almighty, when the woman looked at him like that, he was ready to go to hell and back for her.

"It feels like you don't want to talk either." She laughed softly, and her fingers trailed along his erection in a leisurely manner. Iain's hands grabbed at her waist, but she eluded him to move her body downward until she was kneeling between his thighs. "Not this time, Lord Glenburnie. I'm the one in charge now, and since you like to ask so many questions, I have one for you. Should I suck on your cock, my lord, or do you prefer to be fucked with me in the saddle?"

Stunned by her language, his eyes flew open to stare up at her in shock. The naughty gleam in her eyes formed a knot in his throat. He'd heard her mutter curses beneath her breath before, but what she'd just asked him aroused him in ways he'd never dreamed possible. Her smile unrepentant, she quirked an eyebrow upward and wrapped her fingers around his almost painfully hard cock. The confidence in her touch sent another invisible caber slamming into his chest.

"Should I stop?"

The question was little more than a whisper as she locked her gaze with his. The only response he could manage was a hoarse no, and she slowly bent her head to blow a warm breeze over the tip of him. The guttural groan that escaped him caused a low, throaty laugh to escape her, and the instant her tongue swirled around the head of his cock, his body jerked hard against the mattress. She repeated the action, her gaze never leaving his.

Another constricted sound of pleasure rolled out of him as her tongue swept over his skin as if she were licking a spoon clean. The erotic sensation sent his heart crashing into his chest, and his eyes closed as the heat of her mouth engulfed him, burning its way downward to the base of his cock.

Fire surged its way through his blood. It pounded a blaze of lust, desire, and passion into every inch of him. With every sliding stroke of her mouth, she teased and pulled him toward a release he struggled to prevent. He wanted her to saddle him as she'd suggested and ride him hard. He partially sat up to grasp her arms and tugged her upwards.

Without hesitating, she sheathed him with one quick stroke of her body. A shout of gratification rolled out of his throat as her body gripped his tightly. She paused for a moment, and his fingers dug into the flesh of her hips in a silent demand that she move against him. Laughter escaped her as she slowly slid his cock in and out of her buttery core. She seemed to instinctively understand that the slow, methodical way she was riding him was quickly becoming a torture session of need. Desire crashed through him and blinded him to everything except her and the fiery passion she'd aroused in him.

Eyes closed, he thrust his hips up to meet each downward stroke of her body. In the next beat of his heart, she bent her head to swirl her tongue around one of his nipples. The heat of her tongue on his skin made his hands cup her and rub his thumb over one of her nipples as she toyed with his.

The instant she bit down on him, he grunted with surprise. Another soft laugh echoed above him. The moment he looked up at her, his chest tightened in reaction to the knowing smile curving her lips. Entranced, he knew not even one of the fey could capture his imagination the way this woman was as she pleasured him with a deliberate confidence that had him reeling.

"I think you're enjoying this, my lord."

As her muscles contracted around him, she leaned back and increased the pace of her body's strokes against his. The air left his lungs as his gaze focused on the sight of his cock sliding in and out of her glistening folds. Christ Jesus, he'd never seen a more erotic, tantalizing sight in his life. Reaching out, he stroked the rim of her white-hot core.

The gasp of delight she uttered made him rub his thumb over the top of her core again, and she shuddered beneath his touch. Warning shots fired in his head at how close he was to losing himself in her, but he ignored the salvos. Fingers pressing into her lush hips, he urged her to ride him harder and faster. She obeyed his silent command and responded with an unrestrained passion.

Seconds later, her muscles rippled and tightened around his cock as her spasms clutched at him with a force that made him shout with delight. She was exquisite in the way she moved over him, and as much as he wanted to extend this moment of pleasure, he knew he was fighting a losing battle.

In the back of his head, he remembered he'd not worn protection the first time he'd made love to her. Now, as his sacs tightened and drew up against his cock, he quickly lifted her off of him then spilled his seed onto his stomach.

Harsh and ragged, his deep breaths of release mixed with hers as she fell onto the mattress beside him. Without thinking, he reached out to clasp her hand in his simply to maintain the physical connection between them. Lifting her hand upward, he brushed his lips over her fingertips.

At the simple gesture, he heard her draw in a sharp breath, and he immediately turned his head toward her.

Puzzlement and concern crashed through him as her soft profile reflected an emotion that bordered on pain. With his free hand, he quickly reached for a handkerchief off his bedside table to remove his seed from his stomach then rolled toward her. Fingers trailing across her cheek down to her chin, Iain gently forced her to look at him. Whatever he'd seen on her face had disappeared, and frustration snaked through him. Madeline's eyes met his, and she arched her eyebrows upward in a silent question. As he struggled with what he could say to reach the part of her she'd closed off to him, Madeline blew out a breath of exasperation.

"Don't you *dare* ask me if anything is wrong, Iain." The warning was like a claymore hacking the air between them as she turned her head away to stare up at the ceiling.

"Then tell me why ye wish tae leave Muchalls Hall, *mo leannan*? Ye have nae mentioned leaving before," he growled with frustration.

Annoyed and disappointed at her determination to leave Muchalls Hall, the girls—him—he scowled at her. He ignored the fact he'd included himself in the thought. Instead, he focused his attention on his belief that the woman had to have Scottish blood. He was now certain not even his youngest was as stubborn as Madeline.

"I told you why I've decided to leave," she cried angrily. "It's unhealthy for the girls to become too attached to me. And tonight… things are even more complicated now. It's best for everyone that I leave."

"What does tonight have tae do with Grace or Ainslie?" He feigned puzzlement, only to regret it a second later when Madeline inflicted a baleful glare at him.

"You did *not* just ask me what tonight has to do with the girls." The ferocity in her voice made him blow out a harsh breath.

"Aye, it made me sound like an *eejit*."

"I'm hoping that means you just called yourself an idiot," she snapped. "Because it was a ridiculous question.

You know damn good and well what will happen if either of the girls find out you and I… that we… about tonight."

She was right. Iain knew exactly what his daughters would think if they discovered Madeline had been in his bed. Tonight at the dinner table, they'd displayed their determination not to let Madeline leave Muchalls Hall. He wasn't blind to the fact his daughters wanted and needed a mother, but he also knew marrying again was out of the question.

With a mental shrug, he told himself the twins didn't need to know Madeline was sharing his bed. Mocking laughter filled his head. It wouldn't take long for his daughters to discover the truth. Even if Grace hadn't possessed the *an dara sealladh*, the twins were too intelligent not see what was happening beneath their noses. The sigh Madeline released was filled with weariness and resignation.

"I think I should go back to my room," she said quietly and sat upright. He immediately reached out and pulled her back down into his arms.

"Stay, *mo bhòidhchead fuilt dorcha*. I dinnae want ye to leave," he murmured soothingly in her ear as she tried to pull free of his arms. "I give ye my word I'll nae question you any more tonight."

"You promise?" Madeline eyed him suspiciously, her body still slightly straining against his embrace.

"Aye, I'll nae break my word to ye, *mo leannan*."

As her body grew more malleable in his arms, he held her close. He knew beyond a shadow of a doubt that she was deeply troubled. While he'd given his word not to question her any further tonight, he could ask questions tomorrow. Madeline's happiness was far more important to him than it should be, but he'd be a fool not to admit he didn't like seeing her unhappy. The knowledge made a part of his mind clamor for him to stop digging for the truth.

It was a demand he had no intention of obeying. Whatever had made Madeline unhappy enough to decide to leave Muchalls Hall, he was determined to find out why. The sudden warmth of Madeline's arm wrapping around his waist created a feeling of contentment inside of him. The strength of it tugged at a part of him deep inside he knew better than to unlock. Iain dismissed the clanging of alarm bells in his head and closed his eyes.

A quiet sound drifted through the air, and Iain looked down in surprise to see Madeline had fallen asleep. The emotion that suddenly gripped his insides as he studied her lovely features made him swallow hard. Closing his eyes, Iain tried to calm his mind. The last thing he needed was to suffer another headache and have Grace arrive out of the blue with a poultice. His daughter was far too sensitive to the pain of others.

If he were honest with himself, he would admit that his *bhòidhchead fuilt dorcha* was probably right when she said it was best for everyone if she left Muchalls Hall. The voices arguing in his head were loud and clear enough for him to understand the price he'd pay if he asked her to stay. He was far too close to the edge of irrational thought when it came to Madeline, especially when he considered what it would cost him if he let her go.

It was still dark outside when Madeline awoke. Slightly disoriented, it took a moment to register the fact that she was curled up against a hard, male body. What she'd thought had been a dream had been real. Her heart skipped a beat. Dear God, what time was it. Almost as if hearing her silent question, a clock chimed the hour of four.

Most of the staff rose around five, and she wanted to be back in her room by then. Carefully sliding out of Iain's embrace, Madeline laid his arm over her pillow, then slowly left his bed. The pillow might be enough for him not to realize she was no longer lying beside him. Trying not to make a sound, she rounded the bed, grateful for the faint light the embers in the fireplace cast over the floor.

The moment she saw her nightgown and robe lying on the floor, she remembered how quickly they had fallen off her. A split-second later, the memory of Iain exploring her sex with his mouth made the muscles between the apex of her thighs tense and flex with need. She drew in a quick breath and closed her eyes for a moment, then glanced over her shoulder to study Iain as he slept.

If only he weren't so afraid of loving again. Things might have been different for them. The thought made her heart twist painfully in her breast, and she forced herself to dress quickly. It would be difficult to resist him if Iain were to wake up and try to seduce her back into his bed.

Madeline tied the ribbon at the top of her robe and hurried to the door. The hinges creaked softly as she slowly pulled the heavy oak door open. A quiet sound echoed behind her, and she darted a look over her shoulder to see Iain roll over in his sleep. The sight of him pulling the pillow closer to his body caused tears to well up in her eyes. She would never wake up with his arms wrapped around her again.

It was a painful thought that made the tears threaten to spill down her cheeks. The pain of leaving him sliced through her, and she forced herself to peek out into the hallway. The corridor was empty, and Madeline quickly slid through the half-opened door and pulled it shut behind her.

Seconds later, she slipped into her room and closed her bedroom door behind her. For a long moment, she remained motionless with her back pressed into the solid wood barrier. Tonight had been a mistake. She had been wrong to think making love to him this one time would sustain her after she left Muchalls Hall. All she'd done tonight was to create memories that would torture her in the dark for the remainder of her days. They would be a constant reminder of a happiness that could never be hers. A low sound of misery floated out of her, and she flew across the room to her bed.

With a quiet sob, she crawled under the bedcovers to slide between cold sheets. The icy cold was a harbinger of what life would be like when she left Muchalls Hall. It convinced her she would never be warm again.

Chapter 15

Iain leaned back in his chair and stared at the open ledgers on his desk. He'd spent the past three hours balancing the books to ensure his finances were in order, before he created a list of the items he wanted to purchase when he traveled to Amsterdam in another week. While his current state of business affairs was satisfactory, the rest of his life was a different matter altogether.

It had been almost a fortnight since Madeline had spent the night in his arms. Almost two weeks of not being alone with her for even a few minutes to try to persuade her to stay. If things continued as they were, he might have to rethink his trip to Amsterdam. It wasn't unrealistic to believe that Madeline might leave Muchalls Hall while he was away. The idea of returning home to find her gone was not a pleasant one.

The morning after she'd been in his bed, Iain had awoken with a pillow pressed into his chest. Still groggy with sleep, he'd initially thought it was Madeline's soft body he held close to him. Exhilaration had instantly dissolved into irritation and disappointment the moment he realized she was gone.

He understood why Madeline had returned to her room while the rest of the household slept. But his reaction to her having left him was what troubled him. The depth and intensity of his disappointment to awaken and find her gone had blindsided him. Worse, he'd been forced to admit he wanted to wake up every morning with Madeline pressed into his side.

The dangerous thought should have made him feel grateful that Madeline was determined to avoid him. It didn't. Iain wasn't surprised by her determination to avoid his company. But it was her success at ensuring the two of them were never alone for the past two weeks that Iain found frustrating as hell. He was growing more irritable by the day, and it was beginning to show. This morning in the stables, he'd barely kept a civil tongue when Angus had mentioned Madeline's positive effect on the girls.

Until their departure for London, Sebastian and Anna had unknowingly served as one of the primary barriers Madeline had used to keep him from capturing a moment alone with her. She'd even refused his demands she meet with him in his study by sending someone with the excuse that she was busy and would speak with him later.

During the day, his business with Sebastian had prevented him from seeking Madeline out, while in the evenings, she'd either given an excuse not to join him and his friends in the salon or she retired the moment Anna did. On the one or two occasions Sebastian had retired at the same time as his wife, Madeline had quickly said her goodnights as well.

Now in the almost three days since Sebastian and Anna had left to return home to London, Madeline was proving as elusive as ever. With Anna gone, the McFayden's, and the girls had unknowingly taken Lady Starling's place as the wall between the two of them.

Last night his frustration had reached new heights when he'd caught Madeline alone in the salon after dinner. Just as he was closing the salon door to forestall her escape, Angus had interrupted with an update on a new mare Iain had purchased while viewing properties with Sebastian. Annoyed, he'd watched Madeline say goodnight and leave the room.

His irritation at being denied a moment alone with her had pushed him to the point of walking down the hall to her room in the middle of the night. He'd paced in front of her door for at least fifteen minutes trying to decide what to say to her. That he'd actually convinced himself they could have a conversation outside her bedroom door had been ludicrous.

That would have been impossible. Madeline's effect on him wasn't just one of physical arousal. She was the only woman he'd ever met that could make him feel varying degrees of lust, amusement, irritation, fury, and tenderness all within the space of minutes.

It wouldn't have taken much for any discussion to escalate between them. That would have led to their continuing their conversation in her room simply to keep from waking the rest of the household. That, in all likelihood, would have ended in pleasure, but at a cost to Madeline's privacy and comfort.

Despite her independent and straight-forward nature, the balance of power between them would have shifted if he had entered Madeline's room in the dead of night. That he wouldn't do to her. Her bedroom was her private sanctuary. Iain refused to make her feel as if he had the right to enter her safe haven whenever he wanted. It was why he'd returned to his room without even knocking on her door.

With a muttered oath, Iain sprang from his desk chair and strode to the window to stare out at the North Sea. What could he do to convince Madeline to stay at Muchalls Hall? In the back of his mind, a voice told him to admit he cared for her. Iain quickly slammed the door closed on the thought while telling himself Madeline had shown no sign of reciprocating any such feelings.

In the next breath, the word marriage whispered through his head. Immediately, his jaw clenched. He'd vowed never to marry again and with good reason. No matter what his feelings for Madeline might be, marriage meant children.

Another voice chided him for sidestepping the issue of matrimony with the excuse he didn't want to make Madeline with child. Deep down he knew the real reason he'd vowed never to marry again. The quiet rap on his study door made him turn around as he called out for his visitor to enter.

The instant he saw the woman preoccupying his thoughts, it was as if a bolt of lightning had struck his chest. Her gaze met his for a fleeting moment, before she looked away to close the study door behind her, then stepped deeper into the room.

"I need your help," she insisted quietly. Something in her voice set him on edge, and he narrowed his gaze on her.

"My help?"

"I need to go to Aberdeen." The words were the last thing he would have thought to come out of her mouth, and he stared at her in bewilderment.

"Aberdeen?"

At his question, Madeline winced and looked down at a piece of paper she held. She exhaled a sharp breath then moved forward quickly to offer him what he suddenly realized was a piece of correspondence.

"I have an interview."

The quiet statement made him go rigid with tension. Slowly accepting the paper, his gaze locked with hers for a long moment before he opened the folded missive. The handwriting was confident and powerful on the page, and Iain knew without even glancing at the signature that the writer was a man.

Dear Miss Whitworth,

After careful review of your reply to my first letter, I would like for us to meet when I travel to Aberdeen to visit family next week. I believe you and I might be well-suited to work together. I was impressed by the detail of knowledge you included with your correspondence, and I am of the opinion that your skills will be of immense value to me as I expand my practice in London.

A meeting in person will confirm my thoughts as to our suitability of working together. We can discuss the details of employment at that time. if you are amenable to my request, I am free on Thursday afternoon. We can meet in the tearoom of the MacDonald Norwood Hall hotel. You may write to me in care of my sister, Mrs. Andrew Tulloch, Aberdeenshire with the time of your availability this coming Thursday.

Regards,
Graeme Douglas, M.D.

An emotion Iain had never experienced before surged through him at the thought of her in the company of another man. It didn't matter the reason, he only knew he didn't like it. Stunned by the strength of his reaction, Iain looked up from the letter to study Madeline with a possessiveness he knew he wasn't entitled to feel, but felt nonetheless.

She flinched at his look and immediately averted her gaze. The silence in the room was fraught with tension as he slowly folded the correspondence, then extended his arm to return the letter to her. Madeline took a quick step forward and snatched the missive out of his hand then retreated just as fast.

"Can you help me get to Aberdeen this Thursday? I know it's short notice, but I just received Dr. Douglas's letter this morning." Irritated by her request, Iain glared at her.

"Have ye told Grace and Ainslie that ye are leaving Muchalls Hall?"

Iain deliberately avoided answering her question by asking one of his own. How he managed not to raise his voice astounded him because all he wanted to do was rage at her for being so damn determined to leave. His anger strengthened as she shook her head.

"Not yet."

"Do ye expect me tae break their hearts for ye?" Iain snapped. "I'll nae do that, Madeline."

"I didn't ask you to. I just haven't found the right moment to explain things to them." Irritation filled her words, showing she was offended by his suggestion.

"*Explain?* Ye won't even explain tae *me* why ye are leaving, Madeline."

"I've already *told* you why." The vagueness of her fierce reply ignited a fierce anger inside Iain as he glared at her.

"Nae, ye dinnae tell me anything," he bit out through clenched teeth. "And ye have refused to speak with me since ye left my bed almost two weeks ago."

"There wasn't anything to say." Despite the sharpness of her tone, Iain heard something he thought might be pain in her voice. He took a step forward, but Madeline shied away in the direction of the door. "What happened…what happened between us only complicated an already difficult situation."

"How was it difficult?" he snarled. "Ye were happy here."

"Too happy."

"What the *hell* does that mean? Ye are nae making any sense, woman."

"It means the girls weren't the only ones who were becoming too attached."

There was a small catch in Madeline's voice that made him stiffen. Was she saying she had feelings not only for Grace and Ainslie, but for him as well? His chest tightened as he struggled with the ramifications of what that would mean for the two of them. Almost as if she could read his mind, a humorless smile touched her lips. With a soft sound of ironic disbelief, she eyed him mockingly.

"Just because you fucked me, my lord, doesn't mean you have to worry I expect anything from you. We had some great sex. But that's all it was."

Madeline's words sliced through him as if she'd gutted him like a fish and had left an invisible, gaping wound in his chest. It was a tangible sensation that barreled through him and threatened to drive him to his knees. Iain barely had time to register the painful impact Madeline's words had on him, before he was teetering on the precipice of an anger so fierce it threatened to eclipse anything his father had ever rained down on his head.

Iain heard the dark rumble of fury rising out of him as he swiftly closed the small space between them forcing Madeline to retreat until her back was against the wall. One hand pressed into the wood behind her, Iain pinned her in place as he slowly slid his free hand up over her waist to cup her breast. The memory of suckling her taut nipples as he slowly slid his cock into her body's heat aroused him despite his anger.

He tried to suppress his desire, but it was impossible to do so. The soft, feminine scent of lavender and rose petals filled his nostrils, and the sweet smell fired his blood with a need that mixed with his anger until he was hard beneath his kilt. Desperate to avoid revealing how deep her words had wounded him and how easily she could arouse his desire, Iain narrowed his eyes at her.

"Ye have a way with words that belong in a whorehouse, *mo leannan*."

"How typically male," Madeline spat out with disdain. "It's okay for a man to use foul language or have a good time in bed, but God forbid a woman do the same."

"I am nae complaining, lass. In fact, I'm already hard and aching tae be buried inside that sweet honey pot of yours."

Iain smiled with bitter satisfaction at the way her body became rigid, and she straightened to her full height. As his thumb rubbed across a hard nipple, a small gasp escaped her, and he couldn't tell if it was a sound of anger or something darker. In the next breath, her hands tugged his kilt upward.

"Then I'm game for a little up-against-the-wall action if you are, Lord Glenburnie, simply to prove I'm right."

Lust and something else threaded through her words as she wrapped her fingers around his erection. Iain jerked hard at her fiery touch. Madeline tilted her head back to stare up at him, and her sweet mouth formed a silent command that shot an explosive bolt of desire through him.

Without hesitating, he crushed her lips beneath his while tugging the skirt of her gown upward and trapping the material between them. In seconds, his hands were caressing silky thighs, and he quickly lifted her up to thrust his body into hers in one hard stroke. The strangled cry she released against his lips mixed with his own groan of pleasure. Christ Jesus, his body had been craving her since the morning he awoke to find her gone from his bed, but he hadn't realized until now that his craving was driven by something far more potent.

There was a frantic urgency to her unrestrained kisses that stoked the fires igniting inside him as her tongue tangled with his. Every frenzied swirl of her tongue around his tugged an urgent response from him. Their kiss was tempestuous and filled with an unbridled passion that touched something deep inside him.

Arms wrapped around his neck, she pushed back hard against each of his thrusts in a silent demand for more. She was a firestorm of hot need and pleasure wrapped around his cock as his body hammered its way into hers. The intensity of her body's response to his possession was swift, and as her muscles tightened around him, a low, guttural cry rose out of his chest.

Madeline wanted to sob with joy and pleasure as Iain filled her completely. The night she'd spent in his arms had been one of passion and fire, but this moment was a seismic, out-of-control expression of hot lusty need.

It resonated with all the pent-up longing, desire, and pain that had been her constant companion for the past two weeks. In the back of her mind, she heard a voice warning her there would be a heavy price to pay for this lapse in judgement. She ignored it. It was too late for her.

Soon she would be gone from Muchalls Hall, and this brief moment of joy at being connected to him again would be worth the consequences. Her body responded to his thrusts with a frenetic passion that consumed her. Every one of her senses fired mind-numbing sensations across her skin as he drove his body into hers at a furious pace. The first spasm of her climax rippled through her with a wild intensity that made her draw in a sharp breath of ecstasy.

Clinging to him, she gasped loudly as another shudder skimmed its way through her. At her soft cry, his lips bruised hers, while the world exploded around her in one pleasurable, acute sensation after another. Fierce tremors rocked through her as his body hardened against hers, then with a low cry his hard muscles pinned her against the wall in an exquisite moment of release.

The sound of Iain's ragged breathing echoed in her ears as his forehead pressed down into her shoulder. Eyes closed, Madeline drank in deep breaths of air as she slowly regained control of her senses. Remorse tried to set in, but she pushed it aside. As painful as it would be to leave him, she refused to regret giving herself to the man she loved. She would not allow herself to feel shame at having silently declared her heart to him.

Slowly, Iain's body relaxed against hers, and as he retreated from her, Madeline swallowed hard at the finality of it. Her eyes fluttered opened to meet an unreadable dark blue gaze. An emotion flickered in the depths of Iain's eyes, and her heart twisted painfully in her chest. Madeline wanted to believe he was experiencing pain and despair at her leaving Muchalls Hall, but she refused to indulge in the futility of such a thought. She freed herself from his embrace, then bent her head to adjust her clothing as she fought back tears.

The silence in the study was thick with tension, and Madeline quickly gathered her wits determined not to let him see how shattered she was. When she'd entered Iain's study, she'd known he would press her for why she was leaving. Why she hadn't prepared a response he would have accepted was a question she already knew the answer to, but didn't want to admit.

Worse, she'd made the mistake of confessing her heart had found a home at Muchalls Hall. The moment she'd seen Iain narrowing his gaze at her, Madeline had known he was considering the possibility he was included in her confession. Desperate to convince him otherwise, she'd lost control of her tongue. Her grandmother had been right when she'd said Madeline's sarcasm was going to come back to bite her.

Madeline should have known it would be a mistake to tell Iain their night together had been nothing more than a one-night stand. All she'd done was make him angry, and the moment he'd touched her every rational thought had gone out the window. She should have simply left when he pushed her for an explanation.

Perhaps worst of all, she was forced to admit that deep down she'd come to Iain hoping he would give her a reason to stay. Leaving Grace and Ainslie was going to be difficult enough. Walking away from Iain would be the same as having someone rip her heart out of her chest. Fingers trembling, she shook out her skirts then took a step toward the door, but strong hands caught her arms and pulled her back into a hard chest.

"Ye cannae deny there is something between us, Madeline."

Iain's brogue was as seductive as always, but this time she thought she heard something else echoing through it. For a fleeting moment, she allowed herself to believe his voice held the tender, fervent emotion every part of her wanted him to feel for her. A second later, her heart convulsed viciously in her chest until it made her think she was bleeding out because there was no way to staunch the blood flow.

Even if she stayed, Iain Fraser would never allow himself to give his heart to her unreservedly. That fact above all others was why she had to leave. With a firm tug, she pulled herself from his grasp and put a small amount of distance between them before turning to face him. The frustration on his face was mixed with another emotion, but she refused to contemplate what. With a sharp shake of her head, she released a small sound of pain.

"I'm not denying anything, but my mind's made up, and either you're going to give me a ride to Aberdeen or I'll find some other way to get there."

Madeline experienced a small amount of relief at the quiet firmness of her voice. At least he wouldn't see how hard it was to walk away from him. She knew Iain well enough to know he wouldn't hesitate to use that knowledge to his advantage if he thought he could convince her to remain. Without waiting for him to respond, she whirled around and raced from the room.

Chapter 16

Madeline woke up and stared at the ceiling. It was Thursday. Today she was leaving her heart behind at Muchalls Hall. Last night at the end of the evening meal, she'd broken the news to the girls. It hadn't gone well at all. Not even the death of her parents or her grandmother had affected her with such a heartsick savagery.

Grace's reaction had been one of utter devastation. Like her father, Grace had demanded to know why Madeline was leaving. But Ainslie's reaction to the news had startled Madeline. The girl had stared at her for a long moment before turning her head toward her father.

Iain's youngest daughter hadn't said a word, but the anger on Ainslie's face as she'd eyed her father with scorn had made him flinch. The girl clearly blamed Iain for Madeline's decision to leave. She'd tried to make the girls understand they needed a proper governess, but Grace had vehemently rejected Madeline's explanation.

Ainslie's continued silence had troubled Madeline, and even Iain seem worried as to his youngest's reaction to the news. It was as if the girl had reverted into the shell she'd been in when Madeline had first arrived at Muchalls Hall. The fact had almost made her reconsider her decision to leave, but she knew it would be a mistake.

With each passing day, her love for Iain would continue to grow, and the pain of not having him return her love would eventually become more than she could bear. At that point, leaving Muchalls Hall would be even harder on the girls. Seeing their reactions last night had made her want to break down into tears, something she'd avoided until she'd gone to bed. Then she'd sobbed herself to sleep.

Madeline gulped back another bout of tears then slowly climbed out of bed and listlessly went about dressing. She'd chosen to wear what Eileen had referred to as a traveling gown from the trunk someone had pulled out of the water weeks ago when she'd first arrived. Madeline had never understood how the luggage had contained clothing that fit her flawlessly, but over time, just like the mystery of how she'd arrived in the past, she'd simply come to accept it and not question the how or even the why.

Sinking down on the bed, Madeline pulled her shoes on and with the shoe hook, quickly pulled the buttons through the leather slits running up the side. When she'd finished, she sat up and stared off into space. In the back of her mind, she heard a whisper that said it wasn't too late to change her mind.

She quickly discarded the idea. That was the path to a hell of her own making. With a soft sigh of resignation, she moved to the door. As she opened it, a folded piece of white paper fluttered into the hall. Madeline bent to pick it up and saw her name written in Ainslie's childish hand. It was obvious the girl had taken great care with Madeline's name.

Ainslie was always in a rush to finish things, and her handwriting usually reflected that part of her personality. For the girl to write slowly and with care told Madeline how important Ainslie considered the letter to be. Madeline closed her eyes as she hesitated unfolding the paper. Whatever the child had written would most likely bring her to tears. Pushing aside her fear, she slowly unfolded the note.

Madeline,

> *I love ye very much, and I dinnae want ye tae go. but if ye will nae stay, then I am coming with ye. I ken faither*

will try tae stop me, but I will nae let him. I am going tae hide where he will nae find me.

I will wait until I know ye have left with Cecil. then I am going to follow ye on Macklin. please dinnae tell faither. He does nae love me, but I know ye love me very much.

Love, Ainslie

"Oh Ainslie," Madeline whispered, her heart sinking in her breast.

She should have known the child was planning something like this. Ainslie had been far too quiet last night. Fear made her run down the hall, then down the stairs to Iain's study. Madeline didn't bother to knock, and as she entered Iain's private sanctuary, she saw him standing at the window staring out at the North Sea.

The moment she entered the room, Iain whirled around to face her, and Madeline froze at his expression. It was only there for a fleeting moment, but she was certain it had been a look of deep despair. She barely had time to register the thought before a loud sound of anger exploded out of him.

"Why are ye still here? I thought Cecil was driving ye tae Aberdeen," he snapped coldly.

Iain's icy manner made Madeline hesitate. She knew Iain loved his daughters deeply, but if Ainslie were standing in front of her father right now, the girl's belief that her father didn't love her would only be strengthened. Perhaps she should have gone looking for Ainslie alone. Iain's harsh oath punctured the air like a crack of lightning.

"I asked ye a question, Madeline." The sharpness in his voice made her wince.

"It's Ainslie—"

"If ye have come tae tell me how tae handle my daughter after ye are nae longer here, I dinnae need your advice."

"She's *gone*," she exclaimed in a voice filled with worry.

"Gone?" Iain grew very still as he stared at Madeline in confusion.

"She left me a note." Madeline hurried across the room to his side and handed him Ainslie's short letter. "I should have known she was planning something last night when she was so quiet."

"*Christ Jesus*," Iain rasped in a low voice as the color drained from his face. "She could be anywhere, maybe even halfway tae Aberdeen."

"No, I think she's hiding somewhere close by. Close enough to see me…" Madeline's voice trailed off as she met Iain's stormy blue gaze.

"Close enough to see you leaving Muchalls Hall."

The icy words rang out in the quiet of the study as if they were swords clanging against each other in battle. Something flashed in Iain's eyes that any other time might have sparked hope in her. But his cold, dispassionate reply said she was wishing for something that didn't exist. Madeline swallowed hard.

"Yes, or at least hiding somewhere close to the manor until she's certain I'm on my way to Aberdeen."

"Then I suggest ye leave, and I will search for the lass. She will nae remain hidden for long when she sees ye leaving."

Iain stepped around her and strode toward the door. Darting after him, Madeline grabbed his arm and tugged him to a halt. The stony, unreadable expression on Iain's face made her heart clench tightly in her chest. For the first time since deciding to leave Muchalls Hall, she realized Iain couldn't care less that she was leaving. Terrified for Ainslie and furious with herself for being stupid enough to fall in love with a man who didn't care for her, Madeline glared at him.

"If you think I'll just leave without knowing Ainslie's safe, you're—"

"My daughter is nae longer your responsibility, Madeline. But if as her note says, she's waiting tae see ye leave, then leave ye will." There was something in his voice that made her suck in a sharp breath.

"You blame *me* for Ainslie running away."

"I dinnae say that," he growled before his expression softened slightly. "But if ye want tae help me find the lass, then do what she is waiting for. Let her see ye leaving. We will find her then."

Suddenly biting back tears, Madeline closed her eyes and turned away from him as guilt rushed through her. Iain didn't have to say she was responsible for Ainslie's disappearance. It was the truth, she'd done nothing to distance herself from the girls in the past two weeks.

Instead, she'd tried to impress the memory of Ainslie's and Grace's voices, their laughter, and their smiles in her head and heart. Worse, she'd allowed her love for them to show several times. It was no wonder they'd reacted the way they had last night. Iain's hand cupping her chin made her eyes flutter open as he forced her to look at him.

"It's nae your fault, Madeline. The lassies love ye, and I…" Iain stumbled slightly over his words before he continued. "I understand now why ye were worried about how your leaving Muchalls Hall would affect them."

She didn't answer him, and as a tear slid down her cheek, he wiped it away with his thumb. There was a tenderness in his touch that made her throat close up with emotion, but he didn't say a word. Instead, he took her hand and pulled her toward the door.

With the speed of a general acting on new information, Iain had sent Angus and Grace out to search for the girl while he'd ridden Taren out onto the moors. Madeline had wanted to search for the child too, but Iain had insisted she remain at the manor and leave as she'd planned. For the past hour as she'd paced the floor of the salon, Madeline had tried to convince herself Iain, Grace, or the groundskeeper would find Ainslie.

Her fear had escalated when all three of them had returned to the manor a few minutes ago without the girl. Now, as Iain helped her up onto the buckboard's seat, Madeline was trembling with apprehension. Iain's hand squeezed hers tightly, and she gasped as she looked down at him.

"The lass will follow ye, *mo bhòidhchead fuilt dorcha*. I dinnae doubt that."

Despite his calm reassurance, Madeline saw a deep concern in his blue eyes. One that only strengthened her own fear. Cecil climbed up beside her and took up the reins of the plow horse hitched to the wagon. With a gentle slap of the leather against the animal's hindquarters, the vehicle rolled forward, and Madeline's fingers slipped slowly from Iain's.

As Cecil drove the wagon down the driveway to the main road, Madeline's gaze scoured every inch of the landscape hoping to see some movement that might reveal Ainslie on Macklin's back. When they reached the main road, the child had still not appeared. With each creak of the wagon's movement, Madeline's fear grew. They'd gone almost three miles when she saw Macklin.

The animal was standing on the edge of a small copse of trees and shrubbery, and Madeline's heart leapt with relief. Sharply ordering Cecil to stop, she quickly descended from the wagon and ran toward the horse. There was no sign of Ainslie, and Madeline's heart sank.

If she wasn't with Macklin, where was she? The sound of thundering hoofbeats echoed through the air, and she whirled around to see Iain riding his horse toward her. As the gelding slid to a halt, Iain was already dismounting. The moment he landed on the ground he was running toward her.

"Did ye see her?" he asked fiercely as he ran past her to pick up the reins dangling from Macklin's bridle. Iain didn't look at her, studying the leather straps he pulled through his fingers.

"No," she said with a rising panic. "Something's wrong, Iain. I can feel it."

"Aye."

The brusque response was harsh with worry, and he ducked under Macklin's head to walk toward the small clump of trees and underbrush. His head bent, he studied the ground as if looking for something. When he lifted his head, he looked not just worried, but confused.

"What is it?" she asked quietly.

"Macklin appears tae have arrived here on his own. His hoofprints dinnae indicate Ainslie was riding him, and there's nae sign of her footprints."

"But if she's not here… dear God, do you think she was thrown from the horse? She's an excellent rider, but what if something startle Macklin and she lost her seat?"

"It's possible. I'm going tae follow Macklin's trail back tae the manor."

"I'm coming with you."

"Nae, I need ye tae ride Macklin back tae Muchalls Hall—"

"Let Cecil do it."

"The mon's not ridden an animal since he fell off Macklin and broke his arm two years ago, and he's nae longer a young lad."

"You know you're going to need me when you find Ainslie. She's furious with you. If she's not hurt, she might run away from you," Madeline protested vehemently. Iain quickly strode forward and wrapped his hands around her upper arms to give her a hard shake.

"Ye *must* do this *mo leannan*. I need ye tae tell Angus what's happened. There are places ye dinnae know to look for her, he does. The mon knows the moors better than anyone, even me."

With a sharp tug, he pulled her toward Macklin. As they reached the animal, Iain pulled what she now knew was a *sgian dubh* from the sheath at the top of his knee-high stocking. Before she could ask him what he was doing, he used the knife to slice her dress open at the side seam almost to her thigh, then forced her to turn around to do the same on her left side.

"That will make it easier for ye tae ride," he said as he straightened to meet her gaze. Madeline nodded as he formed a stirrup with his hands and helped her mount Macklin. His hand on her thigh, he handed her the horse's reins. "Tell Angus that I am riding along the cliffs back toward the manor, and he should head out toward the cairn. Ainslie likes to race the squire's boy over that ground."

"Find her, Iain. I couldn't bear it if my leaving…" Madeline's voice trailed off as her hands tightened on the reins.

"I'll find her, *mo bhòidhchead fuilt dorcha*. Now, go." The hoarse, dark note in his voice told her how deeply worried he was, and nodding her understanding, Madeline turned Macklin toward Muchalls Hall.

Madeline glanced over her shoulder as she rode away. Iain had already reached Cecil who was waiting by the wagon. She saw him giving the older man directions, before he ran back to his horse. Her heart in her mouth, she urged Macklin into a gentle canter.

The only horse she'd ever been on had been on a guided trail ride two years ago. Now she wished she was as skilled a rider as everyone at Muchalls Hall so she could make the animal go faster, but she was already terrified of falling and delaying the search for Ainslie.

It took Madeline a little more than fifteen minutes to ride back to the manor, although it seemed much longer. Almost as if he'd been waiting on her, Angus ran out of the front of the house with Grace close on his heels. Madeline brought Macklin to a halt and allowed Angus to help her down. It took only a few seconds for her to explain the situation before the groundskeeper was riding off toward the cairn. A small hand slipped into hers, and she looked down to meet Grace's gaze. The look of fear on the girl's face made Madeline pull her close.

"It will be all right, Grace," she murmured soothingly trying to put aside her own fear at the same time. "Is there any place you think Ainslie might have gone to hide from your father?"

"She always goes tae the barn to sit with Macklin or Taren when she's upset," Grace exclaimed. "But she was nae there."

"Is there anywhere else she goes to if she's upset?"

"She likes to go down tae the inlet sometimes, but Angus said she was nae there either."

A chill suddenly scraped down Madeline's spine the moment Grace said Ainslie wasn't at the beach. What was it her note had said? She would hide some place where Iain wouldn't find her. Surely, she wouldn't have gone into the sea cave.

But it was the one place Ainslie knew Iain would never think to look. Horrified that she might be right, Madeline knew there was only one thing she could do. She had to search the sea cave. The sound of a horse made Madeline turn her head hoping it was Iain with Ainslie sitting in front of him. Her heart sank like a stone in water as she saw Ainslie's friend, Ethan Tewel, trotting toward her and Grace.

"Hello, Miss Whitworth," he called out cheerfully. "I came tae see if Ainslie wanted tae go riding."

"Ainslie's missing Ethan, but I think I know where she might be. I need you to ride out to the cairn, find Angus and send him back to the manor. Tell him I'm going to look in the sea cave for Ainslie."

"*The sea cave?*" Grace and Ethan spoke at the same time, and Madeline ignored their horrified consternation and with a sharp gesture, she pointed in the direction she'd seen Angus ride off in.

"*Go, Ethan.* Lord Glenburnie will need Angus's help if I'm right."

The boy nodded his understanding, then turned his horse around and rode away at a hard gallop. Beside her, Grace stood motionless, an expression of shock on her sweet face.

"Grace, isn't there one other horse in the barn?" At her question, the girl simply nodded her head. "Then I need you to ride out to find your father. He said he was going to follow the cliffs as he made his way back to the house. When you find him, tell him I've gone to see if Ainslie's in the cave."

"I dinnae think she would go there, Madeline. She promised *Faither* she would nae ever enter the cave."

"I know she did, but I need to be sure she's not there." Madeline leaned down and kissed the girl's cheek. "Now tell Mrs. McFayden where you're going so Angus knows to go straight to the inlet."

Gently, Madeline pushed Grace toward the front door of the manor then turned and ran around the side of the house and toward the cliff. In minutes she reached the edge of the precipice overlooking the inlet. Clinging to the rope handrail, Madeline quickly made her way down the steep, narrow path to the inlet. As she reached the beach, she ran toward the outcrop.

The moment she reached the rocks, Madeline stared down at the sand. A wave retreated from the beach, and she saw the remaining traces of a small footprint. Her heart began to pound wildly with horror. Ainslie had said it was possible to walk around to the other side when the tide was out, but that wasn't the case now. The water had already risen to beat against the base of the outcrop that formed the natural harbor.

Quickly removing her shoes, Madeline waded into the water and gasped at how cold it was. It was not quite the end of September, but the water felt as if it were November or December. Forcing herself to ignore the cold, she concentrated on moving along the wall of rock to its outermost point. The further she moved out into the water, the colder it became. When she rounded the stone outcrop, she forgot the cold water the instant she saw the wide opening in the cliff wall a short distance away.

Hoping it was the cave entrance, she waded forward as quickly as she could. The water became deeper and the waves stronger the closer she came to the cave entrance. It tugged at her legs with a strength that forced her to fight simply to remain standing. She slipped suddenly, and the water rushed over her up to her chest.

Frightened, she froze where she stood as the vivid memory of being thrown into the water when the sailboat had capsized filled her head. Terror and fear rolled through her in one wild rush until her stomach churned. Desperately, she fought hard to push her anxiety aside by reminding herself she was a strong swimmer. In the worst-case scenario, if she was forced to swim, she wouldn't be in the open water during the middle of a storm.

All that mattered now was finding Ainslie. Madeline knew she would never be able to live with herself if they discovered too late that she had been hiding in the sea cave. If she was inside, Ainslie could easily drown if she didn't get out before the tide came in, and Madeline had no idea how long it would be before that happened.

With each step she took toward the cave entrance, the deeper the water became. Iain had already lost his brother to the sea, and she refused to let it happen to his daughter. As she reached the cave, she peered into the darkness.

"*Fuck*," she muttered fiercely. Why hadn't she thought to bring a lantern with her. She snorted silently as she realized it wouldn't have helped because the water would put the flame out. Cupping her hands around her mouth, she shouted Ainslie's name, but if the girl had shouted a reply, the sound of the waves drowned it out.

Madeline's heart pounded with fear as she moved into the cavern. Once again she called out to Ainslie. In the distance, she could have sworn she'd heard something, but she wasn't sure if it was an echo of her own voice or Ainslie shouting back. Terror skimmed through her, but Madeline continued forward.

With each step forward, her soaked gown slowed her progress. Not only was the material heavy, but parts of the skirt floated on top of the water from where Iain had split the gown up its side seams. The water-logged material pushed and pulled against Madeline with every wave that surged into the cave's mouth.

Frustrated by her slow progress, she knew the heavy material had become a significant disadvantage, and it would only make the situation worse if she didn't do something. The thought made her reach behind her to undo the gown's buttons. Her fingers were numb from the cold water, and when she managed to undo a couple of buttons, she pulled hard at the back of the gown trying to rip it open.

After several tries she felt a number of the buttons give way. It wasn't as many as she'd hoped for, but the gape in the back of the dress was just enough to give her wiggle room. Fighting with the snug, wet sleeves clinging to her skin, she finally pulled her arms free then pushed the water-soaked gown up and over her head. Tossing the heavy dress aside, she was able to move forward more quickly now.

Her eyes had grown accustomed to the dark, and to her surprise, there were holes in the cave's ceiling that allowed light to filter through. As she moved deeper into the darkness, she offered up a word of thanks for the varied sized holes that fed enough light into the cave to see by. A moment later she uttered a fierce curse as water splashed through the holes and doused her. When she'd finished spluttering and wiping sea water out of her eyes, Madeline cupped her hands around her mouth and called out to Ainslie again.

As before, she couldn't tell if it was her voice echoing back at her or if it was Ainslie replying. She thought she heard another shout, but it was indistinguishable and seemed to echo from behind her. Shivering with cold, Madeline continued forward and a few feet deeper into the cave she called out Ainslie's name again. This time she heard the girl's shout, and relief made her sag slightly before she called out that she was coming for her.

Every few yards, Madeline would give a shout out to the girl in an effort to determine how close she was to Ainslie's location. The echoes in the cavern made it difficult to know if she was heading in the right direction as the sounds echoed in front and back of her. She had gone several feet, when the thigh-high, water-filled passage took a right turn.

As Madeline rounded the corner, she saw Ainslie sitting on a dry area of stone. Relieved that she was safe, Madeline rushed forward. She was only about six feet away from the girl when the floor beneath her feet disappeared. Caught unprepared, Madeline sank below the waterline and salt water filled her mouth.

In the next instant, she bobbed back up into the cave. Coughing hard, she tried to draw in air as she struggled against the strong currents pulling viciously at her legs. Panic sailed through her, and in the distance, she heard someone frantically calling her name. Beneath her, the water tugging at her legs won, and the current pulled her downward again. Suddenly, she realized she was drowning for a second time.

Chapter 17

Iain slipped several times as he raced down the sloped path to the inlet. If not for the hemp rope that served as a handrail, he would have fallen to his death because he was moving so fast. But the only thing his brain was focused on was an image of Madeline and Ainslie trapped in the sea cave. If he were to lose them—a voice in the back of his head shouted he would not let that happen.

As he reached the beach, he saw something floating in the water. His heart crashing into his chest, Iain charged into the sea without hesitation. Fighting to remain upright against the currents beneath the surface, he waded deeper into the water. The moment he reached the object, he realized it was Madeline's gown. Fists burrowing in the sodden wool, he jerked his head first one way and then the other.

"*Madeline*," he roared in a state of sheer panic. "*Ainslie.*"

There was no answer to his shouts. Blindly, he plodded through the water toward the outcrop. The sight of a feminine shoe floating in the water near the shoreline heightened his fear to a level that threatened to undo him.

"*Madeline. Ainslie.*" Either they couldn't hear him or they—*no*, he refused to think the worst. "Madeline is an intelligent woman, Fraser. She knows she'll be able to move more easily and faster without wet clothing weighing her down."

The thought made him quickly remove his jacket, shoes, and hose. Knowing he might need his *sigan dubh*, he tucked the blade and its sheath snug between his kilt and stomach. He'd need every advantage if he was going to save them. Over his shoulder, he heard Angus's shout, and he turned to see the tall, burly Scotsman racing toward him. Over the man's shoulder was a large coil of corded hemp. Iain immediately leaped forward as the man reached him and tugged at the coil to find one end of the rope.

"Let me go, Iain," the older Scotsman said quietly as he watched his employer tie the thick cord of hemp around his waist and use a bowline knot to secure it in place. Both men knew the old sailor's knot wouldn't come loose easily.

"*Nae*," Iain snarled. "I need ye tae hold the rope."

"But ye—"

"I'm going after them." Iain met the other man's gaze steadily. "You're stronger than I am. If the cavern fills with water like it did…ye can still pull Ainslie and Madeline out of the cavern faster than they can swim."

"And what about ye?" Angus objected with a shake of his head.

"I might not be as good a swimmer as my brother was, but I'm stronger than Madeline and Ainslie. I'll be all right."

"And the rope? It might nae be long enough, Iain."

"I'll find a way tae secure it inside the cavern if it pulls up short. I trust ye nae tae let go on this end."

"Aye," Angus said gruffly.

Shouts echoed from the cliff, and Iain saw Squire Tewel, his son, and one of Tewel's farm hands making their way down the steep slope to the inlet. Iain turned away, but Angus's large hand clamped down on his shoulder.

"Tewel has rope with him. We'll tie it off, but…" The Scotsman blanched slightly, and Iain patted the large hand on his shoulder.

"Three tugs means the line is secured around Madeline and Ainslie, and ye are tae pull as fast as ye can. At least on the surface they'll have a fighting chance, and the rope will keep them from being swept out to sea if…"

Iain didn't finish the thought. Instead, he whirled around and splashed his way through the water toward the farthest part of the outcrop. Rounding the curve of the rock face he saw the entrance to the sea cave.

Fear flooded through him, and he froze where he was. It took only a second for his head to fill with the image of his brother's lifeless body floating at the cave entrance. He wasn't sure how long he stood there, but the sudden, strong tug on the rope around his waist forced him out of the past. Angus had clearly noticed he wasn't moving and had used the tug to capture Iain's attention.

"Goddamnit, Fraser," he growled. "If ye cannae save them, then go back and let Angus try."

The taunt of cowardice made him blow out an explosive breath of air from his lungs as he moved forward once more. Pushing his way through the water that was almost up to his waist, Iain fought against the unseen currents trying to drag him off his feet. He reached the cavern's entrance in less than a minute and paused in front of the yawning hole. A shudder hammered its way through him as he remembered the moment he'd reached the surface all those years ago.

In the next breath, he saw Madeline's and Ainslie's faces in his mind. The moment their images filled his head, a strange calmness rolled over him. It was as if his terror had become a minor nuisance that his brain had pushed into the back of his mind, so it wouldn't stop him from doing what needed to be done.

Slogging his way through the water that was slowly inching its way up to his waist, Iain reached the portion of the cave where the light from outside was replaced by the limited illumination from the holes in the rock ceiling. His gut knotted with renewed fear as a gushing stream of water poured out of one of the larger holes and drenched his head and torso. He shuddered beneath the cold water.

"*Màthair of God*, move your arse, Fraser. If they don't drown, they'll die from the cold water." Ahead of him, he heard a shout, and his heart slammed into his chest. *"Madeline."*

His loud cry received no answer, and he knew his voice had been drowned out by the sea. Waves were now pounding against the rocks that made up the cavern's ceiling. The noise of the sea and the cavern's acoustics would make it difficult for Madeline to know he was behind her. With a surge of energy, Iain pushed his way quickly forward through the water, ignoring the way the currents beneath the surface fought to halt his progress.

The rope around his waist tightened then abruptly tugged him backward. Immediately, he retaliated with a hard jerk on the thick, corded hemp. Angus tugged on the rope again, this time twice, and Iain hesitated. Had the rope run out? Above his head, water streamed through two holes close together as the waves receded.

Almost as if someone else was guiding his hands, he struggled to undo the bowline knot holding the rope snug around him. Quickly shoving the end of the rope through one hole he pushed his fingers up through the second one to search for the wet hemp. The moment he found it, he pulled it down through the hole then knotted the rope off. He'd need it for Ainslie and Madeline on their way out of the cave.

Continuing forward, he listened hard for Madeline's or Ainslie's voices, but the North Sea was doing its best to drown out any sound. Ahead of him, he recognized the sharp right turn of the dark passageway. The ledge was just beyond it, that and the riptide pool. His heart thundered in his ears as he pushed against the water to reach the turn. A second later, Iain heard Madeline's voice followed by Ainslie's. Suddenly his daughter's voice erupted in shrill screams of alarm. The horror and panic in his daughter's voice as she repeatedly called out Madeline's name nearly pulled every last breath from Iain's lungs.

"Màthair of God, the riptide pool."

Adrenalin crashed through him as he plunged through the water with the strength of a man possessed and rounded the corner of the passage to see Ainslie on the ledge he'd taken refuge on as a boy. The riptide pool had been one reason he'd been too terrified to leave the cave all those years ago.

He was certain the passage of time had made the pool even more dangerous, as the sea would have expanded the two cross tunnels of water under the one leading to the ledge, where his youngest was on her knees. Ainslie was leaning forward her hand outstretched toward a spot in the pool that was churning from Madeline's wild thrashing to reach the surface.

"Ainslie, get away from the edge," he ordered in a harsh, fierce tone. "She'll pull ye in, and ye will both drown."

His daughter jerked her head in his direction, and she began to sob. Despite his wish to reassure her, Iain knew Madeline was his first priority. He saw her bob to the surface, gasping for air before she was tugged down below the water again.

"*Fuck*," he snarled at the unseen enemy trying to pull Madeline to her death.

Carefully he slid one foot at a time to the spot where he remembered the floor ended in front of the deep pool. Madeline's hand suddenly shot up into the air close to where he was standing and slapped at the water as if searching for something to hold on to. His heart in his throat, he lunged forward and wrapped his hand around her wrist.

With a hard tug, Iain pulled Madeline toward him and up out the water. He fell backward slightly before he regained his footing on the rock floor and straightened to pull her close. Coughing hard, Madeline dragged in deep, ragged breaths as she leaned against him.

"It's all right, *mo ghràdh*, ye are safe now." At his soft words, she looked up at him wide-eyed with fear. With a gentle stroke of her cheek, he gave her a quick kiss. "I want ye tae start back."

"No," she said in a fierce whisper. "I'm not leaving you or Ainslie behind."

"Damnit, Madeline. I want ye tae—"

"I'm not leaving, so you can either stand here and waste time arguing with me, or do what needs to be done to reach Ainslie."

With a harsh oath, he jerked his head in a sharp nod and forced her to stand behind him. Across the dangerous pool of water, Iain met his daughter's terrified gaze.

"Ainslie, I know you're scared, lass, but ye will be fine if ye do exactly as I say."

The girl didn't say a word, she simply bobbed her head sharply. Moving to the opposite side of the cavern's passageway, Iain pressed his chest to the wet wall.

"I want ye tae stand against the wall just like I'm doing, lass. Then I want ye tae slowly slide toward me until your right foot is almost on the edge of the ledge."

With another nod, Ainslie did as he instructed, and Iain swallowed hard as he remembered how dangerous the next few minutes would be. If she slipped—he pushed the thought aside.

"That's a good lass. The next part is going tae be difficult, but ye can do this, *mo leannan*. I need ye to stretch out your hand. There should be two indentations in the wall. They're small, like the cubbyholes in my desk."

Ainslie began to do as he said, then suddenly retreated with a look of abject terror on her face. With a violent shake of her head, tears streamed down her cheeks.

"I cannae do it, *Faither*. I dinnae want tae fall into the pool."

"I ken you're afraid, Ainslie. But I also ken how brave ye are. Ye are even braver than your Uncle Thane, who was fearless." Iain flicked his fingers in a gesture for her to come forward. "I will nae let go of ye, *mo leannan*. I love ye, and I will give my life tae keep ye safe."

The moment his daughter's eyes widened in surprise, Iain bit down on the inside of his cheek. He had a great deal to atone for where Ainslie was concerned.

"Come on now, my wee brave lass. I'm right here, I'll nae let anything happen tae ye."

With a small nod, Ainslie pressed her body against the stone then slid her hand forward over the cavern's wall. An exultant smile on her lips, she placed her hand in the indentation then looked at him.

"I found them, *Faither.*"

"That's my bonnie lass. Now I want ye tae stretch out your right leg and put your toes into the nook that's almost directly below your hand." Panic crossed her face, and Iain suppressed his fear and forced a smile to his lips. "Ye can do this, Ainslie."

Slowly, his daughter stretched out her right foot to find the niche Iain remembered from when Thane had talked him through these same terrifying steps.

"Now I want ye tae put your left hand in that small cubbyhole that's next to your right hand. Keep as much of your left foot on the ledge as ye can."

Without questioning him, Ainslie did as he instructed. Behind him, Iain heard Madeline draw in a sharp breath as they watched his youngest clinging to the wall of the cave with the treacherous water churning below her.

"The next thing ye must do will be the hardest of all, Ainslie. Ye will need tae trust me, *mo leannan.* Can ye do that?"

Iain met the girl's gaze across the short, yet perilous space between them. The fear in her eyes made his heart contort violently in his chest. Terrified for her, Iain waited for her to respond.

"Aye, *Faither.* I trust ye." Ainslie's voice was not much more than a whisper, but Iain heard it, and he nodded with approval.

"That's my brave, bonnie lass. Now when I say so, I want ye tae stretch out your right hand toward me. The minute I grab your arm, I want ye tae jump toward me, using your left foot to push off and away from the ledge. Can ye do that for me, Ainslie?"

The girl's eyes darkened with terror, but Iain knew it was nothing compared to his fear of losing her. Without looking away from his youngest, he spoke softly to Madeline.

"Madeline, can ye hold my arm tae help anchor me?"

"Yes."

There was a note of fear in her voice that matched his own, and he felt Madeline's cold hands wrap around his forearm in a grip that was so strong it startled him. Slowly, he slid his chest across the wet rock and shifted his weight toward Ainslie with Madeline pulling against him. Muscles taut with tension, Iain continued to stretch himself forward until his hand was only a couple of feet away from where Ainslie clung precariously to the rock wall.

"Are ye ready, Ainslie?" he asked quietly. The girl flinched, but she gave him a slight nod. Iain's muscles tightened as he prepared himself to pull Ainslie into his chest. "Remember what I said, when I start tae pull ye over here, ye need tae jump toward me. I promise I will nae let ye go."

At his words, the girl gave him a slight nod then slowly slid her right hand out of the rock indentation and toward him. In seconds, Iain's fingers curled tightly around her arm.

"Now, Ainslie."

With a hard tug, Iain pulled his daughter toward him while throwing himself backward at the same time. The two of them sank beneath the waist high water, but Madeline tugged hard on Iain's arm to help him regain solid footing while his other arm remained tightly wrapped around Ainslie's waist.

As he dragged his youngest daughter up out of the water and into an upright position, Ainslie coughed and spluttered for a few seconds before she began to sob. Her arms wrapped tightly around his waist, Ainslie trembled violently as she clung to him.

Iain held his daughter close, while he bent his head to murmur soothing words in her ear. The girl's sobs slowly softened, he felt the tug of the sea against his legs. Close beside him, Madeline touched his arm.

"Iain." The urgency in her voice as she said his name made him look at her and nod.

"Aye." He gently forced Ainslie to look up at him. "We need tae go, *lass*. The hardest part is over."

With a firm grip on his daughter's shoulder, he turned her around and urged Madeline to move ahead of them. Despite the cold water tugging and pulling on them, the three of them made good progress to where Iain had tied off the rope. As he undid the knot, he ordered Madeline and Ainslie to keep going. When he'd freed the thickly laced hemp from the cavern's ceiling, Iain followed them. As he slogged his way forward, he coiled the rope over his shoulder knowing he would need it soon.

They were at least fifteen to twenty yards from the cave's entrance when he saw the water had risen to Madeline's chest, and he could see Ainslie was dog paddling her way forward. Overhead the waves poured a constant stream of water through the holes in the cavern's ceiling, which reduced the light and made it difficult to see.

Iain knew the mouth of the cave was now underwater, and his heart sank. With a sharp command, Iain ordered Madeline and Ainslie to stop. As they turned to look at him, Iain froze. They were almost in the exact same spot where Thane had told him to swim out of the cave and that he would be right behind him. A hard tremor rocked his body, and his breathing became fast and shallow.

"Why are we stopping?" Madeline exclaimed softly as she took two steps toward him. "We need to use what little air is left before we're forced to swim out of the cave."

Unable to answer her, Iain looked at Madeline's frightened expression before he turned his head toward his daughter. Lips turning bluish from the cold, Ainslie's face was calm and without fear as she eyed him with a trust he knew he could not betray. A bolt of energy surged through him, and Iain waded forward. Silently, he pulled Ainslie toward him and wrapped the rope snuggly around her waist. With a hard tug, he turned his daughter toward Madeline.

"Wrap your arms around Madeline's neck, Ainslie."

"But why, *Faither*? I ken how tae swim. Ethan taught me at the pond, and I can hold my breath longer than him." At his youngest daughter's confident declaration, Iain stared at her in stunned amazement. A look of trepidation swept over his daughter's face, before he twisted his lips in a slight smile.

"Why I should be surprised that the niece of Thane Fraser has the same courage and daring as her uncle, I dinnae ken. But ye will need to hold your breath longer than ye ever have before. Do ye understand?"

"Aye, Faither."

"Iain, I don't understand what you're doing." Madeline's voice echoed with fear and angry confusion as she put her arms around the child.

"Angus is on the other end of the rope. Ye will need to swim, but the mon will pull ye at the same time. With Angus pulling on the rope, ye will reach the mouth of the cave faster."

Before she could protest again, he threw the rope over Madeline's head and pulled it taut around her waist so she and Ainslie were bound together. As he worked to secure the rope with a bowline knot, Iain pressed his mouth to Madeline's ear.

"We have about fifteen tae twenty yards tae go before we reach the cave's entrance. There's nothing but water between here and the surface outside of the cave. We will also be swimming against the tide."

"Oh, dear God," Madeline whispered hoarsely.

The knot completed, he squeezed Madeline's hand, then turned to Ainslie. Pulling his *sgian dubh* and its sheath out of his kilt, Iain pressed the knife into his daughter's trembling hands. He bent his head toward Ainslie's.

"Take my *sgian dubh*, lass. Ye may need it to cut ye and Madeline free of the rope once ye are out of the cave," he whispered. The girl accepted the knife and tucked it down into the front of her dress, her eyes glistening with tears. He smiled. "What's this? Tears? Surely that is nae possible. My brave Ainslie is nae one to cry."

The girl blinked rapidly and her trembling lips curved upward. Iain smiled back at her, his heart full of love and pride. She was every brave and daring person he was not. Not even Thane could hold a candle to his Ainslie's courage. Iain kissed her forehead before he took a step back.

"I need both of ye tae take deep—"

"No, we'll not leave you." Madeline's voice was fierce as she floundered in the water, toward him, hindered by Ainslie bound to her by the rope. Despite her inability to move easily, Madeline's fingers wrapped around his shirt sleeve to tug him toward her.

"The passage is nae wide enough for all three of us tae swim through it together. I will be right behind ye." Iain's voice was quiet as he gently forced her to release him.

The desperation and panic on Madeline's sweet features said she was remembering the story he'd told her about the day Thane had died. Something in her gaze made him step forward and cup her face in his hands. Leaning forward he kissed her deeply before his mouth feathered its way to her ear.

"I love ye, Madeline. Dinnae ever forget that, *mo ghràdh*." Iain didn't give her a chance to respond as he hardened his features and took a step back. "Now both of ye take three deep breaths. Madeline, keep your arms outstretched to keep from hitting the walls of the cave, and kick as hard as ye can. Let Angus and the rope do the rest of the work."

His heart hammering in his chest, Iain watched as Madeline and Ainslie did as he commanded. Madeline's gaze remained locked with his unflinchingly, and as she and Ainslie drew in their third breath, Iain tugged hard on the rope three times. A split-second later, the two of them disappeared beneath the water.

Left alone in the dark, watery tomb, Iain tried to drag air into his lungs, but the rising water kept rushing into his mouth. He retreated several feet and struggled to fight off the panic that was tightening muscles already wanting to contract from the cold water. Closing his eyes, he tried to calm himself. If he allowed his fear to win, there was no doubt in his mind that he would drown just as Thane had.

"If ye love the woman, Fraser, then ye need to swim faster than Thane ever could. She's already alone in the world. Ye cannae leave her or your daughters. They need ye tae fight."

Burying his fear as deep as he could, Iain prepared himself for the horror that lay ahead of him. With each deep breath he drew into his lungs, his fear fought hard to hold him back. Resisting the terror trying to take control of his mind and body, he inhaled one last deep breath then dove into the water.

There was no light to show him the way, and he was immediately disoriented. It prevented him from swimming for a moment as his terror tried to tell him he was going the wrong way. A sudden surge of water crashed into his chest and sent him crashing into the stone wall of the deadly passageway.

Iain barely held in his cry of pain, but a small amount of precious air escaped him as he grunted beneath the impact. Stunned, he didn't move for a moment, and disorientation began to set in. Which direction was life or death?

From somewhere far off in the distance, he heard Thane's voice harshly calling his name and ordering him to swim. Turning toward the voice on his left, Iain spread his arms outward allowing his hands to steady himself against the stone walls and push himself forward with every kick of his legs.

Every time the tide surged into the cave and tried to send him backward, he would stop and brace himself against the cave wall. As the strength of the current eased, he continued forward, while using the strength of its retreat to pull him closer to what he prayed was the open sea and a chance at survival.

Suddenly, a ray of light penetrated the darkness in front of him. With a rush of adrenalin, he kicked hard to drive himself forward to what his brain said was life. He was just on the edge of the light when the burning sensation clutched at his lungs.

It instantly exploded to engulf his chest as if someone has set his insides on fire. His body reacted immediately on instinct and tried to breathe in air where only water existed. Again, he heard Thane's voice ordering him to swim, but he couldn't move his limbs. All he could do was thrash about as his mouth opened and tried to breathe in air. Slowly, the light in front of him disappeared just as the air in his lungs had. As everything grew dark, Iain stopped fighting the pain. Images of Madeline and his daughters laughing flashed through his head, and he quietly gave himself up to the water with a resigned sense of peace.

Chapter 18

Madeline gasped for air as her head popped above the water. Against her chest, Ainslie moved slightly, and Madeline tried to shake the child.

"*Ainslie*, breathe sweetheart. It's okay to breathe."

The girl suddenly coughed and water spluttered out of her mouth before she dragged in a deep breath of air. Relief spiraled through Madeline at the sound, and she closed her eyes for a brief moment. The rope was still pulling them away from the cave, and she caught it and tugged on it several times. As the wet hemp went limp in her hands, she awkwardly turned around in the water to look toward the cave. Where was Iain? Her heart pounded wildly in her chest when after several seconds he didn't rise above the surface.

"Oh, dear God." At Madeline's hoarse exclamation, Ainslie shouted for her father.

When he didn't reply, the child uttered a strong curse word and Madeline stared down at her in shocked surprise. The girl grimaced beneath her governess's gaze then reached for something inside her dress. In seconds, Ainslie raised her hand, and a silver blade glinted in the sunlight.

"Where did you get that?" Madeline gasped in horror before she read the answer in Ainslie's dark violet eyes. She immediately turned her head toward the cave's entrance. There was still no sign of Iain, and her heart thudded with fear. Ainslie had already begun to saw against the wet rope, but her movements were slow and jerky as the child was shaking so hard. Madeline was trembling almost as hard from the cold as well, but the thought of losing Iain sent a surge of heat and energy pulsing through her veins.

"Give me the knife, Ainslie." At Madeline's quiet command, the girl jerked her head up. "It's going to be all right. I'm going to cut myself free and go back for your father."

Without a word of protest, the child handed her the knife. The handle was heavy and awkward in her hand, but Madeline closed her fingers around it in a death grip. The blade was incredibly sharp, and while it took several precious seconds to cut through the sturdy rope, she finally freed herself. Iain had wrapped the rope around Ainslie's waist twice, and the fact he might have expected this moment flitted through Madeline's head. With the bowline knot no longer holding the rope in place, Madeline handed the knife back to her young charge, then tried to tuck the free end of the rope into the hemp wrapped around Ainslie's waist, but the girl slapped her hand away.

"*Nae.* Ye *must* go after *Faither.* Please Madeline, ye have tae save him." The guilt on Ainslie's face was so stark, Madeline thought the girl might go after Iain herself if she didn't move quickly. With a nod, she pulled away from Ainslie.

"Tug the rope three times, and Angus will know to pull you back to the beach."

The moment the child bobbed her head, Madeline turned away and swam toward the mouth of the cave. The last time she'd been this cold and exhausted had been the night Iain had pulled her from the sea. With a resolve that gave her the ability to overcome her body's protests, Madeline swam toward the dark hole.

The tide pushed her forward, then tried to pull her away, but she fought the water with a determination she knew came from adrenalin. It was a source of energy that wouldn't last, and she forced herself to remain focused. As she reached the cave entrance, she saw what looked like white caps created by something in the water. Praying it was Iain swimming toward her, Madeline swam forward several strokes.

The tide rolled into the cave and over her head, the current trying to press her down. She fought back and kicked her way back up to the surface. Only a couple of feet away, she saw Iain's dark head being pushed down into the water and toward the back of the cavern. Desperately, Madeline swam two more strokes forward and pulled his head above the water. To her horror, he didn't drag in a breath, but remained still as he floated next to her.

"Iain," she screamed with a grief that sliced through her with the sharpness of his *sgian dubh*. She shook him slightly, and when he didn't respond, fiery anger spread its way through her limbs. "Oh no, you don't, you arrogant Scot. I will not let you get away with saying you love me only to die on me."

One arm wrapped around his neck, she pushed her way through the water as if she were fighting to win a triathlon. Every second was precious now if she was going to get him to shore in time to save him. She was almost halfway toward the outcrop of rock that enclosed the inlet when she saw Ainslie bobbing in the water in almost the same spot where she'd left her moments ago. Furious, Madeline glared at her, but the child scowled back with a look that mimicked her father's.

"Ye need my help."

Despite her anger, Madeline knew the girl was right. Without thinking twice, she pulled Iain closer to his daughter to press Ainslie's chest into her father's back. As quickly as her cold limbs could move, Madeline wrapped the rope around father and daughter twice.

"Keep his head above water… as best you can." Madeline's teeth were chattering almost as badly as Ainslie's.

"But how… will ye—"

"Don't say another… goddamn word, Ainslie. You're in enough trouble… as it is. If you don't do what I say, I'm…

going to paddle your ass until you… won't be able to sit down… for a week."

The girl's eyes were wide in her face as she silently nodded her agreement to obey. Madeline gave three hard tugs to the rope, and father and daughter slid through the water at a rapidly increasing pace. Fear driving her forward, Madeline swam after them as fast as her contracting limbs would let her.

Weariness flooded her body with a suddenness that made her flounder in the water. The adrenaline that had allowed her to reach Iain had run its course. Instinctively, Madeline knew she wouldn't make it back to the beach if she tried to swim around the outcrop of rocks. With several lethargic strokes, she headed straight toward the rocks, where she wrapped her fingers around some seaweed to hold her in place for a moment.

A wordless prayer of gratitude moved Madeline's lips for the brief respite as she drank in deep breaths against the rocks. She was trembling badly, and she realized she was still in great danger. The water was cold, and while it had been bearable in the beginning, her prolonged exposure meant that hypothermia would set in soon, if it hadn't already. Eyes closed, she rested her forehead against a smooth, flat section of the rock and tried to move, but exhaustion and the cold proved a difficult obstacle to overcome.

It was all she could do simply to drag herself forward along the outcrop using the rock face to steady her. The memory of Iain's lifeless body made her release a sob of pain, and she tried to move faster. Did Angus and the others know CPR or was she the only one who knew what to do?

Frustration sailed through her at how little she knew about medical history and how slow her body moved. Shouts erupted in the air from the other side of the rocks, and Madeline heard Ainslie and Grace shrieking her name. Their cries were stark with grief, pain, and fear. Instantly, the life went out of her. Oh God, Iain was dead. Just as he'd been unable to save his brother, she'd been unable to save the man she loved.

Grief swelled up inside Madeline, and she threw her head back and released a scream of sorrow that echoed wildly over the sound of the sea. It was a primal vocalization of her heart breaking. Sobbing hysterically, Madeline's cheek stung as it scraped across the rough surface of the outcrop.

Never in her life had she ever wanted to die until this moment. And she craved death now. Ached for it. Every part of her was dead, and she allowed her fingers to slowly loosen their grip on the wet stone. Tears were still streaming down her cheeks, when she heard shouts from up above. Slowly raising her head, Madeline didn't recognize the two men shouting, and she ignored their cries.

In a listless movement, she bowed her head again silently wishing them to go away. She was too tired, too numb, too dead inside to care if someone wanted to save her. She didn't want to be saved. Overhead, she heard Ainslie's voice shouting her name, but she didn't look up. The small measure of relief that the girl had made it safely to shore, was swiftly replaced with a pain so terrible she had no words to define it. Madeline sobbed again as Iain's face filled her head.

"Madeline, take the rope, lass."

Angus's voice was loud and sharp as wet hemp slapped against her back. She lifted her head to stare upward. Through her tears, she saw a blurry shape she recognized as the tall Scotsman. Madeline rejected his command with a slow shake of her head.

"I have nae seen such a bull-headed lass in my entire life," he shouted angrily. "Ye and Iain deserve each other. I hope the two of ye make each other miserable until your dying days."

For a moment, Angus's words echoed in her ears like an annoying fly buzzing about her head. As each second ticked by, she slowly absorbed the Scotsman's words. He said he wanted her and Iain to make each other miserable. How was that possible? Madeline's head jerked up as she stared at the man dangling the rope against her back. Had he just said Iain was alive?

"Aye, so, ye finally see the lay of the land, dinnae ye, lass. Now, put ye head and arms through the loop." Something almost like laughter echoed in Angus's voice as he nodded toward the rope hanging against the rock face. "If I dinnae get ye up here then down tae the beach, Iain is apt tae try and fetch ye himself, and the mon is just back from the dead. He's nae in any shape tae do that."

Iain was alive. The thought skimmed its way across every nerve ending in her body until she was tingling all over. Joy warmed her blood, and her lethargy gone, she obeyed Angus's instructions. When she reached the top of the outcrop, she staggered a few feet toward the opposite side of the outcrop's flat surface to look down at the beach. Iain was lying in the sand, nodding at something Grace was saying to him.

Almost as if he sensed her watching him, Iain turned onto his side and tried to push himself up on his elbow. Her heart swelled as she drank in the sight of him. He was alive. Closing her eyes, Madeline murmured her thanks to God. In the next second, a small frame latched onto her. Ainslie's arms were tight around Madeline's waist as the girl looked up at her. Tears streamed down Ainslie's face, and with another prayer of gratitude escaping her lips, Madeline hugged the child close.

Unable to tell if the girl was crying out of reaction to her ordeal, fear, or happiness, Madeline didn't question Ainslie. The sudden wave of dizziness that rolled over her made Madeline stagger a few steps to one side to remain standing. Angus uttered an inaudible curse and gently pried Ainslie away from her.

"Ethan, help Ainslie back down tae the beach, lad," he said as he swung Madeline up into his arms. "I'll see Madeline gets down there safely. "

Iain's youngest daughter nodded and with her friend's arm around her waist, Ainslie slowly walked toward the face of the cliff. Madeline murmured a soft protest as the tall, brawny man swung her up into his arms and followed the children. The moment he scowled at her dissension, she winced.

"If ye think I am aboot tae listen tae the lad rail at me for nae bringing ye tae him fast enough, then ye are as tetched in the head as he is."

The grumpy yet affectionate growl in the man's voice made her bite back a smile as he headed toward a natural slope of stone that was a path down to the inlet. As they reached the sand, Madeline quietly asked the Scotsman to set her down. Sand squished between her toes as she staggered forward as fast as she could to where Iain laid next to a roaring bonfire someone had built.

The moment she reached Iain, she sank down to her knees beside him. Tears blurred her vision as she bent over him and kissed him gently. Fingers brushing across his forehead and cheek, she caressed him tenderly just to prove to herself he was alive and well.

"I thought I'd lost you," she whispered with fear as the memory of the terrifying moments they'd just survived increased the tremors rocking her body.

"Ye almost did, *mo ghràdh*, but ye saved me so Angus could beat the life back into me."

His voice was gravelly, and it held a note of pain that made her carry his hand to her mouth. Iain's lips twisted in a smile that was half amusement and half pain, as he watched Angus drape a heavy blanket over Madeline's shoulders. She had been trembling violently from the cold, exhaustion, pain, and fear for minutes now, and the warmth of the blanket emphasized how cold she really was.

"Ye need to change out of that wet undergarment," Iain said quietly.

"Here? Now?" Her eyebrows shot upward as she eyed him with amused disbelief.

"There is nae need tae worry I will accost ye, *mo ghràdh*," he snorted softly with laughter. "I'm exhausted and in tae much pain tae do nae more than hold your hand."

"*You* might be, but if you think I'm going to undress and wear nothing under this blanket with other men around, then—"

"I have rethought my suggestion and agree ye should nae undress here. Instead, I want Angus tae take ye back to the manor tae change and sit in front of a warm fire."

"And you?" Madeline nodded toward the blanket he was lying on and the one draped over him. His bare shoulders were exposed to the fire and the sunshine above. Iain smiled teasingly at her.

"The fire already has me feeling warm again, although I think it may be days before my chest stops hurting."

"Well, I'm not leaving you."

"Does that mean ye intend tae stay at Muchalls Hall?" The quiet question made her eyes meet his before she looked away.

"Yes," Madeline replied softly as she focused her gaze on the flames of the fire that was thawing her muscles.

It was impossible to leave him now. Although he would never marry her or want them to have children, she didn't care. As long as he loved her, it would be enough. Grace and Ainslie had already become a part of her soul, and she would love them as her own. Strong fingers entwined with hers, and Iain squeezed her hand tightly in his.

"Ye will nae regret it, Madeline. I will never let ye regret staying, *mo leannan*." The fervent promise in his voice made her turn toward him. Just seeing him alive and well made her happy, and she smiled.

"I could never regret loving you, Iain."

A gentle touch on her shoulder made her turn her head. Grace stood staring down at Madeline, the remnants of fear on her lovely face, while Ainslie stood shivering inside a large blanket next to her twin. Without hesitating, Madeline smiled and opened her arms to the girls. The twins immediately threw themselves forward, and they clung to Madeline as if they never intended to let go.

Her heart swelling with love, she tightened her embrace around them and looked over their shoulders at Iain. Their gazes locked, and Madeline drew in her breath at the love reflected in the dark, stormy depths of Iain's blue eyes as his hand reached out to capture hers. As his fingers tightened around hers, she knew it was a silent promise that he would never let go as long as he still had breath in his body.

Chapter 19

Iain jerked awake from the nightmare he'd been having. The sun hung low on the horizon and filled the master suite with a soft glow. An incoherent whisper next to him made him turn his head toward the sound. Madeline lay on the opposite side of the bed with Grace and Ainslie lying between them.

When they'd returned to the manor, Ainslie had been almost hysterical when he'd tried to convince her to nap for a few hours. The child had been terrified to leave him or Madeline. Grace had been almost as upset as her twin. At their reaction, he'd looked helplessly at Madeline until she'd told his daughters she would take a nap with them.

Her suggestion had been a source of immense relief for him. Even though her exhaustion was apparent, the fear in her eyes warned him she would balk at leaving him just as Ainslie had. At that point, he'd admitted to himself that he was equally unwilling to let the three of them out of his sight.

Without thinking twice, he'd ordered them into his bed. Madeline's eyes had widen with alarm as she'd glanced at Bridget and Eileen bustling about the room, but he'd shrugged his indifference. To his and Madeline's amazement, Bridget had looked up from insisting Ainslie finish her hot soup to agree with his decision.

Iain had expected silent disapproval from his housekeeper, but the alacrity with which Angus's wife had agreed with his decision had left him speechless. At his amazement, the housekeeper had eyed him with amusement and murmured that she had no doubt that his bed would be much warmer in the near future. Although the girls hadn't heard the woman's observation, Madeline had been close enough to hear the remark.

The moment Madeline's cheeks flushed with pink, he'd grinned at her. She'd immediately shaken her head in amused disgust, then turned her attention to putting the girls to bed. With the three of them, fully clothed, tucked in beneath the sheets and several blankets, Bridget and Eileen had left Iain sitting at the fire to stand guard.

The girls had fallen asleep almost as soon as they were tucked beneath the sheets. But Madeline had remained awake much longer. The two of them hadn't spoken, they'd simply been content to look at each other. The love in her soft brown eyes had warmed his heart almost as fast as the fire. Before long, Madeline's eyelids had drooped, until with one last sleepy smile, her eyes had drifted shut.

Iain had maintained his vigil for almost an hour before exhaustion had him on the verge of falling asleep in his chair. Gathering several of blankets off a nearby chair, he'd lain down on top of the coverlet next to Ainslie and fallen asleep.

Now as he studied the three most important women in his life, Ainslie moved beneath the covers as a soft moan blew past his daughter's lips. Gently stroking her brow, Iain murmured words of quiet comfort until she fell quiet once more.

He didn't move for a moment, because every time he did so, his entire body ached as if he'd been throwing cabers one after the other for hours. His chest was the most painful. It hurt like hell from where Angus had pounded life back into him. The four of them had returned to the house together, when Madeline's response to his third demand that she and the twins return to the manor reinforced her previous two refusals.

Iain's gaze settled on Madeline's face again, and his heart tightened in his chest. Today's near tragedy rested on his shoulders. First with Ainslie and her belief that he didn't love her, then Madeline believing the same thing. If he'd not been so stubborn about admitting how much he loved her, she would not have been so eager to leave Muchalls Hall, and Ainslie would not have run away. He'd almost lost both of them.

The thought chilled him.

The logs burning in the fireplace popped and sizzled as the flames ate away at the thick chunks of wood. A second later, the blaze made a log suddenly shift position, and Iain lifted his head when it fell with a thud onto the hearth. It had been several hours since Angus had brought Iain back from the dead.

Careful not to make the mattress shift position as he climbed out of bed, he bent over Ainslie to pull the covers up to her neck, then reached across her do the same for Grace. Unlike the twins, Madeline had the blanket pulled up over her ears, and he smiled as he realized she might steal his covers in the middle of the night. He would have to hold her close every night if he wasn't to freeze to death in bed. His smile broadened at the thought.

Wrapping a blanket around his shoulders, Iain returned to his chair by the fire, then settled his gaze on Madeline sleeping so sweetly in his bed. The idea of holding her close as he fell asleep every night and waking to the sight of her beautiful smile was a happy one. The rest of his life would be spent proving his love for her. It was an emotion that ran deep within his soul.

Staring into the fire, he frowned slightly as he contemplated their future. Would she fight him on not having children? The idea of losing her in childbirth made him close his eyes with a terror he knew could easily drive a wedge between them. Although he'd overcome his fear of water to save her and Ainslie, the idea of watching Madeline grow heavy with child filled him with dread.

He could fight the sea, but he was powerless if something went wrong during childbirth. Watching Flora die without having the ability to save her had been difficult enough. The thought of something similar happening to Madeline was unthinkable.

"Faither?"

The soft, tentative word broke through his thoughts, and Iain turned his head to see Ainslie standing a few feet away. The moment their gazes met, guilt and shame swept over the girl's face, and she immediately bowed her head.

"Come here, Ainslie," he whispered, stretching out his hand to her, but his youngest remained rooted where she stood. "It's all right, my brave, bonnie lass."

At his quiet reassurance, Ainslie lifted her head. Eyes wide in her face, she stared at Iain, and he flicked his fingers to encourage her to come to him. Tears rolled down her cheeks as she ran forward to wrap her arms around his neck.

"I am so sorry, *Faither*. I dinnae mean tae break my oath tae ye. I am so sorry."

Her words were almost incoherent through her quiet sobs, and Iain pulled her tight against his chest. Closing his eyes, he remembered the fear he'd experienced in the sea cave as he'd seen her on the rock ledge with the whirlpool between them. That same fear had returned as he'd tied his youngest daughter to Madeline. It had been the brutal realization that he might not save her. But he had. He'd saved them both. A tangible sensation of relief pummeled its way through him at the sobs whispering out of her. It had been terrifying to drown, but he would willingly do it again a thousand times over if it meant keeping her, Grace, and Madeline safe from harm.

Pulling the girl down into his lap, he closed his blanket around the two of them and remained silent as she wet his shirt with her tears. She cried for a long time, and when her sobs eased, he tightened his embrace as she lifted her head to look at him.

"Do ye ken how proud I am of ye, my bonnie lass."

"I dinnae ken how. Ye drowned because of me." The words were a mere whisper of a sound, and Iain squeezed her tighter.

"Aye, but Angus brought me back."

The only response he received was the sound of her sniffles, and a vise wrapped itself tightly around his chest at the memory of how close he'd come to losing her. Silence filled the room again, and Iain tried to think how best to frame his words so that his youngest understood how much he loved her.

"Ainslie, I want ye tae know I love ye very much. It's why I followed ye into the sea cave."

"Were ye nae afraid."

"Aye, I was terrified," he replied as a wry smile touched his lips before he grew sober. "But I ken ye were in danger, and that's all I could think about."

"But Madeline came for me."

"Aye, but even if I had ken for certain Madeline was trying tae reach ye, I would still have come for ye, *mo nighean luachmhor.*" Ainslie's eyes widened as he said the words, my precious daughter, in Gaelic. "Because I love ye even more than Madeline does. When ye were born, I vowed I would give my life tae keep ye and Grace safe, that's how much I love ye."

Tears made Ainslie's eyes glisten as she stared up at him in disbelief. Her expression made him wince as he brushed a stray lock of hair off her forehead.

"Ainslie, I need to know why ye think I dinnae love ye. Is it because I am stern with ye, lass?"

His daughter stiffened against him, and his fingers gently tipped her chin up so she was forced to meet his gaze. She blinked rapidly in an obvious effort to fight back tears.

"How can ye love me if I am why *Màthair* died?"

"*What?*" Iain's head jerked to one side in astonishment as he stared down at her. "I dinnae understand, lass."

"I heard ye tell Angus a long time ago that *màthair* was nae strong enough deliver two bairns." A small hiccup escaped the girl as she bowed her head. "I ken then that if I had nae been born, *Màthair* would still be here for ye and Grace."

Stunned, Iain stared down at his youngest in horrified disbelief. When had he ever said such a thing to Angus? If he had, he was certain it had not been said in the context Ainslie had come to believe. With a sharp shake of his head, Iain captured his daughter's chin and forced her to meet his gaze.

"Whatever ye heard, Ainslie Fraser, ye misunderstood my words. I have *nae ever*—" he said in a quiet, firm voice. "I repeat, *nae ever*, blamed ye or your sister for what happened tae your *màthair*. It's true that she was nae very strong. But that is nae your doing. I would have done everything in my power tae save her, but there was nothing I or the doctor could do."

As he finished speaking, a voice in the back of his head reminded him that he *had* possessed the power to save Flora. But if they had not had children, he would not have Ainslie and Grace. It would be different with Madeline. Experience had taught him how dangerous it would be for Madeline to have his child, and he intended to take every precaution to ensure that didn't happen.

"Will Madeline die like *màthair* if she has a bairn?" The question made him shake his head with determination, but as he opened his mouth to speak, Madeline answered the question for him.

"I just survived the North Sea for a second time. I think I've proven how feisty I can be when it comes to not dying anytime soon," she said softly. Iain looked up and met her gaze. For a moment, he was certain he saw pain flickering in her eyes as she met his gaze, before she turned her attention to Ainslie. "And *you* are asking *too many* questions, young lady."

"Aye, Madeline will be with us for a long time." He smiled up at her, and once more he could have sworn he saw pain flickering in her gaze before she lifted several locks of Ainslie's hair and shook her head in amused consternation.

"Right now, I think it's time for you to take a bath. Your hair looks like a bee's nest."

A quiet giggle escaped Ainslie, to which Madeline smiled mischievously. Stretching out her hand, she caught his daughter's hand in hers and pulled Ainslie to her feet. The girl didn't argue and headed toward the door only to stop suddenly in mid-stride. Ainslie abruptly spun around on her heel, then hurried back to Iain and wrapped her arms around his neck in a tight hug.

"I love ye, *Faither*," she whispered in his ear before bolting from the room.

The moment Madeline took a step forward to follow Ainslie, Iain reached out to stop her. As his hand caught her arm to hold her in place, Madeline's smile made his heart swell in his chest.

"I love ye, *mo ghràdh*," he replied softly as he smiled up at her. Wrinkling her nose in mock disapproval, Madeline gave him a quick kiss.

"I need to learn Gaelic so I know when you're saying something sweet or when you're calling me something like a Sassenach *eejit*."

"I'm nae sure I like that idea. I enjoy seeing your eyes flash when ye are angry or excited," Iain said softly.

With a gentle tug on her arm, he pulled her toward him while sliding his hand down to lift her hand up to press his lips against the inside of her wrist. Unable to resist, his tongue swirled a circle across her skin. The sound of a sharp inhalation made him raise his head and grin at her, enjoying the desire he saw flare in her eyes.

"They're flashing right now, *mo leannan*, but I dinnae think with anger." He chuckled as she tugged free of his grasp.

"Arrogant Scot," she muttered as she stalked away, but just before she walked out of his bedroom, Madeline glanced over her shoulder, and he saw the smile curving her sweet lips.

Chapter 20

Madeline stood outside Iain's study for a long moment debating whether to interrupt him. It had been almost a week since the terrifying incident in the sea cave, and they'd yet to find a moment alone to talk.

She pursed her mouth at the thought. That wasn't exactly true. Iain had tried for the past two nights after dinner to pull her into the salon to speak with her, but she'd put him off with either an excuse that the girls needed her or she was tired.

Both reasons were true, but she could tell he was growing frustrated that they hadn't been alone other than for a brief embrace, before one of them was needed elsewhere. The girls were deeply traumatized by last Thursday's events. Ainslie in particular remained constantly at Madeline's side or her father's.

In the early morning hours, the night after they'd escaped drowning, the girl had started experiencing nightmares from which she'd awoken screaming in terror. To make her feel safe, Madeline would sit with the girl into the early morning hours so she was there to calm Ainslie's fear if the child woke up in a state of panic. Even Iain was not fully recovered from the incident. It had taken him over two days to recover from being brought back from the dead.

She knew his chest was still sore from where Angus had desperately pounded Iain's chest and ribs to remove the water from his lungs and revive him. Madeline had been worried about him contracting pneumonia, but he showed no signs of being ill other than wincing with pain if he moved the wrong way.

He'd tried to hide it from her and the girls, but the third time she'd seen his discomfort, she'd insisted on wrapping his ribs just in the event he'd experienced a partial fracture. With her sleeping patterns disrupted by her watching over Ainslie at night and worrying about Iain, she was dragging by the time Iain had felt better.

But it hadn't just been her caring for Ainslie and a lack of sleep that had made her avoid speaking at length with Iain. She was still coming to grips with her decision to remain at Muchalls Hall as Iain's mistress. Madeline didn't regret the choice she'd made, nor would she change her mind either.

She loved Iain and wanted to spend the rest of her life with him. But Madeline couldn't help being worried about what the girls would think about the arrangement, not to mention Mrs. McFayden and her disapproving looks.

Now, as she stood outside Iain's study, she forced herself to quietly open the door to peek inside. His head was bent over papers on his desk, so she began to retreat not wanting to disturb him.

The moment the door creaked softly, Iain lifted his head and met her gaze. In seconds, he was up from his desk and striding quickly across the floor to pull her into the study and then his arms. As his mouth claimed hers, Madeline willingly gave herself up to his caress. Passionate and heady, his kiss left her breathless when after a long moment, he lifted his head to smile down at her.

"I have missed ye, *mo ghràdh*." Iain brushed his fingers across her cheek, then chuckled as she opened her mouth to question him. "It means, my love."

"I love the sound of it and its meaning. It's beautiful," she said with a soft sigh of pleasure. Iain kissed her lightly, then caught her hand in his and pulled her toward his desk.

"I have something for ye."

Iain picked up a square jeweler's box from where it sat on top of the desktop and opened it. Nestled inside the dark blue, silk-lined box was a silver brooch. The jewelry was a crown of rubies resting on top of two interlocking hearts.

"It's beautiful," she exclaimed with delight. Her fingers brushed over the silver jewelry as Iain lifted it from the box.

"It's a Luckenbooth brooch. It belonged to my *màthair*. My father gave it to her when she accepted his marriage proposal."

"Thank you," she said softly as he pinned the brooch to her dress.

"I've already sent Cecil tae the church with my request that the priest post the banns. When I return next week, we'll go tae Aberdeen and shop for a ring."

Confused, Madeline stared up at him with a frown. She had no idea what banns were, and the mention of a ring instantly made her feel as if he were giving her jewelry like a man with a mistress usually did. With a shake of her head, Madeline drew in a breath and swallowed hard as she pressed her hand against his heart.

"I don't need you to give me jewelry, Iain," she declared softly. "I chose to stay because I love you."

"I dinnae understand, *mo ghràdh*. Do ye nae want tae marry me, Madeline?" The question made her stare up at him in amazement.

"Marry…? Are you asking me to marry you?"

"Dinnae I just say my father gave the Luckenbooth brooch tae my mother when they became engaged?" Eyebrows arching upward, he shook his head.

"Yes…but, you said…I don't understand," she whispered as hope suddenly unfurled inside her heart. "You said you wouldn't marry again."

"Aye, but that was before I fell in love with ye, Madeline."

"But… you don't want…" The moment her voice trailed away, he narrowed his gaze at her.

"Children? Aye, I have nae changed my mind about that," he said firmly. "We will use protection tae ensure ye dinnae carry a babe. I almost lost ye in the sea cave, I'll nae risk your life with a bairn. But I intend tae marry ye, *mo ghràdh*. I'll nae risk another man trying tae take ye from me."

"Another man?" She laughed with a light heart as she realized Iain was giving his heart to her completely with his proposal of marriage.

"Aye, I dinnae enjoy how I felt when I read that doctor's letter tae ye. I will nae let another mon have your heart. That belongs tae me, just as mine belongs tae ye, *mo ghràdh*."

Tears blurred her vision as he verbally expressed her thoughts. Iain uttered a low sound of concern before he pulled her into his arms.

"What, *mo leannan*? Why are ye crying?"

"Because I'm happy," she choked out before drawing in a deep breath. "I never thought I would hear you say such wonderful words."

"And they're true, *mo ghràdh*. Every one of them. It might have taken this stubborn Scot a few days tae come tae my senses, but I know it would nae have been long before I followed ye. And I would nae have allowed ye tae refuse coming home tae Muchalls Hall with me." Iain grimaced slightly then chuckled. "And that is the last time I will admit tae being stubborn."

"But you're *my* stubborn Scot, and I wouldn't have you any other way," Madeline said softly as she pulled his head down to kiss him.

It was a gentle caress that slowly deepened as Iain's arms tightened around her. Melting into the heat of him, her lips parted beneath his. Spice and evergreen scents brushed over her senses, and the tart, tangy flavor of cinnamon danced across her tongue as it tangled with his in a passionate kiss that made her sex tighten with anticipation.

Everything about him was hard male, and she reveled in the strength and fire of him. A large hand slid across her breast, and she moaned with need. Iain lifted her off her feet and turned her around to sit her on the desk. There was a hunger in his kiss that matched her own. Eager to touch him, her hand slid down and under his sporran to stroke his erection beneath the green plaid wool of his kilt.

A dark sound rumbled in his chest, and with a sound of frustration, he caught her hands and bent them behind her back. Iain's mouth trailed across her cheek then brushed against her ear where he nibbled on its lobe.

"Please, Iain," she whispered as she nipped at the side of his neck.

"Nae, lass. Nae here. I dinnae want someone to interrupt us. I want ye in my bed with nothing between my mouth and your silky, sweet-smelling skin," he murmured as he kissed her again. His mouth crushed hers in a fierce caress before he lifted his head and drew in a deep breath.

"Ye are truly one of the fae, Madeline Whitworth. The next three weeks will seem like an eternity before I can show ye every night and morning how much I love ye."

"*Three weeks?*" she exclaimed. "Are you going to be gone that long?"

"Nae, *mo leannan*, but once I have ye in my bed again, it will nae be easy tae let ye leave me in the morn. And I'll nae sneak about in my own home."

"I've already done that," she murmured as she stretched her neck so her lips could kiss the sharp, angular line of his jaw.

"Aye, but I dinnae think ye would be comfortable about the arrangement, especially where Ainslie and Grace are concerned. Your reaction when I mentioned they dinnae need tae ken was enough tae tell me that."

His thoughtfulness and understanding made Madeline's eyes water again. Iain shook his head slightly and sought her mouth once more in a teasing kiss before he raised his head with a look of regret.

"But I will nae deny that it will test my will power for the next three weeks not tae steal down the hall to make ye mine in every way I can think of." The rueful note in his voice emphasized he was not looking forward to the next three weeks. Madeline felt the same way. As he released her hands, she reached up to wrap her arms around his neck.

"Perhaps a midnight picnic in the trees near the pond would ease your appetite," she murmured and smiled as his expression brightened.

"Aye, a blanket is all that would be required, because I could feast on ye for the rest of our lives, and still not have enough of ye." The wicked gleam in his eyes made her laugh, before her fingers caressed his face.

"I love you, *mo ghràdh*." Madeline winced at her poor pronunciation. The Gaelic endearment sounded nothing like what Iain had said. He laughed at her look of disgust, and when she glared at him, he gave her a quick kiss.

"It was a good first effort, *mo bhòidhchead fuilt dorcha*. I've nae doubt ye will improve, and I ken the girls will enjoy helping ye learn the language."

"Enjoy poking fun at me, you mean." Madeline shook her head with amused disgust.

"Aye, that they will, but they will love ye all the more for trying. Shall we tell them the news now or at dinner?"

"Now," she said with a smile. "Then we can ask Mrs. McFayden to make something special for dinner, to celebrate."

"Then prepare yourself for shouts of excitement, *mo leannan*. Grace and Ainslie love ye almost as much as I do." With a smile, Iain pulled her along behind him as they left the study to find his daughters.

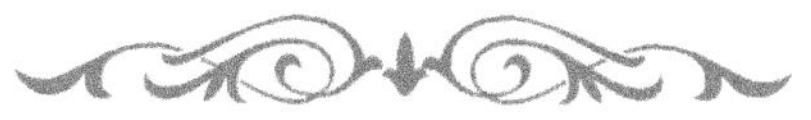

Chapter 21

April 1897

"Damn it to hell," Madeline muttered as she stabbed her finger with the needle.

She was grateful the girls had gone riding with Ethan. The two of them had started a money jar that required her to drop ten shillings into it every time they heard her use a foul word.

In the six months since she and Iain had been married, the twins had already earned ten pounds off her. The first time Iain had dropped her first payment of coin into the jar, he'd arranged for her to have a monthly allowance.

When she protested, he'd laughed and said he was certain most of it would wind up in the jar. He'd laughed even harder when she'd insulted him for teasing her, then had kissed her until she couldn't think straight.

She shook her hand as if it would ease the stinging then examined her finger for blood. Seeing none, Madeline winced, then scowled at the needlepoint that was supposed to be the beginnings of a decorative pillow. Somehow, she was going to have to convince Eileen that needlepoint was something she would never excel at.

Outside, the sound of hoofbeats coming up the drive from the main road whispered through the air, and Madeline lifted her head in surprise. Had the girls returned already? A second later, her heart sank at the more likely explanation that someone had come to call. Immediately, she wished Iain was home. He'd gone to Belgium on business five days ago, and wasn't due home until the day after tomorrow. The thought of entertaining a stranger was not a pleasant one.

The first several weeks after the banns were posted and their marriage, neighbors had descended on the house to extend their well wishes. Madeline was certain some had paid a visit simply to inspect her, especially several of the younger women who'd accompanied their mothers. If looks could have drawn blood, she would have died bleeding to death on the floor.

With a sigh, Madeline rose to her feet and walked to the parlor window. Fingers pulling back the sheer curtains, she drew in a sharp breath of surprise and happiness. Iain was home sooner than he'd said he would be. Madeline whirled around then froze where she stood. As much as she'd longed for Iain's return, Madeline had dreaded it as well.

For the past two days, she'd tried to think of a way to tell him about the baby. Accidents happened, but Iain had made it clear in word and action that he didn't want her to have a baby. Madeline bit down on her lip as she hurried toward the salon doorway eager to see her husband, but dreading the moment she told him she was pregnant. As Madeline entered the main hallway, Iain strode through the door.

Happiness lit up his face as their eyes met, and he closed the distance between them in three quick strides. A moment later, strong arms wrapped around her, and Iain swept her off her feet and swung her around in a circle. Laughing as she looked down at his rugged features, her heart expanded as if it might burst in her chest. Despite her troubled thoughts, being in Iain's arms again filled her with a joy she'd never dreamed possible before she'd arrived at Muchalls Hall. The moment he set her down, he kissed her deeply then lifted his head.

"Did ye miss me, *mo bhòidhchead fuilt dorcha?*"

"Yes, terribly," she whispered as she pulled his head down to hers and kissed him again.

Teasingly, the tip of her tongue slid along the seam of his lips until he parted his mouth, and their tongues mated in a passionate dance. Lost in the heady male scent and taste of him, Madeline's heart skipped several beats, as his hand slid up over her waist until his thumb was rubbing the underside of her breast. Eager for his touch, she thrust her hips forward, and she was satisfied the moment she felt his erection pressing into the apex of her thighs. A dark rumble rose in his chest, and he quickly pushed her away from him.

"Ye are enough tae drive a mon mad, Lady Glenburnie." Iain ran his thumb over her bottom lip, his eyes dark with the same hunger stirring inside her.

"Then why push me away, Lord Glenburnie?" she murmured with a teasing smile.

"Because the wicked, sinful things I want tae do tae ye at the moment can only be done in bed, *mo ghràdh*." He grinned at her and tapped the tip of her nose with his forefinger before he bent his head to nibble at her earlobe. "Would ye like me tae describe in detail everything I intend tae do with ye tonight, *mo leannan*?"

Iain's teasing conjured up images in Madeline's head that made her draw in a quick breath. The man had a way with words that set her on fire. Already she was aching with need. A knowing grin on his face, he winked at her, and Madeline scowled at him in frustration.

"You did that on purpose," she muttered with annoyance.

"Dinnae ye once tell Grace and Ainslie that anticipation is part of the fun."

"Hmm, I suppose that depends on what one's anticipating." Madeline blew out a puff of air as she directed a grumpy glare at him before she retreated from his arms with a laugh. Reluctant to separate herself from him completely, Madeline linked her arm with his as they walked into the study.

"Was your trip successful?"

"Aye, I acquired almost everything I wanted. Although, I had to settle for a third less of the steel I wanted to buy, but other than that, I did quite well." Iain grinned with satisfaction. "There will be money for repairs and improvements to the manor, a new wardrobe for ye and the girls. And I will finally nae have any debt hanging over my head."

"I don't need any new clothes," she said with a smile. "But the girls most definitely need new dresses. Ainslie seems to have grown two inches almost overnight. Her ankles are showing under her skirts, and poor Eileen is appalled."

"I have a feeling Ainslie is going to follow your example in all things as she grows older."

There was an odd note in his voice, and Madeline unlinked her arm from his to halt in the middle of the study. Iain didn't look at her as he continued to make his way to the desk, where he pulled papers from his pockets and dropped them onto the desktop. Uncertain whether he was criticizing her or simply resigned to his youngest's sometimes reckless behavior, Madeline frowned.

"Are you saying I'm a bad influence on her?"

"What?" Iain's head jerked up at her quiet question to stare at her with a dumfounded look. "Of course, not, *mo bhòidhchead fuilt dorcha*. I think ye are an excellent influence on her. But all this talk of her becoming a horse doctor, I had hoped…"

"That she would be willing to settle down and have babies?" At his small shrug, she smiled with relief and shook her head. "Ainslie will be fine. I wouldn't be surprised if she becomes a veterinarian *and* settles down. She knows what she wants and is not afraid to go after it."

"Perhaps," Iain said with a skeptical look. "She's always been strong-willed."

"Oh, *that's* not on *my* head," Madeline laughed. "She gets *all* of her stubbornness from you. There's no doubt she's her father's daughter."

Iain grinned as he circled his desk to catch her hand in his and pull her toward the fire. He sank down into his favorite chair, then tugged her down into his lap. Madeline wrapped an arm around his neck and smiled at him as he studied her with amusement.

"I will nae argue with ye on that point, but I reserve the right tae do so in the future."

"You'll lose the argument every time, and you know it."

Her laughter made him shrug slightly as he grinned up at her. The sudden image of a little boy grinning up at her with stormy blue eyes just like Iain's made Madeline look down at the large hand holding hers. Her face must have revealed her troubled thoughts despite her efforts to hide them. Iain's grip tightened around her fingers.

"What's wrong, Madeline?" When she didn't answer his question, he cupped her chin with his hand and forced her to look at him. "Tell me, *mo ghràdh.*"

Madeline winced then quickly broke free of his embrace to stand up and begin pacing the floor. The moment she did so, Iain was on his feet with startling speed. Strong fingers dug into her shoulders as he stopped her and forced her to face him. Heartsick and uncertain how to tell him the news, Madeline helplessly met his gaze.

Almost as if he could read her mind, his dark blue eyes darkened as he looked down at her stomach. A second later, he released her and took two steps backward. The tension vibrating off of him was a tangible sensation, and a shiver skimmed its way down her spine.

"When?" His voice was devoid of emotion, and Madeline flinched.

Did he blame her for becoming pregnant? Her heart sank at the thought. Her hand pressed against her stomach, Madeline swallowed the knot in her throat that was beginning to choke her.

"Around the end of October," she said quietly.

"How?"

The single word question echoed sharply in her ears. It wasn't just the harsh note in his voice that left her feeling as if he'd hit her. It was the growing suspicion that he blamed her for getting pregnant. Shock held her rigid as she stared at him in disbelief. The silence grew between them like a rubber band being stretched until it was on the brink of snapping back into shape with a painfully unpleasant sting. A sudden burst of anger spiraled through her, and Madeline narrowed her gaze at him.

"*How?*" Madeline heard the icicles dripping off the word. "Are you suggesting I planned this? That I did something to make it happen?"

When he remained silent, Madeline drew in a sharp breath of pain. He *did* blame her. Speechless, Madeline stared at him in horrified disbelief. How could he think her capable of deceiving him in such a way?

In an explosive move, Iain whirled away from Madeline and strode to the window overlooking the North Sea. One hand pushing aside the drapes, his fingers curled around the window frame. Even as careful as he'd been, he'd failed. He'd failed to keep her safe. Only one other time had he felt this powerless, and that was the night he'd watched the life drain out of Flora. The memory made him grow cold.

He would lose Madeline the same way.

He'd been so careful, and yet he would still lose her. The fact could not have been more visceral if it had not been a sharp *sgian dubh* slicing through Iain's gut. He closed his eyes at the fear crawling through him. The one thing he feared even more than water was losing Madeline. He turned around to face her, but his beautiful wife was no longer in the room.

Stunned, he remained motionless as he remembered the wounded look of pain on her face when she'd asked him if he thought she'd done something to deliberately become pregnant. A question he'd not bothered to answer because he'd been reeling from her news. Iain uttered a fierce oath and strode out of the study to find her.

When he stepped out into the hall, Madeline was nowhere to be seen, and he quickly crossed the entryway to look for her in the salon. The empty room only emphasized the fear that was threatening to control his every thought and movement. This is what it would be like when he lost her. It was a realization that became a physical sensation. It gnawed at his insides with a viciousness of a wild animal attacking him.

Iain strode quickly toward the stairs and took the steps two at a time then made his way down the hall. As he quietly opened their bedroom door, Iain saw Madeline sitting on the edge of the bed with her head bent. The defeated slump of her shoulders made his muscles knot with pain.

The door clicked behind him as he closed it, and although he saw her body jerk, she didn't move. Slowly, he moved forward to kneel at her feet. A shudder rippled through her as he took her hands in his.

"I am an arse, *mo ghràdh*. Ye are nae tae blame. I am." His soft apologetic words made her head come up with a jerk. Cheeks wet with tears, she looked pale and drawn. Her appearance made him feel even worse than he had a moment ago.

"Neither one of us is to blame, you, arrogant Scot," she snapped with outrage as she tugged free of his grasp. "Accidents happen, but that you thought I'd deliberately done something to become pregnant—"

"*Nae*, I *dinnae* think that, *mo leannan*," Iain said firmly as he caught her hands in his once more.

Madeline tried to free herself from his grip, but he held fast refusing to let go of her. When she turned her head away from him, Iain squeezed her hands tightly in an effort to make her meet his gaze.

"*Look at me, Madeline.*" When she didn't move, Iain roughly tugged on her hands. "I *said, look at me!*"

Slowly, she turned her head toward him, and he flinched beneath the cold, dispassionate look on her beautiful face. He swallowed hard as he stared at her, drinking in the delicate curve of her cheek, the wounded shimmer in her brown eyes, the taut line of her full mouth. How could he make her understand what it would do to him when he lost her?

"The *only* thought in my head when ye told me about the bairn, was how will I live without ye." Fear made his voice crack as he met her stunned gaze. "Ye are everything tae me, *mo ghràdh*, and losing ye will be my undoing."

Iain bowed his head and buried his face against her hands which had fallen into her lap. A shudder rocked through him as she bent over and kissed the top of his head.

"Oh, Iain, you mustn't think like that. I'm not Flora. I'm strong, and I'm healthy," she whispered as she wrapped her arms around his shoulders. "I believe with all my heart that everything will be all right, my darling. Won't you please try to believe it too?"

The heartfelt plea in Madeline's voice made Iain raise his head to look at her. As their gazes met, she cupped his face with her hands and leaned forward to kiss him softly. When she pulled back from him, Madeline's expression pleaded with him to do as she asked. Closing his eyes, Iain dragged in a deep breath before meeting her gaze again. With a nod, he silently agreed to her request. He could only pray she was right.

October 29, 1897

A loud wail filled the air as the next Baron Glenburnie tested the power of his small lungs. Relief barreled through

Iain as he watched Madeline heave a sigh then fall back into her pillows with a smile. Her hand clasped tightly in his, he leaned over her and kissed her brow.

"Are ye all right, *mo ghràdh?*" Iain's gaze searched her features for any sign of pain or discomfort but saw nothing. She looked up at him with a radiant smile.

"I'm exhausted, but it was easier than swimming in the North Sea during a storm."

The reference to their battles with the sea made him smile as he kissed her gently. As he straightened, the midwife moved toward the bed and placed their son in Madeline's arms. Sitting in a chair beside their bed, Iain leaned forward to stroke the child's cheek with his finger.

"Thank ye, *mo ghràdh.*" His soft words made her look at Iain in surprise.

"For what?"

"Ye have tolerated an ill-tempered Scotsman for the past seven months," he muttered as his mouth tightened in a grimace of self-disgust. "And now ye have given me a son who is as bonnie as his mother."

"Ill-tempered?" Madeline arched her eyebrows at him with a look that said he'd been more than irritable, especially in recent weeks. "Don't you mean unreasonable, grumpy, and in general, a horse's ass?"

"Aye, all of those." He jerked his head in agreement, and Madeline reached out to touch his cheek.

"Every time you snapped at someone, I knew it was because you were worried you would lose me." Brown eyes luminous with love and understanding, a small tremor vibrated through her fingers to his cheek. "And I've never felt more loved in my entire life."

"I love ye, *mo bhòidhchead fuilt dorcha.*" Iain covered her hand with his, then turned his head to press his lips against her palm. Looking back at Madeline, he saw her smile mischievously.

"Isn't it time our daughters met their little brother?" At her question, Iain grinned.

"Aye, I'm surprised Ainslie has nae charged in here already." At the sound of his father's voice, the newest resident of Muchalls Hall scrunched up his face and wailed for a second time. Iain eyed his newborn son with amusement. "Well, now, Andrew Thane Fraser. That's a war cry any Highlander could be proud of."

Madeline laughed as she bent her head toward the baby, while Iain strode toward the door. As he stepped out into the hall, Ainslie and Grace sprang up from the floor where they were sitting.

"Can we see him, now?" Ainslie exclaimed impatiently. Iain stared at her in surprise as she announced her new sibling was a boy without having been told anything. She grinned at his astonishment and bobbed her head toward her twin. "Grace told me."

The moment his gaze fell on his oldest daughter, she shrugged sheepishly, and Iain laughed as Grace hurried forward to hug him then darted past him. Ainslie did the same before bolting after her sister and making a beeline for the side of the bed opposite Grace.

Arms folded across his chest, Iain leaned his shoulder against the doorframe to watch his daughters admire their new brother. The lad was still crying, and Iain heard Ainslie ask to hold the baby. With a smile, Madeline gently transferred their newborn son into his sister's arms. The moment Ainslie cradled her brother against her, the baby grew silent.

Startled, Iain looked at Madeline who met his gaze with equal surprise. She rolled her shoulders in a small shrug before answering a question Grace asked. As his oldest daughter moved around the bed to sit closer to Ainslie and the baby, Iain crossed the room to sit beside Madeline again.

Iain took the hand his wife offered him as he sank down onto the mattress beside her. One arm wrapped around Madeline's shoulders, Iain pressed his lips to her temple. The soft sigh parting her lips echoed with happiness, and the sound made a knot form in Iain's throat as his eyes met hers.

Radiant with joy, Madeline's brown eyes were luminous with love, and she stole his breath away.

Unable to speak, Iain swallowed hard as she snuggled into his side. Neither of them would ever know or be able to explain how she arrived at Muchalls Hall, but it didn't matter. The North Sea had taken a great deal from him, but it had also given him a precious gift when he'd pulled Madeline from the water. A gift he would cherish the rest of his life.

$\mathcal{A}$uthor's $\mathcal{N}$ote

LANGUAGE
The Gaelic included in this work are derived from
different resources, including, but not limited to, Outlander
Wiki, Outlander lists, Dwelly's great Scots Gaelic - English
dictionary, and Omniglot online encyclopedia

mo leannan — sweetheart
mo ghràdh — my beloved or my love
a shùgh mo chridhe — my dearest or my darling heart
mo chridhe — my heart
mo brèagha dìthean — my beautiful flower
mo bhòidhchead fuilt dorcha — my dark-haired beauty
mo muirninn — my darling
mo nighean dubh — my dark-haired lass (for a daughter)
cairn — stone mound marker for memorial / boundary
faither — father

faither (colloquial Scots) is used primarily in northeast
Scotland (Aberdeenshire and surrounding areas)and the
Shetland Islands.

fuddy-duddy originated in American English
around 1871. It is more than possible that Anna would
have encountered the word in her travels with her uncle on
the Falcon (Forever Yours).

FORMS OF ADDRESS FOR SCOTTISH BARONS
Scottish barons style their surnames similarly to Clan
Chiefs, with the name of their barony following their name,
as in Iain Fraser of Glenburnie or Iain Fraser, Baron of
Glenburnie.

Formally in writing they are addressed as The Much Honored Baron of Glenburnie and their wife is referred to as Lady Glenburnie or The Baroness of Glenburnie. The phrase Lady of Glenburnie is incorrect unless the lady in question holds a Scottish barony title in her own right.

Verbally, Scottish barons may be addressed with the name of their barony, as in Glenburnie or simply as Baron with nothing else following, which if present would suggest a peerage barony.

SPORTS IN SCOTLAND

Football was invented in Scotland, and they were the first to use the passing game. Organized football in Scotland occurred in the 1800s, and the Aberdeen University club was founded in 1872. The length of the Scottish football field is approximately the same as that of American football fields (100 yards). The history articles I found simply explained the history of the game and the development of teams and championships played. They did not give an overview of the game in the late 1800s. However, images I found as far back as the 1880s make it appear that the game is soccer even though they called it (and still do) football.

THE NORTH SEA

The North Sea is ranked the deadliest and most dangerous body of water on the globe. The water is always rough due to the construct of different shorelines, distances between shorelines, colliding currents flowing from the Atlantic Ocean, Norwegian Ocean, Skagerrak Strait, and the Strait of Dover, and overall weather conditions.

The water temperature in the North Sea near Aberdeen for the month of September and October averages between approximately 55-65 degrees depending on weather patterns.

Creative license was taken with the capsizing of Madeline's sailboat in present day. A master sailor would have technology available to know in plenty of time if there are any storms brewing in open water. That knowledge would have ensured the captain could take appropriate action sooner to protect his guests from any storm danger.

HYPOTHERMIA

Hypothermia from exposure to cold water can set in as quickly as the first hour or two, not in minutes as some might think. A healthy person can survive over an hour in waters 60 degrees and lower, and this is specifically referring to individuals in open water. Water closer to shore will actually be colder than open water due to air currents that affect the movement of water.

COLD WATER SHOCK AND INCAPACITATION

Cold water shock and incapacitation are more likely to cause death during water accidents as they are the instigators of the final outcome, which is drowning. Cold shock response can be overcome by most people simply by controlling one's breathing and not succumbing to panic.

Cold water incapacitation occurs when the body draws blood away from the extremities to protect the main organs. Without sufficient blood flow, one's limbs will begin to contract and movement becomes difficult. Eventually swimming is impossible with drowning the end result.

Since Madeline, Iain, and Ainslie are *not* neck deep in cold water for any great length of time, incapacitation would take longer to occur. Additionally, adrenalin can also play a role in one's survival and ability to rescue someone else, such as Madeline displays.

While cold water incapacitation can make it difficult to walk after being pulled from the water, I believe it reasonable to assume that Ainslie would recover more quickly than Madeline and Iain, specifically because she was able to walk into the caves before the tide began to come in. She didn't get wet until Iain helped her navigate around the tidal pool safely.

With regard to Iain drowning and being resuscitated in a believable fashion, I used the factor of cold water as the saving grace when it came to his survival. When the body's temperature drops low enough, the major organs, including the brain, are protected for a limited amount of time.

In the book's two water incidents, all the above factors allowed me to create what I believe was a realistic scenario of events. These events allowed me to show the character's growth, while creating positive outcomes with no negative or prolonged aftereffects. At the very least, my research allowed me to write the water scenes in a way that most readers will find realistic and/or possible events and outcomes.

Other Titles by Monica Burns

THE RECKLESS ROCKWOODS SERIES

Obsession #1
Dangerous #2,
The Highlander's Woman #3
Redemption #4
The Beastly Earl #5

THE RECKLESS ROCKWOODS

The Next Generation

Scandalous #6 (Jul 2023)
Masquerade #7 (Dec 2023)
Brazen #8 (Jul 2024)
Reckless #9 (Dec 2024)

THE RECKLESS ROCKWOODS NOVELS

The Reluctant Rogues

The Rogue's Offer #1
The Rogue's Countess #2

FOREVERMORE SERIES (TIME TRAVEL)

Forever Mine #1
Forever Yours #2
Forever My Lass #3
Always Yours, #4 (TBA)

SELF-MADE MEN SERIES

His To Command #1 (Novella)
His Mistress #2

STAND ALONE TITLES

Kismet
Mirage
Pleasure Me
A Bluestocking Christmas
Love's Portrait
Love's Revenge

THE ORDER OF THE SICARI SERIES

Assassin's Honor #1
Assassin's Heart #2
Inferno's Kiss #3

About The Author

Monica Burns is a bestselling author of spicy historical and paranormal romance. She penned her first romance at the age of nine when she selected the pseudonym she uses today. Her historical book awards include the 2011 RT BookReviews Reviewers Choice Award and the 2012 Gayle Wilson Heart of Excellence Award for Pleasure Me.

She is also the recipient of the prestigious paranormal romance award, the 2011 PRISM Best of the Best award for Assassin's Heart. From the days when she hid her stories from her sisters to her first completed full-length manuscript, she always believed in her dream despite rejections and setbacks. A workaholic wife and mother, Monica is a survivor who believes every hero and heroine deserves a HEA (Happily Ever After), especially if she's writing the story.

Find all the ways you can connect with Monica on the next page.

www.ingramcontent.com/pod-product-compliance
Lightning Source LLC
Chambersburg PA
CBHW060907210726
48293CB00006B/1996